STATION BREAK

STEVE FRIEDMAN AND *ROSEMARY FORD*

STATION BREAK

A NOVEL

St. Martin's Press
New York

STATION BREAK. Copyright © 1993 by Steve Friedman and Rosemary Ford. All rights reserved. Printed in the United States of America. No part of this book may be used or reproduced in any manner whatsoever without written permission except in the case of brief quotations embodied in critical articles or reviews. For information, address St. Martin's Press, 175 Fifth Avenue, New York, N.Y. 10010.

Design by Dawn Niles

Library of Congress Cataloging-in-Publication Data

Friedman, Steve.
    Station break / Steve Friedman and Rosemary Ford.
       p. cm.
    "A Thomas Dunne book."
    ISBN 0-312-08895-7
    1. Television journalists—Fiction. 2. California—Fiction. I. Ford, Rosemary. II. Title.
PS3556.R5643S7   1993
813'.54—dc20   92-44190
                                                                         CIP

First Edition: March 1993

10 9 8 7 6 5 4 3 2

ACKNOWLEDGMENTS

My thanks to Beverly Friedman, who makes everything possible, to David Black, who made Mary Reed a reality, and to Tammy Brown, who makes order out of chaos every day.
—Steve Friedman

My thanks to David Black, whose patience and encouragement were always appreciated. Also to Jay Adkins, a dear friend and unexpected muse. I am indebted to the following people for their unique and valued contributions: Michael Bailey, Maureen Baron, Tammy Brown, Ed Carney, Gene Cassidy, Gerard Ciermans, Adam Dawson, Thomas Fasano, Patrick Franklin, Lev Fruchter, Don Kaplan, Bevin O'Brien, *Plan B*, Bipin Sangankar, Don Van Dyke, Mary Ann Wong, and Tim Yates. Finally, many thanks must go to Tom Dunne and Reagan Arthur at St. Martin's Press for their suggestions and care. Finally, I am deeply grateful to Steve Friedman for his support and good humor, and for giving me a chance.
—Rosemary Ford

STATION BREAK

ONE

A FOGHORN SOUNDED on the San Francisco Bay, and gulls screamed over the early-morning traffic. On the night table, the liquid crystal figures of a digital alarm clock glowed like embers: 6:59 A.M. Then, like a magician who winks before an old trick, the numbers blinked and changed. Immediately, the insistent tones of a radio announcer filled the room: *"At four o'clock this morning as he was leaving the radio station, Feld was taken to the nearest hospital where he is said to be recovering from a shoulder wound. Police say . . ."*

A slender hand emerged from a tangle of sheets on the bed and began to grope among the many items heaped on the night table. It knocked against half-sealed jars of cosmetic creams, tipped over a bottle of prescription tablets, scattered pens, and leveled a small mountain of files and notebooks before it finally seized a slim black-and-silver panel. Mary Reed extended the remote control like a wand toward the end of the bed, and with her right index finger depressed the button labeled "Power."

Three television monitors, stacked one on top of the other, faced the bed. Lowering the remote control to activate the two remaining monitors, she pulled a pillow from under one shoulder and squashed it behind her tousled blond hair. The glassy gray-green screens in front of her dissolved into a snowy electrical night that grew rapidly lighter. Form and color poured evenly down from screen to screen until the entire column filled with bright moving pictures. Mary glanced at the clock as the figures slid to 7:01 A.M. Pushing the hair from her eyes, she turned up the volume on one of the monitors.

"*Good morning, welcome to 'Today' on this Wednesday morning . . .*" She flipped to the next screen. "*. . . Continuing my three-part interview . . .*"

"*Can you say Egg McMuffin?*" Mary got up as the commercials started and put on a robe. In the kitchen she pulled out a box of Kellogg's Frosted Flakes and sighed as she thought of the calories. Okay, she told herself, as she shook the cereal into a bowl, you can have some if you go to the gym at lunch today. And tomorrow, she added punitively as she added skim milk. She brought the cereal and a cup of black coffee back into the bedroom.

Completing her morning ritual, Mary headed toward the door of her apartment to pick up the newspapers that lay on the mat outside. On her way back through the living room, she paused for a moment to look through the window. It faced a wide, quiet street lined with the pastel-painted buildings and miniature palm trees that typified the Marina District of San Francisco. Overhead, a pale sun struggled with the fog.

In the living room there were stacks of videocassettes, reports she had made in San Francisco and, before that, for the local television station in her hometown of Portland, Oregon. Portland had been her first full-time job after graduating at the top of her class from Stanford. Her major had not been journalism, which, of course, she took, but radio-television, which had become her life. Three months ago, when she had turned twenty-five, the young reporter vowed that she would work on finding a story big enough to catapult her to a job in network television.

Sitting in her bedroom, Mary shoveled a spoonful of cereal between two perfectly shaped lips and focused her green eyes on the front pages of the newspapers spread out in front of her. They included *The New York Times, The Washington Post, USA Today,* and the *L.A. Times,* as well as the local Oakland and San Francisco papers. The television played in the background: *"And we'll be back after a station break."*

Mary peeled off her robe and let it fall on the floor alongside the other garments she had abandoned when, after a long day's work, she had collapsed onto the bed. After showering she dressed quickly, tugging her underwear from disorganized drawers, then snatching a suit from her overflowing closet. The jacket was a soft green gabardine that accented the color of her eyes, and the matching skirt wrapped around her waist to end well above her knees, revealing long, shapely legs. Mary eyed herself critically in the mirror, tweaking the fabric and pulling the jacket down so that it fit the curves of her body like a glove.

Satisfied, she slid a trench coat from its hanger, pushed her feet into a battered pair of flat driving shoes, and picked up her attaché case. Walking to the middle of the room, she plucked the remote control from the table and shut off the power.

Mary turned her green Mustang convertible onto Bay Street and picked up the radio set hooked-up in her car.

"Ron, hi, it's Mary Reed. What's new?"

"Morning, Mary," Ron answered. Ron was the daytime assignment editor at Channel 6, responsible for assigning reporters and camera crews to new stories as they broke. Mary had arranged with him to give her an update of what was going on each morning, and also to give her an idea of her schedule for the day. The meager resources of the local television station were not squandered on support staff, and reporters were expected to organize themselves.

"You know that late-night talk-show host, Marvin Feld?" he asked.

"The gay guy?"

"He was shot leaving the radio station early this morning. He's okay, the wound turned out not to be serious. I sent Roberti over to the hospital to cover it."

"Do they have any idea why? I mean, was it a mugging, or was someone out to get him?"

"We don't know yet."

"Bizarre. Anything else?"

"No more stories. You're set up for promos, then you need to get out to the airport to cut the on-air bridge for part four of the airport safety series. Oh, and Wyatt wants to see you sometime this morning." Wyatt Andrews was the news director at Channel 6.

"Thanks, Ron. Listen, I'm on Columbus now and the traffic looks reasonable, I'm sure I'll be there in ten minutes. Can you tell makeup to stand by? I can do the promos and then I suppose I'd better meet with Wyatt before going to the airport. Ask him if nine-thirty is okay. Also, we need to finish editing parts three and four this afternoon. Make sure Nina and Elizabeth know." Mary swore. "Sorry, Ron, some jerk is cutting me off. Got to go."

"Okay, see you soon, Reed."

On either side of the street were billboards the size of buildings. Some carried advertisements for cigarettes, others for gasoline or Scotch whisky, and some advertised the local Channel 6 news. BEFORE YOU GO TO SLEEP, WATCH MARY REED, the bold letters commanded. A flawless face, ten times larger than life, ballooned above the words. Mary Reed had much of the pert, cool beauty of a young Grace Kelly; her eyes, in particular, had the same sparkling and intense quality that could light up the screen. A smile played around the corners of her mouth and high on her left cheekbone was a beauty spot. The young reporter got a lot of mail about her beauty spot.

The figure gripping the wheel of the Mustang convertible, however, bore only a faint resemblance to the billboard photograph. The woman in the car was frowning as she negotiated several lanes of traffic. Her eyes looked small, her face was pale and rounder than the one in the photograph, and her uncombed hair was pushed into an unruly bunch at the back of her neck.

Channel 6's offices were located downtown in the Embarcadero Center. The *Herald,* the newspaper that owned the television station, had invested in the space when it was built. Although it was the television station's revenues that enabled the prestigious but insolvent newspaper to exist, Channel 6 was considered a necessary evil by most of the *Herald*'s board of directors. They, along with many in the print media, condemned television news as sensationalist and flashy. When the idea of a new building was suggested, Channel 6 employees were delighted. They had been longing to move out of the inconvenient, tiny offices they had been squeezed into at the newspaper's neo-classical headquarters. Unfortunately, though, the poorly designed work space in the new building was a daily reminder of the board's lack of enthusiasm for their most profitable enterprise.

Mary parked her car in the underground garage and walked to the elevator, producing her identity card for the security guard, who broke into a broad smile when he saw it. "Sorry, Miss Reed, I didn't recognize you."

She ran into the makeup room next to the studios. "Good morning, Agnes."

"Hello, honey." The makeup woman looked up from her magazine. "Come on, sit down there." She threw a large square scarf around Mary's head and fastened it tightly. Mary pulled out her makeup box and Agnes poked through the bottles and tubes, the colored pencils, and flat cases of powder and shadow to find what she needed. Once she was in Agnes's expert hands, Mary relaxed and began telling her stories about the people she had interviewed. "Did you know that the chief psychiatrist at Patterson Clinic likes wandering in Golden Gate Park at night dressed like Marilyn Monroe?" she asked.

"Well, they're all crazy, those shrinks, I've always known that," Agnes commented as she plied her fingertips and brushes across Mary's face.

Mary nodded at a picture of a film star she had just noticed in an opened magazine. "Agnes, are you aware that that woman is a dominatrix?"

"Oh, please!" Agnes shrieked with laughter. "You're a piece of work!"

With darkened brows, mascara on her eyelashes, and subtly shaded color on her lids, Mary's green eyes danced into prominence. Gradually, the contours of her face were defined with shadows and her lips softly outlined to bring out their fullness. Finally, the hairstylist cajoled her hair into a shape that would not move, even in a high wind. Nobody failed to recognize Mary Reed when she sailed out of the makeup room.

Mary walked into the studio and greeted the production crew by name. Her producer, Elizabeth Platt, was waiting.

"Hi, Elizabeth. How was your weekend?"

Elizabeth made a face. "Looked at apartments the entire time."

"Find anything?"

The producer shook her head. "Did you get a chance to ask Mark about his?"

Mary raised her hand in a gesture of exasperation. "Oh, God, I forgot!" she said. "Never mind, he's coming up this weekend. I'll ask him then."

"I hope it's not too much trouble," Elizabeth said with a slight edge in her voice, "but if you get a chance it would be great."

"No, it's no trouble," Mary said. "I just forgot." Elizabeth's sarcasm was lost on Mary for the same reason that Mary had forgotten her request. Mary was not unkind, only a little selfish; she only really paid attention to other people if they could help her in some way, and the nuances of the producer's mood did not register on that scale. "I'll let you know on Monday."

"Thank you, really. I appreciate it."

"So, I think we can get these promos over fast," Mary changed the subject. "What've we got? A ten and a thirty, right?"

"Yes. We'll do the thirty-second one first. Here's the script," Elizabeth said.

Mary read the script and laid it down on the table. "What's the footage?" she asked.

"Eight seconds of nighttime landing, six inside the cockpit and six inside the air-traffic control room."

Mary thought fast. "Listen, why don't we cut the two six-second spots to four, make it move faster?"

"Mmm," Elizabeth murmured.

"What are we doing about the end?"

"We've come up with a couple of ideas," Elizabeth said. "But before I run them past you I thought you might have some thoughts."

"What about fourteen seconds of people, just ordinary people, boarding planes? Do we have enough footage for that?" asked Mary.

"Sure," the producer said, though she was frowning.

"Trust me, Elizabeth, it'll be good."

Mary watched as the tape was edited. When the newly created tape was ready, she signaled for it to run and, leaving her script on the table, ad-libbed the voice-over as she watched the pictures.

"But these people are not aware that they are playing Russian roulette every time they board a plane," she wound up.

Elizabeth Platt recognized with some bitterness that she would never have the natural talent of someone like Mary Reed. She had heard few people who could ad-lib a narration with Mary's ease and style, and she watched the reporter with a look that expressed equal parts of envy and admiration. They ran the track back. "Perfect," Elizabeth said. "I don't know how you manage to get the timing dead on." "Thank you." Mary flashed her a radiant smile. "Now, I suppose we should do the ten. What do we have for it?" she asked.

"Well, I lined up the landing shot and then we've got the two interviews. You know, the one where the pilot said the air-traffic controllers don't have any idea what they're doing and the one with the controller who got mad and said the pilots were just a bunch of overpaid cowboys who don't give a damn about safety," Elizabeth said. "I thought we could make something out of that," she added. Elizabeth hated the tentative way she sounded, but Mary made her feel less sure of her instincts than any other reporter she had worked with.

Mary looked meditatively at the screen. "That would be dramatic," she said. "But it's not really what we're doing. The report is about fear, not about people bad-mouthing each other." Elizabeth nodded and waited for Mary to decide what she wanted to do. To other people, Elizabeth gave the impression that she was in charge, but in the studio there was no doubt who was boss. Mary Reed wanted complete control over everything she did. It was her face, she argued, and her voice that the public identified with the reports; she got the blame if they were bad and the credit if they worked. The team players had trouble with that concept but her skill and professionalism usually helped her get the best out of the people she worked with.

"I'd like to try this," Mary said to Nina, the editor. "It might work. Start with two seconds of the landing, then intercut with the faces of passengers—get the smiling ones, the kids." Nina started to work. "That's it," Mary said, excited. "Great, Nina. Now don't show the plane landing, keep cutting away just as it's about to touchdown. Yeah, maybe this way we'll make ten seconds last forever." Mary screened the tape from the beginning. She looked inquiringly at Elizabeth.

"Okay." The producer nodded.

Mary laid down the voice track. *"Will this plane make it? We'll show you the odds behind every safe landing tonight at six on Channel Six."*

"You did it again. One take, Mary," Elizabeth said with a forced smile when she heard the track. She wished that just once Wyatt Andrews's darling protegée would fall flat on her cute little face.

"Great. Listen, I've got to run. I've got a meeting with Wyatt. Then I'm shooting an on-air bridge for part four at the airport."

"When do you want to edit?" Elizabeth asked.

"Can you do it around one, Nina?" Mary asked the editor. They both agreed. "See you later, guys. Thanks, everyone." Mary headed toward the door.

"One take Mary," a production engineer echoed as the reporter quit the studio. "I'd sure like one take with you, beauty," he muttered.

"Dream on, Billy," Mary said over her shoulder as she strode down the corridor.

"Way to go William," said a colleague, chuckling because Billy was young enough that the tips of his ears had turned a bashful pink.

Mary traveled down to the eighth floor in the elevator and walked through the noisy, open newsroom to the executive offices beyond it. The news director's office door was open and Wyatt Andrews was on the telephone when Mary breezed in. He signaled for her to sit down and she perched on an uncomfortable chrome and leather chair in front of his orderly desk. The walls of the office were covered with the awards that the news division had received over the six years Wyatt had been director. Mary's special reports on AIDS the previous year had won the station three local Emmys. She wanted the airport safety series to be there, too.

"Mary." Wyatt finished his call and leaned toward her. "The airport pieces are the best you've done for us yet. When you had that air-traffic controller showing us how close it's cut in that room it really scared me."

"Well, I know you're just saying that because you know my contract only has five more months to run," Mary said with a teasing smile.

"Compliments from me aren't going to get you to spill ink on our contracts," he replied. "I know that if L.A. or New York call, you'll be out of here. And if they don't," he added, "you'll probably kill yourself."

Mary's eyes met the faintly mocking look of the fifty-six-year-old man who had taught her more about journalism in the last two years than she had learned at school or even in the two years she worked in Portland. "Oh, no, that's not true," she said. "I want to be buried here." She kept a straight face.

The gaunt, gray-haired Wyatt knew his job. It was to find young reporters like Reed, people with brains and looks who could grow under his guidance and help him keep the station in first place. He knew that he could only keep the Mary Reeds of this world until they were ready for the glamour and money of the bigger markets.

Wyatt Andrews had once worked for one of the major networks. His task had been to punch up its lackluster morning news. What the New York executives neglected to mention in the interview, however, was that it intended to leave Andrews's predecessor in the same position and let the two men fight for the top job. This method of running an organization, modeled on Darwin's theory of natural selection, was based on the premise that the better fighter makes the better manager. For a year Andrews battled his way through conflict after conflict in the office, while his wife tried hard to find something to like about New York City. When the position of news director at Channel 6 was offered to him, he heaved a sigh of relief and returned to his hometown.

"Listen, Mary, I'm going to tell the people in programming that we'll make your airport reports into a half-hour special. They'll love the demographics, there's a natural middle-class audience for it out there. And it's a great piece for the May sweeps." The sweeps, periods in February, May, and November, were conducted by an independent company, A.C. Nielsen, and measured the number of viewers for each show. These figures then determined the station's advertising rates. "Can you get that together by Saturday?" he asked.

"Well, I've still got part five to cut. It's in good shape. If you get me Nina and Richard to edit a couple of evenings, we can have it for you in time."

"Great." Wyatt leaned back in his chair. The meeting was over. Mary stood up.

"Now, there's just one thing, Wyatt," she said, turning back to him, "I want the press to see this."

"It's already too late to get them to write anything for the Saturday papers and they're not going to show up Saturday afternoon just to screen your report," Wyatt argued.

"Why don't we delay broadcasting it for a week?" Mary put her hands on the back of the chair and pushed down on them. "We can screen it a week from Saturday. That way all the newspaper people get a chance to see it beforehand. It will still be near the beginning of sweeps month, and the piece isn't topical."

"We've already run a couple of promos," Wyatt objected although he saw the value in Mary's argument. Her mind ran on a dual track: the journalism mattered, but only if it got attention.

"Okay," he said with reluctant admiration. "You win."

"Thanks, Wy." Mary gave the news director a big grin and walked out of his office at her usual high velocity.

Andrews looked out of his window for a moment. The woman sure had guts, he thought, he just did not think she was mature enough yet to handle the big leagues. Channel 6, where she was everybody's little sister, was the right environment for her right now. You only had to look at what happened to Jessica Savitch, he concluded, as he usually did when he thought about his star reporter's career.

At around one P.M. Mary came back from the airport with a roll of tape for the fourth part of her airport safety series. The tape contained the on-air bridge: a simple shot of Mary, who narrated the link between the two segments of the story. Mary made her way to the editing complex, a maze of tiny dark rooms to the right of the newsroom. Andrews had allocated Mary a producer to edit her pieces—a privilege not extended to the other reporters—and Elizabeth Platt was waiting for her in edit room five, along with Nina Basalt, who was the best editor at Channel 6.

"Can't find the interview with the air-traffic controller," Nina was saying.

"Try the second roll," Elizabeth replied as Mary shot into the room.

"Sorry, guys. Got held up," Mary said. "What's happening?"

The three women closeted in the dark office started on the drudgery of making exciting television out of six reels of half-inch videotape. Many reporters wrote a script and gave it to their producer and editor to link-up with appropriate footage. It was a method that went back to the early days of television when scripts were written with the literacy and detachment of a print article. For Mary, however, and others of her generation raised on the powerful images of advertising and MTV, the pictures were the medium, and the script was created to serve them.

"If you put reel three up there," Mary said, "I think we have a better shot of the air-traffic control center on it. We can use it to intercut with our stuff on reel six inside the American Airlines cockpit."

"Okay," Nina agreed.

As they looked at reel three, a satisfied smile spread across Mary's face. She had already edited the piece once in her mind while they were shooting it. Now she knew instinctively what the finished report would look like. She glanced around the tiny edit room and thought of it as heaven; it was exactly where she wanted to be, exactly what she had been dreaming of doing since high school.

"Yeah, good idea," said Elizabeth, who had the difficult task of staying in favor with Mary while impressing Nina with her authority. She usually failed to do either.

"Okay, now, Nina, try to build the sequence . . . more . . . start with six or seven seconds, first the air-traffic control room, then the cockpit . . . now, cut it down. Make each shot two or three seconds . . . more tension . . . make us feel it . . . put us there in that cockpit. . . ." Mary rose out of her chair as the sequence came together. "Good, great, terrific!" In her excitement Mary snapped the pencil she was holding in half.

"Wait a minute," Elizabeth said. "Go back to that second to last cut, the edit didn't take."

Elizabeth was right. At the point where the tape had been edited the picture was jiggling. Nina ran the pre-edited tape through the time-base corrector, a machine that strengthened the electronic signals on the videotape. Then she re-edited the tape. This time the cut held.

"Good," Elizabeth said.

After two more hours of pulling out pictures and adding sound bites from different interviews, Mary left Nina and Elizabeth to put the finishing touches on the piece. In her cluttered ten-by-six-foot office, which was the envy of other reporters who worked in the newsroom, Mary worked on her ideas for the script.

"Hey, Mary?" Paul Berman stood in the doorway of Mary's office, and pushed the door open. "You got anything for tonight yet?" Paul produced the eleven o'clock news where Mary was guaranteed airtime in a spot Andrews had named "Nightbeat."

"What about following up on that corruption story that the *Herald* did last week?"

"That's old news, Mary. Even the *Herald*'s stopped covering it. 'Least I don't remembering seeing anything on it this week," Paul said, leaning against the wall.

"Right, that's what interests me. They dropped the whole investigation like a hot potato. There's got to be something there. Listen, do me a favor, Paul. I've got to get this script in shape, so we can run part four of the airport piece on the six o'clock news tonight. If you don't come up with anything, when I get off the set at six-thirty we'll talk some more." Mary gave Paul a hasty smile and turned back to her typewriter.

Ten minutes later Wyatt Andrews knocked on the door. "How much longer before I get to see part four of your brilliant series, Reed?" he asked. He perched on the corner of her desk.

"Give me ten minutes to finish the script and about twenty for Nina to lay it in. What about four o'clock?"

"That's right, edit late and I can't change much," the news director said.

"Oh, Wyatt," Mary said girlishly, turning to face him. "You give me too much credit."

In the edit room Elizabeth and Nina looked up as Mary entered.

"Okay, let's try it. Nina, lay it down. Afterwards, Wyatt wants to screen it."

As the pictures rolled, Mary read her nine-page narration. The words fit perfectly with the footage, and Mary uttered them fluently. She noted that the timing between the interviews worked well.

"Best piece of the week, so far," Wyatt said to Mary a half hour later. "Elizabeth, Nina, good work." He left the edit room, followed by Mary.

"Mary, there's a call for you!" someone yelled as she entered the newsroom.

"Mary Reed? Leo Roth, I'm an agent with Chichester Williams. I'm here on personal business and I happened to see the report you did last night. Let me ask you, are you represented?"

"I've been thinking about it. Other people from your office and from ICM have called me, but I think I'm going to wait 'til I leave San Francisco."

"Let me give you my number. If you change your mind or if you have any questions you think I can answer, give me a call. I'd be happy to meet with you anytime you're in L.A."

"Sure." Mary doodled on her script as the agent recited his number. She was not ready for an agent, not yet, and when the time did come, she was going to aim higher than Leo Roth.

TWO

JIM WILKES WALKED into his house in the Sunset neighborhood of San Francisco. "You leaving?" he asked his daughter. She had come into the hallway at the sound of his entry.

He pronounced each word distinctly, but the care that he took with his speech told Katie Wilkes that her father had been drinking for a while, maybe all day.

"Yeah," she said. "Dinner's all ready. Just heat and eat." She grinned and patted the tight blond curls that circled her face. "I'll be back around twelve. Mike's driving me."

"Okay, hon." She started to go. "Oh, Katie?" he called after her. She stopped. "Did I get a call from a man called Johnson, Finn Johnson?"

"Oh, yeah. Said he'd call back tonight."

"Thanks." Wilkes nodded. His daughter was visiting him for a week over a school holiday, but he had a suspicion it was more to see her old boyfriend Mike than her father.

Wilkes listened to her footsteps as she walked to the front door. "And you'd better not be any later than that, girl," he called after her. "Or Mike Ascona's ass is in a sling."

The burly man walked with some difficulty to the kitchen at the back of the small frame house, opened the refrigerator, and pulled beer from its plastic loop. He slapped the door shut with the broad palm of his hand and lumbered out onto the back porch. As the screen door closed behind him, Wilkes gulped from the chilled can. He moved to sit down, then paused, remembering there were no longer any chairs on the back porch. Nevertheless, Jim Wilkes, halfway drunk, glanced furtively at the emptied space to the left of him, just in case. Perhaps the patio table that wobbled and the four fold-up chairs with seats and backs of woven aqua plastic had returned. And perhaps he was going soft in the head, Wilkes mocked himself.

Dolores had taken almost everything when she left him last year, including Katie; cleared out anything that was not bolted to the floor, he joked afterward. A few things he had replaced but the rest he lived without as a way of defining her absence. In his heart it was still a wonder to former detective James John Wilkes that the proud and gorgeous Dolores Davis had stuck around with him as long as she had. You had to love cops to marry one, and Dolores had had little patience for the demands the police force made on her husband and on her. She had threatened to leave him a thousand times, but when several pounds of quality Columbian cocaine was planted in his filing cabinet at the department, he told her to get the hell out. He said it would get worse; he had been framed, next they will hurt you, he had argued. Scornfully, she had refused to listen. She had dug in, stood by him, she even cried heartrendingly during his trial. Every week of his twenty-eight months in the slammer she had visited him.

Then, a month after his release, she had packed their home into crates and, suddenly, she was gone.

Wilkes raised his beer can to the mystery of woman.

The phone rang and when Wilkes answered it he heard the voice of his former partner in the narcotics squad, Eddie Martinez. He was now a homicide detective in his hometown of Bakersfield. "Hi, pal. How are you doing?"

"Fine," Wilkes said. "Listen, I'm in the middle of something, Eddie. Can I call you back tomorrow?"

"Sure, pal. I just called to see how you were doing. But if you're busy that's okay. Just call me, okay? Don't be a stranger."

"Yeah, I will. Thanks." Wilkes put down the phone with relief. He knew that his old partner was worried about him, but Wilkes felt he had reached a place where no one could help him.

He stumbled down the steps into the yard. The California evening was cool and clear, and Wilkes shivered as he swayed past a dusty azalea bush. A fly buzzed through the air around his head, settling for a second now and then on his stubbly jaw. Wilkes tossed his head but the irritating noise came back immediately. He sprung back, raising both hands in boxer's fists. "Okay, fly. Come and get it," he muttered when he heard the insect again. He moved forward, jabbing at his unseen tormentor and fell back, all the while hurling insults at the creature. His arm swung out in a loose left hook. "You're dead meat, pal."

Wilkes used to box. You could tell by the way his feet danced as he punched, carrying his weight with a practiced lightness. He had been an amateur heavyweight champion, weighing two hundred pounds. Now the scales tipped over the two-thirty mark on account of the extra years, a bad diet, and too much beer.

Yesterday, Wilkes lost his job. He had been a nighttime janitor for an armored truck depot in downtown San Francisco. The night shift ended at eight yesterday morning but he was nowhere in sight when his replacement arrived. One of the cleaning women had found him later, slumped in a mop closet in a leaden alcoholic slumber. The crisply suited personnel manager did not waste time. "You're fired, Mr. Wilkes. No excuses," he said. Wilkes's slack features had twisted into a look of hatred the young black executive knew only too well, and he had turned briskly on his heel and walked away.

As he stumbled around the shabby yard, Wilkes's boxing frenzy abated as abruptly as it had started. He was panting for breath and sweating heavily. Holding the rail, he lowered himself onto one of the porch steps. His bloodshot eyes dimmed with tears. He was surely a man to be pitied—ex-champ, ex-cop, ex-husband, ex-janitor—there was the story of his life.

Wilkes stumbled into the kitchen. On the counter he saw a note Katie had left him: "Please remember to eat, Dad." He was never hungry these days. The telephone rang and Wilkes jumped to get it. "Hello . . . Johnson?"

At midnight when she arrived home, Katie Wilkes was not surprised to find that the food remained untouched, nor that her father was asleep in the living room bathed in the pale radiance of the television that was rerunning an episode of "The Honeymooners." What startled her was the smile that lit his large, rough face, a smile she had not seen in a long while. Katie turned off the television and went to go find a blanket for her father.

Wilkes drove down a dusty exit off Route 40 into the southern California desert. Twenty miles into nowhere, fifty yards past a gas station, he rolled off the road. On the other side of the road stood a derelict general store and behind it, a little to the right, he could see a wash hung out to dry. Children were playing in the dirt in front of the store. Above a crumbling porch faded letters spelled the name BOB'S CAFE AND INTERNATIONAL RESTAURANT. Wilkes had found his destination.

He parked his car in front of the café and got out, glad to pull his long legs out from the cramped space beneath the steering wheel. He walked to the porch, took the steps in a single bound, and stepped into the gloom of the shuttered café, pausing at the doorway to accustom his eyes to the dim light.

"Well, fucking A, if it isn't Jim boy," drawled a voice from behind the counter at the back of the room, which Wilkes now saw was filled with tables and chairs but empty of people. "Six-foot fucking-two of cop."

Through the gloom, Wilkes could make out the black hair, blunt chin, and pale, cloudy eyes of his former cellmate. "Finn Johnson, you grow since we last met?" he asked. "Or were you hankering after the sound of breaking bones?" Wilkes held up his fists in mock menace. "Can still pack a good punch, you know. If you come out where I can see you."

"Want me to worry, cop?" Finn Johnson swiftly raised a semiautomatic over the countertop and, pointing it at Wilkes's chest, pulled back the slide.

"Wha'd'ya think?" Johnson said, holding Wilkes's gaze. "Know that game kids play? Put your hand out like a stone, and the other kid has his like a knife, and you won 'cause the knife don't cut stone." He paused. "You got the fists but I got the weapon." The slow smile that was Finn's facial signature spread across his face. "How do *you* figure it, cop?"

Wilkes kept staring. "I figure it's assault, most likely with an unlicensed firearm. Now, cut it out, kid. Didn't your daddy tell you not to play with a loaded gun?"

"Who says I'm fucking playing?" Finn sneered.

There was a bullying note in his voice that was new to Wilkes, who stayed in the doorway. He opened his hands, and now he waved the broad palms at Finn in a gesture of surrender. Light seeped over the top of the grimy shutters and spilled onto his shoulders.

Finn frowned. Suddenly he lifted the gun and aimed it between the ex-cop's eyes, but Wilkes's training stood him in good stead and he barely flinched.

"Ha!" Johnson laughed, breaking the tension. He tucked the gun into his belt. "Want coffee or something?" he asked, nodding at the pot behind him.

"Sure could use something cold. You got a beer?" Wilkes asked, as he cautiously advanced a few paces into the room.

"Here." Finn's movements were quick and graceful. Compared to Wilkes, the young man seemed slight, but the taut way he carried himself signaled his muscular strength. He wore jeans and a loose, unbuttoned shirt over a torn T-shirt.

Johnson walked to a table with the can and put it down. Through half-closed eyes, he watched as Wilkes pulled out a chair and stretched for the beer that he gulped eagerly.

" 'While since I saw you," he said. "Be three years now." Finn shook his head. "Bad memories," he said. He was silent. "Saved my butt a couple of times. I don't forget that," he added, looking away.

"That why you didn't shoot just now?" Wilkes asked. He wiped his mouth with the back of his hand.

Finn did not answer. He leaned back on a nearby table.

"Heard you were involved with that guy whose tapes you used to listen to," Wilkes continued. "What's his name? Redenbacker?"

"Radamacker," Finn corrected him.

"Yeah, that's the one. Used to talk about the chosen white race and burning your driver's license. That him?" asked Wilkes.

"Jerry thinks there's a lot of shit coming down today."

"Can't argue with the guy there," Wilkes said. "Listen." He looked at Finn. "What I need are weapons, cars, and some men who could handle a job."

"Yeah?" Finn crossed his arms.

"I got something for us," said Wilkes.

"Don't need your two-bit bullshit, man," Finn said coolly. "I'm into a different kind of gig now."

"I know, I know," Wilkes said soothingly. "That's why I'm here. Listen, I heard about your people through Danny, Danny Stevens. He told me it was you that creamed three million from an armored truck about three months back.

21

Right? It was on the news. Happened not far from here." Wilkes played his trump casually.

"Douche bag's been talking." Finn eyed Wilkes with a flicker of real interest. In the old days, he had looked up to Wilkes. It was not only that the ex-cop had saved him from some heavies when they were in the penitentiary together, it was the attention Wilkes had paid him, showing him a few tricks of self-defense, the best way to use his wiry strength. Finn had started to work out every day. He used tapes, Madonna or Jerry Radamacker. And after Wilkes had teased him for a time, he even started to wash himself occasionally. Self-respect, Finn remembered the older man saying to him. Don't let them take away your self-respect. That was what Radamacker was saying, too. Finn looked across at Wilkes and seeing the extra weight, the telltale signs of drinking, he wondered briefly, where the self-respect had gone.

"Listen, Johnson. I got you and your people a mother of a deal." Wilkes paused. "I reckon around twenty-four million. Enough for everyone."

"Where someone like you get that sorta action?"

"Been working at the Goldor security depot. Nighttime janitor." Wilkes looked at Finn and plunged on. "Depot's where the trucks load and unload. Few days ago they fired me. This nigger came . . ." Wilkes trailed off. "Anyway," he began again, "I contacted a few people I knew and your name came up. Also made a little investment in the project."

Wilkes saw Finn frown. "No one knows what's up," he said, "I paid up and was real careful. Now I got truck schedules that are good for two weeks. Plus I got an idea of how the alarm system's laid out. Look," he pleaded, "I know the building. When I wasn't smashed I'd be checking the place out, thinking how easy it was for someone to break in and surprise me. Never imagined I'd be the one breaking in." Wilkes shrugged. "Then I talk to Danny, and I get to thinking how you might have the right backup for this job."

Finn pulled out a chair opposite Wilkes. Twisting the seat around to face him, he straddled the seat, putting his arms along the top of the backrest. His eyes were half-closed. "Keep talkin'," he said.

In the kitchen of Mary's apartment, Mark Ashfield was listening to music as he made a sauce for the red snapper he had prepared for dinner. He was wearing a denim shirt, navy sweater, and jeans, the casual clothing that suited his tall, loose-limbed frame best. His hair was light brown, straight, and when it fell into his eyes he had a habit of brushing it away impatiently with the back of his hand. Sailing had tanned his face and left a permanent tracery of smile lines around his striking blue eyes.

The music that issued from the speakers in Mary's living room was the aria "Stride la vampa" from *Il Trovatore,* hauntingly sung by Mark's mother, Dawn Ashfield, a former mezzo-soprano with the San Francisco Opera Company. The music was conducted by Mark's father, who had been a conductor with the company. Three years ago, both his parents had been killed in an automobile accident near Houston while his father was on tour. He and his sister had been devastated by the destruction of their close-knit family. Mark had been twenty-seven, just about to graduate from journalism school, a profession he had chosen after several years racing and cruising on the sailboats he loved. A few months after the tragedy, he moved back to his native San Francisco to be near his sister and grandmother, and took a reporting job at the *Herald*'s city desk.

As he laid the fish on a platter, the aria reached its passionate climax. It was only recently that Mark had been able to listen to his parents' recordings again. "Avenge me," his mother sang. And by letting her sing, Mark felt that in his way he was avenging her. The low and thrilling voice, which was part of his earliest memories, would not be silenced forever by a drunk driver.

He glanced at the clock, nearly eight. Mary was late as usual. He was annoyed that she had not thought to call him. Mark had met Mary almost a year ago when they had both been covering a story on corruption in the mayor's office. They had been seeing each other as regularly as their jobs permitted ever since.

The front door opened. "Mark?" He heard Mary's voice.

"Here," he said, wiping his hands on a towel and moving toward the door. Mary flew into the kitchen and stood for a moment looking at him, her face flushed and happy. Then she hugged him, covering him with kisses. "I'm sorry I'm so late. That idiot Berman kept me for ages to talk about the eleven o'clock show." She stepped back. "How are you, stranger?" A plastic shopping bag dangled from her wrist. "I bought some great wine, and some dessert of course. So," she said. "How is big, bad L.A.?"

Mark had turned back to the counter where he started to prepare Mary's favorite spicy Roquefort cheese dressing. "L.A., let me see, how is L.A.? Well, perhaps you can say it's about as intellectually stimulating as foam rubber, but nothing like as useful." He was thinking that he should know by now that Mary had little idea of time, especially where work was concerned, so he did not make an issue of it. Still, he was irritated.

"You really hate it, huh?" Mary watched him affectionately, letting him sulk. She always forgot how good-looking Mark was when she had not seen him for a while. She walked up to his bent back and squeezed her arms around him, laying her head between his shoulder blades. "I missed you so much," she said. "We haven't seen each other for almost a whole month."

Mark twisted around in her embrace. He was frowning slightly as he bent down to kiss her. He straightened up and with his thumb softly traced the curve of her lower lip, looking at her with thoughtful absorption. She looked back at him steadily, giving him time. Mark liked the way she had of being wholly present when she was with him. "I missed you, too," he said, forgetting his mood. "A lot." His eyes recovered their gentleness as he smiled. He tipped up her chin and kissed her very deliberately until she gasped for breath.

"Mmm," she murmured suggestively. "We're going to have the best weekend. When do you have to go?"

"Late Sunday, there's a flight around nine I can take."

"Thank God for Southwest Airlines! You know, I wonder if we'll end up seeing each other more now that you live several hundred miles away and we have to make time for each other."

"Could be." Mark laughed. He had been transferred to the *Herald*'s L.A. bureau a month earlier when the former bureau chief had "gone native," and started writing screenplays instead of newspaper stories. For Mark the job was a promotion, but it was also a question of paying dues. He could have refused the assignment, but his boss had made it clear that this would not be the correct approach to an ongoing career at the newspaper. "Forget this candy-assed beat, go to L.A. and do something real," his boss had told him.

"Let's eat," Mark said. He poured dressing over the salad. Mary picked out a corkscrew from the drawer and started to open the bottle of wine.

"By the way," Mary said, "I spoke to my mother today. She sends you her love."

"Ah, the wonderful Sonya," said Mark as he tossed the salad.

"Oh, you two are too much!" Mary fished out the cork. She supposed she should be pleased that her boyfriend and her mother got along so well, but sometimes she felt a little jealous of their rapport. "Anyway, she's going nuts about the arrangements for Dad's party next month. I told her you might not be able to make it because of that convention you're covering."

"Oh, I've found out that it ends at noon on Saturday so I can take a flight up in the afternoon."

"Oh, that's great! She'll be so pleased. They adore you, you know."

"And why not? I'm pretty adorable."

Mary groaned with mock exaggeration. She poured two glasses of wine and sat down at the table.

"Tell me everything about L.A." said Mary. She took a sip of wine.

"Oh, God. I really don't want to talk about it now. It's going to be a challenging city to write about. Oh," he said suddenly, "the good news is I've found a house. It's in Brentwood. Two bedrooms, a pool. Ideal."

"When do you move in?"

"End of the month."

Mary put down her fork. "You know, this is delicious," she said.

"Well, one of us should be able to cook," he joked.

"I don't have time," Mary said, immediately defensive.

"You make time to go to the gym, but you don't make time to cook. One of them isn't important to you. Isn't that the way it works?"

Mary fidgeted. "Please don't lecture." She leaned forward. "I'm trying to make a career, you know. And it's not that easy. A lot of people would be very happy if I screwed up." She paused. "Anyway, I find time for you." Her eyes flashed at him.

"Sometimes," he said. Mark was unruffled; this was an old conversation. "Sweetheart, I know you want to succeed and I do know how difficult it is, but I just don't want you to lose sight of other things. There's a whole world out there that has nothing to do with television. Be a shame if you missed it."

"I suppose Amy cooked," Mary said, referring to Mark's previous girlfriend, who he had lived with for a year.

"Yep, and I put on fifteen pounds." He smiled and held out his hand. "Come here and give me a kiss."

"I would rather die," said Mary, turning her profile to him.

"You should have been an actress, you know that?"

"That's what I originally wanted to do," she said. "When I was twelve I wanted badly to be Meryl Streep. I grew my hair long so I could look like she did in *Manhattan* and then I saw *Sophie's Choice*. I had a Polish accent for weeks."

Mark laughed. "Oh, my God, you would have been terrific." He watched her get up and go to the sink. "You want water?" she asked.

"Sure," he said. He went and stood behind her. "But, first—" he said. The sentence was left unfinished. He grasped her around the waist and hoisted her on to the countertop. "What are you doing?" she asked, giggling. One of her shoes fell on the floor and she edged the other off with her stockinged foot. She felt Mark's strong, sensitive hands slip from her waist, stroking the curve of her hips and pressing against her legs, then they pushed upward under her skirt along the inside of her thighs, forcing her knees apart. Responding, she wove her legs around his back and pulled him closer. "So," he whispered as she felt his hands suddenly traveling up her back under her blouse, "how much did you really miss me?" Mary smiled as Mark looked into her eyes and, one by one, he unhooked the buttons of her blouse.

Mary's beeper, which was in her bag, suddenly shrilled.

"Oh, God," she groaned. She took his face in her hands and bent to kiss him. "I'm so sorry," she said.

Silently, he lifted her down and watched as she went to the telephone and dialed the assignment desk at Channel 6. "Hi, Don. . . . Yeah. . . . Are Hutch and Riggins available? . . . Okay . . . I'll call you when I get there." She tucked her blouse into the waistband of her skirt.

Turning to Mark, she said, "I have to go."

"I gathered," he said.

"I'm sorry," said Mary. "It's rotten timing. But this is serious. You know that radio guy, Marvin Feld, who was shot a few days ago?"

"My God. What happened?"

"Well, this time, they got him. He's dead. They found him by his car in a parking lot."

Mark groaned. "Oh, no!"

"Mark, what's the matter?"

"Oh, it's just that I knew Marvin. Went to school with him." Mark sat down heavily. "You know, in a funny way it's absolutely typical of him to die like this. He was always such a wiseass clown and he did some crazy things. You know in those days most people just didn't admit being gay but Marvin had no problem with it. I liked him for that. He liked me, too, for some reason. We'd have lunch about once a year."

"Oh, darling, I'm so sorry. If I'd known I wouldn't have blurted it out like that." She put her arms around his shoulders and hugged him tight. Gratefully, he folded his arms around her waist, laying his head against her. "Thank you, honey," he said after a while. "But you have to get going."

"I know. Would you like to come along with me, for company or something?"

Mark shook his head. "No, it's okay. Think I'll stay here and make a few phone calls."

"I'll see you after the show then." She kissed him tenderly.

Later that evening, Mark switched on the eleven o'clock news. Mary was reporting live from the studio. *"It seems a group called the New Brotherhood have taken responsibility for the death of Marvin Field. In a recent show, Feld had commented that the Bible should only be read by people with powers of abstract reasoning . . ."*

Mark sat among the debris of their interrupted dinner. He looked through the pages of notes that he had made during several telephone conversations that evening. They constituted the beginnings of research into a story he wanted to write about Marvin Feld. He leaned back and sighed. Tomorrow he would find out more about the New Brotherhood.

Outside the wind picked up, slapped through the riggings of boats moored at the Marina, and whipped against the steel cables of the Golden Gate Bridge.

THREE

IT WAS JUST past noon when Wilkes drove his rented Skylark past the gas station and Bob's Cafe. The road ahead of him licked through the sand like an asphalt tongue. The desert landscape was unfamiliar to the cop who had spent most of his life in the city, and the silence unnerved him.

He had watched a nature program once about a flower that bloomed in scrub like this. It reproduced by bursting into flame, the seeds scattered by fire. He pulled at the air-conditioning lever; it was down as far as it could go.

After the meeting, Johnson had told him he would be in contact if the deal was on. Wilkes rented a motel room in Barstow and waited. The previous night Finn had informed him that Jerry Radamacker wanted to speak with him in the desert hideout. A beat-up pickup passed him going the other way. Wilkes knew that he was doing this because of Katie. He was past feeling much, but he wanted something for her. Glimpsing the 9-mm automatic half-concealed under his jacket on the seat beside him, he sighed, and a look of regret dulled his face for an instant.

Wilkes knew that if they pulled off the robbery he would be an obvious suspect, so he had made arrangements to disappear with his share of the cash and skip across the border. In Mexico he had a few contacts and he reckoned he could hide while the heat was on. That was as far ahead as he could think for now. He felt as if part of his brain were shut off and would not let him plan beyond a certain point.

In flat, disjointed sentences Finn had told Wilkes a bit about Radamacker. He had taught college, now he was affiliated with a white supremacist church and believed that the white North American Christians were the chosen race. "The rest," Finn said, "the niggers, Chicanos, chinks, and all come from the bad guy, the one in the Bible, the one who got a mark. Cain." Radamacker, it seemed, had written a book about what was going to happen to these unsuspecting descendants of Cain and everyone else who did not agree with him.

At biweekly rallies held around the state, Jerry searched for new recruits. He looked for white unmarried men under forty. The candidates had to pass a mental and physical endurance test, and if they passed, they became part of the paramilitary unit that he personally bankrolled. Some of Radamacker's men lived in the compound, or in desert towns, others stayed in the major cities, coming out when called upon. Radamacker funded his operations through armed robberies, and he had dabbled in counterfeiting. This last piece of information Wilkes knew from his pal Danny Stevens.

When Finn talked about Radamacker's ideas he was vague about their ultimate goal.

"We are always preparing for action," Finn told Wilkes, "when the time comes, we'll be there."

"And what do you do now?" Wilkes asked.

"We done some stuff," Finn replied. "Jerry likes us to signal our presence, that's what he calls it." Finn looked at Wilkes. "We select targets. People we don't like."

Wilkes waited.

"You know that talk-show host got killed? Had a show on the radio? Big mouth, always yapping on about some fucking thing. Fucking Heeb." Finn spat.

"The one they found in the parking lot with a clip of bullets in his chest? That was Radamacker?" He waited for an answer.

"Jerry don't kill," Finn said flatly.

Wilkes was staring at Finn. Who did the killing? Who else have you killed? he wondered numbly. He decided to keep his mouth shut in the future.

Wilkes pulled over and took from his pocket the map he had drawn from Finn Johnson's directions. Satisfied he had got it right, he continued along a dirt track that curved around a mountain. On the other side of the mountain a wide valley opened up and stretched into the distance. Below him, Wilkes saw a cluster of buildings huddled together on the valley floor. It looked like a military base except for a church that dominated the drab concrete buildings around it. Wilkes could make out the concave expanse of a satellite dish on top of the church. He drove slowly down the track and round to the gateway. Ringing the compound was a high wire fence not visible from a distance.

The large gate at the entrance was closed. Inside, two guards watched the car pull up. After consultation, one of them stepped through a small door cut into the gate and walked toward the car. Both guards were wearing military-style clothing. As the guard approached the car, Wilkes found himself smiling at the man's motley outfit, which was made up of various items of army issue taken randomly from different decades, ranks, and climates.

Wilkes wound down his window. "Come to see Jerry Radamacker," he said.

"Yes, I've verified that," the guard said, standing by the car. "Would you step out?"

Wilkes did as he was told. The guard frisked him and searched his car.

"You can go in now." The guard waved at his mate and the large gate swung open. Wilkes drove in.

"Go to the parking lot to the left of the church," the second guard told him as he drove past.

As Wilkes parked by the church, a small, fat man dressed in the black garb of a minister was struggling down steps that led from the main door of the stone church. The rotund clergyman scurried toward the car, pulling out a handkerchief to wipe his face as Wilkes swung the car door shut.

"So, you must be James Wilkes," the minister said. Wilkes nodded curtly. He was no lover of the church; there had been little enough evidence of the hand of God in his thirty-nine years of life, and he was pretty sure he was not about to find it now.

"Finn Johnson told me you were expected," the minister said. "I'm Thomas Taylor, the Reverend Thomas Taylor." The pale, self-styled cleric extended a plump pink-and-white hand toward Wilkes, who squeezed the soft flesh reluctantly.

"I'm sorry you missed my Sunday sermon this morning," the minister said in a flat Texan accent. "I believe I expounded upon the topic of redemption by grace in quite a novel way." The minister rubbed his hands together; he was always looking for new recruits. Wilkes loomed over him, staring at a point on the minister's right shoulder.

"I see you're looking at the emblem of our church," Taylor said approvingly. The small gold cross had a strangely twisted configuration that Wilkes did not recognize. "I designed it myself," the minister continued, "according to ancient texts."

Before Wilkes could reply, he saw Finn walking toward them. "Cut the bull, Taylor," Finn said as he got closer. "Cop didn't come here for a sermon." Finn stopped about ten yards short of the mismatched couple and hooked his thumbs through the belt loops of his jeans. Jerking his head to indicate that Wilkes should follow, he turned and started walking toward the church steps.

"Before you go, Mr. Wilkes," the minister said. "I'd be gratified if you would take this." Taylor held out a folded pamphlet. "Contemplate it at your leisure. It may prove to be of comfort."

Wilkes slipped the paper into his jacket pocket without looking at it. He hurried after Finn's retreating back.

"It's been a pleasure talking to you, Mr. Wilkes. I wish you the best of luck," the minister called out.

Finn waited for Wilkes to catch up with him.

"So, where are we going?"

"Come on." Finn raced up the steps, and Wilkes followed at a slower pace. Finn walked past the main entrance along the length of the rectangular church and ushered Wilkes through a door in the side of the back wall.

They were in a high-ceilinged vestry behind the nave of the church. Next to the doorway, high shelves were untidily stacked with hymnals and sheet music. Opposite, under a high window, sat a large cherrywood chest.

The young man walked over to the bookshelves. Brushing the worn, blue-backed books to one side, he pushed a button. Wilkes stepped back involuntarily as a portion of the floor in front of him slid smoothly open to reveal a rusting iron spiral staircase that penetrated the hill.

"Go on." Finn nodded to Wilkes.

Wilkes descended the narrow, curling stairway and waited at the bottom for Johnson. It was cool and damp under the church and pitch-black until Finn located the light switches. Wilkes was sweating; he felt confined. Finn joined him and walked down a short corridor toward a large freight elevator.

"What *is* this place, Johnson?" asked Wilkes.

"Some comedian built it." Finn smiled. "Think that's a joke, right? But it's a fact. Guy gets wound up one day about how there's going to be a nuclear war, or something like that." Finn shrugged. "Comes out here to the fucking middle of fucking nowhere, and he builds himself a place to hide. Must've had a few dogs with him. Should see the amount of dog chow down there. Jeez!" He paused. "What a wacko, eh?"

"Some comedian," Wilkes commented.

Finn pushed the elevator button. "It's the minister's place. Comedian guy left it to him when he croaked," he said. "Taylor built the church and a house. Jerry built the rest when he came here. He keeps his office down here. Place gives me the fucking creeps."

The elevator rose noisily to their level. It looked old.

"Is it safe?" Wilkes asked.

"Oh, man!" Finn said, exasperated, and stepped in.

Gingerly, Wilkes got into the elevator and Finn pulled the gates closed. As they shakily descended, Wilkes noticed a date scored into the control panel: 1962. He was a boy then, but he remembered one summer night all those years ago when he looked at aerial photographs of gray warships pushing through a wrinkled gray sea on the seven o'clock news. Other grainy photographs showed military installations, and big black arrows pointed to the possible location of missile silos. The young Jim Wilkes was at his friend Artie's house because, unlike the Wilkes's, they had a television set. The two families sat in Artie's mother's curtained living room watching while the newscaster told them that the ships belonged to the Russian navy and they were headed toward Cuba with a bellyful of nuclear missiles.

The elevator bumped to a stop. Finn tugged the gates back. The television comedian must have panicked over the Cuban Missile Crisis, Wilkes thought, and built this weird fallout shelter in the middle of the desert. Just like Artie's mother who had started going to the supermarket three times a day until you could not get into the basement for cans of pineapple chunks.

Wilkes had to keep his head down because the ceiling was so low. Finn stood in front of a large, heavy door. As Wilkes looked up, the door swung open.

"Jim Wilkes," announced Finn, waving at Wilkes to go through the door ahead of him.

"Why, it's the detective," intoned a mocking voice familiar to Wilkes from the tapes Finn had played over and over again the year they were cellmates.

The voice was like a river, ever-changing yet always carrying the same resonant timbre. Sometimes it rang out deep and plangent, at other times it tripped lightly and swiftly. Inmates smuggled the voice from cell to cell. On the tapes Radamacker talked of winning and losing, about the Bible and the white man, about a new world that would rise up from the American wasteland, the bald eagle become phoenix. Wilkes saw the tapes calming men with hope at one moment, agitating them with righteous anger the next.

"Jerry Radamacker." A thin man in a cheap navy suit emerged from behind a large, littered desk top and extended his hand. Wilkes had imagined a bigger man. Radamacker was about five ten, his narrow frame exaggerated by the ill-fitting suit. His chest, however, was broad and his upper body well-developed by exercise, which accounted for the volume of his voice. He wore wire-framed glasses and his skin was pale and pitted with scars.

Radamacker's desk was covered with papers, maps, empty milk cartons, and videocassette tapes. Behind his chair, an American flag hung limply from a wooden pole. It could have been the district attorney's office, Wilkes thought, except for the location. And the video technology, he added when he turned to his left and saw a floor-to-ceiling, wall-to-wall bank of television monitors.

Jerry noticed Wilkes's stare. "I've got a closed circuit system around the base. Wouldn't want to miss anything," he said. "Of course, I get regular television, too. And cable, and I get the network feeds because of the dish." He sat down in the chair behind his desk, gesturing for Wilkes to sit on the flimsy fold-out chair in front of him.

Radamacker was watching a San Francisco station. A blond woman stood with a microphone in front of a large building where a candlelight vigil was being held for the murdered talk-show host. He turned the volume down. "Hymie fag," he commented. "Belongs dead." He winked at Johnson who smiled.

"Go on," Radamacker said to Finn.

"Yeah. I'm going to the range." Johnson closed the door behind him. Jerry looked at Wilkes sharply. "You know what's worse than a fag?" He paused and looked away. "A nigger woman," he said with violence. "Look at that Winfrey woman, Aunt Jemima I call her. She's destroying families around the country. You know how she does it? She shows children how to run up bills on their parents' credit cards. It's true!" Radamacker's eyes blazed, though his voice was steady. "She did a show on it!

"That's what happens," he continued, "when you let the Negroes out of their cages. They don't know how to control themselves. Why should they? They don't belong."

Radamacker grinned mirthlessly at Wilkes. "People are surprised when they hear me say that. They figure I've got no compassion. But I see the big picture. I realize that they don't know how to act decently because they have been oppressed for so long. So"—Radamacker fixed Wilkes with his glittery stare—"So, I say send them back to where they came from. Let them go back to Africa. And we'll take the whites. That's what they want, right? I wrote a book, you know. Show you how the world should be. I'm a professor. Did Johnson tell you that?"

Wilkes nodded.

"An engineer. I taught college. Taught and wrote a book. I'm a Renaissance man you might say." He paused. "But I learned the hard way, I know what it's like on the streets. You know Chicago?" Wilkes shook his head. "Can be a tough place for a kid to grow up. Book learning won't help you there, just being on top. I never got caught, that was my secret." Radamacker looked at Wilkes thoughtfully. "Have you got what it takes?" he asked. "Don't answer," he said, as Wilkes struggled to follow him. "We'll find out soon enough."

Uncomfortably, Wilkes shifted his weight. Radamacker's mood suddenly became businesslike. He picked up a hundred-dollar bill from the flotsam on the desk. "What do you think of this?" He gave the banknote to Wilkes.

Wilkes studied the bill. He rubbed it between his thumb and forefinger. "Good way to get noticed," he said finally. "Your machines are old," he explained. "The ink isn't applied right."

Jerry barked a short, hard laugh. "Thank you, Detective." He leaned forward. "Now, Finn told me you have a lead to the real thing," he said silkily.

Wilkes pulled a piece of paper from the pocket of his denim jacket and smoothed it with the palm of his hand over his knee in an attempt to flatten out the creases. "I have the schedule for the trucks through next Saturday. They change every week, sometimes more often. I think—"

"A drinker. That's what Finn told me." Jerry's face was agitated. "Milk. You should drink milk." The muscles in his face relaxed a little. "Milk kills the chemicals they put in our water to brainwash us." He paused.

"Yeah," said Wilkes cautiously, not looking at Radamacker directly. "The way I see it," he continued, "is this—the only times I've known Goldor to change the schedule was when they just had a problem and they got suspicious of something. Now, the building won't hold any surprises for me, but we'll need someone who's good with electrical work and at least two other men. We'll have to deal with four guards and a nighttime janitor. 'Course, we'll also need radios and getaway cars." He looked up. "Listen, Goldor depends on no one knowing the schedules or the security system, and I know them both. It's a chance in a lifetime!" Wilkes finished his recitation and shifted his weight back. He looked squarely at Radamacker. "I'd want a fifty-fifty split," he added.

Radamacker leaned back and, resting his elbows on the arms of his button-back leather chair, brought his fingertips together. "The way *I* see it, Jim," he said softly, "is that I'm putting my men on the line for a delivery you think might not even happen if Goldor gets 'suspicious of something.' In addition, I am providing all the support with no money down." Jerry tapped his fingers against one other. He looked across the desk. "Do you believe in revolution, Jim?" he asked.

"What d'you mean exactly?" asked Wilkes.

"Do you believe that without crime in our city streets, without corruption in our public officials, without pollution in our lakes, and hormones in our sirloin steaks, this mighty land would stand above all other nations? Do you believe that?" Radamacker's voice had risen excitedly. He got up and started pacing in front of the video screens.

"Well, sure, sure I do," Wilkes said hesitantly.

"Did you know that the military has canceled all leave for the first three months of next year?" said Radamacker. He stopped in front of Wilkes and looked at him, his gray-green eyes as glassy as marbles. "Did you know," he said, thumping the desk with his fist, "that Saddam Hussein has injected a new strain of AIDS into the American people? Did you know"—his hand crashed against the surface of the desk again with a force that scattered papers to the floor—"that the Federal Reserve is going to issue new, blue money in two years' time?" Radamacker's breathing was hard and ragged, and he glared savagely at Wilkes without seeming to see him.

Wilkes was silent. He was terrified that Radamacker was going to completely lose control. For the first time he noticed a small picture of Adolf Hitler on the wall beside Radamacker's desk.

Radamacker started pacing again. When he spoke his voice was lower, but it was tense with pent-up rage. "But of course you can't know these things yet." He spat. "It takes study to learn the pattern. You see," he said as he gestured at the monitors, "everything you see on the tube is controlled. The Jews have gotten a lock on the communications industry. You can't trust anything you see anymore. Jim, Jim, there's so much to explain." His hands jerked with agitated gestures.

"Perhaps you would like to come to one of my meetings. You'll see how everything is part of a plan."

He turned to face Wilkes. "I'm going to fight them, Jim. I'll fight for a free America." A manic smile slashed across his face. "You could be part of the struggle, you know. It's people like you who make America great, Jim. Don't let the international tricksters rob you of your birthright. If you come with us, Jim, we'll fight for you." He pulled Wilkes to his feet by his jacket collar.

Wilkes kept his head down. He talked slowly. "What you say is very interesting, and I'll consider it in my own way. But I came to you because of the job. Do we have a deal?"

Radamacker released him and walked behind his desk. Jim sank back into his chair. "Thirty-five percent," he said briskly. "And I'm being generous. But thirty-five percent of nothing buys less than nothing, which is what you'll be if something goes wrong." He paused. "Thirty-five percent." Radamacker was dismissive. He looked absently at Wilkes, an expression of delicate distaste shading his face. It was as if the big, awkward man had suddenly become an object of pity and aversion, an old bear dancing at the end of a tattered rope.

"Okay." Wilkes felt exhausted by the interview. Radamacker suddenly grew genial. He stepped around his desk and clapped the ex-cop on the back. "I'm going to put Johnson in charge of the operation. He'll be in the field, and I'll oversee from here. You stay here at the base now, and we'll plan the whole thing. We could be ready to strike in a day and half." He motioned for Wilkes to follow him out of the office.

Radamacker led him past the elevator and into a long tunnel. Wilkes kept bumping his head on the ceiling while Jerry waved an ineffectual flashlight in front of them. They were heading westward through a secret passage that connected Jerry's office with his living quarters, and they emerged in the basement of the largest of six, poorly constructed shacks that lined the rim of the compound.

At the back of the shacks, a piece of scrubland thirty feet wide ended in a high wooden fence. The fence enclosed the shooting range where Finn was practicing. A group of men were working on the engine of a jeep; two more sat in the shade of a back doorway reading comic books. As Radamacker and Wilkes walked across the strip, the men gave loose salutes that Jerry returned.

"Got to have discipline," he commented. He walked toward a door in the fence and paused. A shot rang out. "Johnson!" he yelled.

Finn opened the door from the inside. He looked at Radamacker, who nodded, then his gaze widened to include Wilkes. Content with what he saw, Finn cracked a lazy smile. "Like to feel the kick of a nine-millimeter Browning?" he asked Wilkes. "Think you can handle it?"

"Sure." The ex-cop stepped inside the shooting range. Finn walked toward a booth at the back where several cases had been laid out, some with their lids flipped open, others sealed. Finn lovingly lifted the Browning Hi-Power from its velvet-lined case.

"This babe's a beaut," he said, handing the weapon to Wilkes, who took the gun and rolled it in his hand to feel the heft of it before he loaded a clip.

"Why don't you try it from twenty feet," Radamacker said, indicating a line in front of the nearest target.

Wilkes moved forward slowly. He saw half a dozen targets staggered down the length of the range. Each stood six feet tall and had been cut to resemble the outline of a man facing front, arms akimbo, feet planted solidly apart. Tacked onto each frame were sheets of paper painted crudely with the uniform of a California police officer. Patched to the forehead and over the heart of each figure were the white-and-black circles of a bull's-eye. As Wilkes neared the twenty-foot line, he saw that the faces of the dummy cops were painted with the features characteristic of six ethnic groups.

Wilkes shuffled onto the line. Before he aimed, he looked back over his shoulder. Finn was slouched against the fence, buffing his gun with a soft cloth. Jerry stood beside him, staring unblinkingly at the ex-cop.

"You have a problem?" Jerry Radamacker threatened, smooth as axle grease. Slowly, Wilkes shook his head.

"So, shoot, why don't you?" he ordered. "Blow the enemy to hell."

FOUR

"YOU CAN JUST feel the tension in this arena! How about that! He nearly went over the rope. Weighs upward of 400 pounds! Using that nerve clasp under the arm! Kicks the midsection!! Headbutts him . . . and again! Now he picks him up . . . drops him down . . . and . . . look at that! He goes to the ropes! And he's going to do it again! He's done it again! He's on the floor! And he's not getting up! And yes! We have a new champion!

"And that's sports for tonight, Charlie."

"Well, that was quite a performance, Joe, what . . ."

"No, it's no good. We have to kill number sixteen." In the control room, producer Paul Berman looked at his director Mike Duvall, who nodded. Berman spoke into the microphone, connecting him to Charlie Monroe, the eleven o'clock news anchor. "Let's kill the reader on the water shortage and go straight to the weather."

Monroe was not pleased to lose even a minute of his precious airtime. "I'm an anchorman, not a traffic cop," he grumbled.

Mary Reed detached a microphone from the folds of her dress and headed toward the control room without saying a word. Inside the small, cool room, lit cathode-ray blue by a bank of monitors, she made straight for Berman who was sitting between Duvall and Ginny MacIntyre, his writer on the show.

"Sure we can't cut out of Ray's report early?" Berman asked Ginny as Mary approached him.

"No, no. We have to keep it all, it's impossible to cut it any more," Ginny responded mechanically. It was the third time in the last two minutes that Berman had asked her the same question.

"Jesus, it's going to be real tight," the producer said. He leaned back in his chair and stretched his back. "Hello, there," he said greeting Mary, who had been standing behind him for a few moments. "Nice piece about City Hall you did tonight. You've got some great sources."

"What did you mean before?" asked Mary, ignoring the courtesies.

"Listen, Mary," Berman said with a sigh, "we've got to keep your pieces down. I'm becoming a time merchant here. I had to kill Charlie's reader just to give you an extra thirty seconds on your report. I can't keep winging it, you can appreciate that." Berman was trying to control his temper but the effort was making him sweat. He pushed his hand through his wiry black hair.

"Ten, nine, eight . . ." the associate director counted down.

Mary clenched her jaw. She was pale under her studio makeup, but the eleven o'clock news was now on the air again and she could not argue her point. She drew herself up. "Some of us," she said haughtily, "are trying to report news, not wrestling." As Mary swept out of the control room, Ginny MacIntyre raised her eyebrows.

"So, you want to be a producer?" Berman grinned at Ginny. He picked up the red telephone. "Hey, Charlie," he said. "Remember, the reader's gone. Go straight to the weather."

"Wyatt?" Mary was on the phone to the news director at his home. "You see my piece just now?"

"Hello, Mary," Wyatt said with mild resignation. He motioned his wife to go back into the living room, where she was serving coffee to their dinner guests.

"Did you see it?" Did you like it? Was it too long?" Mary asked rapidly.

"It was great, Mary." He paused. "Really," he added, when Mary didn't say anything.

"Berman said I've got to keep the reports down to exactly three minutes. It can't always be done, you know."

"No story exists that can't be made shorter, you know that," said Wyatt evenly. He had made it a policy to interfere in the mechanics of a news show as little as possible, which removed him from this type of petty bickering and gave his good producers the freedom to grow.

"Well, I hope you enjoyed the wrestling highlights," Mary said irritably, sensing that she was not getting anywhere.

"I couldn't give a damn about the wrestling highlights!" Wyatt sighed. "But the audiences love them. Come on, Reed, give me a break."

"Well, you're going to get an extra three minutes and thirty seconds of wrestling highlights when I'm gone."

"Listen, you've been working hard, Mary. Sweeps start soon. Take the rest of the week off, give yourself a break."

"If you say the same thing tomorrow morning, I might believe you," Mary said. "Good night." She hung up.

"Who was that, dear?" Wyatt's wife, Ann, asked as she poured her husband a fresh cup of decaffeinated espresso.

"Mary Reed." Wyatt drank deeply.

"And what's she complaining about this time?" Ann asked with a knowing smile.

"Thirty seconds."

"Oh." Ann turned to her guests, who had started to leave. "So soon?" she asked them.

Mary's Nightbeat report was one of the main reasons the eleven o'clock news on Channel 6 was often the top-rated show. Andrews had recognized that most late news shows were a rehash of the earlier programs and, to counter this, Mary's pieces were designed to give the impression that the reporter had been pacing the streets of San Francisco between seven and eleven every night. In addition, the three-minute segment had become the perfect vehicle for city news stories that would otherwise be buried by national events, which took precedence in the earlier shows.

In order to showcase his star reporter, Wyatt ensured that Mary's pieces either led off the news or came right after the first commercial break. At first, the late news anchors objected to playing second fiddle but Wyatt prevailed. "This is not a democracy, Charlie," he told one anchorman. "I make the rules, you follow them. If you don't like it, you're free to go." That was a year ago, when Nightbeat had first started. Now, Mary was a staple of the eleven o'clock news, to such an extent that Wyatt had seen research indicating that some viewers thought that Mary actually anchored it—which was just what the regular anchors had feared, of course.

The news director was also aware that the reporters on the late news were resentful of Mary's three minutes of virtually guaranteed airtime. Three minutes were a significant percentage of the half-hour news program; if you took out the time used for commercials, sports, and weather, there were precisely fourteen available for programming. What reporters resented even more, however, was that when Mary's reports fell through, Andrews had suggested that she use those of the other reporters, which she repackaged so that it looked as though she had done them. Some people grumbled and some of them left, but most stayed because it was always more fun to work for a number-one show.

Not that Mary actually tramped the streets of the city from seven to eleven looking for stories. Unless a story broke late, she and the eleven o'clock producer, Paul Berman, usually decided what they wanted to do by six-thirty. They would take a tape from the library, and put together the body of the report, edit it, and record a new narrative track over it. Mary went to the studio or outside location at ten-thirty and did a fifteen- or twenty-second introduction to the tape, which usually ran about one minute. Afterward, she wrapped up the report by answering a question, often prearranged, from the studio anchor. The anchor playing the straight man to a knowledgeable reporter was a classic routine heavily relied upon by local news stations. The system worked well, and Mary usually got time off for dinner between seven and ten before winding up her working day after the eleven o'clock show.

Wyatt Andrews lay awake in bed, listening to his wife's light snores. His own working day was not short, but as he stared at the ceiling thinking of Mary's long and demanding hours, he shook his head. For all the glamour and attention, hers was not a job he envied; he had seen too many kids burn out under the strain. Wyatt looked at the clock. The following day, he had a meeting with his boss, the station manager, who would try to pare the news budget once again. He had lost some good people this year because of the budget cuts, and he did not relish losing any more. Andrews sighed, then turned on his side to welcome sleep.

"Oh, Paul," Mary said. It was the afternoon of the following day, and Paul Berman had dropped by Mary's office. "I've got something for you." She handed him a rectangular package, elaborately gift-wrapped.

"It's not going to explode, is it?" he joked. "One of those bombs that kills television producers but leaves tall buildings standing?"

Mary laughed. "Well, I thought your kid might like it."

"The Hulkster!" Berman said, unwrapping the package and holding up a framed photograph of Hulk Hogan.

"I thought maybe we could interview him on 'Nightbeat.' "

"Hey, for Hulk Hogan you get four minutes," Berman said.

"Witnesses!" Mary shouted. "I need someone to hear you say that, so you can't worm out of it when the time comes!"

"Seriously, Mary. When it's important, you'll get your thirty seconds. All you have to do is ask. Just give us a little warning, that's all." His tone was light but firm. There was no point antagonizing Mary again, but every now and then he liked to win a point or she would walk all over him.

"Thank you for my photo," he said, holding her peace offering to his chest. "Josh'll really get a kick out of it."

Through her open door, Mary watched Berman melt into the newsroom as she punched a number on her phone. No pictures adorned the four walls of her office. The only item that betrayed its occupant's identity was an eight-by-ten photograph of last year's Emmy Awards ceremony. Mary had carried off the prize for investigative journalism with her four-part special on AIDS, winning the awards for reporting, writing, and producing. It was the first time in San Francisco's history that one series had taken the three top investigative awards. The photograph, tacked crookedly to the wall behind a cluttered credenza, showed the reporter and her award-winning editor, Nina Basalt, holding the statuettes. When you looked closely, you could tell that Mary's face had been chubbier then, her smile less practiced. In the last year, she had outgrown the last vestiges of adolescent awkwardness.

A large vase filled with withered flowers—the gift of an admirer—stood on the corner of her desk. Eventually a colleague would throw the bouquet away with an exasperation that Mary would smile at without understanding; she had not noticed. Videotapes, books, and papers littered the surfaces of her office, including the floor. The Channel 6 cleaners had instructions banning them from entering the office and disrupting her idiosyncratic filing system.

With the phone cradled between her shoulder and ear, Mary paced back and forth in her stockinged feet. Stretching the telephone cord to its utmost, she reached the door before turning and padding back behind her desk to glance at the monitor in the corner. John Ransome, the network anchor, was reading the evening news.

She hung up and dialed again. "Mark, hi. I read your piece in the *Herald* today. It's really excellent. The way you described the candlelight vigil his lover arranged for him instead of a funeral was amazing."

"That was a good part," Mark agreed. After doing some extra research, he had written a moving and clever piece that did justice to the angry humor of Marvin Feld, the slain talk-show host and his ex-classmate. The *Herald* had run it that morning.

"This group, the New Brotherhood. You didn't find out much about them?"

"You can tell, huh? Kept running into brick walls with those guys. No leads panned out. That'd be a major point of research for the book—"

"The book?" Mary asked.

"Oh, didn't I mention it?" Mark said with a rehearsed casualness. "I got a call from a publisher in New York. They're interested in a full-length biography, want me to write it. Wouldn't that be something?"

Mary experienced a twinge of envy of which she was instantly ashamed.

". . . We could write it together," Mark was saying.

"Is this another of your ruses to get me into print journalism?"

"You're a fine writer, Mary, and you're learning to be a good journalist, too. You should find out what a real reporter does for a living one of these days."

"Oh, I do plenty of real reporting on television, thank you," said Mary, rising to the bait despite herself.

"Television reporting is an oxymoron. Television is about emotion, not news. Did you know that the amount of information conveyed in the evening news is equal to about a third of one newspaper page?"

"So, where were you during the major events of your lifetime?" Mary countered. "I bet you were glued to the tube during Watergate. And"—Mary drove her point home—"when you heard about the Tiannamen Square protest, did you buy a paper or did you watch one man stand up against a tank? One picture told the story far more eloquently than words."

"Yes, but then what? You guys"—Mark was well into his stride when he started referring to her as "you guys"—"you guys capture a moment like that and then you unplug your blow-dryers and you're off to the next photo session."

"In that particular case, I think they banned all cameras and all reporters. The picture had scared them."

"Maybe, but still you get my point. Television news is skewed by its emotional content . . ."

"A little like this conversation," Mary suggested.

"I've been ranting, haven't I? It's all the excitement."

"Listen, are you still on for next weekend?"

"You mean your father's sixtieth? Sure, I'm coming up on Saturday afternoon."

"Excellent. I'll meet your flight." Another call came in. "I've got to go. Congratulations, sweetheart, I love you. Call me later, okay."

"Ms. Reed," a female voice said. "I have some information you might find interesting."

"Really," Mary said.

"I'm calling from home. It's about the School Board. I couldn't call you from there—someone might hear me." The woman sounded more and more agitated.

"Take a deep breath," Mary advised.

She waited for the women to collect herself. "Now tell me what's going on." Mary pulled her notepad toward her and started writing.

FIVE

FINN JOHNSON WAS talking about the time he and four of Radamacker's men robbed an armored truck on the road. "Guess the dummy couldn't read. Had this sign, see. Wrote it myself before we left the compound. It said 'Get out or die.' Moron fucking sat there staring at the sign like a fucking zombie. Didn't budge an inch. What a dickhead." Finn shook his head at the man's folly.

Wilkes nodded. The two were sitting on low campstools in the basement of Radamacker's safehouse in San Francisco eating hamburgers. It was a few minutes after two A.M. on their second night in the city. The night before, they had done a dry run of the Goldor security depot robbery that Wilkes had planned with Jerry and Finn. Everything happened just as the ex-cop had said it would, and tonight they were going to pull the job. As Finn and Wilkes waited, Red and Caban, the two other men Jerry had assigned to the operation, were at the Goldor depot defusing the alarm system. In an hour the men in the safehouse would join them.

"Real pea brain, eh?" Finn said with wonder, pulling himself out of his reverie to look at Wilkes. He was chewing his burger with his mouth open. "Sprayed the fucking truck with bullets. Have to use armor-piercing bullets to get through those vans. Man, they rip through manganese steel like it was butter. Truck looked like a slice of Swiss time we were through. Fucking asshole guard didn't stand a chance."

"Thought they banned those bullets," said Wilkes. He was not that interested in how Finn got the illegal ammo, but they had time to pass and he was getting sleepy, a sure sign he was nervous.

Wilkes remembered the day he was given a cell with the slight twenty-five-year-old. Finn had said nothing for a month, and Wilkes was too involved in his own predicament to bother with his silent cellmate. One day, however, when he saw Finn was getting badly beaten up, the ex-cop placed his heavyweight's bulk between the boy and his tormentors. It was the sort of impulse a man without a badge should try to restrain, but Wilkes had not learned that then.

After that, Finn began to talk to his rescuer. He would talk for hours at a time, then he would say nothing for a few days. Wilkes did not offer much of a response, but for Finn it was enough that he listened to the young man's broken stories, tolerated his moody silences.

Over the months Finn told the ex-cop about his life. How he grew up on a farm in rural Iowa; how when he was twelve his father walked out of the door without saying a word and was never heard from again. How six months later his mother went into the orchard, put the barrel of a pistol into her mouth, and pulled the trigger. The boy found her under the apple trees when he came home from school. Finn remembered it was May because the white blossoms from the trees had dropped on her legs. He tried not to look at the mess the lead had made of her head. In the kitchen he sat and waited for his sister to come home from school. Mary Ellen was two years older and would know what to do.

    His sister was not afraid to look at their mother. She said that what had happened to her would be their secret. So they buried her under the apple trees and began to run the farm themselves. Few people questioned the children's absence from school and no one thought to make the trip out to the remote Johnson farm to check them out. It was only a year later when the bank looked down its columns of figures and noticed something awry that someone went out to see what was going on. Two days later the men from the bank drove back with the law in tow. The bank took the farm and the sheriff took the Johnson kids and placed them in special schools.

    Finn was arrested three years later after he tried to blow up a cash machine. The cash machine belonged to the bank that had taken the Johnson farm, but that did not figure as an issue in the trial. Finn was given a suspended sentence and sent to reform school. Mary Ellen had run off to Chicago by then. For a while she sent him letters filled with schemes for him to join her in the city but her last letter was different. "Don't look for me here," she wrote. "If you saw me now, I'd hate you. Make believe I'm dead."

    When he left school, Finn went to Chicago but his sister had vanished. He drifted west and became good at stealing cars, tuning them up, and selling them. By the time he reached California, he had seen the inside of a few county jails on charges of auto theft and illegal weapons possession. Twice he jumped bail; and in Chas, South Dakota, he escaped jail.

    When Finn reached California, he felt happier because he liked the climate. He started working in a used-car dealership, supplying cars for Armenian-born Bibi Bibielniks. Things were good for a while because Bibi had no children and liked having the young man around. Then Bibi found that Finn was stealing money from the business. There was a fight in which the Armenian pulled a gun, but it was Finn who pulled the trigger, lodging a bullet in the older man's spine. In the hospital Bibi lapsed into a coma and had remained unconscious for the two years Finn had been in jail on charges of robbery and attempted murder. The sentence maddened Mrs. Bibielniks, who wanted to pull the plug on the life-support system that kept her husband alive and pin a murder charge on Johnson. Every week she sent Finn a note in prison swearing vengeance on him and his unborn children.

Finn had the idea that if he just kept quiet, everyone would leave him alone. But he soon attracted the attention of one of the fiercer inmates and in the first few months was raped three times. The fourth time Wilkes stepped in. The man who had raped him was black, and afterward Johnson talked endlessly to Wilkes about how he would be revenged on Big Mo.

In the mornings Finn started to exercise with a Walkman in his ears. That was when he discovered Jerry Radamacker, the voice that seemed to say everything that Finn thought but had not found the words to express. Wilkes had no patience for Radamacker, which was maybe why Finn never told him about an event that was to change his life.

It happened one hot afternoon as Finn lay on his bed listening to a new Madonna tape. All of a sudden the song stopped and it seemed to Finn that then he heard another voice. It was the voice of . . . well, he did not exactly imagine that it was His voice, most likely He would send down one of His Lesser Angels to talk to a jailbird like Finn Johnson. But Finn heard the voice of the Lesser Angel, or whatever, and it said many things in a strange tongue.

He strained to hear the voice in the clamorous cell block that stank of men and industrial disinfectant until, gradually, he started to make out English words. "Finn Emory Johnson," the voice addressed him, "you will be released from jail soon. Ahead you have a long, arduous journey and it will be necessary for you to carry a firearm with you at all times. Whatever people say or do to you, you will never give up your weapon. If you do as I say, you will be rewarded hereafter . . ." The voice faded and then drifted away. When Finn glanced down at the controls on his Walkman, the tape was still although the play button was down.

A few weeks later, Bibi woke up from his coma, right as rain. Johnson's lawyer got the charges reduced and Finn was eventually released. Their parting was unemotional, but Wilkes found he missed the young man's nervous energy, his strange, slow smile.

The ex-cop looked over at Finn. "What did Radamacker mean by calling you his brother?" he asked.

"Yeah?" Finn was finishing his fries. "He said that?" Finn balled his napkin and threw it into the corner. "Brothers in blood," he said seriously. "Cut ourselves and all." He paused. "I protect him. Feels safe with me around. I carry the gun, Jerry feels good."

Finn drained his can of soda just as a high-pitched buzz sounded. Tossing the can, he walked through a low cement archway into a small, recessed space in the corner of the basement where a short-wave radio stood.

Red and Caban called in from the Goldor depot to report on the first step of their operation. Radamacker never used the telephone company. In his office he had explained to Wilkes how the Zionists had infiltrated the telecommunications industry and used code phrases to communicate with one another. Jerry told Wilkes that when a telephone operator tells you to "Have a nice day" it means that the Zionists were signaling for renewed slaughter of the Aryan race. *They make little effort to conceal themselves,* Radamacker had said, *so confident are they of success.*

While Finn was speaking into the radio, Wilkes pushed the last mouthful of his hamburger and bun into his mouth. He stared at the crates and boxes that filled the basement. Wilkes had identified some of the boxes earlier, when Finn was speaking to Jerry: machine guns, antitank weapons, boxes of explosives, assault rifles. He saw one he had not noticed before and kicked at it, too lazy to get up and look. It was a small square carton, and nothing had been stored on top of it. As the box tipped over sideways from the impact of his kick, Wilkes caught it with his left foot and dragged it toward him. The cardboard flaps parted, spilling thousands of polystyrene beads like foam across the concrete floor. Wilkes cursed and steadied the carton. Curious, he fished among the beads for contents. His hand resurfaced holding a small, glass bottle of vitamin tablets. Vitamin B_{12} he noted as his shoulders heaved with silent laughter.

Finn stood in the archway. "Man! Clean that shit up. We're out of here as soon as we get the okay from the commander." Radamacker liked to be called commander during an operation.

"That was Red?" Wilkes asked.

"Yeah. Caban's in the building. Red set off the alarm again at ten forty-five, and the cops just showed up. Took them three and a half hours this time. They got to figure the alarm's on the fritz by now." Finn looked at Wilkes. It was Wilkes's idea to set the alarm off deliberately several times to make it look as if it were broken. The first time the cops came in twenty minutes. Now, if Finn and his men accidentally tripped off an alarm, the police would take their time.

"Great idea I had," said Wilkes. He started trying to sweep the tiny white balls into a corner with the broadside of his foot.

"Red said dismantling the alarm was a piece of cake," said Finn. He turned back to the radio.

Wilkes stretched a dark cotton sweater over his head and pulled it down over his chest. He slotted his old S&W 9-mm automatic on his hip. It was the one he had used when he was on the force, and it made him feel better to have it riding with him now. He patted the pocket of his jacket to make sure the ski mask was there and slipped his hands into a pair of leather gloves.

"All set, partner?" Finn asked, coming back. He was

smiling and his eyes, usually cloudy, were bright. "The Commander said it's go."

Wilkes drove toward the north end of the deserted financial district where garbage trucks were noisily digesting yesterday's newspapers and parked the stolen Chevrolet on the street while Finn checked with Red on the walkie-talkie. Wilkes got out. He was gasping for air, and his legs were shaking. He closed his eyes and tried to take slow, regular breaths until Finn was ready.

The two men slipped silently along the sidewalk on sneakered feet. An occasional car thrummed past them. A derelict held out a hand for money and blessed them when they passed her by. At the corner of Sansome, just before Lincoln Street, Finn turned around sharply, skipped a couple of steps to regain his balance and walked rapidly backward for five or six paces while his eyes darted around him.

"Okay," hissed Finn, taking Wilkes's arm, and the two men ducked into a dark alley. He pointed at a door made of large iron panels, tall and wide enough to fit a truck.

Wilkes nodded, his mouth dry.

"I'm going to signal," Finn whispered. Taking a flashlight from his pocket, he directed it at a window on the second floor. After a thirty-second pause that felt like forever, a crack opened at the bottom of one panel and grew wider.

"Now," ordered Finn when the opening was a foot wide. Wilkes rolled himself lengthwise through the opening. He came to a halt just as Finn, who had done the same, bumped into him. The panel dropped back into place, leaving Finn and Wilkes to grope in the dark until a flashlight beam picked them out.

"You guys okay?" asked Red, standing over them. He wiped his forehead with the hand that held the flashlight so that the beam bounced around the cavernous interior of the depot, catching the white letters of Goldor's insignia on the side of an armored car that occupied most of the visible space.

"I was real worried about that door panel, but it opened fine," said Red.

"Okay," Finn said. He jumped up suddenly. "What's that fucking red light over there?" he whispered savagely into Red's ear. "You told me the janitor would be taken care of." He had grasped Red's forearm and was pinching the skin hard with his fingers.

"Only me." Tony Caban stepped forward, a thick cigar in his mouth.

"Put that fucking thing out right now, dickbrain," Finn hissed. "No, give it here. I'll do it."

"Sorry, I'm sorry, okay?" Caban mumbled.

"He took them from the office, that's where we was waiting."

"You could blow the operation, jerkass." Finn ground the cigar under his heel until the persistent red glow was extinguished.

"Okay, it's nearly four. You got your hoods?" Finn paused. "You waiting for a sign from Jesus or something? Put the motherfuckers on and get into position," he hissed.

While Wilkes pulled out his mask, Finn, Caban, and Red unfolded black cloth cowls and put them over their heads. The hoods were square at the top with triangular holes over the eyes. Silently the men moved into their prearranged posts.

An hour later, Finn and Wilkes still stood shoulder to shoulder in the darkness. Wilkes had cramps in his foot.

"They're late," Finn whispered. He barely shaped the words, but Wilkes heard the threat implied in the statement.

At that moment, they heard footsteps, and a light illuminated the vault where they were hiding. A uniformed guard wearing a heavy holster around his midriff checked the space. He nodded and two men entered followed by a second armed guard. All four wore the white Goldor letters stitched to the tops of their sleeves.

One of the two unarmed guards walked up to the combination lock on a safe in the back of the room and dialed seven numbers. He stepped back for his colleague to complete the sequence, which he did not know, and waited for him to swing open the heavy iron door.

"Now!" commanded Finn loudly. The four masked robbers jumped out in a fanlike pattern. Red and Wilkes overpowered the two unarmed men and slapped handcuffs on their wrists.

"Drop your fucking weapons." Finn threatened the guards with the long nose of his M-16 machine gun. "And, don't move unless you want your balls blown off," he added.

Caban moved in as the buckles of the guards' holsters clunked on the floor.

"Close your eyes. Keep them fucking shut. This ain't no joke!" Johnson screamed, his voice muffled by the hood. Caban bound the guards.

"Okay. Turn around. All of you." Finn lined up the four Goldor men against the wall with their backs toward him. "Move it, brothers," he said to his own men over his shoulder.

Wilkes, Caban, and Red started loading the van with bags from the opened safe. "I said, move it," Finn hissed angrily. The three heaved sacks more rapidly from hand to hand.

"Okay," Johnson snapped. "Let's not get greedy."

The human chain broke. They had carried off about three-quarters of the bags from the safe. Red and Caban pushed a last load into the back of the truck and got in.

Wilkes stood by the driver's door. His ski mask was hot, and sweat misted his eyes. He pushed a hand under the mask to wipe his eyes.

"Get in," Finn ordered him.

There was a sound from one of the guards. Finn's body tensed. "Someone say something?" he said menacingly to the four men against the wall.

As he pulled up his mask to mop his face, Wilkes saw one of the guards looking at him. Wilkes's eyes were wide with horror; he was fixed to the spot.

"Get the truck outta here. Wait for me outside in the alley. I got some business to finish inside," Finn muttered.

Wilkes was driving Finn down Route 5. The four men had dropped the truck under the Oakland Bay Bridge and were driving back along separate routes in two cars. Finn and Wilkes had the money.

"He recognized me," Wilkes said. His hands gripped the steering wheel so that the knotted muscles on his hands were white. His knee shook uncontrollably as he concentrated on driving the car.

"Fucker can't talk," said Finn. He sounded bored. "Not now he can't."

"What d'you mean?" Wilkes asked but even as he spoke he understood. "You blew them away? That's why you stayed there at the end?" Wilkes turned his head from the road to look at Johnson. "All of them?" he asked.

The radio played rock music. "Remember Big Mo." Finn said finally.

On either side of the freeway, tan-colored hills rolled into the middle distance like the rounded flanks of ponies. The sun had risen to its full height.

"Pull over," Finn said after a while. "I need to take a leak."

SIX

FROM THE CAB window Mary studied the familiar streets of Portland. She was looking forward to going home. Tonight was her father's sixtieth-birthday celebration. There would be a dinner for the family's closest friends and relatives followed by a party.

Hillary Reed came from an old family in Portland. He had been an idealistic young lawyer in the sixties and had worked for several years as a public prosecutor. When Mary was four years old, he took the natural step for a man of his background and position and joined his uncle's law firm. His experience as a prosecutor and his conscientious, deliberate approach to the law stood him in good stead in the firm and he quickly became a partner. He further enhanced his community standing by taking on the occasional pro bono case. A staunch Democrat for years, Hillary Reed had become disillusioned with the party after Carter's presidency, and he not only voted for Reagan but ran on the Republican ticket for a judgeship. He got the post and since then had run unopposed.

The Reeds had a house in the West Hills section of town, and they belonged to the exclusive Multnomah Athletic Club. Mary was sent to Catlin Gable private school, and Hillary Reed was delighted when she decided to go to Stanford, his alma mater. Although his profession had made him wary of journalists, the judge was enormously proud of his daughter's achievements. If he had known more about her workaholic habits, however, he would have been appalled. Everything had come easily and naturally to Hillary Reed, and he would not have expected it to be any other way for Mary.

The cab pulled up to the fine turn-of-the-century Victorian house where Mary had grown up. As she closed the gate, the heavy wooden front door of the house swung open and a tall, blond woman untidily dressed in a sweater and slacks came running toward her.

"Mary, honey, I'm so happy you came early." Sonya Reed hugged her daughter vigorously.

"Mom," Mary protested, untangling herself from her mother's embrace, "I saw you two months ago, and you call me every week."

"I know," Sonya said, dropping her arms, "but you're my little baby, remember."

"Not anymore," Mary said firmly. She picked up her bag.

In the large kitchen at the back of the house Sonya prepared her daughter's favorite childhood lunch, a tuna sandwich and a Diet Coke.

Sonya was a beautiful woman, whose classic bone structure revealed her Slavic heritage. Sonya Reed, née Rashish, grew up in the blue-collar St. John's neighborhood of Portland. Although she had never quite been accepted by the West Hills elite, she was not one to worry about public opinion. In the early years of her marriage, Sonya studied for her Ph.D. in education, and after Mary was ten she took a part-time job teaching emotionally disturbed children. She read voraciously, and made no secret of her dislike of television.

From across the counter, Sonya eyed her daughter critically. "You look tired, honey," she said with her customary directness.

"I always work better that way," Mary countered. Although she was an only child, she and Sonya were not close. Mary felt that her mother could have done something more with her life, but she had settled for being the wife of a locally prominent man. Mary did not want to fall into the same trap. Sonya's vocal dislike of television made it hard for her to accept what Mary was doing, and she showed little interest in the career that was taking her daughter farther and farther away from home.

"Listen," Mary said. "Mark'll be arriving around six-thirty. I'll pick him up at the airport. Dinner's at seven, right? Might mean we're a little late by the time we've changed." She sat down on a stool and took a sip from the glass of Coke her mother had put out for her.

"That's okay. I'm just glad you both can make it. How is Mark?" Sonya asked, pushing the sandwich toward her daughter.

"He's settling into L.A. I think." Mary's parents had met Mark when they had visited San Francisco several months earlier, and he had won Sonya's heart by getting the best tickets in the house for a new production of *Cosi fan Tutti.*

"I hope you get to see each other sometimes," Sonya said. "This two-city relationship sounds awfully difficult."

"It's really not as bad as we thought it was going to be. He's always coming up during the week on business, and we've been spending at least two full weekends a month together. I saw his new house last week. It has a pool and a barbecue, naturally. Very southern California!" Mary made a face.

"How would you feel about moving there?"

"Well, my contract runs out in a few months, so who knows? It would be a great place to be. It's the second-largest market in the country."

Sonya was loading plates into the dishwasher. "Second-largest market for what, dear?"

"Television, of course," Mary said impatiently. She took the last bite of her sandwich. "Where's Dad?"

"Golfing with the new chairman of Louisiana Pacific, Charles . . . Charles something, I forget. He wasn't expecting you till later, but he'll be back soon."

Mary stood up. "I'm going to unpack my things."

Sonya called after her. "It might be a good idea for you to get out of the house this afternoon. The caterers are coming in at four and it'll be chaos."

"Caterers?" Mary asked. "I thought it was just a family affair with people dropping by later."

"Well, it's changed a little," Sonya said sheepishly. "I started thinking how your father's going to be running for re-election later this year. The last two times he ran unopposed, but this year there are a couple of people who could trip him up."

"You're becoming a political wife," Mary commented. "Makes a change from Tupperware parties."

"Mary, I have never in my life attended a Tupperware party," Sonya said, rising to the bait.

"Chill out, Mom, it was only a joke." Mary laughed. "So, who's coming?"

"Well, quite a few people, over a hundred I think after dinner. I invited some of your friends so that you and Mark won't get too bored."

"Is Eva coming?"

"Yes, and Johnny," Sonya said.

"Oh, good. A hundred people. Mom, you must be a wreck!"

"I am, a little," Sonya admitted. "But I think it's necessary," she added decisively.

"It's a good thing I brought my green dress," Mary said. "I'd better go hang it up."

"Oh, that reminds me," Sonya said. "Could you help me find something to wear, honey? You're so good at that."

"You mean you went to all this trouble and you didn't buy anything?" Mary said incredulously.

"It's been crazy. Anyway, you know I hate shopping."

"Don't worry, Mom, we'll find you something. Will you need any other help?"

"No, dear. I want you to have a rest this weekend."

Mary went upstairs to her bedroom to unpack her things. The large sunny room still looked the same as it had when she left school. Silver-framed pictures of Mary, from tomboyish child to Stanford valedictorian, lined the white marble mantel. Only the posters had been taken down and rolled up in the closet. There were pictures of the Beatles, John Lennon in particular. Although Mary was not even born when the British group first captivated American audiences on the Ed Sullivan show, she grew up loving their music and idolizing John Lennon. Over her bed was a signed photograph of John Elway, the Denver Broncos quarterback. A graduate of Stanford, he was Mary's hero while she was there, and she became the envy of every girl on campus the day she managed to get an interview with the brawny sports idol for the school news show, which was aired on a local station.

Mary heard the front door slam, and she quickly finished her task. She walked to the top of the stairs and saw her father setting down his golf clubs at the foot of the stairway. Hillary Reed was of medium height, with a solid build. His large-featured face was heavily lined, and in repose seemed forbidding. As he caught sight of his daughter, however, a smile transformed his expression and his pale gray eyes lit up with pleasure.

"Hi, Daddy!" Mary said delightedly.

"Mary, you're here!"

Mary ran downstairs and went to hug her father. "Happy birthday!"

"Thank you, honey." He stood her at arm's length. "I swear you get more and more like your mother every time I see you. Come, come in here a moment." He led her into his book-lined study. "Tell me, what's going on? You came up by yourself, eh?" He looked at her as he settled himself into a faded red sofa.

"Yeah. Mark's arriving later this evening and I'm going to pick him up," she answered as she sat down beside him.

"Good. Told your mother, didn't you?"

"Of course, Dad." Mary rolled her eyes.

"I don't really understand why she's driving herself crazy over this birthday thing," Hillary said with mild perplexity, "but she's quite determined about it." Smiling, he spread out his hands and shrugged.

"That's Mom," Mary said. "So, how's your game, Dad?"

"Bad day today, bad day." He chuckled. "Hit one clear into the woods. You know the little copse on the ninth? My game is pretty much like the weather, one day it's sunny and cloudless, the next it rains all day—no good reason, just happens that way." He looked at his daughter. "It's grand to see you, you know. Should come up more often. Your mother worries about you."

"Well, I'm here now, aren't I?"

The judge nodded and smiled. "I was thinking that maybe we could go fishing tomorrow."

"Sure, that'd be nice." They had fished together since Mary was a young girl; it was the way Hillary Reed had gotten to know his precocious daughter, forming a bond that would be hard for either of them to break. Now it was their way of staying in touch.

Their conversation was interrupted a few minutes later when Sonya appeared in the doorway. "The caterer has arrived. Hillary, don't forget that you promised to pick me up some fresh strawberries. Mary, are you going to stay?"

Mary got up. "No, I guess not. I think I'll head downtown and see if anybody's around at KGW. Can I use your car?"

An afternoon rainstorm had darkened the day, but downtown Portland was bright with the colored lights of bustling stores, when Mary pulled the car into the parking lot in front of a three-story Victorian house that KGW had adapted for its use. KGW was the local network affiliate where Mary got her first full-time job in television, and she always visited the station when she was in Portland. Her father had pulled strings to get her the job, and her concession to him was that she would never cover a story in his courtroom. The connection had raised a few eyebrows at first, but Mary quickly overcame any doubts about her performance by incredibly long working days and her willingness to perform any task, however lowly.

Initially Mary was a production assistant, numbering scripts for the newscasts. She began writing copy on the weekends when help was in short supply, and six months later she started filling in on-air with her own stories. The camera loved her face, and she learned to slow and deepen her speaking voice. The illusion Mary gave on-camera was that she was talking directly and intimately to each viewer. By the end of her two years in Portland she had developed the onscreen presence that Wyatt Andrews had recognized as star material when he saw her tapes.

Mary smiled as she spotted the guard whose fleshy hand was supporting his nodding head. She cleared her throat, and the guard jumped up.

"Why, Mary Reed," said the old guard.

Mary took his hand and planted a kiss on his cheek that made him blush.

"You here long?"

"Over the weekend. Just thought I'd look in on the old place."

"Well, come back again soon."

Mary turned toward the stairs to climb to the newsroom on the second floor. As usual on a quiet Saturday, only a few people were around. She walked to the news desk. The weekend assignment editor was buried in a newspaper but did a double-take when he looked up and saw Mary.

"Hey, Mary Reed! Back to where it all began."

"Hi, Calvin. How are you doing?"

"Fine." Calvin, like many television news people, had started as a newspaper reporter in the late fifties. His thinning hair and the lines around his eyes gave his sixty years away.

"You caught any big ones lately?" she asked him. Calvin was an avid fisherman.

"This big"—He spread his arms wide—"a couple of weeks back. You look great, Mary. Why you up here?"

"It's my father's birthday. Who's around?"

"Carey's anchoring, of course. You know Bill Thomm, he around when you were here? Young kid, he's producing the weekend news. We've got a new sportscaster, an ex-Trailblazer center, and Vic's still doing the weather, but they're not here today of course."

"Where's Carey?"

"In editing, I'll let her know."

"No, don't tell her. I want it to be a surprise." Mary flashed him a smile. "See you later." She walked toward the editing rooms.

When Mary had started in Portland, Carey Alexander had been the top news reporter. Carey not only looked like Elizabeth Taylor, she was sassy and hardworking to boot. As a television reporter, however, Carey had one significant flaw. The camera is a fickle instrument that can make mousey women glow and lovely women look ordinary. Carey Alexander, who could turn heads on the street, did not project well on screen. It flattened out her face, distorting her features, and no amount of careful lighting and makeup could correct it. Carey also had another problem: you could see her eyes move as she read the Tele-Promp-Ter.

Put off by Mary's background, the older woman had all but ignored her, until the day they worked on a triple murder story together. Mary's tireless research, her ability to make people talk, and the dedication she showed, impressed the older reporter, and she asked that Mary work with her again.

Over time Carey taught her how to handle the cameramen on an assignment and how to use her looks to get a story. "Make a guy feel," she would say with a knowing look, "that if it wasn't for this story, you'd be in bed with him." Mary would look startled. "And then, baby, the minute you're finished, get the hell on out." Carey also gave advice about handling producers. "Always oversell your story, make them put it high in the program, not down there with the cooking and flowers. And always, always," she emphasized, "ask for thirty seconds more than you want."

In the editing room, Carey taught her to cut down on the fruitless hours of editing the rookie reporter habitually spent to cut a story. She said that a piece could only hold three or four ideas, that you would never use all your research and that in cutting and re-cutting a story you often lost your initial idea.

Despite the ten-year age gap, the two women had become good friends, and regularly got into the town's gossip columns. Their friendship was strained, however, when a young lawyer, Paul Jacobs, started to go out with both of them. After a while, Paul and Carey began seeing each other alone and Mary, feeling left out, had had to find other entertainment. Paul eventually left Portland, but things were never quite the same again. She and Carey continued to work on stories together, but their working partnership suffered.

More and more, Carey became irritated by Mary's suggestions on how to do a story and envious of the growing respect for her at the station, where she had been promoted to a full-fledged reporter. Mary did not pay much attention to her friend's hostility until the night when Carey took a story Mary had put together on the mayoral elections and re-cut it for the six o'clock news. That left Mary without a story at eleven. Later, the weekend anchor spot opened up, and Carey used everything in her power to edge Mary out of the running. When Carey finally landed the job, Mary started to look for another position.

After standing a few minutes outside the editing room, Mary saw the door open, and, as Carey came out, Mary jumped out in front of her. They hugged each other a little self-consciously.

"You look great, Carey," Mary said, noticing that her friend seemed happier than when Mary had left Portland. Mary sensed that Carey, now in her mid-thirties, had accepted that she, like hundreds of other highly competent men and women on local news stations around the country, had gone as far as she could.

"Thank you, darling. You, of course, look fabulous!" Carey said, looking critically at the poised woman in front of her. Carey might have succeeded in edging Mary out of a job in Portland, but she knew she had lost in the long run. If she kept her head, Carey thought to herself, Mary Reed would go far.

"What a surprise! So, what brings you to the sticks?" asked Carey.

"My father's sixtieth."

"Well, I'm glad you could find time to drop in," Carey said with a trace of irony.

"I couldn't come and not see you."

"Mmm."

The conversation halted. "What were you working on?" Mary asked, nodding at the editing room.

"A piece on serial killers. Have you heard about the one 'round here? I've got some good material and just finished editing the first three parts. It's on tomorrow."

"Can I see?" Mary asked.

"Sure. Hey, Ken?" Carey called to the young man at the editing machine. "This is Mary Reed. Once a peon at KGW, now on Channel Six in San Francisco."

"Hi, Mary," Ken said, getting up from his machine to shake her hand.

"Listen, show her the first three parts of the report. I've got to get madeup and check the script for the six o'clock. Mary, catch up with me in the newsroom afterwards."

"Okay."

Ken offered her a chair, but Mary preferred to stand.

"I'll show you parts one and two, the third isn't finished yet."

"Sure."

Mary walked up and down the editing room and watched the tiny screen. The report was superbly crafted. Prostitutes in Seattle, who knew the victims, were the focal point of part one. Carey's spare, effective narration was juxtaposed with interviews with an articulate and sensitive police lieutenant, the mother of one of the victims, and the mother of a convicted serial killer, all of which combined to make the piece special. Pacing in the darkened room, Mary also saw how she could make the story better. She felt it needed one element to make it perfect: an interview with a convicted killer.

After the tape was finished, Mary went to the newsroom where Carey was reading her script.

"Well, what did you think?"

"It's great, really first-class, Carey. Listen, I'd like to buy the tape, I could adapt it for San Francisco."

"You can have it."

"No, let me pay for it. We have a budget for stuff like this." It was not true, but Mary felt that breezing in and taking her friend's work did not look good.

"Mary, just take it. Ken will make you a copy."

Mary asked Ken to run a copy. She made out a check for five hundred dollars and stuffed it in his shirt. "That's for good work. Take everyone out to dinner on it."

"Well . . ."

"Listen, I'll be watching the news in Carey's office."

Afterward, Mary walked toward the newsroom. "Good show, Carey," she said.

"Thanks."

"Well, thanks for the tape, it's dynamite. We'll do you proud."

"Great. Can you stay for a drink?" Carey asked.

"I've got to get going, I'm afraid. How about tomorrow night?"

Carey shook her head. "No can do."

"We'll make it next time I'm up."

"Okay, kid. By the way, I've got a new significant other. Tom. He's a great guy. Has three boys, wife died. Maybe some day you'll come back for my wedding." Carey smiled coyly.

"Wouldn't miss it for the world!" Mary kissed her old friend with a sudden impulse of warmth. She left the building, clutching the tape.

The encounter with Carey had made her thoughtful. She couldn't help feeling that her friend's life was over, whereas she was within reach of everything she had ever worked for. Mary suddenly longed for Mark's reassuring presence. There was something about the way he saw things straight and managed to make sense of them for her that she needed right then. She pressed the gas pedal and sped toward the airport.

In the Reeds' elegantly appointed home, the hum of conversation grew louder as the evening wore on. The guests included relatives and family friends; Hillary Reed's former law partners; other judges; a few of the civil lawyers with whom he worked; Charles Snow, the new chairman of Louisiana Pacific; and many of the town's other prominent citizens.

Mary worked the party dutifully.

"So, there you are, Mary. Been looking forward to seeing my favorite gal."

She turned around and looked up into the heavy jowls of Bill Waters, head of Reidel Enterprises, who was fond of reminding her of how as a child she once walked into his office and asked his secretary to take a letter for her.

"Hello, Mr. Waters," Mary said.

"That's some dress," he continued, leering at her and bending so close that she could smell his whiskied breath.

"Mary, come over here." The voice of her childhood friend Johnny Preble punctuated the din of the party. Happy to escape, she joined Johnny and a crowd of her childhood friends.

"Say, Mare," said Johnny, after kissing her with the languid grace that characterized all his movements. "You want to go out with us? Thought we'd get a group together and hit one of the clubs in St. John's. You want to come?" He tipped his head back and drew on his cigarette while looking at Mary through half-closed eyelids.

"I don't know. Well, maybe. Actually, we haven't done that in a while," she said, warming to the idea.

"Hey, Mary, did you hear that Elaine and Richard were getting engaged? Her father's furious," said her childhood girlfriend, Eva.

"I can imagine," Mary said.

"So what's the story with Mark?" asked Eva. "He's a real hunk."

"You think so?" Mary was secretly pleased.

"Like you don't know!" Eva laughed. "Come dancing with us," she begged. "It'll be such fun."

"Okay. Wait here a minute, I'm going to tell Mark."

In the main room, she spotted Mark easily because of his height. He was leaning against the fireplace, talking to her father. Mark hated dressing up but he had brought a sports jacket along for the occasion, and Mary thought he looked devastatingly handsome, with his immaculately white shirt open at the neck and his rugged face animated with feeling. She wound her way through the crowd toward him.

"Am I interrupting?" she said, slipping her hand under Mark's arm, and smiling affectionately at both men.

"You're the only person who couldn't interrupt this conversation," said her father warmly. With a stab of pain he did not bother to analyze, he looked at the two happy faces in front of him and acknowledged that they made a striking couple. Mary wore a strapless green taffeta cocktail dress with a full skirt and tight-fitting bodice. She had swept her hair up for the occasion with a matching green ribbon and wore a pair of drop pearl earrings her father had given her for her sixteenth birthday.

"Your father and I were talking about fishing," Mark said.

"I thought the three of us could go together tomorrow," the judge said, "unless you have other plans?"

"Oh, no, that's a great idea," she said with a questioning glance at Mark.

"It's fine by me," Mark said, nodding his agreement.

"Good, well I'll see you at ten o'clock sharp." He started to move off.

"Mark, do you want to go dancing? Johnny's getting a group together."

"If I can dance with you." He grinned.

"Oh, I saw you with Eva, by the way. You seemed to be getting along quite well." She punched him playfully on the arm.

"Well, if she's going, why are we waiting?" Mark put his arm around her shoulder and smiled down at her.

"I want to show you something, okay?"

"I haven't got much choice, have I?" Mark said good-naturedly. They had left the club, and Mary was driving.

"Mark, you were so good tonight, with all those boring people I introduced you to, and all I've wanted all evening was to be with you alone."

Mark looked at her profile in the dark as she drove the car up the curving mountain road. "The feeling was mutual, I assure you," he said.

"Here," Mary said, pulling in front of a crudely built wooden house. "This is our mountain cabin. I wanted you to see it."

The ground floor of the house consisted of a large living room with a fireplace and open kitchen and small bathroom. Mary walked in. She shivered in her party dress and light coat.

"Come here," Mark said, and put his arms around her.

"Why don't we light the fire?" Mary said.

"Okay," Mark agreed, and they went hunting for wood and kindling. Soon Mark, who was squatting in front of the fireplace, rolled back on his heels, satisfied that the wood was burning.

Mary was sitting on the rug with her legs drawn up. Flames lit the milky planes of her shoulders and neck with amber and rose, and soft shadows smudged the familiar lines of her face, making it mysterious. "You're so beautiful. And at the moment you look like an oil painting," he said, "something by Sargent with that dress." He reached over and brushed her cheek with his fingers.

"You know," Mary said looking up at him, "it's quite a compliment for Dad to invite you on a fishing trip."

"Do you ever think of a future with me?" Mark looked into the fire. "I mean marriage, children, things like that?"

Startled, Mary turned to look at him. "I love you, Mark, I really do," she said slowly. "In all the right ways, too. I like being with you, knowing you're there, talking, all the things we do. You've just been there." She shrugged, running out of words. "I don't know about a family, though . . ." Mary was frowning.

"Well, we don't have to have children for a while!" Mark said with a trace of a smile.

"Could you be married to someone with my job?" she asked, still frowning.

"You mean someone as driven as you? Of course, I respect it much more than you give me credit for. I just don't think it's the only thing in life."

"I know. It just feels that way sometimes," Mary said candidly.

"Listen, Mary, all I'm asking you to do is to think about it. I wanted to say something. I feel we've come to a place where we should know if we were going to move forward or not."

Mark leaned over and pushed the coat from her shoulders. He looked into her eyes. "I love you, too, Mary," he said. "You drive me crazy sometimes, but there's something so completely alive about you, it's . . . well, you're . . . magnificent." He covered her neck with teasing kisses, then urgently pushed her to the floor, inching her dress over her waist and hips and legs and kissing her all the while. Mary touched the top of his head with her hand and arched her back with pleasure.

Something about the night, their stolen time in the cabin where she had spent happy times as a child made Mary abandon herself to their lovemaking more than usual. Mark felt her giving herself to him. "Yes, my dearest," he whispered, "let me have you." He looked at her tenderly. Her eyes were wide and wild. "Yes," she cried out, holding him close to her.

They lay on the rug in front of the dying fire and Mark curled himself around her, laying his cheek against her hair. "Just promise me you'll think about what we talked about," he whispered.

"Well, it's been lovely to see you, darling," Sonya said as she hugged her daughter. It was a foggy Monday morning and they were at the airport. She turned to Mark. "I hope you'll come again soon. You have an open invitation. And feel free to suggest it to this one"—she nodded at Mary who was already taking their bags out of the car—"she needs to be told to take a break sometimes."

"Okay, bye, Mom, take care. I love you." Mary waved as they walked through the automatic doors. "I'm just going to make a quick phone call," she said to Mark once they were inside the building. "Why don't you grab us some coffee?"

Mary found a telephone and dialed the assignment desk in San Francisco. "Ron, it's Mary. . . . No, I'm still in Portland. My plane leaves in fifteen minutes. Listen, I've got a good story on serial killers. Can you get someone to do some research? I want to find a killer who'd be willing to do an interview. . . . What? . . . No, I haven't heard. . . . A security depot robbery? When? . . . How many bodies? . . . Listen, Ron, put me through to Wyatt. I want to work on this story. . . ."

SEVEN

IT WAS JUST after midnight and downtown Bakersfield was rowdy. At the Twin Palms Bar there were few customers. Dean Carroll, commonly known as Slim, mopped the bar with a filthy rag and wondered how long it would be before nobody sat on the slashed vinyl barstools and drank warm beer and diluted liquor; the Palms was not what it used to be.

"Give me another," said a thickset man at one end of the bar.

The man leaned back. "You know why I came here, Slim? I like water in my whisky and here I get it without asking." The man barked. "Ha, ha!" He looked around for someone to share his humor. "Hey, doll!" he called, catching sight of a woman in a red dress at the end of the bar. "Want a drink? You look like you could use one."

For the moment, Darlene Travis ignored the joker at the other end of the bar. The dark, greasy roots of her dyed blond hair were visible as she bent her head to search for matches among the contents of her purse, which she impatiently scattered on the countertop. Finding what she needed, she shook the hair from her eyes and, putting both elbows shakily on the bar, absorbed herself entirely in the task of lighting a cigarette.

There was a time when Darlene Travis had been attractive and she still applied her makeup theatrically, ringing her filmy, blue-green eyes with thick black circles and reddening her cheeks with a thick paste of rouge. The corners of her painted lips turned down, lending her the wistful look of a sad clown at a circus.

"Tell the fat guy to shove it," she said thickly, looking with unfocused eyes at the bartender. She could feel the rush of the drugs in her system, but could not hear how her speech was slowed and skewed.

At a corner table Tony Caban was working on getting drunk. Radamacker always forbade women and drink for a week before a job and now they had some celebrating to do. As planned, they had unloaded their half of the money from the robbery in the San Francisco safehouse under Johnson's supervision. All the money, that is, except for the fistful which Caban convinced Red that no one, not even the watchful Jerry, would miss. Caban loved the feel of the glossy fresh-stamped bills and had run his palm appreciatively over them before slipping them into a bag that he had kept hidden. They had switched cars again and now they were on their way back to the motel.

"Did I ever tell you about Myra?" said Caban leaning toward Red after draining his fourth shot of vodka. "What you say we go visit her after this? Gotta believe me, man, she is something. One night we came down here, me and Andy and that new kid. We—"

"Where she live?"

"Edge of town. I tell you, me and Andy—"

"You boys all on your ownsomes?" Darlene Travis sat on a neighboring table, crossing one leg over the other to expose half a yard of narrow thigh, thinly encased in sheer black nylons. A string of glittering diamonds ran up the outside of each stocking from the ankle, and Red found himself staring at the place where the diamonds disappeared into the red dress.

"Sure, and that's how we're staying." Caban looked at Darlene's tall, skinny body with disgust. He drained the last of the vodka from the glass.

"You truckers?" asked Darlene.

"Yeah. Hey, bartender, give us another round for the road." He turned toward Red. "Let's get the hell out of here, Red. Get us some real action."

"Bring me a gin with the vodka," Darlene called out. She looked at Red and smiled her sweetest smile. "You dance, Red honey?" she asked. Red glanced at Caban who shook his head in exasperation.

Darlene fished for a quarter in her purse and then slowly wobbled toward the jukebox. She started to dance alone, wrapping her arms around herself and closing her eyes.

"*. . . Just call me angel of the morning, angel . . .*"

Slim brought the drinks to the table. Red's shoulders were swaying to the music. After a few moments, he hauled himself to his feet and, grasping Darlene awkwardly around her waist, began a shambling dance with her.

"*. . . touch my cheek before you leave me, baby . . .*"

Caban wiped his mouth on the inside of his wrist. "Jesus, Red," he said, "what are you doing?"

At the bar the thickset man was telling Slim about the glory days of the oil business. "You got to remember," he was saying, "back then most anybody could get a few bucks together and go drilling experimental like." Slim nodded automatically while keeping his eyes on the rest of the room. In one corner a couple was making out. At the back of the main room the arch of an old doorway led to a smaller room where a noisy crowd was finishing up an evening at the pool table. They filed out past the bar.

One of the pool players pulled on Darlene's arm so that she spun away from Red and slapped into him.

"Leave me the fuck alone, Joe," she said sloppily. She straightened her back and walked away. Another song began playing as she walked toward Caban, Red following. "You boys play pool?"

Caban looked at her quickly. "Sure," he said, surprised. "You want to play?"

"I only play for money," Darlene said.

Caban scratched his chest and then turned his head. "Two beers," he ordered Slim. He looked at Darlene. "And a gin for the red dress here." Caban picked up his drink and moved into the back room.

Fifty minutes later Darlene had won two hundred dollars. She had beaten each of them once although Red was winning this game of eight ball.

Caban had been silent for a while. He was sitting on a chair, pulling every now and then at a bottle of beer, and looking without expression at the game. "Where you learn to play pool, red dress?" he asked finally. She did not seem to hear him. His eyes narrowed. "You think you can fool us, but we've got more money than you could ever dream about, so you can . . ." The end of Caban's sentence became a mumble and his head slumped against his chest.

"Your friend should lay off that drink or we're going to have to carry him out, you know that?" She looked at Red who was chalking his cue. He had stopped drinking.

"We're closing now, boys. Drink up," Slim called from the bar.

Caban lurched toward the bar. "Give me another bottle of vodka, Mr. Bartender." Slim shook his head. "Come on, man." Caban crashed into the barstools, knocking one over. "Shit!"

"Move on now, we're closed," Slim said. He looked toward Red. "Get your friend the hell out of here, I don't want any trouble."

Red was pushing Caban into the car when Darlene came toward them, swaying like a string puppet in her red stilleto heels.

"Red, honey," she said. "You boys'll give me a ride home, ain't that so?"

"Where d'ya live?"

"Down the highway, not far."

"This ain't no taxicab, lady. C'mon, Red. What were you waiting for?" Caban grunted and tried to pull the door closed.

Red looked at Caban and then at Darlene who was standing by the car. "Get in," he said to her.

As Darlene squeezed into the front seat, Caban was mumbling. "Man, you know, I can't believe this. Listen, I'm telling you, Red. You drop me off at the motel first, okay? I'm not getting lost in downtown Bakersfield with you for Chrisake. I mean, what are you thinking, man?" The words came out fast and thick, but Red seemed to understand.

Caban drained a bottle of beer that he pulled out of his jacket. As he lurched across Darlene to throw it out the window, she saw the gun in the inside pocket of the jacket. In her head the words of the song were playing, protecting her—
"... *Just call me angel of the morning.* ..."

"So if you don't drive trucks, what do you boys do?" asked Darlene.

"Oh, this and that," Red said.

Caban's head had lolled against Darlene's shoulder and she thought he had fallen asleep. Then he started touching her. Unsurprised, she pulled away but Caban grunted in annoyance and, putting his hand around her thigh, pulled her to him. Clumsily he probed and pushed against her worn, pale flesh, pressing his body along hers with feeble, drunken desire.

"You know maybe the slut ain't so bad," Caban mumbled.

Red stopped the car in front of a motel. "Okay, Caban. Here you are. Get out." He did not look around but sat and stared at the flashing sign outside the motel.

"Okay, okay, man. I'm going. You coming?" he asked Darlene after tumbling out of the car.

Darlene looked at Red, who shook his head. "I don't think so," she said, laughing at him.

As Caban stumbled into the motel, Red turned to Darlene. "Listen, sugar, you want another drink? I've got a bottle in my room and I'm in the mood to do a little celebrating."

"Sure." Darlene looked at him slyly. She needed another hit. "Let's have us a real good time."

The compound was quiet. Thomas Taylor clambered up the tiny spiral staircase that led from the elevator by Radamacker's underground office to the back of the church. He was panting from the exertion and a film of perspiration covered his pink face. At the top of the stairs he paused and pulled out a large white handkerchief to mop his forehead.

Taylor worried about the way Jerry Radamacker had been talking recently. The minister used to enjoy their wrangling about doctrinal matters, but now that Jerry was talking about a time for action, Taylor had grown concerned. Patience and preparedness, he counseled, but Jerry simply looked at him and gave him a closemouthed smile.

In the main doorway to the church, Taylor stopped again, this time to polish his misted glasses with the handkerchief. Beyond the compound he could see the scrub stretching across the valley bed. " 'And it was commanded them,' " Jerry had quoted to him from the Bible a few minutes earlier, " 'that they should not hurt the grass of the earth, but only those men which have not the seal of God on their foreheads.' "

In the west, the sun slid toward the desert floor like an egg into a skillet. Immediately it was dark. The dumpy minister shivered; in ten years he had not gotten used to the sudden onset of night at the compound.

"Any word from Red and Caban?" Johnson asked Radamacker.

"They'll be in tomorrow. Stopped in Bakersfield." Radamacker was sitting at his desk, his feet up on the table. His attention was on the monitors in case the robbery story came on the local news. *"In Marin County the homeless are counseled by a trained psychologist. Susan Moss speaks to two homeless . . ."*

Johnson wandered around the room restlessly; he picked up some papers on Radamacker's desk and put them down again. His eyes glittered and there was a strange fixed smile on his face. Finally he broke the silence. "Man, look at me, why don't you? I need to talk to you."

Radamacker raised his eyebrows and turned his head slightly toward Johnson. "Talk to me, brother," he said slowly, enjoying Finn's discomfort.

Johnson began haltingly to describe the robbery. His voice was flat and without expression but as he spoke he seemed to calm down. He leaned against the door looking straight at Radamacker's shrewd eyes, but seeing instead downtown San Francisco, a dark alleyway, smelling fear in the sweat of his men, noticing with distaste the splotches of blood on his sneakers.

"So, you went back into the vault after you loaded the car?" Radamacker softly prompted.

"Yeah, they was tied up in that room back to back. So it was easy. One bullet for the black guys. In one head and out the other." Johnson illustrated his shot, squinting as he lined it up.

"You're sure they're dead?" Radamacker's attention remained partly on the monitors.

"Sure as can be. They were moaning and all, so I finished them off."

"And the other two?" Radamacker asked casually.

"One of them was white. . . ." Johnson's fingers drummed restlessly at the edge of Radamacker's desk.

"But you remembered what I told you?"

"Yeah," Johnson said, barely audible.

"And what about the cop?" Radamacker asked, his eyes boring into Johnson, seeing everything.

Before the robbery, Radamacker had spoken to Finn when they were on the shooting range. "In the months ahead it's going to be necessary to take life," Radamacker had said. "Now I'm going to tell you something—and I'm preaching you nothing but God's own truth. Killing happens in the mind, you know that. It's not enough to have a weapon. It's in the head, Johnson, it's the headwork makes a thing happen." Then Radamacker had paused, and very slowly he said, "And sometimes, boy, you're going to have to wipe out a white man." Finn had stared back at him. "I know it's hard to believe it, but there are white men who would stand between us and God. They want to stop us and we can't let them. Jim Wilkes is one of those men. He's stopping us from doing God's will. I need you, Finn Johnson, to prove to me that you are a true leader of our brotherhood. You are going to send the big man off, boy. Liberate him from the bonds of life." Radamacker had stepped back. "And I don't want excuses." Finn knew what happened to people who brought back excuses: Jerry liberated them from the bonds of life with the aid of a firing squad.

Aroused from his reverie, Johnson became aware of Radamacker's mesmerizing stare. "What about the cop?" Radamacker asked again.

"It's okay," he said, "I wasted the cop."

"Good," Radamacker said, leaning back in his chair and bringing the fingertips of his hands together. "Good." Radamacker visibly relaxed.

Finn looked down at the desk top, avoiding Radamacker's gaze. The television monitors flickered.

"Tell me about it," Radamacker said. His voice was casual, but his eyes never left the face of the younger man. It was an important moment. Radamacker had forced Johnson to cut his strongest tie to the world outside the movement; now he would be utterly dependent on Jerry.

"Okay, so we're driving down the freeway." Johnson started pacing around the room. "And I ask him to stop," he continued, "I say walk down there a little, stretch your legs while I take a leak." He looked toward Radamacker. "Then, I wait for him to come back. I have my piece out, real casual, like I'm checking it out, you know." He mimed the scene, his weight on one leg, hip thrust up, playing with his gun.

"He doesn't get it at first. He's walking back and he looks dazed-like. Comes real close to me, then the motherfuck says, 'You really did that, didn't you? The guard recognized me and so you blew them all away?' He's looking at me, weird-like.

" 'Told you already, I says.' Finn's face was flushed and his words came faster and with more emphasis. 'I wasted the guards on account of the color of their fucking skin. Ain't got nothing to do with you.' Then I put the weapon to the cop's head, real gentle, see. Wilkes looks at me. Thinks I'm fucking joking. 'Told you before not to play with guns,' he says, and he moves his face right close to me. I can see the hairs hanging out of his nose. The guy fucking thinks I'm joking.

"So I lets him have one, sudden in the leg. Falls on his knees. All of a sudden he's scared. He's shitting in his dumbfuck pants, begging, blubbering like a fucking baby. That really got me. A pathetic fucking baby. That's when I start to let him really have it." Finn stopped. He stared at a place past Radamacker's head.

"But you want to know what really disgusted me?" he continued, although his eyes remain fixed beyond Radamacker. "I used to respect the guy. We was pals, sort of, inside. I wanted him to die nice, like a man. But the motherfucker couldn't handle the fear, went out like a squealing fucking pig."

Radamacker stayed quiet for a bit. Then he got up and walked over to the door. "You did real good, brother," he said, gripping the boy's shoulder.

He took a step away from Johnson and then turned suddenly to face him. "And how do you feel, boy? You remember what I said about that?"

"You mean about feeling clean afterwards?"

Radamacker nodded.

"Feel clean, I guess. Yeah, yep. That could be. Clean, eh?" Johnson smiled; his eyes had lost their glitter.

Radamacker's mouth moved in an imitation of a smile. "Okay, Johnson. Now go get some rest. You look like you could use it." He pulled open the door to his office and ushered Finn out.

For a long time, Radamacker sat at his desk, staring into the room. He was thinking of the first time he had killed a man. He had been eleven, a morose, silent child, whose main interest had been the elaborate chemistry lab he had set up in the basement of his family's small house in the poor white Chicago neighborhood where he had grown up. For the third time in one week the local gang had stolen his books as he came home from school, and had beaten up the underdeveloped boy so badly that he could not open one eye and had to have twelve stitches in his lip. For the next two weeks he worked in his basement lab on a secret project, a bomb that he detonated in the gang's headquarters. The leader had been killed instantly; two other boys were injured. Behind his thick glasses, Jerry had betrayed not a flicker of emotion as he watched them carry the bodies out of the debris. Inside he exulted, for he felt born again. In time he had taken over leadership of the gang, which he trained in acts of vicious racial violence. Radamacker's grades never suffered from his extramural activities and the neighborhood folks still considered him the shy, rather sweet-faced boy who had grown up among them. Jerry Radamacker learned early how to live a double life.

After a while, he got up and turned out the lights in his underground office.

Clouds scudded across a blue sky and white caps frothed on the surface of the San Francisco Bay where Mary and Mark were sailing. Across the water, sunlight bathed the ridge of Marin County and the bright buildings of Sausalito where they were headed.

"What's this?" Mary asked, turning the pages of a slim, red paperback.

"It's research on the Feld murder. A manifesto by the right wing. I'm trying to understand how these people think."

"What's it about?"

"The end of the world as we know it. The author claims it's fiction, but it's rather like Lenin trying to write a romance, since it's actually a blueprint for revolution."

Mary flipped casually through the pages. "What is this 'demographic warfare' he keeps mentioning?" she asked.

"Well, basically, this guy wants to purge the population of the world, which means that they finally hang half of the population of L.A., wipe out New York City and Israel, oh, and sizable portions of Russia and Africa—it was written before the Soviet Union collapsed, of course. He probably wipes out about sixty million people by the end of the book."

"How does Feld fit into all of this?"

"I guess he's part of the Jewish conspiracy that runs the media. No matter that the guy was as marginal a member of our society as you can get, for these people he is part of the power elite that is strangling our country."

"How?"

"With pornography, for example. They detest pornography—I've heard of incidents where these guys have put bombs in porno theaters."

"Good for them," said Mary feelingly. "But they don't really like women, do they? It doesn't fit."

"No, women are merely carriers of future Aryan men as far as I can see."

"Madonnas, not whores," Mary commented.

"You've got it." Mark adjusted their course to round the headland. "What's interesting to me is how they've taken over some of the left-wing rhetoric of the sixties. They denounce materialism and the government as stridently as any Tom Hayden. And in the teeth of a period where excess and greed have become the norm, they are crying out for spiritual values." He paused. "This may sound bizarre," he said, "but I sort of understand what they mean. It's just their solutions get them way off-base."

"And their analysis. As you pointed out, Marvin Feld was hardly the voice of a conspiracy," Mary said dryly. "How's the investigation going, by the way? Have they found any witnesses?"

"No," Mark said, sighing. "They thought they'd found a woman who saw a car pull away when Feld left the station, but it didn't pan out. You know what someone told me though? Apparently, when they found him, there was a noose around his neck. They've been holding the information back to use as a check against phony claims."

"He was shot though, wasn't he?"

"Oh, yes," Mark said grimly. "You saw the photos. Twenty bullets. He was definitely shot."

Mary pulled a stray lock of hair out of her eyes. They were approaching their destination. "You want to take down the mainsail?" she asked, tossing the book into the cabin.

At six o'clock the phone rang in Master Sergeant Casey's office at the Presidio. Straight-backed, with a face tanned and scrubbed like saddle leather, Kevin Casey looked younger than his forty-eight years.

The San Francisco Presidio boasted the highest ratio of officers to enlisted men of all the U.S. Army stations. Its verdant golf courses, pretty red-stone buildings, the riding academy, and main parade area ringed by California's fine Spanish mission architecture all made it a sought-after posting.

Casey enlisted when he was a boy of eighteen, but it was not until he went to Vietnam in the early seventies that he found his true vocation. In Saigon, Casey had started an operation he continued to the present. In Vietnam, a supply sergeant soon learned that inventory, which Stateside had to account for on triplicate forms, was easy to scavenge. Working out of the supply offices, Casey cleaned up the hardware and got it back to the States with considerable ingenuity. His most successful method was to invent a soldier who had been killed in action and to ship back a coffin filled with hardware packed like body parts, which was picked up at the airport by a contact masquerading as a grieving relative. When the army busted someone for using the same idea to transport heroin, Casey reluctantly stopped using it. The other things he found, the radios, medical supplies, spare parts, Casey sold to the Viet Cong. Casey had been born cynical, but the war gave him his excuse. Now, he reckoned, they owed him.

Paradoxically he had been a good soldier, which was the reason he was not forgotten when he went back. "If I have anything to do with it, you're going to get your dream sheet, Kevin," Colonel Nugent told him when he left. "What you did for me and our men out there won't go unrecognized. You'll be riding ponies on the Elysian fields before long." It took a few years, but finally Casey got the papers posting him to the Presidio, and he had been there ever since.

During the last decade, he had put on a couple of pounds and had gotten a little greedier. He had ten bank accounts—nine overseas—and in two years he planned to retire from the army with a pension.

The phone rang a second time and then stopped. Casey stood up. It was the end of the day but you could still shave with the crease in his fatigues. He picked up a sports tote that held a change of clothes and headed toward the gym. Fifty minutes later he drove down Broadway and pulled up to a pay phone. Glancing at his watch, he noted that it was seven twenty-two. The phone rang, and Casey got out of his car and picked up the receiver.

"Okay, Sarge. I can see you. You alone?" Harry Bleech asked from his vantage point on the corner.

"Yeah, I'm alone," Casey said impatiently.

"Okay. Well, we're watching and if anybody follows you they'll be seen plain as day, got that? I'll meet you under the bridge in exactly twenty-five minutes. Won't take you longer than that to get there. You're more than two minutes late, we're gone, okay?"

"Okay, okay." Casey got a little tired of these military theatrics, but the bozo kept coming up with the money. Casey had checked into Bleech's Idaho operations and he had a suspicion that Bleech could not come up with the type of money he was asking for without a partner, but it was not in Casey's interests to find out much more. He got in his car and drove away.

It was dark by the time the master sergeant reached the meeting place under the Bay Bridge. His loafers slipped on the loose dirt and pebbles.

"You know," he said when he got within earshot of the two men huddled together, "you've got to do something about those camouflage uniforms. Stick out like sore tits, you do. I can see exactly where your men are." Bleech glowered at Casey. "Only town in the goddamn country where people wouldn't look twice at a bunch of guys standing around with leaves on their clothes," Casey added, grinning. He enjoyed baiting Bleech.

As Casey drew close, Bleech motioned to the man standing next to him, who went up to him and patted him roughly down the outside of his body. Casey smiled. "So, how're you doing?"

"Just fine," Bleech said gruffly.

Bleech knew Casey from Vietnam. Bleech had been a clerk in the army and by the time Bleech arrived Casey was already a legend. Whatever you wanted Casey could get. The young man from Idaho had studied the sergeant intently. In time, he had learned enough to set up his own small-time operation, running liquor mainly, some drugs.

"I've got some real beauties for you this time," Casey said.

"You got the antitank weapons."

"Yeah, and a couple of M-79s."

"How do you do it, Casey?"

Casey shrugged. "Same deal as before," he went on. "I get half the money now, half before you pick the stuff up. Oh, and you only got ten days this time."

Bleech nodded. "What's this ten-day shit? You never did this before."

"Listen, this shipment fell into my hands, Bleech. The Oakland terminal's filled with men transferring, which meant the hardware got shipped to us. Now, I have a limited time to work with this stuff. You have to get it out of there by the end of next week."

"I guess it'll have to work. I'll contact you in two days, so you can tell us which day is good," said Bleech. He handed Casey a brown paper package containing the money.

"Thanks. Oh, I almost forgot. Here's something for you."

Bleech took the envelope Casey extended to him. Inside were two sets of eagles, the type that army colonels wear on the shoulders of their jackets. Bleech looked pleased. "Thanks, sir," he said, but Casey had already faded into the darkness.

In a safehouse in the city, Bleech talked on a two-way radio to Jerry Radamacker, his partner in the deal and the man who was fronting the cash. "We're all set," Bleech said. "He'll let us know when in two days, but we've got to get the stuff in ten." There was a pause as the radio signals were received.

"What do you mean ten days? Who says?" Radamacker's voice was harsh with suspicion.

"That's what the man said. Has to be moved on."

"This hasn't happened before. What's new, Bleech?"

"This is some hot shit, Jer. Think about it. It's going to be the biggest motherfucking stunt we've pulled off."

"And the biggest motherfucking fuck-up. Harry, your ass is hanging out there. You got my men and my money, but you cross me and I'll find you wherever you hide your dumbfuck tail."

Radamacker's voice was filled with menace and Bleech hung up the radio with hands that shook. He knew Radamacker's methods.

Detective Eddie Martinez, formerly of the San Francisco Police narcotics squad, now in homicide in Bakersfield, parked his cream Plymouth Fury outside the flat-roofed, three-story concrete building where Darlene Travis lived. On the car's back bumper was a sticker: SCHOOL'S IN SESSION, DRIVE CAREFULLY.

It was ten in the morning, and Martinez had been up all night. He was wearing a brown sports slacks and a polyester-blend plaid jacket that his wife had given him for his birthday a month ago. Usually his jackets were altered so that the right side accommodated his holster and gun, but Tina had forgotten to fix this one. He noticed irritably that the lining was already wearing away and he sighed. His wife would really prefer it if he sold insurance in the new plaid jacket.

Martinez checked his watch and calculated that he was already owed two hours overtime. He had been on duty since midnight, checked two homicide scenes, and talked to fifteen people who had not seen anything.

He walked up the metal staircase on the outside of the building and down the walkway on the second floor to Darlene's apartment. With the flat of his hand he whacked the gray metal door. "Come on, Darlene, wakey, wakey." He heard nothing. Cursing under his breath, he leaned his head against the door frame and started to kick the door, rhythmically speaking between kicks. "Get-up-and-open-the-door-Dar-lene, before I break it down."

"Hey, mister, stop making such a noise, I've got a baby up here," a voice from the stairway above yelled at Martinez.

"Come on, Darlene," he said through clenched teeth.

He heard a scrabbling sound, a muffled voice, and he jerked his head back, stepping away from the door, rolling onto the balls of his feet. Even after ten hours on duty, he was still a cop.

"I'm telling you I got nothing," Darlene said listlessly, letting the officer in.

"You got less than nothing," Martinez corrected her. He walked to the middle of the room which smelled of acrid perfume, sweat, and rotting food.

"Screw you." Darlene sat down on a bed, and picking up a nail file she began sawing at her pointed gold nails. "What you want anyway?"

"Hot coffee, eggs, and clean sheets. But before I get that I got to talk with you." Martinez walked to the table and rummaged through old boxes of doughnuts, Styrofoam cups, and Chinese food cartons. He turned around. Darlene was wearing a filthy blue wrapper that kept falling open. "What I don't want, Darlene," he said, "is to look at you. Tie that thing up." Sullenly, Darlene complied. "Heard some news about a friend of yours, Clarence Hoover."

"Ain't no friend of mine."

"Where does he hang out, Darlene?" said Martinez.

"What'd he do?"

"Had a little disagreement with his lady-friend. Now, where does he hang out, Darlene?"

"I told you I ain't seen him."

Martinez grabbed a chrome tube of lipstick that was lying on the table. He started writing a word on the mirror behind him. "Maybe you forgot this word." The stick broke as he wrote the *O* of Chino, the women's state penitentiary. "You want your old room back?"

"I heard he left town."

"Yeah?" Martinez put his right hand on the handcuffs that dangled from his waist.

Darlene's eyes narrowed; the cop was getting serious. "Listen, I don't know from Clarence Hoover, and I don't hang out with his crowd anymore but maybe I got something else for you. Two guys, a few nights back. I met them playing pool at the Palms. One of them was bragging to me about how they robbed a bank or something."

Martinez released the handcuffs. "Where? Which banks, Darlene?" He suddenly felt tired, banks were of no use to a homicide detective.

"Don't know."

"You haven't told me anything I can use."

"Maybe it was a security truck. Got to give me something for this," she said. "I got evidence."

"Listen, Darlene, you're going to have to tell me more than this diddly-squat stuff."

"I'm telling you I got evidence," Darlene pouted.

Martinez weighed the situation. 'Then maybe I can talk to a guy and we can get something out of it for you. So, put on a dress, look like a person, will you? I'll meet you in fifteen minutes."

"I'm not getting into that fucking copmobile."

Martinez started to go. "Move your ass, Darlene."

"Chill, Eddie. I'll be at the third booth of the Big Donut in twenty minutes."

"Fifteen," said Martinez and started to walk toward the door. The Big Donut served two purposes for Darlene. First, the booths were tall enough that you could not see who was talking, and second Darlene, like any junkie, needed sugar. Martinez figured he could use a coffee at the department's expense as well as another hour's overtime.

At the doorway the detective turned back, Darlene was still filing her nails. "I said move your ass, Travis," he snapped before slamming the door behind him.

EIGHT

HARRY BLEECH WAS at his Idaho base camp when Radamacker called him on the two-way radio.

"You got a date yet?" Radamacker barked.

"Tuesday. But it's going to cost us a little more."

"What the fuck's wrong now, Bleech?"

"Jer, Jer," Bleech's voice came confidently through the speakers. "You're getting a lot of stuff with this shipment. Don't sweat the extra cash."

"It's the sudden increase, Bleech. What's the story?"

"It's like coffee, Jer, bad harvest and the prices go up. There's been a lot of demand for these babies. But, listen, if it's too much for you, just say no. We could find someone else. You're just my main customer, there are others."

"No, it's okay," Radamacker said too quickly. He fiddled with the dials as the sound faded. "Listen, same drill as before, right? You and two men meet up with Johnson and two of my men in the safehouse and plan it from there, okay?"

"Yeah. Over."

"I'll be calling you. Over."

"Hey, Jer?" Bleech paused. "God be with you."

Radamacker sat at his desk a while, mulling over the bad feeling he had gotten from the conversation. Bleech was not quite a fool, but, he knew the man had no instincts. Radamacker was sure it was his instincts that separated him from other men, predominantly an instinct for survival that over the last few years had ensured his success with massive cash robberies and weapons deals.

Radamacker had met Bleech when they both belonged to the same tax-protest group in northern Idaho. After the group broke up, Bleech stayed in Idaho; a fertile recruiting ground for the Aryan Crusaders, a survivalist outfit he had founded. Radamacker was about to join Bleech when he met the California-based Thomas Taylor and became fascinated by the minister's unusual philosophy. Taylor offered the intense young man the use of his desert hideaway, and Jerry seized the opportunity to found his own group.

Although he had his ideological differences with the Aryan Crusaders, whom he privately called a bunch of hippies, Radamacker had stayed in touch with Bleech. In the last year the effort had paid off, and Harry had led Jerry to several big arms hauls through a contact he had at the Presidio. Radamacker, as usual, had nothing to do with the actual deals; Bleech set them up and, Jerry reasoned, he should take the risk. He separated himself from the crime as carefully as he had from the Goldor robbery.

Jerry walked toward a refrigerator at the back of his underground office. The room felt quiet and safe. He looked around at the walls carved out of rock and a door that could probably stop a tank, and felt secure. He gulped some milk straight out of a carton. On one of the monitors the word

95

Roundtable was spelled out in gothic script. Jerry, looking up, turned up the sound and the strident theme music of a late-night cable show filled the room. " *'Roundtable' presents Armageddon,"* announced the titles as they swam across the screen. *"Tonight we will visit the predicted site of the world's end and then we'll go back to the studio for a roundtable discussion with Reverend Thomas Taylor and Richard Yarrow. Also—"*

"Armageddon, bah!" Radamacker turned off the power to all the monitors so that the room was lit only by a lamp on his desk. He sat at his desk in the shadows for a long time, his legs extended across the desk top. Pressing the fingertips of each hand lightly together, he looked into the darkness.

He had money and soon he would have the right weapons. If all went well at the Presidio he would be ready to begin his life's work sooner than he had thought possible. The first step in Jerry Radamacker's master plan was a daring attack on one of the nation's major sources of crime, corruption, and spiritual degeneration: Los Angeles. He stared up at the ceiling of his underground office, saw that he could now do something big, and the muscles around his mouth contracted as if with pain, baring his teeth. Radamacker was smiling.

Mary picked up her raincoat and slipped into a pair of flat leather shoes. In the bathroom she reapplied her lipstick and ran a comb through her hair.

It was seven o'clock, time for the local station to switch to network programming while the staff shrank to skeleton size. Mary walked toward the newsroom. On her left, a light burned in one of the tiny editing rooms and she heard a low sound as an assistant producer and editor searched the archives for footage. The huge, open newsroom was deserted, except for one writer who tapped the late-night news onto a keyboard and a producer who was researching a piece he was shooting the next day. The building clicked and whirred; the doors of an elevator ground as they closed, warm air whispered in the heating ducts.

At the top of the barnlike room, near the wood and glass

double door opening into a reception area, the gently curving front wall of the assignment desk stood like the bridge of a ship. It always reminded Mary of a taxi dispatcher's booth. Besides answering the two-tier bank of telephones, the assignment editor also had radio contact with all of the camera crews and reporters. Every morning, a list of the day's stories and the whereabouts of each reporter and crew was posted. If a story broke that day, the assignment editor and producer would decide who could best cover it. At four-thirty, just before the five o'clock news, the pandemonium at the desk reached its peak. Phones rang without pause, while support teams of directors and production assistants waited anxiously in the newsroom for their tapes to come in.

During the day, two assistants worked on the desk, helping with the flow of events and coverage. The important, daytime shift lasted from seven in the morning until five, when the five o'clock news went on the air and the six o'clock show was sewn up. Don Cross came in at three-thirty and overlapped with the daytime editor, so that when things were really hectic there were two editors. Cross left at eleven-thirty, after the late news, and the nighttime assignment editor took over the desk until seven the next morning. If the night was quiet, he wrote five pages of his novel about a sensitive, abused child growing up in ancient Egypt—which, except for the setting, was a literal account of his own upbringing.

Now, more than three hours into his shift, Don Cross knew the worst was over. All that remained was the eleven o'clock news, and Mary Reed's Nightbeat spot was the only segment that could turn up any surprises. This night, like most others, Nightbeat's camera crew was the single unit working, though another crew stood by in case of an emergency. Cross angled the reading light over the *Racing Form.* The light reflected off the cheap, shoe-polish hair dye with which he periodically coated his carefully combed hairs. He had a habit of lifting his glasses with his thumb and forefinger and rubbing the sides of his nose where the frames had dug into his skin. The round lenses jumped up and down as he thought about putting twenty clams on March Folly in the fifth race at Golden Gate.

Purposeful footfalls padded past the front of the desk.

"Good night, Mary," Don Cross said without looking up.

"How do you do that?" Mary asked. "How did you know it was me?"

"Ah, I see everything, child. It's my Indian blood. I see, for instance, that tonight you will shortly meet two men—one strong like young tree of oak, the other wise like standing mountain—and I see . . . I see . . ." Don Cross made cutting motions in the air with the edge of his palm. "I see charcoal-broiled meat and onion rings," he finished quickly.

Mary laughed. "Does that mean that Hutch and Tommy finally called in?"

"They got caught in traffic, but Hutch said there was no way they would miss their date with you."

"Well, I'm going over to the Market Diner," said Mary. "If they call in again, let them know I'm on my way. I'll be back around ten."

"See you." Cross returned to his paper. Behind him on one of the monitors, John Ransome finished reading the evening news for the network in New York. Cross folded his newspaper neatly and picked up the telephone to call in his bet.

"What I mean," said Hutch, "is what goes through their minds when they pull those kinds of stunts? I mean, like yesterday, we did that piece on the police commissioner, right? About how he's been taking bribes. I mean this is practically a national story. And we did this great three-minute segment, busted our guts to get it in under the wire. And they run thirty seconds of it so they could fit in a story about a kid with bone marrow disease."

"Kids who overcome diseases; that sounds like one of Randy's ideas," Mary said. Randy Martin was the owner of Channel 6.

Hutch lifted his hands in the air, palms upward. "I mean it just don't make sense, that's all."

"You know what else was wrong with that piece?" said Mary. "They should have run a picture over the sound bite of the commissioner, the first time, when you hear his election speech. It looks bad the way it is."

"Not all reporters are editors, too, you know, Mary," said Hutch, quick to spot the criticism.

Mary was sitting in the Market Street Diner with Bill "Hutch" Hutchings and Tommy Rigson, the regular Nightbeat camera crew and, in her view, the best crew at Channel 6. She took Hutch and Rigson out to dinner about once a month. They did much of the work for her spot every night, choosing the best background, wrapping buildings around her, setting up the lights, while Mary simply showed up half an hour beforehand. Mary genuinely liked these earthy men, and used the dinners as a way of repaying them. They, for their part, were flattered by the time she gave them.

The garrulous Hutch was an old-timer. Channel 6 still had a few of them around, protected by union contracts, which meant a hefty paycheck, fancy benefits, and a generous pension. And hell, they deserved it. Some of them had been in the industry forty years. Of course, the corporate people, the number-crunching "veeps," hated these relics from the past buried in the lower strata of their balance sheets. Because, as any M.B.A. worth the letters could immediately see, beneath these fossilated figures, billion-dollar pension funds had collected like oil under the bedrock of the corporation.

Producers worked around people like Hutch, whose suggestions and requests were politely listened to and then quietly ignored. So the veterans turned around and talked to anyone who would listen and, once you got past the refrain of "Hey, pal, one, two, or three years and I'm out of here," they had some great stories. These people had been there in the early days, fresh out of high school or the military, when television was a prodigy newly born. The days of John Cameron Swayze's "Camel News Caravan," Ed Sullivan, Jackie

Gleason; when live television was the place to be. Things had changed a lot since then, they would say, nothing could rival the excitement and tension of a live variety show in the days when live really meant live. They were television's oral historians, full of jokes and stories three decades old.

Hutch had always been in news, working through the sixties and seventies as a sound man. His partner, teacher, and friend Tommy Rigson was one of San Francisco's legendary cameramen, along with Ron Everslage and Jim Watt. Their work brought the flower children of Berkeley to life, and then, as the peace movement became more militant in the late sixties, they recorded battles in the streets and the increasingly bitter confrontations between idealistic youth and a hard-nosed Texan president.

Now Hutch was teamed up with his former colleague's son, Tommy Junior. Rigson Senior had left for the world of movies in the mid-seventies, just about the time that television discovered videotape and film became a dinosaur for news coverage. In Hollywood, Rigson was hired as a realism consultant by several major movie directors. His task was to add a documentary accuracy to celluloid fantasy, thereby making the illusion seem more real, or reality more illusory, depending on which way you looked at it. Fortunately for Rigson Senior, a great many people looked at the films he worked on, and he had become extremely successful.

The decor was fifties' retro; burgers were served by a waitress in red pedal pushers and sneakers. "When I was growing up," Hutch commented, looking around him, "they called these places dumps."

"Are you complaining?" asked Mary, who would pick up the tab. "Listen, if you want to eat French, I'll order some fries."

Hutch laughed, watching her bite into her burger. "I finally figured out how you could eat so much and never gain a pound," he said. "It's that sushi you reporters like—gives you parasites. It's the parasites you're feeding with all that food you put away." Hutch's own waistline indicated that sushi was not his food of choice.

"Rachel did a piece on that a couple of months back," said Mary.

"Sushi, they call that a news story? Women, that's what's wrong. It was easier in the old days when there weren't all these ladies all over the place." It was an old complaint and Mary had heard it many times before.

"Well, Hutch, welcome to the twentieth century," Mary said. "Women are going to stay in television and you're just going to have to accept it." Mary smiled. She knew not to take Hutch seriously when he started talking like that. The bottom line of their friendship was a shared professionalism, which Hutch's opinions and the fact of her gender could not shake.

"Isn't that right, Tommy?" she asked turning to Rigson, who had been silently ingesting a half-pound bacon cheeseburger.

"Well, I don't see any problem with women." Rigson did not speak often, and when he did he was slow and deliberate. The two men were a study in contrasts. Hutch's dark hair was graying and although his shoulders were relatively strong from carrying camera equipment, his legs were thin from lack of exercise. If Hutch stood sideways, he looked as if he had swallowed a bowling ball that was lodged in his belly; it came from a combination of Miller beer and middle age. Rigson, on the other hand, had the blond good looks that were typically Californian. Muscular and tan, his jeans and T-shirt were obviously chosen to reveal rather than cover his well-honed body. Channel 6's makeup woman, Agnes, commonly referred to Rigson as God with a microphone.

"That's because you don't know what it was like before," Hutch said to Rigson. "News was a man's game. No disrespect to you, Mary, you do a fine job. And I know there's no turning back the clock, but that's just the way I feel."

"We know how you feel, Hutch," Mary said. "By the way, did you see the documentary on public television last night?" she asked. " 'Storming the Barricades,' I think they called it.

Had some of your dad's pieces." She nodded at Rigson. "Was that when you were there, Hutch? There was a great bit from the People's Park."

"Oh, my," said Hutch. "That was a while ago." He pushed his plate away. "That the one with the long close-ups on faces in the crowd?" he asked. Mary nodded. "Christ, I remember shooting that with Tommy. Those godawful ten-ton cameras and the trouble we had editing that film.

"We were in the Park all day. Once the film had been developed and we were back at the studio we saw what a bitch it was going to be to edit. With tape, you can fudge these things, but with film, early morning looks like early morning—there's that clear, pale light—and by eleven you could see the light was harder, more yellow, and the shadows change. It was hell trying to match up the edits. So we cussed and moaned and then we decided to go with it and do a piece showing how the mood changed as the day went on. You could see how the anger sort of came and went; people got sleepy and bored, some got high. We found a couple of faces that, by chance, we had shot through the day, and we did the story with cuts of the faces from the beginning to the end of the day. Those long shots and close-ups were something else." Hutch leaned back. "Intense," he added.

"I can't imagine working with film," said Mary. "It's so slow. How long did a story take?" she asked.

"Well," said Hutch. "Say you shoot at three, and you get it back to the studio by three-thirty, then it takes forty-five minutes to process and you start editing around quarter after four. If a story was real big, the station sent out a remote truck. We'd broadcast live with film inserts. But the trucks were expensive, so most stories didn't get the truck."

"It wasn't news, it was olds!" Mary laughed.

"Yeah, I guess," said Hutch, smiling. "But it was beautiful. Some of those pieces are classics now. When tape came in things really changed. I mean, before we had reporters who could write, really write good stuff, and they had to do investigative work, too, and edit their work. Now, all a reporter has to do is introduce a piece of prerecorded tape 'live' from somewhere. They're performers, not journalists."

"There's still room for someone who can be both," Mary said evenly.

Hutch looked at her. "Maybe you can pull it off," he said holding her eyes with his. He shrugged his shoulders. "And maybe you just think you can."

He looked away again. "You want to know what I miss most about film?" he said. "It looked so good. I mean in the People's Park piece you could see the emotions on people's faces because the film had texture, it had depth and complexity. Tape is so goddam ugly."

"But tape is light, it's instant, you know right away if something is wrong, instead of shooting for a whole day and finding that the film was bad or something."

"Yeah, I remember a day when it got jammed in the camera but we didn't find out till we got back," Hutch agreed.

"And it's easy to edit, you can reuse the same shot as many times as you need to . . ."

"Yeah, and look how that's abused." The old cameraman was enjoying his role.

"What do you mean?" asked Mary.

"I'm talking about when tape came in with live minicams in the seventies. People'd do almost anything live, just for the novelty of it. There'd be a cat up a tree and the local station would cover it. 'Live from a front yard, we were looking at . . .' "

"And the car wrecks," Mary chimed in. "I remember all those car wreck stories." She put on her reporter's voice. "I'm coming to you live from somewhere between exit eight and nine on the Van Buren Freeway. Incredibly, the driver of what was formerly a Chevy Nova emerged miraculously unscathed after a nasty collision with this badly buckled barrier."

"And what about . . ." Hutch dropped his voice to a confidential hush. "Joe Schmoe was a quiet man, so people who knew him say. And no one can offer any reason why he should barricade himself in his own house with an M-16 and his neighbor's dog."

"That's the one where you get leg cramps from crouching behind a parked car across the street all day and the minute you decide to call it a day, the guy decides to come out and shoot himself on the front lawn because he wants to be on television, and the competition gets the story," Mary said.

Hutch grinned. "See, it's not what it used to be."

"Oh, Hutch. You've got to move with the times," Mary said.

"Hey, I move with the times, look at me, I'm here, aren't I? Though I tell you, seventeen more months and this sucker's history. But even this"—he jerked his thumb in Rigson's direction and back at himself—"this two-man crew is gone already. They're getting real keen on one-man crews, you know, sound and camera all in one—" He was interrupted by the beeper slotted on to his jeans. "Well, better go see what this was all about," he said, ambling toward the door and the telephone in the van.

Mary, who was watching Hutch's face as he spoke into the two-way radio in the front of the van, groped in her pocketbook for her wallet. "Let's go," she said, getting up and acknowledging Hutch's excited gesticulations from the front of the van. Mary paid the check and joined her crew outside.

"There's been an explosion at the Presidio," Hutch explained, gunning the van.

Mary jumped in. "I'm going with you guys, it'll take too long to get my car."

"Reed?" It was Don Cross on the two-way radio.

"Give me the headset? . . . Okay. . . . Cross, what's going on?"

"There's been an explosion at the Presi—"

"I know. Anything else on it?"

"Not at the moment. We picked it up on the police radio. Hutch? What's your ETA?"

"Ten minutes, we'll be ready to go on the air in twenty minutes max," answered Hutch.

Mary took the headset back. "Cross, we could go on at eight fifty-eight. We'll preempt the network news update with ours. If you tape the nine o'clock show. What is it? Oh, yes, that cop show. Tape it on two tapes, then when I'm through, you can roll the first tape from the top and keep taping the rest so the audience won't miss it."

Typically, Mary was taking charge, not only of reporting the news, but also programming the station. She not only knew what show was on that evening, but could interrupt network programs with perfect confidence. Cross smiled to himself, he liked her attitude. "Are you sure you'll be ready?" he checked.

"Bank on it."

"Okay. Hutch, Reed, my ass is out there for eight fifty-eight. Make it happen." Cross relished the action, which felt something like the old days at the network in Los Angeles. The tension had made him sweat, misting up his glasses, and he polished them roughly on his jeans. If Hutch and Mary did not deliver a live news bulletin, he could be responsible for several hundred thousand blank television screens around nine o'clock.

As the van rounded the last curve, the news team saw the flickering orange light of the Presidio fire. A fire truck came screaming round the corner, narrowly missing Hutch, who cursed and then followed it into the barracks. The place was thick with uniformed people—the military, police, and fire fighters swarmed around the flames, like shadows in hell. Hutch parked the van and Mary jumped out of the back. The furious noise of the fire obliterated all but the shrillest sirens.

" 'S'hotter than a tamale here," Hutch muttered. He looked around for a good spot for Mary to stand.

"Hey, Freddie!" Mary spotted a fire marshal she knew. He was leaning against a truck. "The last time I saw you you had a cat in your arms."

At the station owner's request, Mary had done a soft piece on the city's fire marshals several months earlier. "Seems like a long time ago, Mary." Mancusi's face was grim.

"So, what's the story here?"

"Wish they'd let me know." Mancusi spat out a piece of chewing gum. He indicated several fire trucks and men standing idle behind him. "We've got a bonfire that's roasting God's toes, and the FBI is checking it out before they let us anywhere near it. It's the stupidest thing I've ever seen."

"The FBI? What've they got to do with it?" Mary asked, surprised.

"A lot it seems."

"Hutch, let's set up here with the flames in the background. Tommy, tell Cross we're going to be ready on time. Oh, and tell Cross to send two, no three, more units out here. We need some decent pictures for Chrisakes." Mary looked through the video camera for a good background. "What kind of building is it?" she asked Mancusi.

"Warehouse," he replied. "Must have had a lot of powder stored there to burn like this. I can't think what would make such a blaze."

"Two minutes, Mary," said Rigson.

"What about the fire? How long will it take to get it under control?" Mary was putting on the microphone as she spoke, tucking the wire under the fold of her raincoat lapel.

"It's hard to say without going in there. They have to let us at it first. It's hard to call, probably at least an hour before we get the flames under control and then . . . oh, looks like we're on." Mancusi walked toward an official who was beckoning him over.

"Thanks, Freddie," Mary called after him.

"Thirty seconds to go, Mary. Are you ready?" Hutch prompted.

"Yeah, tell Cross we're going to run for four minutes. When I start, pan off me, and zoom in on the flames. When I say 'There had been no official statement,' come back to me tight, and make sure you end up tight on me." Mary's voice was strong and authoritative. This was her element.

At Channel 6, the news flash notice was on the screen

and an announcer said smoothly, *"We interrupt our regular programming for this news bulletin."*

"I'm Mary Reed at the San Francisco Presidio, where fire fighters are battling the raging inferno you can see behind me..."

Mary checked her time on a small stopwatch palmed in her left hand, setting her own cues by glancing at it periodically.

"Federal agents are rumored to have been in the Presidio earlier this evening, causing speculation that they were involved in the fire..."

"Damn you, bitch," Bud McClelland, case agent, FBI, allowed himself to curse under his breath. He turned to Derek Chin, chief of the San Francisco Police Department. "So, she heard we were involved."

Chin said nothing. *"Fire officials say that it will be at least an hour before the fire is under control and a more formal investigation can take place. I'll be here, along with the rest of the channel six news team. We'll report again at ten and, of course, we'll have a complete report at eleven o'clock. For now, this is Mary Reed, live..."*

"Organize a press conference, Derek. Make it for ten o'clock and say nothing." McClelland was annoyed.

"Call from Washington, sir," a voice announced on his intercom and Carson picked up the telephone.

The police chief left the FBI offices and headed toward the Presidio.

The stopwatch in Mary's hand flickered at three minutes and fifty-nine seconds. As soon as she heard the announcer, Mary peeled off the wires.

"Hutch." Cross came through on the two-way radio. "Did the other two crews arrive yet?"

"Yeah, just got in."

"Were they shooting? Can you get Mary for me?"

"You want me to get Mary or monitor the other crew?" asked Hutch irritably.

Mary appeared at the back of the van and grabbed the headset. "Listen, get another live crew over here. I'm hearing a lot of speculation that there's some bodies in the building. This is going to be a big one. Trust me. I'm going to put one crew out on the wharf to get some wide shots. I want the other two with me."

"Why?"

"Listen, there's going to be a press conference, there'll be—" Mary broke off suddenly. "Sorry, Cross, got to go. Don't forget to get me that crew." Mary strode off and the camera crew followed her with difficulty. Like iron filings to a magnet, reporters from all around ran toward Derek Chin.

"What's going on, sir?"

"Was anybody inside the warehouse when it blew?"

"Is this a military matter?"

"I'm sorry I can't comment on this at the moment. There'll be a press conference at ten. I hope we can answer all your questions at that time. Now, excuse me. Excuse me, let me get through." Chin was fighting to get through the crowd around him.

Mary signaled to the cameraman to her left to zoom in and get a tight shot of the police chief's closed face.

"We've heard rumors that the FBI are involved in this, Mr. Chin." Mary paused.

"As you say, rumors, Ms. Reed," said Chin, exasperated by the crush of people around them. "And if you quote rumors in public, you'd better substantiate them. Good evening."

Chin finally wrestled through the crowd and disappeared into the police line. A moment later he re-emerged and headed for his limousine. Mary ordered her crew to shoot the car as it pulled away. Chin's presence and his anger were uncharacteristic—as a rule, he did not like to get his hands dirty.

NINE

THE PRESS LOOKED on from a distance while teams of fire fighters moved purposefully around the warehouse. Mary was standing by the van talking to Cross on the radio when she noticed that suddenly there were no more people near the warehouse. An eerie tension thrummed in the air for a second or two. Then an explosion deafened her. Instinctively she dropped to her knees as the upper floor of the building folded and fell in a spectacular display of pyrotechnics.

Most people nearby reacted to the noise in the same way as Mary, some even lay on the ground. The veteran Hutchings, however, loped toward the warehouse with his camera, hoping for a good shot. Two other crews followed him closely.

It was as if they had a reflex that moved them toward situations from which most people naturally fled, and, like flies to honey, these few dark figures flitted toward the place where the noise and the heat were most intense and the pictures were the sweetest.

Fire fighters and the military combined to cordon off the warehouse where the fire raged and had succeeded in containing the blaze so that it was not spreading.

David Roberti ran over to Mary. "You okay?" he asked. The fortyish round-faced reporter had started at Channel 6 many years earlier, and now the street-smart Roberti was one of Channel 6's top reporters. He had hair that never lay flat and his clothes were often out of fashion, but his rough style made him a welcome relief from some of the male models who populated eyewitness news teams from coast to coast.

She nodded.

"I was just talking to someone," he said. "Apparently, they thought it would be safer if they blew up the second floor since it was going to come down at some point without their help."

Mary nodded, getting up and patting the dirt off her knees. Hutchings came back to the van.

"How was it?" asked Mary.

"Hot." Hutch grinned, his face grimy from smoke. He patted his camera. "Got some great footage."

"Let's run it to the studio," said Mary, "right away, so we can use the pictures when we go on next. What's the news on the press conference, David?"

"Think it's going to be at ten," said Roberti.

Hutchings walked off to unload his tape to a runner, who would rush it back to Channel 6.

"What is going on here? Can you make any sense of it?" Mary asked Roberti.

"Well, I know you said that there were FBI agents around earlier. I heard it was the bomb squad."

"That's wild. Does it mean that the fire wasn't an accident?"

"Could be. Or maybe there were detonators in the warehouse. I'm not an expert." Roberti shrugged.

"Either way, it's strange. You know, I've just remembered something. I saw someone in the car with Chin when he came by before who looked familiar. I couldn't place him at first, but I think it was Ralph Wade's aide, Daryl. I met him at one of those parties Wade likes to throw." Ralph Wade had been a congressman for San Francisco for the last fifteen years. He was known for his flamboyantly liberal politics and great parties.

"Wade, huh? It must be serious."

Mary beckoned to a second camera crew. "Listen I was talking to a fire marshal when we first got here. I want to see if he'll do a piece on camera for us."

Mary and Roberti approached the burned-out warehouse and the cordoned area around it. "Now, where's Freddie?" Mary scanned the faces until he saw Mancusi, talking to a sandy-haired reporter who was scribbling furiously in his notebook.

"Who's that?" asked Mary, nodding at the reporter.

"Don't know."

Freddie Mancusi looked up as Mary approached. He nodded at the young reporter, who looked up gratefully at the fire marshal and stabbed his narrow notebook into his pocket. "Thank you, sir," he said. He shot a nervous smile of recognition at Roberti and Mary and walked off.

"Freddie, this is David Roberti, my colleague."

"Pleased to meet you," Mancusi said.

"Who was that kid?" Roberti asked.

"One just now? He's from the City News. I think he said his name was Sweeney."

"Smart," added Mancusi. "Physics major or something. Figured there had to be a bomb because of the way the fire spread."

"That's what I heard," Roberti said.

Mary was looking at the warehouse, where men in silver and orange protective gear were walking around the fire which had virtually spent itself. "That the bomb squad?" Mancusi nodded.

"Can you shoot that?" Mary turned excitedly to Hutchings. "Get those guys on tape, will you? This is important." The crew walked toward the warehouse, dodging officials for a good angle.

"Freddie, would you do a short interview for Channel Six? Describe the fire, what your men have done to contain it. That sort of thing? I won't ask you to speculate."

"Sure thing."

Roberti offered to send another crew over to Mary and Mancusi and disappeared for a while. After the interview, Mary returned to the van. The beeper was sounding in the front seat. She picked up the two-way radio from the seat, and heard Wyatt Andrews at the assignment desk.

"There's been another explosion, Wyatt. They set it off to stop the warehouse collapsing unexpectedly."

"You got pictures?" he asked.

"They're on the way to you right now."

"Good. City news service says there'll definitely be a news conference at ten o'clock. I want Roberti to go on with you then."

"Okay."

"You got three crews now, right?"

"Yeah, Wyatt, all here and working hard."

"Okay. So you anchor the ten o'clock. Put Roberti at another location. Make it look like we've got the story covered."

"Excuse me, Wyatt, we *have* got the story covered. What's on the other stations?"

"Some pictures, but no reporting. We're way ahead. Stay on it, Reed. But, remember, no speculation, just the facts ma'am. We'll go on at nine fifty-eight fourteen over the network news break and we'll run for five. See you out there in ten, Reed. Break a leg."

Mary ran over to Roberti. "David, I'll set up here for the update. You go down to the main conference area in front of the main gate. Looks like there won't be any more flames, but I'll get the warehouse in the background. I'll set the scene, and then at ten o'clock straight up, I'll throw it to you for the press conference. Get the first question in on casualties. They still haven't said if anyone was inside when it blew."

"I've been doing some more talking, Mary. Everyone's sure there were people inside. Would they hold a news conference at ten o'clock for a fire? Not a chance. The question is how many people and who."

"You said it," Mary agreed.

Mary, getting ready for her next report, was checking out her equipment. She pinned her microphone to the lapel of her jacket, and adjusted the volume on the IFB in her ear. This was the device that allowed her to hear information from the control room back at the station. As she was reapplying her makeup, Paul Berman, who was producing the bulletin, told Mary she had two minutes.

At 9:58:14 the Channel 6 bulletin slide came up and the announcer came up with the familiar announcement: *"We interrupt our regular programming for this news bulletin."*

"I'm Mary Reed, back at the Presidio where there's been another explosion since I last talked with you an hour ago."

Wyatt Andrews, standing in back of the control room, loved that line. In the breaking story, Mary established herself right away with the television audience with "the last time I talked with you," and he admired the "an hour ago" part because that informed the viewers at home that she had been on the scene and on top of the story already, and she did it all in six seconds. The footage of the second explosion, which reached the studio minutes before the broadcast, popped up on the screen as Mary continued to talk.

Mary, looking at the monitor on the ground right next to the cameraman, saw the tape on the screen. *"This happened about thirty-five minutes ago. As you can see . . ."*

Mary was not just reporting, she was talking to her audience. The secret Wyatt taught her when she came to Channel 6 two and a half years ago was that many television reporters did not play to the image, so their words were delivered without regard to the picture on the screen. Mary was putting Wyatt's lesson into practice now as she comfortably talked over Hutching's footage: *"We still don't know what caused all this and, even more importantly, we don't know if there was anyone inside when the first explosion occurred shortly after seven o'clock tonight."*

She was ad-libbing. Although there wasn't a script, Mary talked as if there was. There were no stammers, no pauses—Mary just pressed on.

"The rumors here, and I must say there are plenty of them, put federal agents inside just before the first blast. But, that's only one of many rumors without any confirmation."

Again Andrews was pleased. Mary was able to speculate without committing herself. By indicating that her remarks were hearsay, she was letting her audience know what the people at the scene were thinking while at the same time protecting herself. If the story turned out differently, Mary would be able to say that the rumors proved untrue.

"But now officials may be ready to talk. For that part of the story, let's go to the Presidio's main gate and Channel Six reporter David Roberti."

"Mary, the public information officer of the Presidio, Major William Rogers, and city police official Hal Morris are set to hold a news conference."

Roberti turned toward the two officials. These were two perfect public-relations types. Tall, muscular, and white, one was dressed impeccably in a suit, the other in full military uniform.

"Mr. Morris, what caused the explosion and was anyone inside when it blew?"

"David, I don't know. And we won't know until the fire is properly extinguished and we can go inside."

"Major?"

"I agree with Hal. And any speculation from anyone will be just that, so don't do it."

All of a sudden Mary's face appeared on the Channel 6

screen. Wyatt glanced at three monitors to his left and saw that the other stations in town were now on the scene and they were staying with the news conference. The latest footage from the Presidio was being broadcast from the van, so Mary could control what appeared on the screen from the machine in the van. Wyatt held his breath. "This better be good," he mumbled to producer Paul Berman.

"*It's clear that the two public information officials aren't going to give the public any information,*" Mary said to the camera. "*As I said, the FBI were allegedly seen around the scene of the crime this evening. Fifteen minutes ago Channel Six took these pictures.*" Mary gestured to Hutch to run the tape from the van.

"What is she doing?" Berman in the studio had no idea what Mary was going to do next. Obviously, she had not had time to run this tape over to the studio, but she had not told them about it either.

"Easy," said Wyatt. "Let's see what she's up to."

"*This tape shows the distinctive orange-and-silver fire gear of what I have been told is the FBI's bomb squad. They have been prominent in the investigative work here and have been allowed primary access to the site. It seems that the explosion might have been caused by some sort of bomb although the FBI . . .*"

Beads of sweat broke out on Andrews's forehead. If Mary was right the Presidio fire could be the start of a major story and not just a spectacular one-night affair. But if Mary was wrong, he was in for a tough time.

"*Live from the Presidio this has been David Roberti and Mary Reed from Channel Six news. We'll be back with more on our Nightbeat Report on the Eleven O'clock News.*"

Mary hit 10:03:14 exactly. She had done it again. Andrews hoped Mary's journalism turned out to be as good as her sense of timing.

"Reed," Wyatt boomed into the two-way radio. "Great stuff. It's got to be right is all. What's your basis for the bomb story?"

"The FBI squad, the intensity of the fire, the way it spread."

"Not enough."

"Get off my case, Wyatt. I used all the right words. It's a rumor. And, anyway, I'm right, I know I am."

"You better be. Listen, you work on getting some confirmation, and I'll work on it from here. Maybe we can run a carefully worded piece without proof. Check in later."

"Okay."

"At eleven we'll have a cold open with a live shot of the Presidio. You'll do eight minutes then we'll put the other news on. I asked Berman to call you in ten minutes to coordinate. Do as much live as you can."

To start a newscast with a live report was a courageous gambit. The anchors in the studio would resent it, but Wyatt was confident that Mary and the story merited such showcasing. He set the two-way radio carefully on the edge of his desk. A production assistant poked her head around the door. "It's Randy for you."

Although he was expecting the call, Andrews still turned a shade whiter than pale. "Okay. Listen, tell everybody in the newsroom to hunt for confirmation on the bomb report."

He picked up the telephone. "Hi, Randy."

Randall J. Martin, Jr., was the thirty-five-year-old owner of Channel 6. It was his grandfather who built the *Herald* into the city's dominant news source in the thirties and forties and his father who expanded the business in broadcasting during the fifties and sixties. For his thirtieth birthday, Randy was made chief operating officer for broadcasting in the family run business. He ran Channel 6 and the stations in Portland, Seattle, San Diego, and Phoenix. For Martin, life was breakfast at the country club, lunch at the men's club, and dinner with a few friends at his house in Hillsborough, the lush suburban neighborhood where Bing Crosby, Randolph Hearst, and baseball star Ricky Henderson, made their homes. To say that Martin, the well-groomed image of a perfect WASP, was born with a silver spoon in his mouth, was to understate how easy it had been for him. For Martin, running the television station was a mixture of business and pleasure. Owning a network affiliate in a major city was a license to print money and, even in the days of cable and video rentals, the profits were still forty to fifty cents on the dollar. In addition, Martin could call up the network people in Los Angeles when he needed a favor, perhaps some soap-opera star to emcee a charity event.

Like many station owners, Martin was a well-respected pillar of his community. To him, news was money. He liked the ratings high but he did not want to ruffle feathers in the power centers of the city where he was an honorary member. Instead, he liked the news to report on positive things and he liked it to be uplifting, too. Recently, he had Andrews run a series on the city's unsung heroes which included the wives of coast guards, police dogs, and volunteers at the city's hospitals.

"Hey, Wyatt. I'm watching our station here and it looked like that Reed girl beat the hell out of the other jerks on this Presidio thing."

Wyatt knew that he was hearing a preamble to the attack and he silently willed his employer to get to the point. Andrews had some work to do before the eleven o'clock show and a three-martini telephone call was not going to help him.

"Thanks, Randy." The Martins liked to be called by their first name because they felt it made everyone part of the family, their family.

"But I've just talked to the mayor's office, Wyatt. His people are mighty upset . . ."

Wyatt thought about how the rich spoke: earlier in the conversation it was "that Reed girl" and "this Presidio thing," now the mayor's office was "mighty upset."

"I'm telling you, no more talk of bombs. We can't have Channel Six scaring the shit out of people by making them think there are bombers in the city."

Wyatt understood immediately that the mayor had spoken to Martin and that Martin, who might need the mayor in his next ribbon-cutting ceremony, had promised him something he technically should not do: he had promised the mayor that he would muzzle a reporter. Wyatt sighed. One of the reasons the news director was in San Francisco and not at one of the major networks was that he straddled the middle. In a conflict, such as the one he had right now, where the interests of journalism clashed with those of the management, he tried to please both sides.

And so, with another sigh, Wyatt, having caved in to Mary, caved in to Randy. "Okay, Randy. Unless there's proof, no more bomb reports. Talk to you later."

Randy Martin put down the telephone and left his den. His wife looked at him nervously as he returned to the dining table and Martin gave her a reassuring smile. Before sitting down again, the station owner leaned over and whispered to the mayor that he had taken care of that Reed girl's report on this Presidio thing.

There were now ten people in the newsroom, and all of them were working the telephones. When a big story broke, employees who were not working came in to help. Producers, reporters, technicians, all wanted to be part of the action. To miss working a major story was a fate worse than death, especially when it meant getting paid time and a half.

"Anybody got anything on the bomb report?" Andrews yelled to the newsroom. No one answered. Wyatt looked at the clock: ten thirty-five.

"Wyatt, there's a man called Ivory Joe for you." The production assistant looked at Andrews, hesitating over the name.

Ivory Joe was the code name used by mayor's press secretary, Bill Hunter. He was Wyatt's "Deep Throat" at City Hall. The nickname came from the fifties rock singer Ivory Joe Hunter, a San Francisco favorite. Hunter only used the alias in times of crisis.

"Ivory, what's going on?"

"Can't say, but Reed is causing problems."

"Is she right?"

"Can't say."
"Can't or won't?"
"Both."
"So?"

"Look, don't run this story. It's too hot. We don't understand this bomb business but some feds were killed. A sting that went bad. I'll talk to you first thing tomorrow morning, seven o'clock. Remember, Andrews, the mayor wants a lid on this."

Wyatt heard the click of the telephone as Hunter hung up. Nothing he had heard could be reported, that was his deal with the press secretary. He had ten minutes until the broadcast and still no official confirmation. He picked up the two-way radio.

"You're right," he said to Mary, "but I can't get confirmation."

"What about running it as rumor?"

"I'm afraid I can't do that, Mary."

"I'm not backing off. This is hot. It could be a major story, Wyatt."

"All I'm saying is that we need confirmation before we can go with your gut. If we're wrong, people are going to make us pay. No leaks, no scoops, no interviews, nothing. It'll be cold out there, Mary. They'll kill us on the street." Wyatt paused. "Mary, can you hear me?"

"Sorry, Wyatt, I was talking to David. Here's an idea. We saw a City News guy, Sweeney. He heard about the bomb squad from the same source as we did. Check the wires, he might have filed his report."

Wyatt turned off the radio. He got someone to check the city news wires, but no report of an explosion caused by a bomb at a Presidio warehouse had been filed. Wyatt now knew Reed was right, but his job was on the line if he let her speculate at eleven o'clock. He tapped the City News desk number on his telephone.

"Mr. Sweeney, please."

"Sweeney, here."

"This is Wyatt Andrews from Channel Six. Listen, are you reporting on any suspected bombs at the Presidio?"

"I'd sure like to, but I don't have any confirmation."

"Well we do, and we're going to report it on the eleven o'clock news."

"Yeah?"

"The only way you can beat us is to file right now. You can quote unidentified sources. Do it, it's a scoop."

Sweeney scratched his head for a few seconds. He knew that Wyatt Andrews was not giving him a scoop so much as protecting his broadcast. The City News service, which all radio, television, and newspapers had in their office, was not Wyatt's competitor. However, Sweeney knew something was going down at the Presidio and all his reporter's instincts told him to publicize it, even at the risk of his boss's wrath. Besides, he might want a job at Channel 6 one day.

"Okay. I'll file now."

Andrews burst out of his office. "Get me the City News on the computer," he said to an idle assistant. Wyatt was computer illiterate and longed for the old days when news wire machines printed out the news on yellow paper lined with carbon. In those days you could feel the news as if it were happening right there on those large, noisy machines. Now it was like going to the bank, with account numbers and a foolish password he could never remember.

As the green letters snaked across the screen, Andrews relaxed. Sweeney had come through; Wyatt owed him. It was three minutes before the eleven o'clock news when Wyatt read the report to Mary. She would run the story, he would keep his job, and the views would know a little about what really happened.

"Your deal, right?"

"Yeah."

"Did he open his eyes?"

"No."

"Gin."

The door opened and a surgeon, the chief resident and a nurse entered a private room in the University of California Medical Center, where two federal agents were playing cards at the bedside of a man they had named J. Adams. Of the eight men who were found in the Presidio warehouse, three were FBI agents. Two of the bodies, both terrorists, were pulled out of the flames alive, but one had died during the night. Adams was now the sole survivor of the Presidio blast.

It was the evening after the explosion and the patient, who had spent eight hours on the operating table, was expected to come out of sedation soon. He had a breathing tube in his mouth which hooked him up to a respirator; a needle dripped glucose into a vein in his arm; a naso-gastric tube was stuffed through his nose and into his stomach; a catheter, pinned behind his collarbone, measured his feeble heartbeat; and another catheter, in his hip, dripped urine into a hanging bottle. J. Adams might have been alive, but he was not in good shape.

The pretty redheaded nurse, who had been sitting at the patient's side, rose to greet the doctors and her replacement for the nighttime shift. "He's still sedated," she said unnecessarily to the surgeon, gesturing at the patient. The doctors began to check the patient's vital signs, making notes on the clipboard and exchanging comments in low voices.

Ned Rigby, known as "Sly" because a lazy eye gave him a shifty look, closed the fan of cards he had just laid on the chair between him and his colleague, gathered the pack, and put it in his jacket pocket. He watched with studied casualness as Adams was examined.

A head bent round the door and beckoned Rigby into the corridor. He stood up. "Stay here, will you. Be back soon," he said to his fellow FBI agent, Ted Begay.

In the hallway, Rigby saw several policemen in uniform stationed at strategic positions, while a few plainclothes detectives roamed through the corridors. The Bureau had set an entire wing of the hospital off-limits, and even the medical staff had to pass a checkpoint before entering the wing. Rigby and his boss, Frank Carson, walked toward a small alcove stuffed with a brown vinyl sofa where, for the moment, no anxious relative or friend was sitting. The deserted corridors accentuated the institutional drabness of the hospital, but neither Carson or Rigby noticed such things.

"Anything new?" Carson asked, raising one pale eyebrow to emphasize his question. Carson was assistant supervising agent, or ASAC, in charge of the Presidio case, and he reported to Case Agent Bud McClelland. He had been transferred from Washington and put on the case that morning. His predecessor was one of the agents killed in the Presidio explosion.

"Not really," said Rigby. "Seems like we'll have to wait a few days before they can take the respirator out and we'll see if he can talk any." He paused, but when Carson remained silent he added, "The doctor doesn't hold out much hope."

"We don't need the guy to dance!" Carson snapped. He was frowning and the pink lines on his forehead were furrowed in concern. "We've just got to keep that twitching inventory of body parts alive long enough to give us some more names. Three agents are dead because of a loused-up operation. Casey's vanished without a trace. Washington's in an uproar, the attorney general's office is on my tail. We've got to produce something quickly."

"What about the guy that died last night—anything on him?"

"McClosky. Found his records, he was in the military so we got his prints and dental records. Plus he has a rap sheet, armed robbery, that type of thing. Nothing on him for the last couple of years."

Carson glanced around before pulling out a manila envelope. "Okay," he said. "Here's what we know about this Adams character. Casey gave us some information, not much, but it's all we have. Real name is Harry Bleech. Knew Casey from Saigon. Casey thought he might be fronting for someone, but Casey didn't ask questions as long as he got the money. It's all here." Carson tapped the envelope against Rigby's chest. "Read it and weep."

Carson looked at his watch. "I've got to make a call to the mayor's office. That reporter on Channel Six really isn't helping us. If we don't know what happened, how can we tell the press? What a job, eh?" Carson bustled down the corridor, and Sly Rigby rejoined his partner and studied the dossier on Henry Bleech.

In the second-floor hospital cafeteria the redheaded nurse, Frances McCarthy, sipped a cup of lemon tea.

"Hi, Fran. You on the late shift again?" Emma Michaels sat down heavily opposite her friend. "I'm just about to start. You got any hair spray?"

"In my locker," said Frances.

"I ran out, and I've just noticed this pen mark on my pocket seam, which the dragon lady is going to notice," Emma said irritably, looking down at her otherwise immaculate uniform. "I reckon it'll come out okay with the hair spray."

"I'm just about to go," Frances said, finishing her tea. "Come back down with me to my locker, and we'll fix you up."

"Where are you working these days?" asked Emma as they got into the elevator.

"Oh, they're moving me about a bit," Fran said vaguely. She had been told not to say much about what she was doing.

"I hear they've got five people up there in the wing they've closed off?"

"Just one," said Fran, then realized what she had done. She laughed nervously. "They told me not to say anything."

"What's so special about this patient?" asked Emma.

"You ask me, the poor guy's nearly dead, but they won't give up till they can make him talk."

"Who's they?"

"The police, I guess." Fran looked down as another nurse got on the elevator.

"So, what did this guy do that the police were so interested?" asked Emma when they arrived at Fran's locker.

"You know that thing at the Presidio?"

"The explosion, you mean?"

"Yeah, well, this guy was involved in that." Fran gave her friend the can of hair spray and closed her locker.

"Young guy?"

"More like fifty, I'd say. He's really fighting."

"I think it's terrible that they close off a whole wing of the hospital like that for some criminal. What about the other poor patients that can't get care?"

The redhead shrugged. "I don't know, Emma. That's the way it goes, I suppose."

"Yeah, well, thanks for everything, Fran. You're a pal."

At seven o'clock the control room burst into spontaneous applause. Upstairs in the newsroom, Wyatt Andrews shook everybody's hand. For the second day in a row Channel 6 and Mary Reed had beaten out the competition in their coverage of the Presidio story. That morning the ratings came in from the previous night. They were broken down into fifteen-minute segments that showed that Channel 6 had an 18-percent share of the audience at nine o'clock that went up to 24 percent during the first interrupt. At ten o'clock the share went up to 32 and at eleven o'clock it climbed to 50 percent, meaning that half the households in San Francisco were watching Mary Reed. Wyatt hoped tonight would be as good. Mary had forced the authorities to release more information and had put together a special report that Andrews aired at six with updates at eleven.

When big stories break, local news stations get their chance to shine. Most of the time they deal with the same material as the other stations and the only difference among them is in their presentation. That is why so many shows devoted attention to a goofy weatherman and a good-looking male and female anchor team to convey the reassuring illusion of a cozy on-set family. However, Wyatt believed that a big news story covered well was the way to be the best, and in the Presidio fire he had achieved it.

"You coming to Schroeder's, Wyatt?" Paul Berman stood in his doorway.

Andrews's phone rang. "Sure, see you there in a minute." He picked up the telephone. It was Irwin Hansen, Wyatt's old Columbia Journalism School classmate, who was currently news director for Channel 3 in Los Angeles.

"Irwin, how are you?"

"Fine, Wyatt. You?" Hansen replied impatiently.

"I'm doing fine, Irwin. Heart's not great, I've been told, but I'm really feeling good. Judy's doing well, too. 'Course she misses the kids . . ." Andrews deliberately stalled his old classmate, knowing that Hansen would not have called unless he wanted something, and Wyatt had a good idea what he was after.

After graduating from Columbia in the fifties, Wyatt went to CBS and Hansen got a job with NBC. Their friendly rivalry had been a bond that had lasted the thirty-five years they had been in the business. Now both men were in their mid-fifties, both working in the demanding, budget-conscious world of local news. Although Wyatt had never made it in the networks the way Irwin had, he figured that he ended up with the better deal; he would take San Francisco over Los Angeles any day.

"You know, Wyatt," Hansen finally interrupted him. "I'm glad to see that you're still capable of kicking the network's ass. Reed's coverage of the bombing was terrific, just terrific. I'd like her on my six o'clock show tomorrow."

"What happened? The network cut the budget for their number-two market? You don't have any reporters left?"

"Hey, don't make me beg. I want her, she's good." Hansen paused. "Come on, Wyatt, you're a reasonable man. Can I count on her for tomorrow night?"

Wyatt knew that Hansen was perfectly capable of contacting Mary directly if he refused, so he capitulated. "Well, since we go back so many years, Irwin. . . ."

"Good."

"Good for you maybe, I don't know how good it is for us."

"Listen, Wyatt, I owe you."

"Yeah, yeah, yeah. Hey, stay in touch, will you?"

At one in the morning David Roberti stumbled into his one-room apartment in the Castro District of San Francisco. He had been drinking. Negotiating piles of papers with little success he fell onto his bed. The room was spinning dizzily. "Maybe if I lie down . . ." he mumbled. Before he could try it, the telephone rang.

"Davey?" said Emma Michaels.

"Yeah," Roberti said slowly.

"Are you drunk?"

"No. Well, maybe, some. Yeah." Cautiously, Roberti lay down. "What's up, Emma?"

"You've got to cut down. For your own good."

"Okay, nursie. Enough. What's cooking?"

"You know that Presidio fire?"

"Uh-huh."

"I got a lead for you. Seems there's a survivor and he's in the hospital here."

Roberti jerked his head up, then winced because it hurt. "Yeah?"

"Yeah?" She imitated him.

Roberti was sitting up. "Any details"

"Man's around fifty. He's in bad shape."

"Listen, thanks Em. This is great."

"Okay. Good luck, honey." Emma Michaels returned to her shift, shaking her head in concern over the reporter she once loved.

With difficulty Roberti opened his window made stiff by many layers of paint, and noisily breathed in the chilly night air. He looked at his bed sadly, knowing that he would not get much sleep that night.

TEN

"GOOD MORNING, THIS is Channel Six and we interrupt our regular morning programming for this news bulletin. Here is William Reese."

"We now have the latest in the San Francisco Presidio explosion. We go live to U. Cal. Medical Center and Channel Six's Mary Reed. Mary?"

"William, I've just come down from the fourth floor of the hospital where the FBI has sealed off an entire wing from the public and from all hospital staff whose services are not needed. It seems that one of the suspected terrorists survived the blast. We don't know his name. All we know at this point is that he is in extremely critical condition and he is a man of about fifty years of age. Calls to the police department and the city attorney's office have not been returned.

"No mention of the survivor has been made by the authorities but, as I said, the elaborate security measures and the extensive official presence in the hospital seem to indicate that what my sources tell me is true: there is a survivor from the Presidio explosion.

"In a statement released yesterday, the police department did not mention a survivor. What they did say was that they believe that five armed men broke into the Presidio on Thursday evening intending to steal weapons from the army base. They were caught in the act and in the shoot-out set off the explosion that we witnessed last night. The statement says that three federal agents were tragically killed in the explosion along with the five terrorists."

"So what you're saying, Mary, is that you believe that there is a survivor from the catastrophe who is being kept under strict surveillance in the hospital but officials are not confirming this information?"

"Correct, William. Now we will be following this exclusive report throughout the morning and I'll be giving you new details as I get them."

"And what about the terrorists, Mary?"

"Well, word is that they were connected to a drugs and arms outfit run out of a Central American country, but we'll have a full report on Channel Six news at five o'clock. For the moment, this is Mary Reed reporting live from the University of California Medical Center Hospital."

Mary stood on a semicircular patch of grass outside the hospital entrance and smiled into the camera. David Roberti was impressed despite himself. He had worked on his lead the night before, but when he told the news director about it during a meeting first thing that morning, Andrews had suggested that Mary take it over, with Robert giving her all the help he could. Mary had anchored the breaking story, and Andrews wanted to strengthen her identification with it. The reporter had not fought the decision. He recognized that Mary's star was rising and he was happy simply to play a small part in a big story. In a couple of hours Mary had corroborated his lead and put a piece together, which meant that at twenty-five she was probably a better reporter than he would ever be. He picked up his phone. David Roberti had learned he could not compete with a pretty and competent woman.

In a private room on the fourth floor of the hospital, Frank Carson sighed and swiveled around in his chair to face his two agents. His neck hurt from craning to see the television, which was strapped across the top corner of the room. Sly Rigby and Ed Begay, who were perched awkwardly on the bed, turned their heads to face him.

"So, how'd she hear about Bleech?" asked Begay.

"Oh, any number of ways. A good journalist will have contacts in as many places as possible, isn't that so?" Rigby answered his partner and turned to his boss. "What do you want to do?" he asked Carson.

In response, Carson picked up the telephone and punched out a number he clearly knew by heart. "Hi, Bill?" he said to the Mayor's press secretary. "Frank Carson. Listen, we're going to give a description of the survivor to City News. That Channel Six reporter's got wind of his existence and we're going to have to release this information or we'll look like idiots. . . . No, we really didn't want to do this before because we hoped he would give us something, but really the guy's on the way out, the doctors don't give him much longer and we haven't learned squat from him . . . okay . . . yeah . . . bye."

As Carson finished, a nurse came in with a breakfast tray of coffee and three inedible danishes wrapped in plastic. Carson rubbed his neck. He swilled the coffee doubtfully, then took a large gulp, which seemed to give him new energy. "Okay, guys. Something smells here. The warehouse never should have blown like that. We have no idea where Casey is. We have too many goddamn questions and no answers. Answers are what we've got to find."

Wyatt Andrews looked at the spread sheet on his blotter and absently circled two figures with a pencil. It seemed that he either had to cut down his promotion budget or cut down on the number of hours he could have a crew out on the street. This was not a decision they ever discussed in journalism school, but it was one he had become accustomed to making. The news director's intercom flashed and his secretary announced that the mayor's office was on the line. Andrews picked up the telephone. It was Bill Hunter, complaining about Mary's latest report.

"Bill . . . yes, of course I authorized it. . . . No, I know, but Reed is my best reporter, I'm not going to sit on her. . . . No, not this time. You owe me one . . . sure, tell the mayor to give a full accounting on TV but make it soon. That'll get him off the hook. . . . No, if the FBI and the military want to stonewall, let them, but get your boss away from the whole issue. It's going to be election time sooner than you think. . . . Okay . . . yeah . . . bye."

"Thank you." Mary Reed turned to face the camera, microphone in hand. *"I've just been talking with Police Chief Derek Chin. The police department has released a description of the man they say is the sole survivor from the Presidio explosion. He is in critical condition here at the University of California Medical Center. This is Mary Reed, for Channel Six, News at Five."*

Jerry Radamacker looked into Mary's lovely green eyes and imagined she was looking back at him. He had watched the reporter who had been stalking his story with the single-minded determination of a predator continuously throughout the day. And now, finally, Jerry saw that she was telling him what he should do, she was saying to him—of course, she had to do it silently—she was telling him, *telepathically*, that he had better get to the survivor, pull the plug before the guy let on too much. Thank you, Radamacker mouthed toward the woman on television, thank you.

Radamacker turned away from the screen, his jaw working obsessively as he paced up and down his office, glancing up every once in a while to look at the door. When door opened, Finn walked in.

"Where have you been?"

"Practicing on the range," Finn answered. He looked closely at Jerry.

"I need you here, with me," Jerry barked. "That's your job, protecting me. Anyone could walk in here when you're gone." Radamacker fought to regain his composure. "Bleech survived," he said at last, pointing to the monitors.

"What do you mean?" asked Finn.

"I mean he survived the explosion, you idiot. He's the only one who fits the description, and he's alive in some hospital in San Francisco. He wasn't blown to bits, get it?" Radamacker yelled, losing his temper. "We could be in serious danger."

"But they can't trace it to you," said Finn.

"What if he says something?" said Radamacker. "What if he tells them about me?"

Radamacker was still pacing. He stopped and looked up suddenly. "Finn, I want you to go to San Francisco. We've got to get rid of him before he blabs."

"How we going to do that?"

"I have a plan," he said. "I'll tell you about it tonight. We can't take any chances."

He looked back at the monitors. "Oh, and when you're in San Francisco, I want you to find out everything you can about this reporter Mary Reed."

As they walked toward the rusty elevator, Radamacker put his arm around Finn's shoulders. The younger man relaxed.

To the right of the church behind the minister's house there was a one-story cement building where the leader and his men ate and held meetings. As Radamacker and Finn entered, about fifty men milled around, picking up food from the kitchen hatch and sitting at long tables. Radamacker walked to a small table that was raised on a low dais at the end of the room. Finn sat down beside him, reassured by the awkward shape of the gun at his side.

Thomas Taylor approached the table accompanied by a large, red-faced man.

"Jerry." The large man held out his hand and smiled with easy geniality.

"Glad you could join us," Radamacker said. "Sit down."

"Thank you." Horace Wickstrom sat down with surprising delicacy, distributing his bulk evenly on the uncomfortable metal chair beside Radamacker.

Originally from Alabama, Wickstrom had been Grand Dragon for the California Klan for several years. He had met Radamacker in a tax-protest group in northern Idaho. For the moment, he fixed televisions and broadcast a right-wing cable talk show called "Roundtable" from his garage in San Diego. Wickstrom now paid his taxes, and he was thinking of running for political office.

The minister sat down beside Wickstrom and blessed the plates stacked with chicken, sweet corn, cranberries, and mashed potatoes blanketed in a creamy cheese sauce. Hungrily, Finn started to eat.

Wickstrom was talking about the furor caused by "Roundtable." Protest at the extremist views advocated in his show were pitted against First Amendment principles, which bound the cable companies to give uncensored airtime to people regardless of their political orientation. So although the cable company broadcast "Roundtable" in Southern California, they did it at four in the morning when they figured that the fewest people would watch it.

"We're trying to take the show into the Northwest now," Wickstrom was saying. "Crowded market up there, very crowded." He shook his head so that the loose, grayish wattles on either side of his chin swung from side to side.

"I got a friend in Seattle, a lawyer. He might be able to help you there," Radamacker said. He had hardly touched his food. "I'll give you his number before you go."

"Thanks, Jer. You know, Taylor here pulled off a real good show last week. I've been getting some letters on it."

Taylor ate slowly but with great determination. He

paused in his systematic chewing. "And how much am I vilified by the ignorant?" he asks.

Wickstrom looked at Radamacker. "This man's got education, Jer. I like that." He turned to Taylor. "I don't rightly know what you mean there, minister." He pitched a forkful of mashed potato into his mouth. "Some of the letters were pretty angry, if that's what you're driving at. I had my girl keep them like you asked."

"Thank you, Horace. I have a special use for those names."

"You going to send them birthday cards on April twentieth?" Wickstrom joked.

"Something more sophisticated, I think," said Taylor diffidently.

"Well, you're welcome to come back on another show. And, Jer, I'd really like you to consider it. I've heard you speak, you'd be real special." When Radamacker did not reply, Wickstrom pressed on. "Think about it, Jer, just think about it."

"I told you before, I'll go on the show after you play my video."

"Oh, yeah, the video." Wickstrom scratched his head.

Finn got up to get another plate of food and Taylor followed him. Absently, Radamacker tapped his fork against the side of the plastic plate. He looked into the distance.

"Jer," Wickstrom began, seizing the opportunity to talk to Radamacker alone. He took out the napkin from his collar and wiped his mouth, watching Radamacker sharply all the while. "Been hearing a lotta rumors about you lately . . . like you're mixed-up with Harry Bleech and the Presidio break in. You're an intelligent man. You gotta be careful with this type of stuff."

"Yeah?" said Jerry. "And what have you done recently?"

"We've got to stick together, Jer. You go out on your own and you're lost, you know that? Like Harry."

"Patience and preparedness, right?" Radamacker said.

"Just like the minister keeps saying." He watched as Taylor and Finn returned to the table.

"Maybe you'd consider a donation to run the video," said Radamacker, changing the subject.

Wickstrom looked hard at Jerry. "Means a lot to you, this video? It's good, I'll give you that. Where did you learn to produce such stuff?"

"Used to work at the local television stations when I was in college. I did sound. I'd stay there late and mix tapes for myself. It's professional quality, you know. Not like most of the crap you broadcast. No offense, Horace, but it's not exactly slick."

"It's okay, Jer. You don't have to explain. Listen, I'd do it for you. But I gotta think about my reputation." He shook his head. "I don't know, seems like the minister here's got the right idea: shoot everyone and let God sort 'em all out."

"All talk," Radamacker said with a wave of his hand. "There comes a time when real white men have to act." He stood up. "People like you need me, Wickstrom, remember that." Radamacker left the room. Finn hurried after his leader, catching up with him at the bottom of the steps to the church.

"That you, Johnson?" he asked, peering through the dusk with shortsighted eyes until he made out Finn's face. "You can leave me alone now. I've got some work to do. Come down to the office at midnight, we'll talk about what you're going to do in San Francisco." Obediently, Finn melted back into the darkness.

Radamacker arrived at the underground office just in time for the eleven o'clock news. He watched Mary Reed like a man mesmerized.

"There's been a break on the San Francisco Presidio explosion case. Our local affiliate in San Francisco has learned that there is a survivor from the explosion. We go now to Mary Reed, reporting to us from the University of California Medical Center in San Francisco . . ."

Mary and Wyatt Andrews were watching her appearance on the network news in the news director's office the following evening. It was her third day on the story and her first appearance ever on national television.

"Couldn't cut you out of that one," said Andrews as the segment ended. Mary was now firmly identified with the Presidio story, which was what every station wanted to do with a breaking story, whether it concerned hostages in the American Embassy in Iran or the private life of a local sports hero. Because of this, concerned citizens called her with information. More important, however, the network had respected Mary's work on the story, and so they had not replaced her with a network reporter. These reporters were often called fly-bys—when something important happened, the network would jet them up from Los Angeles for some "drop-in" journalism. They would stand outside the Channel 6 building to lead into a story that was essentially a rehash of the local reporter's work.

When Mary got back to her office she found a sheaf of calls congratulating her on her spot on national television. She leaned back in her chair. Her face looked drawn and there were dark hollows under her eyes, which makeup only partially concealed. She kicked off her pumps. The phone rang.

"It's been quite a day, Mary."

"Who's this?"

"A friend, Mary, a friend." Jerry Radamacker's voice purred over the telephone line.

"What do you want?"

"The survivor of the Presidio explosion . . ."

"What about him?"

"He's dead."

"What?"

There was silence on the other end of the line, and then Mary heard a dial tone. Her mystery caller had hung up. Wearily she stood up and prepared to leave, then sat down again. She left a message on Emma Michaels' answering machine asking her to contact her if there was a change in Bleech's condition.

Mary walked to the assignment desk. "Ron, I need a wake-up call at eight please," she told the assignment editor.

She took the elevator to the garage in the basement of the building. Throwing her coat into the back of the car, she slid into the driver's seat. Mary sped out of the garage and punched her favorite rock and roll station on her radio, turning it up loud. The lights of downtown San Francisco flickered. As she stopped for a red light, Finn Johnson eased a blue Chevrolet out of a side street and pulled up behind her as the lights changed.

At home there was a message on Mary's machine from Emma Michaels. "The Presidio survivor is dead."

Mary was doodling on a pad in her office. She had run around all day trying to find a lead on the Presidio story, and failed to turn anything up. The FBI would not even speak to her and no one else seemed to know anything. She considered the possibility that her Nightbeat spot might have to be about something different. The phone rang.

"Mary?"

"Hello. Who's this?"

"Don't you remember me?" Mary recognized the voice of her mystery caller. "So, did you call the hospital?"

"Yes."

"Do you want some more information, Miss Reed?"

"Maybe."

"I could tell you, for instance, that you bought pizza on your way home last night. Medium, extra cheese."

Mary breathed in sharply.

"Don't worry, Mary. I consider this privileged information."

"Who are you?"

"I'm a patriot."

"What's that supposed to mean? This isn't the Revolutionary War."

"Isn't it, Mary. Isn't it?" She heard the dial tone, and sighed in exasperation.

Ten minutes later the telephone rang again.

"Don't you want to talk to me?" asked the mystery voice.

"Why do you keep hanging up?"

"You think I'm an idiot? Let you trace the call? Come on, give me some credit, Mary."

"Listen, if you have some authentic information, give it to me. If not, I shall inform the police that you are harassing me."

"Whoa, there. Steady on. I told you, privileged information. Okay. I could tell you who planned the Presidio arms deal. I could tell you that the armed forces couldn't keep a mouse out of the country if they wanted to. I could tell you that the U.S. military is run by guys who would sell their birthright for a few thousand dollars. That's what I could tell you."

"Okay, so tell me." Mary heard the dial tone. Ten minutes later the phone rang again.

"Will you put this on television?"

"Sure, if it checks out."

"Dead man's real name was Harry Bleech. Ran some two-bit organization in Idaho."

"What kind of organization?"

"Harry was a patriot. He's for me."

"What is this patriot business? Who are you guys fighting?"

"The federal government and all it stands for. Did you know that all our legislation, the gun laws, the Federal Reserve have been run by an international caucus for the last hundred and fifty years? It's the Jews that started it, and the only person that ever tried to stand up against them was The Great One. He saw what they were doing and tried to stop them and look what they did to him. You think the collapse of the savings and loans institutions was an accident, Mary? Think again."

Mary hung up. The man was a lunatic. When the telephone rang again, she looked at it doubtfully. Reluctantly, she picked it up.

"Check this out, Mary. You're going to like it."

"So what's all this about Harry Bleech?" Mary's voice was low.

"Bleech came to me a year ago. Says he's got a chance to score some weapons but he doesn't know how to raise enough money. Not too sharp, Harry. So, I show him what to do. I get the money. We work out details. I'm the commander. He knows that. But this time, this time turns out the operation's a sting. FBI gets in on it. Must have turned that asshole Casey. So Harry gets blown to pieces."

Mary was chewing her thumbnail. "Who's Casey?" she asked but Radamacker had already hung up.

"So, who's Casey?" Mary asked again when the phone rang a few minutes later.

"I give up, who is he?" Mark shot back jokingly.

"Oh, Mark. I was just about to call you. The weirdest thing is happening. I've got a Deep Throat on the Presidio story. I spoke to him yesterday and he predicted that the survivor would die. Now, he's giving me names. . . ."

The next day Mary sat in the friendly, old-fashioned atmosphere of Taditch's Grill with David Roberti. They were talking about the Presidio story.

"So, I pulled the jacket on this guy Bleech." Roberti took a sheaf of papers out of a manila envelope. "It checks out with your source. The guy ran some outfit in Idaho. Have you heard of the Posse Comitatus?"

She pushed her plate away and looked at her notes. "Aren't they the ones who believe in pro se representation in court, and all that survivalist stuff?"

"That's it. Well, this Bleech guy had the same idea. He gave it a military twist by training his adherents and threw some bullshit religion in. He attracted quite a few lost souls and made some money off them. The guy was no fool. Or maybe it's more along the lines that nobody ever lost money underestimating the intelligence of the American public."

"Twain, right?" Mary smiled. "Okay, but where's the connection with the Presidio?"

Roberti hesitated. "I don't know the exact connection. But look at it this way: these guys are into weapons. They hate gun control; want to have their own little armies. It makes sense that they would do some sort of deal like the Presidio one. The question is where did they get the cash?"

"My Deep Throat is claiming that he put up the money." Mary paused. "What do you think?"

"Well, this Bleech character doesn't sound like he had enough on his own," Roberti said. "Of course, it's always hard to tell with these people, they don't exactly keep records with the IRS. Listen, it checks out so far."

He beckoned the waiter over. "Coffee?"

Mary nodded. When the waiter had gone, she leaned across the table, frowning. "David, what do I say if Wyatt asks me where I'm getting all this from?"

Roberti looked at her. "The information is good, that's the main thing. As long as it's accurate it doesn't matter if little birds are singing it to you."

"Well, I'm not going to tell Wyatt it's some guy I've never even seen."

Roberti took a gulp of his coffee. "Andrews needs deniability. That's his best job protection in a situation like this. He doesn't need to know how his reporters get their stories. And, it's much better for him if he can shrug his shoulders and plead ignorance when Randy Martin comes down on him like a ton of bricks."

"I guess," Mary said.

"I know," said the streetwise reporter. "Looks like you've landed another hot lead, Mary." Roberti drained his coffee. "Go for it," he said.

Mary had just sat down in her office when there was a knock on her door.

139

"Ned Rigby, FBI, ma'am," the man said, flashing his badge.

"Are you the one who called earlier?"

"Yes, ma'am. We'd like to talk to you about the robbery at the Presidio." Sly eased himself into the tiny office, making room for his partner Ed Begay. The two agents loomed over Mary.

"What do you want to know, Mr. Rigby?"

"You called our office earlier today, was that so?"

"Yes, that's right. I was interested in checking out some information I'd got."

"You usually have a segment on the eleven o'clock news, that right, ma'am?"

"Yes."

"And when do you usually record it?"

"Depends if it's a live piece or taped."

"Is it live or taped tonight?"

"Taped as a matter of fact. I just did it."

"Do you like being a reporter?"

"Listen, I don't know what the hell you guys are after, but you'd better stop wasting my time and get to the point."

"Where did you get the information you gave the police department, ma'am?"

"A source. I don't have to tell you guys. This is First Amendment stuff. You can't get that information out of me. My source is confidential."

"This source, ma'am. Used it before?"

"Listen, I'm interested in the information, not the source."

"So you call the police department with a name. Is that right, ma'am?"

Mary was exasperated. "Who is this guy Casey that he's so important to you?"

Rigby raised his eyebrows and Mary realized too late that she had just revealed that she did not know who Casey was. "Listen, I'd like you to leave now. I don't have to talk to you." Mary stood up.

"Yes, ma'am. Thank you, ma'am." Rigby was about to follow Begay out of the small office, when he turned. "Ma'am? If you think about this some more and you feel you want to tell me something new, here's my card. Give me a call. Any time."

Rigby walked out of the room followed by his partner. A second later, Begay reappeared. Mary had sat down, feeling suddenly exhausted. "Miss Reed?" Begay looked at her mournfully. "I came back because, well, because I have a friend who's a real fan of yours. He won't believe I met you. Could you sign this for me? To give to him, I mean."

Mary looked at him sharply, then signed her name on his newspaper.

"Thank you, ma'am."

The two agents walked down the hallway.

"Can't believe I got her autograph," Begay said.

"We're going to get more than that."

"What do you mean?"

"We're going to watch that broad. I want her phone records. It was yesterday I'll bet. I figure someone got through to her, gave her Casey's name, and she called the police department to check it out."

"Think she'll contact us?"

"She's the stubborn type. Never admits she's wrong. In my opinion, she's headed for trouble."

Wyatt met Mary as she came out of the studio after her Nightbeat spot. He congratulated her on another scoop. Mary had revealed the real identity of Harry Bleech and given a detailed report on the Aryan Crusaders. The next day the FBI would be forced to release yet more information on the Presidio incident. When he asked about her source, Mary lied and told Wyatt that she had an informant inside the police department.

As she neared her office, Mary heard her telephone ringing. It stopped and then rang again a few minutes later and she picked it up.

"So we're in the news again, Mary." It was the smooth voice of her anonymous source.

"Listen, I want you to tell me everything you know about the Presidio operation."

Mary listened without interrupting while Radamacker, sensing her interest, detailed each step of the military-style maneuver. As she listened, an idea formed in Mary's head. It was brilliant, daring, provocative, and it could be good journalism.

"Will you repeat everything you've just told me in front of a TV camera?" Mary asked.

There was no response and Mary thought her caller might hang up.

"Well," said Radamacker finally. His voice sounded faint; for the first time she had startled him.

"Well, I just might do that," he said.

ELEVEN

MARY WAS STANDING on the southwest corner of Union and Geary near Union Square. This was what her mystery caller, the commander, had told her to do the previous night. Mary wondered if she was crazy. It was nine-thirty on Monday morning, and she was waiting for her two camera crews to show up. Only Channel 6's top reporter could arrange to get two camera crews for an interview, and she still had had to pressure assignment editor Ron Corvis to get them. Wyatt Andrews would be back from a weekend trip mid-morning. Mary was happy he was not around, if she could not ask him if she should do the interview, he could not say no.

Mary looked around her. It was a foggy June morning.

Sales assistants were filtering into the big department stores in Union Square, mixing with a few early tourists, who spilled out of the nearby hotels. A cable car clattered up the street and over the hill toward Fisherman's Wharf.

Mary was on her second cup of coffee when Hutch and Rigson drew up to the corner in their van, waved at her, and looked for a parking spot. She had requested this particular crew, not only because she liked to work with them but also because she knew that Hutch carried a gun in his van and always went on an assignment with a revolver taped inside his left boot. One of Hutch's best friends, Bob Brown, a cameraman for NBC, was shot to death on an assignment. This was in 1978 when Brown, NBC reporter Don Harris, and Congressman Leo Ryan were gunned down on an airstrip in Guyana where they had gone to investigate Jim Jones and the members of his People's Temple. Hutch's gun would not save him in a similar situation, but the notion of it gave him comfort.

Hutch and Rigson got out of their van followed by Dallas Hall and Mike Ringulet. Mary did not know Ringulet since he was new at the station but she was relieved to see the burly figure of Dallas Hall. Dallas Hall, nearing fifty, was slightly younger than Hutch but he, too, had witnessed most of the major events in San Francisco in the last three decades through a camera lens. One too many stakeouts, or maybe too many nights at the bar, had taken their toll on the ruddy-faced Hall; he was not as sharp as he used to be. Mary watched him get out of the van with his breakfast in hand: a cold can of Budweiser.

"So, Reed, what's the story?" Hall said as he neared Mary.

Mary explained about her mystery caller, Commander Zero, who had agreed to be interviewed.

"Let me get this straight," said Hutch after Mary finished. "We're standing on a street corner with two camera crews and a reporter to interview someone who has probably been calling you from a nuthouse at an as yet undisclosed location. Sounds like a great Abbott and Costello routine."

As he finished, the telephone on the street corner started ringing.

"That's him," said Mary rushing to the booth. "See, he said he'd call at ten."

"Did he say he'd call collect?" Dallas Hall joked.

A few minutes later Mary came back. "He wants us to go to another phone booth. Golden Gate and Hyde, northeast corner. I guess it's near Hastings."

"Tell me you're making this up, Reed. Golden Gate and Hyde? What's with this guy?" Dallas took a last swig at his beer. Mary winced as she thought about how Hall was going to tell this story at the bar. She knew it would receive many embellishments in the retelling.

"Listen, I think there's something to this. I know it sounds crazy but I have this feeling about him," she said.

"Okay, let's hit the next phone booth. Come on, guys." Hutch led the way in his van.

At the corner of Golden Gate and Hyde, Mary and her crews waited for the phone to ring. It was ten-fifteen. A young man in a business suit approached the phone, reaching in his pocket for a coin. "The lady's expecting a call," said Dallas Hall as he blocked the man's path to the telephone. "Try over there." Hall pointed across the street.

The man in the suit started to protest. "Listen," he started to say. Then he shrugged and walked toward the street. "It's a public phone," he said over his shoulder when he was a few paces distant.

"Yeah, yeah. You want me to reach out and touch you?" Hall replied. The young man hurried across the street.

The phone rang, Mary picked it up. "No . . . look. This is ridiculous . . . okay . . . but . . . damn!" Mary hung up the telephone in exasperation. "He just hung up on me. Wants us to go to Sacramento and Van Ness for our next instruction. Maybe you're right. He's crazy."

"Oh, come on, Reed. We can't stop now, we're having

too much fun. Sacramento and Van Ness, huh?" Hall scratched his head.

"Let's go." Hutch was already in the van.

At ten forty-five when the telephone rang on the southeast corner of Van Ness and Sacramento, Mary was there to answer it. She listened carefully and looked anxious.

"What's the word?" asked Hutch.

"He said this was a military operation and when his units move in, we should surrender and go along with them. If we do, he said, no one will be hurt." Mary was clearly worried.

"He wants us to stay here?" asked Hall.

"No. We have to go back to Golden Gate and Hyde."

"You know, maybe we should call the station. This sounds a little whacked-out," Hutch said.

"Yes," Mary said, "I'll get the assignment desk on my car radio. I'll tell them that we're trying to interview someone who has a new lead on the Presidio story and if they don't hear from us in a couple of hours they should call Wyatt and the FBI. In fact, I have the name of the agent in charge of the case."

"Sounds good to me," Hutch said.

The crews and Mary got back into their vehicles and headed back to the telephone booth on Golden Gate and Hyde. As Mary got out of her car, a man with a ski mask, and what she took to be a gun poking through the folds of his leather jacket, jammed her against the door. "Get into the blue car," he said. She looked over at the van. Her two camera crews were unloading their equipment into the back of another van under the supervision of four similarly masked men. Obediently, she walked toward the car, a gun in her back. Behind her, Hutch, Hall, Rigson, and Ringulet climbed into the new van.

"I'm going to have to put something over your eyes," said Finn when he and Mary were in the car. He signaled to a man sitting in the back of the car. He placed a scarf over her eyes and wound several feet of masking tape around Mary's head.

As they drove, Mary tried to keep count of the left and right corners they took, but soon she lost track of the endless turns. The men were silent but they turned the radio up high to blanket much of the noise outside the car, which might give away their whereabouts.

About half an hour later, they parked. Mary was escorted into a building and up two flights of stairs. Behind her she heard the sounds of camera equipment hefted by several men and the exclamations and swearing of her crews, which made it clear that they, too, were blindfolded and were negotiating the stairs with some difficulty.

Mary entered a doorway. "The famous Mary Reed," Jerry Radamacker murmured as he walked toward her. "I'm so glad you could come."

Mary recognized the flowing tones of her mystery caller. "I'm not doing the interview blindfolded," she said.

"You'll do what I tell you," said Radamacker sharply. He caught himself and switched modes again. "Of course, Mary, we'll take your blindfold off when the time comes. In the meantime, take a seat, here"— he guided her down. "We're going to set up."

"Set up?"

"That's right. We're going to set up the cameras and adjust the lighting. We'll be ready soon." Jerry looked over as the camera crews entered. "Okay, bring the equipment over here. Have them stand over there. Listen, boys," he said to the television crews. "I have six men with machine guns trained at your heads. Any funny moves and . . ." Radamacker wandered off toward the other end of the room.

The room bustled with activity. Slack cables slapped against the floor, wires were plugged into place, a tripod clattered to the ground. "Hey, be careful, there," said Hutch, jumping to catch it. All five of them heard the click of a gun and instinctively they held their breaths but nothing further happened.

Most interviews require only one camera crew. The person being interviewed is shot from a camera positioned behind the interviewer and, after the interview, the interviewer will repeat some of the key questions, and stage various listening attitudes for the camera. Called cutaways, these shots are edited into the interview afterward in order to give the reporter a presence in the interview. This method simplifies editing since decisions, such as which person should be on the screen, can be deferred until the tape is brought back to the studio. With two camera crews, both the interviewee and the reporter can be taped at the same time and the viewer gets a more realistic sense of the exchange. Jerry Radamacker had requested two camera crews for his interview and, as Mary sat blindfolded, she wondered where the commander had picked up his familiarity with the technicalities of her profession.

Radamacker told the crews to stand back and he spent ten long minutes fiddling with cameras and sound apparatus. "Okay." He looked up.

Johnson unwound the tape around Mary's head. She looked around her. They were in a large room. The drapes were closed, and the only furniture in the room were two chairs facing each other, a camera trained on each chair. Behind the chairs, on the wall, a large piece of black fabric was hung as a backdrop. This was what Mary saw immediately in the bright glare of the many spotlights that lit up this central area. In the shadows around the room, her eyes started to discern the forms of several men in combat uniform, who aimed the machine guns strapped around their torsos at Mary and her crews. Mary's knees felt shaky, and she chewed on her lower lip. She could feel herself sweating, and, belatedly, she wished herself in another place.

"Take the tape off the crew," Radamacker ordered. Mary turned to look for the first time at her mystery caller as he walked toward her holding out his hand. Mary automatically responded and shook his hand; her mind seemed to be working again after its momentary disorientation. Radamacker was wearing a black mask, but Mary took in his muscular frame, guessing his height to be around five nine or ten. He was dressed in neatly pressed camouflage slacks and a fresh white shirt with a U.S. army colonel's spread eagles stitched onto the shoulders. The mask had slits for his eyes, nose, and mouth. The light shone off his glasses.

"You're shorter than I thought," said Radamacker looking at Mary critically. "And you look terrible. Where's your makeup?"

"You know, we've been on a wild-goose chase all over town, and your men put tape on my eyes. How did you expect I'd look?" Mary snapped.

"We'll give you some time to fix up," Radamacker said soothingly.

"I don't think I care to. I'm a reporter, not Miss America."

"Oh, but you are Miss America, you are," said Radamacker meditatively and his eyes held hers. Mary looked back at the man and heard something plaintive in his voice. Their eyes met. Although she could not articulate what she sensed, she knew she was no longer afraid. Something in his look told her that this man was not going to hurt her.

Hutch started forward as Radamacker took Mary's arm, but he was immediately held back by two of the men.

"Let's get on with the interview," Radamacker said. He was acting like a high school kid on his first date. First he pulled out Mary's chair for her, waited for her to sit, and then sat down himself in the opposite chair. The crews took their places behind the camera. Radamacker explained to Mary and the crews how he wanted the interview to run. He had set up the cameras, and the recorders had been fixed to alter the tones of his voice. "We'll talk for fifteen minutes," he said, and he told the crews to make sure the cameras were rolling and the sound worked. He did not want any zoom shots on his or Mary's face or pan shots of the two of them. The cameras were to stay in place for the entire interview.

Mary noticed that the commander's left hand was trembling with what might be stagefright. He snapped his fingers, and the black backdrop fell away to reveal the American flag. At the bottom of the banner the words *Day of the Rope* had been embroidered in black thread.

"Go," Radamacker commanded.

Hutch looked through the camera lens. The flag was in perfect focus. The cameraman realized that the commander knew his way around a video camera. He looked across at Dallas Hall, whose camera showed a clear, tight shot of Mary Reed with a blank wall in the background. Neither camera picked out any of the armed militia that stood around the walls in the shadows.

Mary counted down to start the interview. "Ten, nine, eight . . ." Her voice grew steadier and stronger as she counted, and she was conscious of the prickle of excitement she always got in front of the camera.

"Wait," the commander ordered. He was rubbing his mask. "I've got something in my eye." He turned around and, lifting the mask, dabbed at his eye with his fingers. His back was turned to the cameras and at a slight angle to Mary. She was looking absently beyond the commander where a gap in the blankets revealed a window and a view of a brick wall. As he straightened up Mary accidentally caught his reflection in the glass of the window. His mask was puckered over his forehead and for a long moment she looked at a man she knew for certain was crazy, but who had the lost expression of a frightened child. Mary suddenly became aware of what she was doing and she started and turned away. At the same moment the commander pulled the mask back over his face and turned to face the cameras.

"Okay, you can start now," he said.

"I'm here with a man who calls himself Commander Zero. He says he is the mastermind of the attempted arms heist at the Presidio last week. That night, a powerful explosion caused the death of eight men, three of them FBI agents. Commander Zero, why should we believe you?"

"In this country," said Radamacker, *"there is a secret pact between the Jews and the blacks, and while the rest of America, while good white people stand by, our country is being sold off piece by piece. The Brady Amendment went through, and the next thing you know a man can't protect his family. This pact, this secret pact has*

to be shown for what it is. We are a nation at war. We white Americans have to claim back the land our forefathers worked so hard to gain and keep. In the—"

"You haven't answered my question, Commander. What did you have to do with the events at the Presidio?"

Hutch had noticed that Radamacker's left hand was trembling; he was itching to zoom in on it.

"What happened in the Presidio was that the FBI screwed up. It was a sting. The survivor in the hospital who died a couple of days ago? His real name is Bleech, Harry Bleech. He had a contact at the Presidio. Now the FBI must have got this contact involved in the sting. He sets up the deal, and Harry walked into it. I told him it smelled bad. But Harry's greedy, see, can't wait to get his hands on the goods."

"Who was the contact at the Presidio?"

"Sergeant Casey, Kevin Casey. And where do you think he is? You can be sure he's safe somewhere in some witness protection program with a new nose and dyed hair."

"What did you have to do with the operation, Commander?"

"Bleech came to me for advice. Guy couldn't rob a candy store. I helped him out, even give him two of my men. Those two men were killed by the FBI. They were good white men, patriots, fighting a war that nobody else will fight so that our children could grow up in streets without crime or drugs or AIDS. The FBI is the plaything of the conspiracy. They developed AIDS to use on their own people so that—"

"Commander, you said that two of your men were killed."

"You want me to identify them?"

Mary leaned forward in a way characteristic of Mike Wallace on "60 Minutes." This was news. There was no way that anyone else could know the identity of the men who were killed.

"These patriots were Eric Schmidt and Red McClosky. They died in the service of their country."

Jerry Radamacker's logic had started to work on Mary. She had to remind herself that she was talking to a man who saw the FBI and the U.S. Army as the enemy.

"This flag," Mary said, gesturing at the backdrop, *"is a symbol of unity. Why are you preaching civil war?"*

"Do you really think so, Mary? Don't you know that the American taxpayer is paying for the leveraged buyouts and corporate takeovers arranged by the Jewish bankers so that the banks and the kike board of directors get rich and fat and the rest of the world gets killed by taxes? And they are letting the Japanese take away the best of our industry, our cars, our technology, the things a working man can be proud of. And tell me, who's making money from selling thirty-dollar tickets to a ball game? Thirty dollars to see some drug-crazed, hormone-altered, overpaid monkey jump up and down between two hoops? We've got to go back to the old days, when America was truly great, when whites had the power. For every Jew in a bank there should be two Americans."

"Jews are Americans," said Mary and instantly regretted it. The man was past reason, she should probably let him rave on. *"The weapons, the weapons you wanted from the Presidio. What were you going to use them for?"* she continued.

"The war, the war we've got to fight."

"Can you be more specific?"

"When you walk into a bad neighborhood and you see six black men, Mary, aren't you afraid? When your children are taught by homosexuals, aren't you worried? When you pay more for your oreo cookies because R.J. Reynolds and Nabisco are passing the buck on to you, aren't you angry? And now Henry Luce's great empire at Time-Life is run by a Jew from Brooklyn, don't you wonder whose news you're going to be reading? I know strong white men who fought for their country in a war their own government decided not to win. They came home, Mary, scarred in body and in mind to the jeers of their countrymen. And then," Radamacker's voice rose, *"they couldn't get jobs because the people they were fighting in the rice fields had moved into their hometowns and had taken their jobs, taken the bread from the mouths of white children."* Radamacker's voice broke theatrically.

"Commander, we have one minute left of the fifteen minutes we agreed upon. I'd like to end by asking you this question. Why

would you come on TV and incriminate yourself in the attempted robbery at the Presidio?"

"We both know that I've taken precautions that will prevent me from being recognized on the screen, including the alteration of my voice. The men that you have seen are also wearing masks so that you cannot identify them. And I'm your source, Mary. I think as a journalist you are interested in protecting your sources." The commander's eyes burned into Mary. "Don't think I won't be watching you, Mary Reed. I'll be watching you."

"One more question, Commander. What do the words sewn on your flag mean?"

"You'll see." Radamacker leaned into the camera. "You'll all see.

"Stop the cameras," he ordered.

TWELVE

"WHY DIDN'T YOU stop the camera crews? You didn't need to let her have two crews!" Wyatt Andrews paced angrily around the assignment desk at Channel 6. "I can't believe you let her go out like this!"

Ron Corvis sighed. "Wyatt, you know how she is. I had six people on hold; she wouldn't let go until I'd let her have what she wanted. She has a way of convincing you to do things that later make no sense. Listen, I told you as soon as I could."

"If anything happens to those guys, I'll fire your ass," Andrews threatened, glaring at Corvis.

A red light flickered on the communication screen in front of the assignment editor. Corvis broke Andrews's lance-like stare in time to see the light and turn his microphone on.

"It's Hutch," Corvis said excitedly to Andrews after listening for a few seconds. "He's talking a mile a minute."

"A loony-toon with a gun. Says he's some commander, part of the Presidio blow up. Can't believe the faggot didn't shoot us—"

"Hutch, calm down. Talk to me slowly."

"Calm down yourself, Ron. Goddamn it! You sit on your pansy ass betting money on the horsies while I'm out here lugging gear all around this idiot town and you tell me to calm down—"

Before Corvis could comment, Andrews seized the mike from him. "Hutch, Wyatt here. Let me talk to Mary now."

On the other end there was silence for a few moments. When Mary came on her voice was calm. "Hi, listen Wyatt, I don't want to talk over the radio. We're all fine, do you hear me? Don't worry. We'll be back at the station in ten minutes and we can talk then. Okay?"

By Mary's tone of measured calm and suppressed excitement, Andrews and Corvis knew that she was onto something big. They also knew that the other stations in town as well as the police monitored their radio frequency and so it was not a good idea to talk at length on it.

In the van, no one spoke as Hutch drove through Union Square toward Channel 6. Rigson played with the camera gear, stowing it more neatly. Mary, sitting in the front beside Hutch, looked out of the window. All of her instincts told her to broadcast the interview, but she had to convince Andrews to see it her way. The van hit the bump it always hit in front of the automatic gate that led into the parking lot under the building. The jolt brought Mary back to the present. She jumped out of the van just as Dallas Hall and Mike Ringulet followed them into the parking lot.

"I want you guys to come with me into Wyatt's office. I think we should all be in on this decision. And I don't want Wyatt separating us. What do you think?" Mary looked at Hutch.

"You're the boss." He and the others followed Mary to the elevator.

"So," said Wyatt Andrews, tight-lipped. "What happened?"

Mary and the four cameramen were sitting on the chrome chairs in the news director's immaculate office.

Mary told him matter-of-factly about the telephone call, about riding around the city from telephone booth to telephone booth, the blindfolds, the interview, the machine guns, and ski masks. Wyatt said nothing during her recitation but sat and stared at each one of the men as she spoke. Rigson lowered his eyes as Wyatt's eyes pierced his with a glance of searching intensity. At that moment Rigson was more afraid of Wyatt Andrews than he had ever been of Commander Zero and his men. Dealing with guns, crowds, fires, and hanging out of helicopters were among the occupational hazards of his trade, but as he sat under the eye of the news director, Rigson tasted a less-exhilarating brand of fear.

Mary finished her description and then got out of her chair. She gestured with her left arm at the men. "Look, Wyatt, these guys didn't know a thing about Commander Zero until it happened. I take full responsibility."

"Mary the Martyr," said Wyatt sarcastically. "How nice of you." He rose out of his chair and, leaning forward, looked at each of them in turn. "Listen," he said angrily. "I don't give a shit who is responsible. You all went through with this thing. I should dump you all, each and every one of you." He looked contemptuously at them. "Who do you think you are? This is a news outfit, not a John Wayne movie."

Mary leaned over his desk from her chair. "I may have been wrong not to tell you, but how did I know if this character was for real? I had to give you some room for maneuver, Wyatt. What if the police or Randy Martin give you hell? You can say you knew nothing about it, right? Blame it on me."

"Listen, Wyatt," Mary begged. "We can talk about this later. Right now I want you to see the tape." She looked at her watch. "It's two o'clock now. We could run it tonight."

"That's decent of you, Mary," said Wyatt, narrowing his eyes. "For the first time today you're letting me in on a decision."

Wisely, Mary kept her mouth shut. She let Wyatt lecture them while she held his eyes with her own, jutting out her chin with stubborn pride.

Finally, Wyatt stopped ranting, he was running out of steam. He sat down in his chair and folded his arms. "Okay, let's see the tape," he muttered.

The camera-men were incredulous, they were waiting for Wyatt to send them home. At a gesture from Mary, Hutch got up and put the first interview tape in Wyatt's machine. As the tape rolled, five pairs of eyes surreptitiously watched the news director for signs of a reaction.

Throughout the fifteen-minute interview, Wyatt's expression remained glacial. Every now and then he wrote a note on his ever-present yellow legal pad, which was neatly placed on the right of his desk. Mary, who had made many moves after deciphering the upside-down scribbles on Wyatt Andrews's pad, did not dare to look. Instead, she glanced under her eyelashes at his impassive face and willed him to use the tape.

"I'll be watching you." The words echoed those of a well-known song and Mary thought of Commander Zero, his moist, helpless look followed by the glassy stare and crazy rhetoric. "Every step you make, every breath you take . . ." Mary shivered and an icy chill ran up her back.

The tape ended. "Gentlemen," Wyatt said, standing up. "I don't need you anymore. Mary, stay here. I need to talk to you alone."

The men filed out without looking at either Wyatt or Mary, who remained seated in her chair. The door closed behind them.

Wyatt got up and sat on the side of his desk, looking down at Mary. "I think you were nuts to go for this," he said, "you need your head examined. Do you think you're immortal or something? No interview is worth dying for. This is television, Mary." Wyatt paused. "Only television." He looked at her hard and then, as if he had seen something he was looking for, broke his stare and walked behind his desk.

"Only television," he repeated, "but I'll admit it's great television, Mary." For the first time that day, Wyatt Andrews allowed himself a thin smile. "I think we should run the interview."

Mary relaxed while Wyatt continued. "This will put us over the top in the numbers. That commander is an asshole, a real hate merchant. Someone has to expose him. Too many people out there are leaning in his direction without any idea of what these wackos are really like."

Mary waited for Andrews's speech to be over. He was pontificating, and Mary was used to the lectures that Wyatt trotted out to justify the business of news which, as everyone knew, was to attract as many viewers as possible.

"I want to run the entire fifteen-minute interview at the top of the six o'clock news."

Mary was stunned. In her wildest dreams, she had not imagined getting so much time.

"Sure, I'll—"

"And I also want you to call the police." Wyatt was thinking out loud. "Tell them you want someone for a live interview, an update on the Presidio investigation. Don't tell them about the commander, we'll run the tape and spring it on them. Put them on the spot. I'll tell Ross."

Adam Ross was the thirty-five-year-old producer of the six o'clock news; he would do what Wyatt told him.

"Now, go to the edit room and put those two tapes together," Wyatt ordered. Mary seemed rooted to the spot. "Off you go, then." She left his office clutching the tapes.

Wyatt waited for a while and then picked up his private telephone. "Bill?" he said to the mayor's press secretary. "You were on target. It is the right wing. We've got some proof. Watch Channel Six at six tonight."

Wyatt started to dial Randy Martin's number. He paused in the dialing to stare out of the window. It could wait,

Andrews decided. He would call later, just before the show was going on-air; it would be less trouble that way.

Andrews stood behind Adam Ross in the control room during the six o'clock news.

"Three-two-one."

"Good Evening," anchorman William Reese said with a smile. *"Tonight we begin with a special report on the Presidio explosion by Mary Reed, one which she risked her life to bring us. Mary."*

"William, for the past several days I've received a number of phone calls from a man who claimed he was responsible for the Presidio break in. This morning he instructed me and two Channel Six camera crews to go to a pay phone near Union Square. After leading us all over the central part of the city, from one pay phone to another, we were detained, blindfolded, and driven to a house somewhere in the city. What you are about to see is the entire fifteen minutes I spent with a man who calls himself Commander Zero."

In the control room, Andrews watched the tape. The altered voice and masked face of the commander made the piece theatrically menacing, but the tight shots of Mary, her tension and her response to his words by turns mesmerized and indignant, became the real drama of the interview. Everyone in the control room was riveted to the screen.

"That was Commander Zero," Mary continued her report. *"Now live from police headquarters we have police spokesperson Hal Morris and we'll speak to him right after these messages."*

Morris was on one of the screens in the control room; his identifying tag on the screen labeled "program." As the advertisements started, he got up from his chair and started shouting at the camera. Nothing, however, reached the control room, and Wyatt allowed himself to smile briefly at the sight of such an eruption of temper without a sound track. Then he grabbed the microphone that hooked him up with police headquarters.

"I'm not going to be a part of this circus," the enraged Morris spluttered.

"Mr. Morris, this is Wyatt Andrews. We need you to stay to give your side of the story. The public needs to know if this Zero guy is for real."

"Thirty seconds," enunciated a voice from the front of the control room.

Ross was listening to Mary. "Reed is asking what's up," he said, looking at Andrews. "Mary," he said into his microphone, "Wyatt is talking to the police guy to try to stop him from walking. We'll let you know. Hold on a minute, I think he's been persuaded to stay."

Wyatt had indeed persuaded Hal Morris to do the interview. The news director looked at the program monitor, and sighed with relief at the picture of Hal Morris behind his desk.

"*Mr. Morris, do the police know who Commander Zero is?*" Mary asked Morris after introducing him.

"*Ms. Reed, I had no idea I was going to follow an interview with some guy with a mask and altered voice.*"

"*The question is, Mr. Morris, do you know who this man is?*"

Andrews enjoyed the way Mary reacted. She was focused and kept control of the interview without letting Morris change the subject.

"*No, the question is do you know who he is. I would like to point out that if what this man is saying is true, then he is a dangerous criminal, responsible for the deaths of eight people and by making him a star of the six o'clock news you have obstructed the course of the law.*"

"*Then, he is a suspect?*"

"*I didn't say that.*"

"*What are you saying, Mr. Morris?*"

"*I'm saying that this interview is over. I will not take part in ambush journalism. Good night, Ms. Reed.*"

Morris tore off the microphone from his jacket collar and threw it to the ground in full view of the camera. In the control room the director ordered the cameras to cut back to a shot of Mary and anchorman William Reese. Ross told the anchorman to interview Mary about what had just happened.

"*Well, Mary. I'd like to ask you a question about what we just saw. Didn't Morris have a point, I mean why weren't the police informed about this Zero guy?"*

In the control room several people heaved with groans. Andrews was not surprised that an anchorman, jealous of the airtime given to a reporter, would want to put Mary on the spot.

"William, I had no idea if this guy was for real. I still don't know. And, as I'm sure you're aware, our job is to report the news, not help out law-enforcement officers."

As the two wound up their interview, Andrews silently applauded her answer. In his view, Mary was a winner. However, he was well aware that in the public's eye both Hal Morris and William Reese had come out better. For them the journalist was arrogant and overpaid; a friend to the liberals and, as such, against the interests of the folks who made up the majority of his viewers.

Frank Carson stopped pacing and watched in shocked silence as a commercial for athlete's foot powder succeeded the local news on Channel 6.

"Where did that woman find this Commander Zero character?" he yelled rhetorically. "Why the hell didn't she tell us?"

Carson kicked the television. "Christ almighty. It's bad enough we have three agents dead without this idiot reporter interviewing a publicity-hungry weirdo, goddamn it!" Carson kicked the television again.

Carson, Rigby, and Begay were sitting in Bud McClelland's office in the FBI's downtown headquarters. Throughout the interview, Carson had been pacing up and down the room with his hands clasped at the back of his neck. Occasionally he would squeeze his arms together and bend his head in anger and frustration.

McClelland, the case agent in charge of the Presidio operation and Carson's boss, had flown to Washington, D.C., the previous night. In Washington, Carson knew, McClelland was taking the heat for the slaughter of three agents in the

Presidio sting operation and the disappearance of Kevin Casey the same night.

Nobody knew what Casey's game was anymore. The master sergeant was not supposed to have been present at the Presidio operation and, as far as they could tell, none of the remains were his, but since that night he seemed to have vanished from the face of the earth. The interview with Commander Zero was the last thing the bureau needed. Carson was fearful, not on his boss's account, but he was worried he would be made to take the fall for this latest fiasco.

"The woman is a goddamn menace to society," he said. "Okay"—he nodded at the telephone, which had lit up like a Christmas tree—"here comes the shit, straight for the fan!" He picked up one of the lines.

"Do you think he's for real?" Rigby asked Begay. "He sounds crazy." He and Rigby were sitting on the sofa surrounded by reams of computer printout.

For the next hour Carson fielded calls from the press and public alike. In addition, McClelland called and screamed for what seemed like a long time; the military wanted to know if they had captured the self-confessed perpetrator of the Presidio breakin; Congressman Wade's aide Daryl called to find out what they were doing to capture the commander; and the Mayor's press secretary Bill Hunter pumped him for details because the Mayor was under pressure to do something. Each of them assessed the damage purely from their own standpoint.

Carson drank cup after plastic cup of coffee until his mouth became furry and bitter and he spat into a trash can to get rid of the taste. He had loosened his pale blue tie and occasionally he stabbed two fingers inside his collar and ran them around his neck to relieve the tension in the back of his head.

"Get the file on the other guy. Not Red McClosky, we have him, but whosaflick," Carson said.

"Schmidt," supplied Rigby. He and Begay left the room.

They would call Washington and in about forty-five minutes the information would come through on the fax machine.

"What do you think, Sly?" asked Begay, turning on the light in another office. "Do we look real stupid?"

"You know, Ted," Rigby said to his partner, "funny thing, but in all my years with the organization, I never knew anyone to give a goddamn if we *looked* stupid as long as everyone's ass was covered. That's the key, partner, smother your derriere with paper and you're okay."

"Stupidest thing we ever did was trust that guy Casey," said Begay. He sat on the desk and looked at the fax machine as if willing it to produce an answer. "He was one hell of an operator. I mean he was bad news, man, just looking at his photo gave me the creeps. You knew he'd screw his grandma if someone paid him enough."

Rigby pushed coins into the soft drink machine outside the office. "Well, either Casey was more scared of someone else than he was of us, or he never meant to hang around and collect his pension anyway." He opened a Coke and slurped it noisily.

Suddenly the fax machine hummed into action and, inch by inch, dossiers on the two dead terrorists mentioned by Radamacker in the interview were disgorged. They had one thing in common: for a varying period of time prior to the Presidio operation there was no record of either man's whereabouts. Rigby grunted and took the sheaf of paper back to Frank Carson.

Carson was on the telephone again with McClelland when Rigby shoved the papers in front of him. McClelland had been working on the case for a year, ever since the military had contacted them because their own investigations had revealed that weapons and ammunition were slipping through the cracks. The big break had been "turning" Casey. The FBI had turned up about twenty-five thousand dollars that remained questionable on Casey's tax returns over the last ten years. This was exactly what they needed. Casey got a lawyer and negotiated a deal whereby he would stay out of jail and receive his pension in return for giving the bureau a few names. Through the master sergeant, McClelland's bureau had nabbed a Syrian arms dealer and a Japanese gangster. These seemed like small gains, however, after the Presidio sting failed and three agents died. Carson sighed. Not since the thirties had so many agents died at one time.

Carson had a hunch that Commander Zero was the mastermind he said he was. There was something he had not told McClelland, because if he had his boss would have mown his ass all the way to Cleveland for dereliction of duty. It was the night Bleech had died: Sly Rigby was sitting at the terrorist's bedside at two in the morning when a policeman had called him out because he thought he had seen a man in one of the corridors. Was it a coincidence that when Rigby had come back Bleech was gasping his last, and the nurse couldn't find the doctor in time to save him? He could never have proved it, but Carson had learned to trust his nose. And if what Zero said about the Presidio operation was true, then the commander had every reason to send one of his men to shut Bleech up before he bleated to the police.

"Frank?" McClelland's voice at the other end of the line roused Carson from his reverie. "We need to talk to the girl, the reporter. Need to know if she got a good look at this Zero guy or if she has a real idea where the interview took place."

"Hold on, Bud. Hey, Sly, what do you think? You think the goddamn reporter's going to talk to us? You met her, what do you think?"

Rigby shook his head.

"Sly doesn't think so," Carson said. "Still and all, she'd be a fool not to. The city's going nuts. This man is a self-confessed terrorist, I mean he practically declared war against the nation and because of him eight people are dead."

A few moments later Carson hung up. "Okay. Tomorrow we're going to pay this woman a visit. If she won't play, McClelland's going to get a subpoena, just in case, and we'll slap her with it, too," he announced.

He got up. "I suggest that the three of us call it a day."

He picked up his tan polyester jacket and, slinging it over his shoulder, walked to the elevator whistling. Carson always whistled when he was in a bind.

Mary's face was pale the next morning when she arrived at work.

"I need to see Wyatt," she said to the news director's secretary. "Now."

"Mary," Andrews said, his eyes lighting up when he saw her. For all the headaches she caused him, he regarded Mary as the daughter he had never had.

"You'll never guess what happened." Mary strode straight into his office and closed the door. "I was getting out of my car just now to come over here, and those two FBI characters from yesterday—agents, I guess—approached me again."

Andrews nodded. The FBI had come to the station the day before and asked Mary if she would testify before a grand jury. Andrews was out of the office, so she had asked them to wait, and had immediately called her father. The judge was incensed. He advised her to refuse to testify and gave her the number of a lawyer who specialized in First Amendment cases. She had explained the situation to Wyatt when he got back.

"I spoke to a lawyer last night, by the way," Wyatt said. "He said the FBI probably wouldn't push it."

"Well, you better show him this." Mary thrust a piece of paper at Wyatt. "I think this qualifies as pushing it!"

Andrews took the piece of paper and read the document, "Subpoena ad testificandum." He looked up at Mary. For a moment her face had lost its defiance, her lip was trembling, and Andrews wondered if she had enough backbone for this ordeal.

"The bastards," Mary said, the color coming back into her face.

"This is serious," Andrews said. "I'm calling Randy."

Wyatt explained the situation and put the phone down. "He wants us to go upstairs," he said.

"So, what would happen if you testified?" Randy Martin asked expansively. Wyatt and Mary sat in high-backed leather chairs in front of his wide mahogany desk.

"No self-respecting source would ever speak to me again," Mary said.

"But people know this man's a criminal," Randy countered. "They would understand that you had to give out any information you know about him."

"That's not the point," Mary said. "It's the principle of the thing. I'd be betraying a cardinal rule of my profession, which is to protect my sources." She leaned forward. "You understand, don't you? It's like a priest going to the cops after hearing a confession . . ."

Andrews, sensing Martin's resistance, tried another tack. "But, Mary, think about it. You've been getting all these hate calls from the public because of the interview, and people are going to hate you even more if you look like you're taking his side. Remember that call yesterday, the one you got upset about?"

"I wasn't that upset," Mary lied.

"What was it?" Martin asked.

"One of the FBI agents who was killed in the explosion, his wife called me, screamed at me for helping the man that killed her husband. You know, the usual flak." Mary turned to look at Wyatt defiantly.

"That's not how you explained it to me," Andrews said sharply. He looked at her, searching her face for the truth.

"Can't you see how you're helping this guy?" Martin said, leaning toward her over his desk. "Interviewing him in the first place was crazy. You gave him credibility. I don't give a damn about this journalists' ethics crap, Mary, you're playing with fire."

"I'm sorry you feel that way," Mary said coldly. "I thought I was doing what Channel Six pays me for and doing it pretty well, too. Wyatt, I thought you were behind me. Yesterday you said you'd back me up."

Wyatt was torn. "I will, Mary." He turned to Martin. "Whatever happens, we really should hire a lawyer right away, Randy."

Mary stood up. "Gentlemen, with or without your support, I am going to fight these assholes. I started something and no matter what you think, it's too late to argue about it now. What I did might not be popular, but I was only practicing my profession, and, as such, I am protected by the First Amendment. I do not have to testify, and I will not." Her eyes glittered with anger as she looked at them. "Now, are you going to help me, or am I on my own?"

There was a long pause. Martin swiveled around in his chair and looked out the window behind him. Finally, he turned back to face them.

"I don't like being pushed," he said to Mary. He turned to Andrews. "Get her a lawyer." Andrews got up. "And keep me informed," he added as they left the room.

Driving home that night, Mary thought about the day's events. Curiously, she was less upset than she had been the day before; it seemed as though something inside her was toughening.

A light flashed in her rearview mirror and Mary looked quickly at the vehicle. For several days now, she had had the feeling that she was being followed. She remembered Commander Zero's words: "I'll be watching you." Mary shuddered, thinking about what the lunatic terrorist might do to her if she talked to the FBI. Was she being influenced by Commander Zero's threat?

Accelerating across the intersection, Mary dismissed the idea. She reached up to push her hair out of her eyes. Her jaw was set. Fighting the subpoena was her only real chance to win something from an ugly situation.

Mary was pleased to see Mark when he arrived shortly before she was summoned before the grand jury. He had come up to San Francisco to support her. As she went into the courtroom, she waved and he gave her the thumbs up sign. Behind him Wyatt Andrews smiled at her encouragingly.

This was her second appearance in front of the grand jury. Two days earlier she had appeared there with a lawyer at the time specified on the subpoena. Her father had recommended George Kobrick, a first-rate attorney who specialized in First Amendment cases. Andrews had hired him at the station's expense. As is customary in such proceedings, the government had granted her immunity from prosecution should she testify, but she had held fast to her refusal. When it became evident to the prosecutor that she was not going to bend in her resolve, Mary was ordered in front of a judge, who had summarily ordered her to testify to the grand jury. Her lawyer had then asked for time in which he could appeal the ruling from the bench, but the conservative judge, who had no patience for the case, had required her to go back to the grand jury the following day.

Pushed by the FBI, the legal system moved as smoothly as a hydraulic piston. If Mary refused to testify a second time, the law was prepared to move very swiftly indeed.

The courtroom door opened and Mary's lawyer motioned for her to follow him.

"Identify yourself," the prosecutor commanded. Mary complied. "Spell your last name for the record, Ms. Reed."

Mary was impatient. She looked at the faces of the twenty or so people who were ranged in rows rather like a college lecture hall. Their faces were not friendly, and they avoided looking at her directly. The grand jury is putty in the hands of a good prosecutor, her lawyer had warned her, they will do anything he or she asks of them. Routinely, Mary answered the questions in the same language she had used two days earlier.

"How did you make contact with the man who called himself Commander Zero, Ms. Reed?"

"On the advice of counsel, I refuse to answer that question."

The prosecutor continued, and Mary automatically gave her responses. "At any point during the interview were you able to see the face of this man clearly?"

Mary looked up sharply. The prosecutor had not asked her this question before. She thought of the commander as he raised his mask to wipe something from his eyes and then she looked the attorney in the eye. "I refuse to answer this question because it infringes the First Amendment."

"I have no choice, Ms. Reed, but to ask you to go before Judge Rawlings."

The judge was not amused to see Mary and her lawyer again. His courtroom was crowded with people and noise, which he detested. And he disliked being pressured. That morning he had already had a call from the mayor urging that he take advantage of the publicity of the case to show the people of San Francisco that every effort was being made to catch the infamous Commander Zero. Earlier that week he had played golf with Randy Martin, who had hinted that he would propose the judge for membership in his exclusive club. Martin did not mention Mary Reed; he did not have to.

At the back of the courtroom Rigby and Begay sat, their backs like plumb lines against a wooden bench that had witnessed both the triumphs and the failures of the legal system.

"Well, Ms. Reed," Rawlings spoke with characteristic sarcasm. "I hope you packed your toothbrush this time, because I have no alternative but to hold you in contempt of my order to testify in front of the grand jury. You'll find out that federal prison is not a particularly pleasant place, but it might be a good spot for you to find out that you're no martyr." The judge eyed Mary harshly over the lens of his half-moon glasses. "Marshals," he ordered the men that stood at the side of the courtroom.

George Kobrick blanched as two federal marshals, acting on the judge's command, came toward the young reporter.

On the steps of the courtroom, Mary nodded at the

Channel 6 reporter, David Roberti, and his crew. When she was sure the camera could see her, she defiantly held up her cuffed hand.

Roberti urged his crew forward. "They are sending me to jail," Mary stated the obvious with dramatic emphasis. "What the FBI does not seem to understand is that if I give up my sources, I won't be able to report anything but the weather."

Other news crews, whom Mary had contacted the previous night in the expectation of winning the case, pushed forward. This could be a better story.

Wyatt Andrews, who had followed Mary down the steps, paused to admire his protégée's unerring ability to turn any event into a media opportunity. What Mary was able to illustrate with uncanny instinct was the Hearst principle of journalism that news is made, not found, and she had wasted no time cannibalizing her own life for newsworthy camera fodder. As she stood on the steps of the U.S. District Court speaking to a clutch of microphones and cameras, her wrist circled by a shiny steel handcuff, Mary Reed was both the news and its reporter.

"She should go into politics," said the station lawyer who had followed Wyatt's gaze and read what he was thinking.

Begay and Rigby slid down the steps with the prosecutor, identical in their dark suits, sober haircuts, and smug expressions. "The law is the law," said the prosecutor into the Channel 6 microphone. "There is no higher authority that protects a journalist more than any other person. We are talking about a self-confessed killer."

"Lackey!" Mark Ashfield yelled, as he chased down the steps after Mary. She turned a pale but defiant face toward him, and he hugged her briefly before he was pushed away and she got into the waiting car.

Mark watched the car pull away with an expression of horror on his face. He had been profoundly disturbed by the scene he had just witnessed, not because he had never heard of such a thing before, but precisely because he had. He was reminded of the stories his parents had told him about the fifties. It was a time that had seemed a world away, but, Mark believed, it had cast its sinister shadow on the day's events. He shook the hair out of his face and walked away, determined to write an incendiary article about Mary Reed's imprisonment.

THIRTEEN

E. J. EDWARDS, the well-known television and entertainment agent, was watching television in his enormous, wood-paneled office in Beverly Hills. The office was located on the third floor of a building he had bought ten years earlier, and named for himself. His client list was among the most impressive in the business, ranging across the spectrum of the news, sports, and entertainment worlds, and on the dark red walls hung signed and framed pictures of everyone he had ever represented.

A former baseball player for U.C.L.A., Edwards, approaching fifty-five, was still trim enough to wrap himself in the loose folds of an Armani suit which he wore, Hollywood-style, with a pale pink polo shirt. A large signet ring adorned his manicured hand and a Patek Philippe watch ringed his wrist. His long silvered hair, which was slicked off a perpetually tan face, was his most striking feature. Long, with a slight wave, it lent him a thirties-style glamour reminiscent of Douglas Fairbanks, Jr., without the mustache.

"Mr. Edwards?" his secretary buzzed him on the intercom. "It's Charles Davis."

Edwards had spotted Davis while he was an anchorman for the local news in Pittsburgh four and a half years earlier. He had placed him at Channel 3 in Los Angeles, where Davis's freewheeling, volatile style had quickly made him the most-watched anchorman on the six o'clock local news. Edwards knew why Davis was calling him. Don Carny's retirement from the late-night talk show he had hosted for over twenty years had given a new urgency to Davis's desire to have his own nighttime talk show. Negotiations with the network had been stalled for some time because they were not sure a local newsman could carry a national talk show.

"Hey, big guy. How you hitting 'em?"

"Long and crooked, E. J. Listen . . ."

Edwards picked up a baseball, signed by Babe Ruth, that he often rolled in his hand as he listened on the phone. During intense negotiations he had been known to pitch it at the solid wood door of his office that bore the indentations of several powerful throws.

"Sure . . . hey, I understand," the agent said after Davis had finished speaking. "Look, I'm having lunch with the network fools next week. I'll talk to them about it. . . . Sure I want to get the ball rolling. You get a divorce yet? . . . No? Listen, big guy, do me a big favor—no, do yourself a big favor, get the divorce, why don't you? You tried, you failed, it's not a sin, you know. I should know. . . . Of course I respect your mother's religious beliefs, your mother is a sweet angel come down from heaven, but she is ruining her son's life. Come on, listen to me . . . listen to me, Charlie, what about the *Enquirer* finding you with that producer you've been seeing? . . . Yeah I know about her. Can't keep a secret in this town, especially not from me, Charlie, you should know that." Edwards's speech was rapid, displaying a parade of emotions for every occasion.

"I'll call you, okay. Next week." Edwards put down the telephone and stretched out his legs. To his right, were three monitors, each screen running a different tape. The first showed Mary Reed reporting in Portland, Oregon, on the second she was interviewing Commander Zero, while the third showed her anchoring the weekend news. He buzzed his secretary. "Get Irwin Hansen on the line," he said. Edwards put his feet on the desk, crossed his arms behind his head, and waited to take the call.

In a profile for *L.A. Magazine*, Edwards had been characterized as a "lone wolf of the old school," as opposed to the large agencies that dominated his business. Apart from his son Brett, a recent graduate from Harvard Law School, Edwards had little other help. His clients now numbered in the hundreds, but Edwards hated to delegate his agenting work. Several agents had come to work for him but left when they realized that there was little opportunity to grow. He survived by regularly adding to his bevy of accountants. The squeeze on his time left some clients disgruntled. When you were hot, the story went, Edwards could not get enough of you; on the way down, he would not touch you.

"Hello, E. J. What's new?" Irwin Hansen, news director for Los Angeles' Channel 3, always picked up calls from the famous Beverly Hills agent. As well as his star anchorman Charles Davis, Edwards also represented sportscaster Bill Bryson and conservative commentator Ralph W. Wilson.

Edwards got to the point right away. "I've been watching the next Barbara Walters, Irwin. Mary Reed, she's the one that interviewed the terrorist in San Francisco. You seen her, Irwin? She's dynamite, a real class act."

"Sure, I know her," Hansen said. "I used some of her stuff on the Presidio story. Wyatt Andrews and I go back."

"Well, I know you're looking for a reporter, and you're not exactly deep in female talent over there. Reed is as hot as you'll ever get. I mean it, Hansen, she's good as well as being gorgeous."

"She's also in jail, E. J.," Hansen objected, "which is not of much use to anyone at the moment."

"There's a hearing coming up in two days. She'll be out, don't you worry. I thought maybe we could encourage her to walk your way but, listen Irwin, if you're not interested I can always call Louis." Louis Peters was Hansen's counterpart at Channel 7.

"Relax, E. J. I didn't say I wasn't interested. Isn't she still under contract?"

"Don't you worry about that," Edwards said breezily. "Have I ever let you down over the little things?" he asked rhetorically.

"Plenty," said Hansen, but he was laughing because he enjoyed his conversations with Edwards, whom he found essentially fair in his business dealings. "Wait a minute," Hansen said suddenly. "Do you actually represent her?"

"I will, Irwin. Trust me."

"Well, perhaps I'll put a call in to Andrews and the two of us will freeze you out of this one."

"Go ahead, try," Edwards said. "What you don't seem to understand is that Mary Reed is already too big for that kind of game. You'll see."

"Okay, E. J. Listen, let's get together next week. And please don't call anyone before we talk."

Edwards put down the phone, and turned up the volume on the Commander Zero interview. As he watched the reporter, the agent and the man battled silently inside him. As a businessman, Edwards was constantly seeking out the next challenge. For a long time now, he had been looking for a client whom he thought had the potential to be the first anchorwoman on the national evening news. And, in Mary Reed he was beginning to think he might have found what he was looking for.

He also found her tremendously attractive. Since his divorce five years earlier and, truth be told, for some time before that, Edwards was often seen around town with the young blondes he favored. One of them, a twenty-one-year-old from U.C.L.A., he had picked out from the cheerleading line at a football game. They had dated for a while and when Edwards had felt the urge to move on, he had found her a job as a weather reporter for Channel 7. They were still on good terms. E. J. Edwards had an uncanny knack for mixing business with pleasure. Sighing, the agent looked at Mary one more time before he walked out of his office to the Beverly Hills Grill for lunch.

Mary could tell it was raining outside. From her seat on the bed she looked up at the small window and stared beyond the prison bars at the teary rectangle of glass. She had been there for a little more than a week, and had adjusted to a routine of regulated boredom with initial bad grace followed by uneasy resignation. Mary was in a federal jail in Pleasanton, a drab coed facility about forty miles east of San Francisco. Mary had spoken to two women in her wing, a tax offender and an embezzler. The guards and warden treated them well; they were not, after all, criminal offenders and, contrary to Judge Rawlings's sarcastic remark, prisoners were supplied with everything, including a federal toothbrush. She pulled at the collarless regulation shift that was chafing her neck. Her Walkman was playing a Spanish language tape, but she had stopped listening to it.

During her time in jail, the young reporter had not regretted her decision to interview the commander. Forgetting the fear she had felt, Mary had convinced herself that the interview had given her the visibility that could lead to her next career move. She was now determined to leave San Francisco.

Mary wondered what time it was. She pulled the plugs from her ears, and swung her legs onto the bed where she lay, one hand behind her head. People had been telling her for months that she needed a break, she thought, unamused at the irony. However, she did feel remarkably well-rested, and good news from her lawyer, George Kobrick, the previous evening had boosted her spirits. Their appeal was to be heard the following day by the Ninth Circuit Court of Appeals and the lawyer was optimistic that the judge would be more sensitive to the First Amendment implications of their case than the hard-line Rawlings.

Mary heard the heavy tread of the guard. "Do you know the time?" she asked.

"Nearly half past."

"You will remember that in ten minutes I have a call to make?"

"Yeah," said the guard. "Won't forget."

That morning Mary had cleared permission from the warden to make this late call to her lawyer who, she said, was traveling. Ten minutes later the guard unlocked the cell and Mary followed him to a large room where telephones lined up along a shelf. Mary brought a pad and a pencil with her along with a sheaf of handwritten notes, the results of a day's labor.

"Going to tell him a thing or two," said the guard, glancing at her notes.

"That's right," said Mary. She was surprisingly tense. She dialed the New York City number she had been given, using the special telephone for prisoners' calls to their lawyers. This line was not as automatically taped as the general line.

"George?" she asked.

"Good evening, Mary," her lawyer responded. He was using the speaker on the telephone and his voice sounded high and faraway; maybe he, too, was nervous. Mary felt her own tension falling away from her as she imagined the scenario at the other end of the line.

"Can you hear me?" she asked.

"We can hear you fine," Ted Koppel said. *"Gentlemen, let us break our discussion of First Amendment principles to talk live to a journalist who is currently defending those rights. Mary Reed is calling us from Pleasanton Federal Prison in California. Or rather, I should say for legal accuracy she is calling her lawyer,*

George Kobrick, who is on the set with us tonight for our panel discussion.
"Mary, how is life in jail?"
"Well, I haven't learned Spanish yet!" Mary's voice sounded high and faraway. "But, seriously, I have to question whether the taxpayers' money should be spent on the $112 per day it costs to keep me in jail, half the price, Ted, of a Harvard education. . . ."

Sly Rigby stepped onto the elevator of the FBI's headquarters in downtown San Francisco feeling glum. In his office he slammed down his newspaper and went to get a cup of coffee.
"You see 'Nightline' last night, Sly?" a colleague asked him.
His teasing attitude grated on Rigby's nerves. "I heard about it," he said crisply.
"Man, that was some stunt. Put her lawyer on the show and called him live. She's no dummy that one. And what a looker!"
Before Rigby could reply, Begay rushed at him and pulled him by the arm into the older man's office. "Sly," he said. His excitement made him breathe quickly. "Glad you're here. Listen something new's come up."
He closed the door in Rigby's office. "There's a detective," he explained. "I was talking with him for the past half hour. You know the guy that died the same night as the explosion?"
Rigby nodded. "McClosky, right?"
"Yeah, Red McClosky. Well, this detective traced him through some counterfeit bills he used in Bakersfield."
"What?" asked Rigby. Begay was speaking too quickly for Rigby to take in what he was saying. "The police were using counterfeit bills? This some kind of undercover operation?"
Begay took a deep breath and started speaking again. "No, no, the detective found some counterfeit bills."
"What do you mean, *found* some counterfeit bills? *Where* did he find them?"

"A hooker gave them to him."

"What the—"

"Quit butting in, Sly. I'm trying to tell you." He paused. "McClosky picked up a hooker up in Bakersfield, gave her the bills. 'Least that's what she told the detective."

Rigby raised his eyebrows. "Why would a hooker talk to a detective?"

"Because she's his snitch," Begay supplied.

"Okay, so the hooker in Bakersfield, who's also a snitch, gave the cop counterfeit bills that whosaflick—"

"McClosky."

"That McClosky gave her. How does he know it was McClosky?"

"He got his fingerprints from the counterfeit he gave the snitch and sent them up to Washington. They contacted us, thought we might be interested."

"Very interested. I think we should talk to this detective in person, Ted. The guy's in Bakersfield, you say?" Rigby made a face. "Let's have him meet us in the L.A. office. See if he can tell us anything else."

Eddie Martinez turned in his chair as the two special agents entered the office where he had sat for the half hour since his arrival at the FBI bureau in Los Angeles. It was two days after his conversation with Begay and he was curious about the FBI's interest.

"Special Agent Rigby," Sly said, extending his hand.

"Detective Martinez," the officer said, standing. "Bakersfield Police Force."

"I understand you have some information that may help us in one of our investigations," Rigby said, moving around the desk and sitting behind it.

"You're working on the Presidio case, right? That's how McClosky died. You think there's a connection or something?" Martinez ventured.

"It's hard to tell," Rigby responded evasively. "Why don't you tell us what happened."

"I'm not sure how it all adds up," said Martinez. He outlined the gist of what Darlene Travis had told him about the trick she had picked up at the Twin Palms. "I have a sworn statement from her," he finished.

"You say this all happened last month, Detective?" Martinez nodded. "In Bakersfield?" It was more of a statement than a question; Bakersfield just did not fit geographically with the Presidio break in.

Rigby looked at Begay. "I wonder if we can identify the robbery, Ted. Go ask for a run on all robberies in the area in May."

Rigby stood up. "Well, thank you, Detective Martinez. This is all very interesting, very interesting." The detective rose also, uncertain what to do. "Now, normally," Rigby continued, looking down at the shorter man, "normally, you'd turn a counterfeit situation over to the Secret Service, but in this case, as it bears directly on our investigation, I think we can take care of it here." Rigby smiled. "Now, do we have a number where we can reach you?"

Martinez took out a card and silently handed it to the federal agent. "Great," said Rigby. "Thank you again." He held out his hand. "And don't hesitate to be in touch if anything else occurs to you. Or if you get any more of those funny money complaints," he added pleasantly.

Martinez nodded. He did not trust himself to speak. "Be in touch if anything else occurs to you," he mimicked to himself. That was what you got for helping the feds, a creepy handshake and a thank you very much, we are going to handle this from now on. Martinez picked up Darlene's statement, which he had left on the desk.

"Oh, wait a minute," Rigby said. "May we have a copy of that?"

"Sure," Martinez said. Rigby disappeared.

A few moments later Begay rushed in with a sheaf of computer printout. "You'll never guess—" he started, then seeing Martinez was alone, stopped.

"Find anything?" Martinez asked, eyeing the paper curiously.

"Well, I'm not sure. Can't find anything in the Bakersfield area. But you remember that big Goldor robbery in downtown San Francisco? That was in May." Begay studied the printout. "You remember it? Killed four guards? They never got the guys that did it except they found the ex-nighttime janitor rotting by Route Five."

"Wilkes?"

"Maybe." Begay looked up. "Can't remember the name."

"Here you are." Rigby returned and thrust Darlene Travis's statement at Martinez.

"Well, I'll be going," the detective said. He nodded at Begay and pushed past Rigby who was standing in the doorway.

Rigby leant back on the doorjamb and watched the detective walk down the corridor. He turned to Begay and raised his eyebrows. "Interesting, huh?" he said.

The telephone rang. Begay picked it up and listened for a moment. Still listening, he covered the mouthpiece with his hand and whispered to Rigby, "Reed got out, the judge went with the appeal."

"Damn!"

Begay put down the telephone, which rang again immediately. This time Rigby answered. "Yes," he growled. "Oh, hi . . . okay. . . . Listen, don't call him back right away. I'm going to ask Carson if he wants us to say anything."

Rigby hung up. "That was Joe. He got a call from some reporter who wants to know if we have any comment about Reed's release."

"What's to say?" Begay asked.

As Rigby dialed Frank Carson's number his hand automatically went to his throat to straighten his perfectly straight tie. "I'm thinking we might want to use this opportunity to leak this connection between the robbery and the break in," he said to Begay. "Reassure people that we're doing something, that we don't need the reporter," he added. "It's Sly

Rigby," he said into the telephone. "Tell Carson I need to speak to him . . ."

"Oh, I see," said Begay. He folded up the fan of computer paper and put it in his briefcase.

Dodging crowds on the streets, Eddie Martinez was thinking about Jim Wilkes. They had been partners together on the narcotics squad in San Francisco before Martinez had left in disgust at the corruption in the department and returned to his hometown. Wilkes had not been as lucky. Martinez knew that his friend had been set up, that someone who did not like what he knew had planted cocaine in the detective's file cabinet. After Wilkes got out of jail, Martinez had called a couple of times but found conversation difficult with his old friend who had become bitter and depressed and, Martinez suspected, was often drunk.

The reason Eddie Martinez bothered with Jim Wilkes was not only that he was sentimental; he knew Wilkes had saved his life. They never spoke about it; it wasn't their way. One night they had been in a drug bust that had escalated into a shoot-out, and Wilkes had stepped between Martinez and a bullet. Wilkes was hit in the shoulder and spent two weeks in the hospital. That was it. A simple, split-second decision that both men knew had saved one life at the risk of another.

The detective found it hard to believe that, low as he had sunk, the ex-cop had turned criminal at the end of his life. Still musing about Wilkes, he got into his car. His mouth was dry, he needed coffee; feds couldn't even offer him a lousy cup of java. Martinez jammed on his favorite country station. Martinez had called Dolores Wilkes after hearing about his old friend's death, but she had been distant and formal with him. Maybe he should pay her a proper visit. It was beginning to seem as though the mystery of his former partner's death might be part of a much larger puzzle.

"I'm glad to be free," Mary was saying. *"Looking forward to getting back to work and continuing to do my job as well as I can."*

Windblown and damp from the rain, Mary Reed was standing outside the federal prison in Pleasanton. A close-up of her face, flushed with pleasure and lovelier than studio artifice could ever make her, swam into one of Jerry Radamacker's monitors. Panicking, he checked to see if his video recorder was taping San Francisco's Channel 6 and relaxed on seeing the red recording light. This woman had gone to jail for him, Radamacker thought, gazing at the screen with something like adoration.

"Have you heard that the FBI have a new lead on this case?"

"I'm sure they're doing everything they can."

Radamacker jumped. A new lead? He paced angrily around the room. Finn, he needed Finn. Where was the man when he needed him? He ripped the videocassette from the machine and put it in the suitcase that lay open on his desk. He unplugged the equipment, closed the suitcase, and took a long look around the underground office before walking out. The heavy metal door swung behind him and he closed the door, securing it with a dead bolt and three bars that fastened with padlocks. "Just try getting into that, Thomas," he muttered after completing the task. Picking up the suitcase, Radamacker walked to the elevator.

"So, you're leaving?" Thomas Taylor looked up as Radamacker came in. He was in his study at the back of the church. "Shall you be coming back?"

"Some day, Tom. We've got work to do together. I'll come back and get you some more recruits for your church." He started walking out of the door.

"Good-bye, Commander Zero," said the minister under his breath.

"What was that?" Radamacker asked, jerking his head around.

"I said good-bye," the minister said mildly. "That's all."

FOURTEEN

"MARY! WELCOME BACK," Wyatt Andrews said warmly. Newly sprung from jail, Mary had gone directly to his office and was still wearing her coat. The news director rose out of his chair to greet her.

"Boy, am I glad that's over," she said. She stepped toward the news director and hugged him. "Thanks for your support, Wy. I would have died without your daily calls."

Andrews smiled. He lowered himself so that he was perched on the edge of his desk in characteristic fashion, hands overlapped on the knee of his raised leg. "You know, we got a lot of calls and letters from people on your side. Not at first," he said with a brief snort, "Randy was terrified for a while. But then things started to turn in your favor." His eyes crinkled. "Well, it didn't help that the FBI looked like total idiots who couldn't catch a goldfish if the bowl was put in front of them." Andrews snickered. "And, of course, 'Nightline' helped. That was a stroke of genius, Mary." Wyatt shook his head admiringly.

"There's a photographer here from *People* magazine to see you, Mary." Wyatt's secretary had poked her head around the door.

Mary groaned theatrically. "Okay, Meryl, tell the photographer I'll be right out." She looked at Wyatt. "They're talking about putting me on the cover."

Andrews smiled. "Great," he said, but he was uneasy; he sensed that Mary might be getting too big for Channel 6. "What are you doing tonight?"

"I thought I'd do a piece on the Presidio investigation. Can I have four minutes?"

"That might be a good idea," said Wyatt thoughtfully. "I'll have a word with Berman. He'll probably want to lead with it: the return of Mary Reed on Nightbeat." Wyatt paused. "What are your plans for the weekend, Mary?" he said in a lighter tone. "Judy and I would love to see you and Mark, if he's in town, for dinner on Saturday."

"Thanks, Wyatt. I'll talk to Mark and let you know." Andrews walked her toward the door.

"You won't believe this," said Meryl as Mary and Wyatt emerged from his office. "But there's a guard downstairs who says he has three hundred roses for you."

Mary looked at Meryl and giggled. "Oh, my God." She rolled her eyes in mock exasperation. "What next?" She hurried down the corridor toward the newsroom.

"Wyatt," Meryl said. "Irwin Hansen from Channel Three in Los Angeles is on the line.

"Mmmm. What? Oh, Irwin Hansen. Okay." He walked back into his office.

"Wyatt." Irwin was congenial. "How does it feel to be standing up for journalistic principles? The local news takes on the big issues. That's like the worm turning, right?" He

185

chuckled; Wyatt did not respond. "Listen," Hansen continued, lowering his voice and becoming serious, "I want you to help me get Mary Reed for Channel Three."

"She's not going anywhere, Irwin," Wyatt said flatly.

"Ach, Wyatt, come on. You know you're going to lose her. Better me than those sharks in New York, huh?"

"We have a contract—" Andrews began.

"Sure you have a contract but that's not going to stop her and you know it. Besides, it's only got three more months to run. Then what?"

Andrews was surprised. Hansen's call was clearly not a spur-of-the-moment probe, he had done his homework.

"Mary Reed is too big for San Francisco," Hansen pressed his point. "The question is not if she'll leave but where she'll go, and that's where you come in, Wyatt."

"She's twenty-five and still wet behind the ears. I wonder if she isn't going to burnout. She's got a lot to learn, Irwin."

"My point exactly. In the wrong hands she'll be ruined. It can happen. I can help Mary, Wyatt. I know that and you know it, too. You'd be doing her a favor. Push her in my direction."

Andrews sighed. "I can't promise you anything. We're in the eye of a storm here, Irwin." He paused. "Sure, I know she's going to leave eventually, but I want to hang onto her here as long as I can."

"Suit yourself, Wyatt. But I'm warning you, I'm going to come on hard. You can be a part of this, my friend, or we can fight. But, let me tell you, this one you're going to lose."

Mary had reached the newsroom when a voice carried over the hubbub. "Mary, there's a man on your line who says he has three hundred reasons why you should speak to him." She looked down at the card she held in her hand. *One rose for every hour you spent in jail,* she read. *With deepest respect, E. J. Edwards.*

Mary went to her office and closed the door behind her. She ran her hand through her hair, sat down and looked at the telephone for a moment before picking up the receiver.

She knew that the agent represented the network's evening newsanchor, John Ransome, as well as Don Carny, the famous talk-show host, and a top woman journalist who now hosted her own weekly newsmagazine show on national television. In his early days, he had been a lawyer for one of Hollywood's legendary silver screen actresses. She reminded herself to keep her head. Picking up the line, she said brightly, "Mr. Edwards, I presume."

"I'm not going to beat around the bush, Ms. Reed. I want to represent you. I think together we can get you to a growth position at a network station in one of the two top markets, Los Angeles or New York. What do you think?"

"Well, I'm flattered by your interest—"

Before she could continue, Edwards cut in. "I'd like you to consider coming to L.A. this weekend. We can talk, get to know each other."

"Uh, well. I don't know. I'm not sure it's a good time for me to leave town. Things are pretty crazy here."

"I'll make sure you're gone for the minimum of time. I'll have my plane pick you up at six tomorrow. You fly down, we have dinner, and you can fly back first thing the next morning. It's a few hours."

"I'm not sure. Is there any way you can come up here?" Mary was trying to get control of the situation. She knew that Edwards never left Los Angeles for any other city but New York, but it was worth a shot. If he agreed, she figured, he must already have a deal for her.

"I'm talking about a major step in your career. Your work on the Presidio story and the courageous stand you took has put you on the national news map, but I've been watching you for longer than that. The airport safety series, the serial killer reports were first-rate. And I saw the city council story you broke in Portland." Mary was gratified. "But I don't think you're going to stop at reporting, Miss Reed. You're anchor material if ever I saw it and I can make it happen for you."

Mary tried to breathe deeply. This was heady stuff. "Okay," she said finally. "You win, I'll come to L.A."

"Best decision you'll ever make," the agent assured her. "My secretary will call you in an hour with the schedule."

"Eddie!" Dolores held her arms open and hugged him warmly. "I'm so glad you came by!"

"You look terrific, as usual," he said. Dolores smiled, and patted her honey blond hair, which was folded in mountainous heights on top of her head. "Why don't you go kidding me," she said. "I've been cleaning all day and I look a wreck, Eddie Martinez. Oh, it's been so long!" she exclaimed, touching his face, her eyes filling with easy tears. "Now, don't stand out there all day, come on in. It's still a dump, but at least now it's a clean dump. You should have seen the dirt. Well, you know what pigs men are when they live alone, don't see a thing it seems, let it all pile up. I just don't know how he could live here. And, you know, he had practically no furniture in the house. It's sad really." She turned her head away, "Katie?" she called in a high-pitched singsong. She turned to Martinez. "She insisted on coming with me. I tried to stop her, I can manage, I said, but she would keep pressuring me. I don't like her to dwell on it. She hasn't been the same since . . ." Once again, tears sprang to her round gray eyes. Dolores had finally ran out of words when her daughter appeared in the hallway. "Look, honey, it's Uncle Eddie, come to visit us."

"Hi," the teenager said shyly.

"Kat," he said, moving over to her. "Can you give your old uncle a hug, for old times' sake?" He put his arms around her. "I'm so sorry, kiddo, about what happened. I wish I would have known." Katie started to sniff and he stroked her hair. "There, now," he said consolingly. "You know I believe you're getting to be the same height as me," he added jokingly. "Soon it'll be your turn to give me piggyback rides."

Katie giggled. "Don't talk stupid," she said through her sniffles.

Dolores watched them, dabbing at her eyes with her sleeve. "It's so good to see you," she said to Martinez. Suddenly she struck her head with her hand. "Oh, what a fool I am. Dinner's in the oven and it's getting burned while I stand here looking at you. Now you are going to join us, Eddie, for a nice home-cooked meal before you go driving back on an empty stomach," she said over her shoulder as she went into the kitchen.

"Well," Martinez demurred.

"I'm not hearing it!" she shouted. "Tina'll never forgive me."

"I can't say no then," he said, walking into the kitchen. "Let me call Tina, though. Let her know what I'm doing."

Dolores smiled indulgently at him. "Sure. You'll have to use the pay phone at the end of the street. We had this one disconnected. Everything's going tomorrow. And we think we found someone to buy the place, but, of course, you never know. Anyway the money's mostly going back to the bank, but it'll help a little. Not me," she said quickly. "But it'll give Katie a start."

"I heard you got married?" Martinez said.

"Well you heard right." Dolores flashed her ring at him. "He's a good man, Eddie. You and Tina should come up and see us one day." Martinez did not respond, and an awkward silence fell on them for an instant. "You'll like this, Eddie," she said, pointing at the casserole. "It's chicken à la king. Katie," she called, "take Uncle Eddie to the pay phone, will you?"

Later that night Martinez drove to Bakersfield through a cool blue night bright with stars. He had enjoyed seeing Dolores and Katie again. During the day he had visited the police department in San Francisco where he used to work. Calling in a favor, he had searched through the clothes that Wilkes had been wearing at the time of his death. In the pocket of the worn denim jacket was a pamphlet that caught the detective's eye. On the back were some numbers scribbled in what Martinez recognized as his friend's inimitable chicken scratch scrawl. He made a copy of the paper.

Eddie Martinez was not an analytical man, and he did not stop to examine the emotions that Jim Wilkes's halting

189

path to a murky end had aroused in him. But one thing the homicide detective knew for certain was that he was not going to get much sleep until he had solved his ex-partner's murder.

Mary drove to the airport on Saturday evening. Mark was away on a story and she had not been able to talk to him before she left. She was nervous, and for a lonely moment she missed being able to talk to him about what was happening to her.

At the reserved parking space at the airport, a pilot greeted her and, taking her overnight bag in his hand, led her on to the tarmac. Emblazoned on the tail of the white Learjet she was being guided toward, Mary picked out the alphanumeric identification N11EJE. Inside the plane the agent's monogram was woven into the upholstery of the cabin and stamped on the black leather of the six seats. The pilot introduced Mary to his co-pilot and the jet, with Mary as its sole passenger, took off for Los Angeles. In the air, the co-pilot indicated that Mary should open the bar in front of her, where she found a bottle of chilled champagne, some strawberries, and her favorite blue corn tortilla chips. Despite her prior determination not to be impressed by anything the agent did for her, Mary was struck by the inclusion of the chips. She wondered how he had found out. Edwards's deluxe treatment of his clients was part of the cocoon he spun around them, binding them to him with silken threads. And Mary, three weeks shy of her twenty-sixth birthday, could not help feeling like a princess.

Sixty-three minutes later the jet landed at LAX. She jumped down the steps and walked toward a white Rolls Royce parked ten feet away. This was all very different from the commuter flights she was used to. "I'm Brett Edwards," a bronzed young man said as he held out his hand. He climbed into the back of the car after her, and kept up a steady stream of small talk during the twenty-five-minute drive to The Four Seasons Hotel.

In her room, Mary changed into a black silk cocktail

dress she had bought for the occasion. After coaxing her hair into place and touching up her makeup, Mary stood back to look at herself in a full-length mirror. Dressed and made-up, Mary's self-assurance made her look a few years older than she was. She was pleased with the dress, which was conservatively cut yet also revealed the lines and curves of her figure, and she indulged her vanity for a few minutes, turning this way and that, practicing her smile in the mirror.

Brett Edwards was waiting in the hotel lobby when Mary emerged from the elevator. Heads turned as the dramatic-looking blonde strode across the carpet, seemingly indifferent to the stir she created. The young man's eyes registered a flicker of interest before he took her arm and resumed his role as her courteous but impassive escort. The car was waiting outside the hotel and drove them to Chasen's restaurant in West Hollywood, a short distance away. "This is where I leave you," Brett Edwards said as the driver opened the door. The car pulled away leaving Mary on the sidewalk. She turned around and walked into the famous establishment.

"Miss Reed, I'd like to welcome you to Chasen's." The maître d' smiled. "This way, please." Mary enjoyed her personalized greeting and followed him down the narrow aisle. On her way she noticed Johnny Carson and his wife, and behind them, the Reagans. "Mr. Edwards, your guest."

Edwards rose from his seat and shook Mary's hand. "Everything okay during the trip?"

"Fine, thank you, Mr. Edwards," Mary said.

"You can call me E. J.," the agent said with a smile. "Everyone else does."

Mary smoothed the napkin that had been placed in her lap.

"I love this place," Edwards said, extending his arm to gesture at the restaurant. "People nowadays, they like Spago or Eureka, but where's the character in those places? And the food. Call me old-fashioned, but I don't like to eat a fish I never heard of before nineteen eighty-six." Mary laughed politely. "Of course, it's not what it used to be," he continued, "I know that. I grew up in this town, you know, Ms. Reed."

"Oh, Mary, please."

"When I was growing up, Mary, everyone came here. Everyone. It's changed, of course. Dave, the original owner—funny guy, but okay if you knew how to handle him—died a while ago, but still," he waved his hand, "it's Chasen's."

The waiter poured Mary a glass of champagne. A few minutes later he reappeared with a salad served with her favorite spicy Roquefort dressing on the side. This time Mary was not surprised; first the chips and now the dressing. The agent had done his homework.

"I can't imagine how you treat people you know well," Mary said as she dipped her fork into the salad.

"I'm a full-service dinner date," the agent said smugly. "But I'll let you choose the entrée."

Later, as Mary nibbled at her poached salmon and Edwards tackled a steak, the agent turned the conversation to business. "I'm not kidding you, Mary," he said. I think you're terrific and I want you as my client. Commander Zero, jail, 'Nightline,' the *People* magazine cover you told me about—they haven't hurt." Edwards waved one hand as he spoke. He leaned forward, gripping the edge of the table. "But as I told you yesterday, Mary, I've had my eye on you for quite a while. I think reporting is your strength, but your anchor potential is phenomenal." He looked straight into her eyes as if reading her mind.

"You know as well as I do," he went on, breaking his stare and leaning back, "that in television most women are either reporters or anchors, not both. The woman that can go head to head with Brokaw or Jennings, both in the field or on the set, will be the one to break the all-male club on the evening news. And you, Mary Reed, are the one I know can do it."

Mary's head was reeling. She blamed the champagne for finding herself at a complete loss for words. "Well," she managed at last, "that's quite a pitch."

"I used to pitch for U.C.L.A. This is no pitch, Mary, it's

what I sincerely believe." He looked directly into her eyes again.

"Well," Mary said. "Well, what about all the others?" she asked.

He ticked them off on his hand. "This one's too old, that one can't report, she's too involved with her family, and the other one has a speech impediment. You could be better than all of them."

Mary ordered some coffee, to clear her head. "How much do you want to be in television, Mary?"

"However much it takes," she said without hesitation.

"Are you prepared to spend the next two or three years living to work, so that when the time comes and one of the big boys' seats comes free, I can push you into it?"

Mary took a sip of coffee. This was hardball, and she needed to think. She sensed the power of the man as he swept her along with the force of his conviction. "I'm flattered, really, by your confidence in me," Mary began, her voice gathering volume as she spoke. "But we're talking about the future. What about now? What are my options at the moment?"

"Okay. Here's my plan. I want you to come to L.A. where you can start as a reporter at Channel Three. It's a first-rate operation and I have some top clients there. Charles Davis, the anchor; Bill Bryson, the sports director; and some others. You've probably heard of Irwin Hansen, the news director. A better man you couldn't find."

"That sounds great," Mary said and smiled. "But is Channel Three aware of your plans?"

E.J. looked over to the table opposite them and nodded. A stoop-shouldered man in an ill-fitting suit stood up and walked to their table. The agent half-rose from his chair. "Mary Reed, I'd like you to meet Irwin Hansen."

Mary was startled. "Hello," she said, taking the hand he offered her. "I wasn't expecting . . ."

"It's okay," Hansen said with a grin. He drew up a chair

and sat down at the table. "I was only listening to every other word you said."

"Okay," Mark said, reappearing on deck with a screwdriver. "So tell me what happened. All of it." She was sitting on his boat in Marina Del Rey. Mark had come back late the night before and Mary had surprised him with the news she was in Los Angeles on a job interview. "Oh, and can you tidy up those lines for me, honey?" he asked.

"Sure." Mary started to describe her wooing by one of television's most powerful agents. She did not tell Mark about the roses and she was matter-of-fact about the trip, these were details she knew would have no impact on Mark, except perhaps to convince him that Edwards was an operator on a major scale. "So, there he was," she said, "telling me I had the potential to become the first woman network anchor and the way I could make that happen would be to go to Channel Three in L.A. as a reporter. And I asked him if he'd talked to anyone over there about it and he just smiled and looked away. I guess he gave some sort of signal because then, lo and behold, there was Irwin Hansen, the news director of Channel Three at our table. I was so embarrassed. I mean all the things Edwards had said to me, he must have heard all that b.s."

"So, it was a set-up," Mark said. He sat down, and began unscrewing a winch.

"Well, yes, I guess. But, listen, Mark. Edwards is, well, he's an agent, right? I mean he doesn't really know anything about journalism. But Irwin has done a lot. He was a top producer in Vietnam. He told me a story about how he went back to witness the fall of Saigon. There were all these names—Safer, Bradley, Cronkite. You know, he took the last helicopter flight out of the city. After that he ran the London bureau for years. He was even in Prague for the spring of sixty-eight. And such a nice guy. Funny looking really, but he's got this lovely kind face. I know I could learn a lot from him."

"So, he told you all these stories so he could get you to

come down again for an interview. Is that what happened?"

"Better." Mary's eyes were bright. "He offered me a job right then, in the restaurant," she said triumphantly.

Mark did not say anything for a while. "What did you say?" he asked.

"I said I'd think about it," Mary said defensively. She was lying. Actually she had indicated that she would accept the job after talking to Wyatt Andrews. Edwards assured her that he would work out the salary and contract terms.

"If you took the job, when would you start?"

"Depends what Wyatt says. I mean my contract still has three months to run, but he might let me go a bit before that."

"I see," said Mark. He got up and walked over to Mary, who was watching him anxiously. He held her chin, tipping her head up toward him and searched her face.

"Is that what you want to be? A female Peter Jennings?"

"What's wrong with that?"

"There's nothing wrong with it. It's just what you have to do to get that worries me." He dropped his hand and folded his arms. "Listen, don't get me wrong. I want you down here more than anything. But my personal wishes aside, is it a good idea for you to move at this point? Wouldn't it be better if you waited a year or two, and got more experience. You know what I mean? Not that you aren't good at the moment, and the way you handled the FBI deserves a medal. I am so proud of you." He looked at her fondly. "Do you understand what I mean?"

"Listen, I'm hot now because of the Commander Zero thing. In a year's time, two years', who knows?"

"That's it isn't it? It's not that you're a damn fine journalist, it's because of the one interview you did that I have no respect for. That's what it takes to be a reporter these days, interview the most wanted man in America, a terrorist killer, mind you, and then you're made. For God's sake, that's not journalism, it's simply pandering to the worst instincts of a sick society."

"Jesus, Mark, give it up!" Mary stood up. "I didn't come here to get a lecture. I know how you feel about that interview, but I wish you'd stop throwing it up in my face every chance you get."

Mark stood up. "Damnit, Mary, you could have been killed. Do you realize that? You put yourself in incredible danger to get that lousy interview. And it worries me that you're capable of doing something like that." His voice softened and he stood in front of her. "I want you here, you understand? Not risking your life with some whacked-out neo-Nazi who wants to be on television." He touched her cheek.

"I know, Mark, I know what you're saying. But it paid off, right? Look, I'm here, and because of the interview I've got a job in L.A., near you." She hugged him.

"So," he said, crouching down again. "You've made up your mind about the job?"

"Yes, and I want you to be pleased for me. In some ways, I'm going to have to work harder than ever now. I mean, people are going to be watching me, wondering if the interview was a flash in the pan." She tucked the end of the last line neatly into the loop she had made. "Mark," she said suddenly.

"What?"

"The rope. You remember they found a rope around Feld's neck? I was just thinking how the flag he used as a backdrop in the interview had the words *Day of the Rope* sewn into it. Do you think—?" Her eyes were round.

"That they're connected?" He finished her sentence. She nodded. "Well," he continued slowly. "It certainly adds up. A lot of the filth the commander was spouting could have come straight out of some of the literature I've been reading. Jesus, honey, it is a wonder they didn't kill you."

"They needed me," Mary said, her jaw hardening. "They used me to get exposure, and they put me in a situation where I had to protect them. But, listen, I told you I saw Zero, just for a few seconds. Not long enough to make a composite, but I'm sure I could recognize his face if I saw it. I went to the police station this week, but none of the photos I saw fit. He trapped me, Mark. I played straight into his hands. Maybe I should consider approaching the FBI."

"You can't," Mark said simply. "You've staked your career—for heaven's sake you went to jail—to defend your right not to reveal your sources. There's no way professionally that you can back down now." He paused. "But you can continue to look at pictures and maybe you should consider going to the Anti-Defamation League. I talked to them about the Feld case. If you're right about Zero's involvement in his murder, they would be very interested to hear from you."

"Okay," Mary said. "At least it's something." She looked away lost in thought. "What happens if he contacts me, Mark? What happens if he decides I know too much and comes after me?"

"I think you've already proved that you won't betray him," Mark said. "Anyway, it'd be too risky for him to go after you."

"I don't know, Mark. That guy's crazy. I saw his eyes." She stared into the water. "While it was happening, each step I took, from setting up the interview right through to going to jail, seemed obvious and natural." She turned her head to look at Mark. "Now I see how this event is going to change my life, and I wonder that I did it so easily."

"It's because you're made of steel, honey." Mark walked over to her and circled his hands around her waist. "Mary, I'm sorry. I've been a jerk about the interview. We won't talk about it again, you have my word." He kissed her, picking her up off her feet in a rush of feeling. "There's a question that's been bothering me," he murmured in her ear. "If you tell me, I promise I won't tell anyone. Really. I just wanted to know if they made you wear pajamas in jail? If you tell me, it'll be just between us, I swear. I know you hate to wear anything when you sleep, but I kept picturing the warden's faces in the mornings . . ."

A slow smile had spread across Mary's face as he spoke. "Oh, really," she said archly. "That's been on your mind, has it?" She took his hand. "Well, if you really want to see what the well-dressed woman wears in her jail bed, you'll have to come with me." Mary pulled him after her down the steep steps into the boat's cabin.

"Was that a call for me?" Wyatt Andrews asked coming out of his office.

"No, it was Mary. She wanted to know if you had any time to see her. I told her to come in at three, after your meeting with Randy."

"Oh, okay." Andrews was surprised. He had always made it clear to his employees that they could come in and see him whenever they liked. Usually Mary took full advantage of his open-door policy to pester him about airtime, or her various conflicts with producers, writers, and editors.

"Wyatt?" Meryl interrupted his flow of thoughts. "It's Irwin Hansen."

"Of course!" he said, understanding the reason for Mary's appointment. And then added, "Goddamn him!" as he walked into his office.

"We got Reed," Hansen said. His tone was smug, Wyatt thought. "Now, how do you want to handle it?"

Andrews knew that the moment had come to stop fighting. "Well," he said. "I haven't talked to her yet. But if she wants to break the contract, I'm not going to stand in her way."

"Wyatt, you always were a mensch."

"I know, I know." Andrews sighed. He dialed Randy Martin's number. At first the owner was insistent that they should fight Channel 3 and keep Mary for the full tenure of her contract.

"I disagree, Randy," Andrews countered. "All we're doing is creating bad blood. There's no difference between now and three months' time. We should let her go. Let her leave on a high. You never know when we might need her again." Martin reluctantly gave in.

Mary walked into the news director's office at three. She was tense. "Hi," she said. "How are you?"

"Fine, fine."

"And Judy, the kids?"

Andrews leaned back in his chair. He was smiling. "We're all fine. Listen, I'll make it easier for you." He plucked a Dodgers baseball cap from his desk and gave it to her.

Mary took the cap with a frown. She twisted it in her hand until understanding suddenly dawned. "You know then? About Channel Three, I mean?"

Wyatt nodded. "When do you start?"

"What about . . . I mean, the contract . . . you mean you'll let me go!" Mary jumped up from her seat and planted a kiss on the news director's cheek.

"Congratulations, Mary," he said, getting up. "And listen, seriously now, if you ever need a shoulder to cry on, I'm it. Don't forget your old friends." She hugged him.

He walked to the window. "So, what do you want to do? How shall we announce it?"

"Well, I've been thinking. I have a couple of pieces I've started. But I'll be finished by the end of next week. So, let's say I leave next Friday." She paused. "There's no point in keeping it a secret, though. We could tell people tonight, maybe after the six o'clock show."

"Sounds okay to me," said Wyatt, gracious in defeat.

Mary walked back to her office relieved that Andrews had been so decent about her going. Now her new job felt more real to her, and she was anxious to get to Los Angeles and start this new phase in her life. Her career was blossoming in the way she dreamed it would, and she would also be living with the man she loved. Mary remembered something she used to do as a young child. When she became conscious of being very happy she would stand still and close her eyes, vowing to remember that moment for the rest of her life. Mary stopped for a moment in the corridor leading to Channel 6's newsroom, and, closing her eyes, recited her childhood promise to herself.

In the office her phone was ringing. "Ms. Reed?"

"Yes."

"My name is Eddie Martinez, I'm a detective." He didn't mention Bakersfield, it was too complicated.

"Yes," Mary said warily.

"I wanted to talk to you. About the Goldor robbery. Happened about six weeks ago."

"I know, I covered it."

"I'd rather not talk on the phone. Can you meet with me?"

"This better be good, Detective."

"I think you'll find it interesting," Martinez said. "There seems to be a link between the robbery and your Commander Zero."

"If you're working with the FBI I can't talk to you," Mary said sharply.

Martinez snorted. "The feds are a one-way street, Ms. Reed. They won't have anything to do with me. No, I'm working on this independently. That's why I called you."

"Listen, I'm interested. But I've got a lot going on at the moment. Why don't you give me your number and I'll give you a call?"

"You won't regret it."

FIFTEEN

"ANY CALLS?" IRWIN Hansen asked his secretary.

Margaret Lynch looked at her boss's stooped figure and wondered how long he was going to last. Hansen was the fifth news director she had worked for in her twelve-year tenure at the station; it seemed longevity was not part of the job description. "Just the dean's office at Columbia. They want to know if you've made a decision about giving that speech to the alumni."

Irwin rolled his eyes. "I forgot to ask Barbara if she wants to make this trip. Remind me of it tomorrow morning, will you?"

He walked into his office, took off his jacket, which he flung on a chair, and loosened his tie. Irwin Hansen was fifty-six and his dark brown hair was liberally salted with gray. In a characteristic gesture, his hand went to smooth the back of his head where a cowlick forced his hair to stand on end and sometimes curled over the back of his ears. Without a jacket his five eight stature was reduced still further by the droop that was especially pronounced in his left shoulder and the middle-aged midriff that swelled over his waistband. The most noticeable thing about him was his watery, vulnerable eyes, which were magnified by the clear-rimmed glasses he wore. His clothes, though expensive, never hung well on a body that was not designed for fashion, and even his tie, knotted now in a perfect Windsor, was a little off-center.

He had just met with station chief Tom Baker to discuss the role of their new reporter Mary Reed. Hansen wanted a general assignment reporter, someone who would cover the news from the street; Baker, the former sales chief, whose eye was ever on the advertisers, had pushed for a reporter who would cover the music and entertainment industries, using the soft-focus, magazine approach of the successful "Entertainment Tonight" show. They had ended the meeting without resolving their differences.

As Hansen stood to leave, Baker had flicked a speck of dust from his immaculately tailored suit, which he wore with a floppy green bow tie. "I see that the ratings are up for the five o'clock show this past month?" Baker had then said, getting up and gathering his papers.

"I think Worth is making a difference," Hansen had replied, pleased at the chance to say something. Rick Worth was his protégé; three months earlier he had promoted the former writer to executive producer of the early show. "I'd like to think about having him replace Paul Gelson on the six o'clock show."

"Will Charles Davis let you?" asked Baker. The six o'clock anchorman was known to favor Gelson.

"I'm working on it," Hansen told him.

"You know, I worry about Davis," Baker said. "He needs a co-anchor."

"Can't do it, Tom. The contract's airtight—I should know, we've gone over it with a fine-toothed comb. No co-anchor. We'd be up to our ears in legal fees if we tried to break it."

Baker sighed. "Listen, do what you think best, Irwin. I bow to your superior experience." Baker had executed a mock bow and headed off toward his office.

Hansen checked his watch. It was nearly five. He had established the custom that between five and seven o'clock only his wife, his daughter, and Tom Baker were allowed to disturb him while he watched the two local news shows he was responsible for. This evening, however, he had invited Mary Reed, who had arrived in L.A. that morning, to join him for the last half hour and then to come to the "surprise" party he knew anchorman Charles Davis was throwing in honor of Hansen's first-year anniversary as news director. He thought it would be a good way of introducing Mary to Channel 3.

The theme music for the five o'clock show sounded. *"Good evening, this is Amber Lyons and Des Westin . . ."*

Irwin sat in his chair behind the huge round desk. On the desk was a white legal-size pad, on which he jotted the occasional note during the show. To his right was a computer, hooked-up to the news wires and through which the news director could send messages to the control room. Close to the computer were two telephones, the second a red one linked him directly to the control room.

The office was large with two windows, one looking out on Burbank and the ridge of mountains that spiked the skyline, the other facing the parking lot. The furniture was a mixture of styles and tastes that the various occupants of the office had left behind. Hansen had filled the office with personal photographs and mementoes; the furnishings he accepted with a shrug.

Irwin Hansen, born Handleman, had come a long way from the streets of wartime Brooklyn, but his illustrious network career had ended after his stint as London bureau chief. Afterward, he had expected a big job on the evening newscast, but it never materialized—some said because of the anchorman's personal antipathy toward him. Instead, Hansen had been offered executive producer at Channel 3 in Los Angeles. Because the local news had started to generate a lot of money for the network, the position came with a generous salary increase, and Hansen accepted. With his promotion to news director, he had won another battle in his long career, yet he lived with the reluctant admission that he had lost the war. Hansen, one year into what he knew was his last job, was often sorely tempted to tell station chief Tom Baker he could shove it before Baker stole his line and dumped him on the streets.

"*Well, Charles, if you liked today, you'll love tomorrow....*" Irwin smiled. It was after six and Bob Coleman, Channel 3's perky weatherman was telling the weather story, California-style: fifteen seconds of reporting and two and a half minutes of jokey patter. Hansen used to wonder why it was necessary to have three weather spots an hour for a climate which, unlike that of the rest of the country, never changed. The research had given him his answer. Next to anchor Charles Davis, the weatherman-comedian Bob Coleman was the station's most popular figure, a popularity that translated into millions of dollars a year in advertising revenues. Hansen had learned to appreciate Coleman's tireless prattle.

The intercom buzzed. It was Tom Baker.

"Listen, Irwin, I've just got a terrific memo from the ad agency," Tom Baker enthused. "I want you to reconsider the campaign we worked up, the one where we make our newspeople more friendly."

"Didn't we discuss this last week?" Irwin said. "I thought the issue was closed. Listen, Tom, as I said before, our reporters are not anybody's friend, they report the news. No one wants to see Charles Davis barbecuing steaks or Bob Coleman fishing with his son. 'Your friends at Channel 3' simply won't fly, Tom, believe me." Hansen's voice was soft but emphatic.

Baker was momentarily silenced by Hansen's response. "Well, all right. But how about if I send you the memo and you can at least read it before you say no?"

"Tom, this idea is only marginally better than the neighborhood one you cooked up last year." Hansen was referring to a campaign Baker had devised where people could send in a card that then would be picked out of a sack on-air. If your name was drawn, the station would broadcast the eleven o'clock news from your living room. The slogan for the campaign was "Channel 3, Our House Is Your House."

"Irwin," Baker said, his overbright laughter trilling on the name. "I really wasn't serious about that one, just wanted to see what you would say. But this one has real possibilities. Come on, just take another look, it won't cost you anything."

Hansen was growing tired of the pushy station chief. "Okay, send it over, Tom." He hung up and shook his head. The intercom buzzed again. "Send her in," Hansen ordered on hearing that Mary Reed had arrived.

"Hello, Mary," Irwin said, shaking her hand warmly. "Why don't you have a seat?"

Mary sat down. She liked the office, it felt comfortable. On the walls she observed pictures of Hansen with several heads of state, as well as some of the big names in television history. Mary became aware that Hansen was watching the monitor intently.

On screen Charles Davis was speaking. *"Let's go live now to Dodger Stadium and our sports director Bill Bryson, Bill."*

"Thank you, Charles," Bryson said. He was standing with a microphone on home plate at the Los Angeles Dodger Stadium. Although he had never played any sport professionally, Bryson had a loose-limbed, athletic build, which he maintained with a lazy exercise regimen of golf, softball with his son, and vigorous spectator sports. Known for his flawless diction, which never faltered even when following the most complex maneuvers in a game, Bill Bryson was admired both within the industry and with his audience of sports fans for his unflappable style and ability to take command of any situation. His encyclopedic knowledge of his field was legendary. "Nobody notices when you forget the name of the French

prime minister," he once joked to Charles Davis. "But if I get a batting average wrong, I get a hundred calls."

"Here in Dodger Stadium," Bryson continued, "It's old-timers' night, a salute to the world champs, the champs of nineteen fifty-five, the Brooklyn Dodgers. . . ."

The black-and-white footage of Roy Campanella, Jackie Robinson, Don Newcombe, and Irwin's personal hero, slugger and centerfielder, Duke Snider, "The Duke of Flatbush," flickered on the screen, riveting his attention. This was what television did best, Hansen thought, it could take you away to where you wanted to be or, as in this case, to where you had been. As Bryson interviewed a stocky, gray-haired Duke Snider about the legendary summer of fifty-five, the year the Dodgers had won the World Series, Hansen traveled back in time.

"That's the news from Dodger Stadium. Now back to the studio and a boy of summer himself, Charles Davis," the black sportscaster joked.

Hansen picked up the red telephone. As usual, it was picked up immediately in the control room by a production assistant who handed it to the show's producer Paul Gelson. "I loved that report. Tell Bill it was the best thing I've seen him do in weeks. Congratulations."

Paul Gelson was both surprised and relieved. Hansen usually called when there was some stylistic or factual error in the program. However, it seemed that his boss had not noticed that the super, or identifying tag, for Duke Snider had not been screened, a detail the picayune Hansen normally spotted instantly. Of course, reasoned Gelson, who had seen Hansen's autographed photo many times, Hansen would have known who The Duke was without a super. He sighed thankfully. "Thank you Irwin, I'll tell Bill. I know he worked hard on that one."

Mary, who had been a little bored by the piece, noted Hansen's interest. "Who was that?" she asked. "The gray-haired guy in the interview?"

Hansen looked at her. "Duke Snider," he said. He picked

up a framed picture, which was prominently displayed on his desk alongside those of his wife and daughter. "I was in journalism school in fifty-five and I went to see every game except two that season. That was before the Dodgers moved, of course," he added. Mary looked closely at the picture. On it Snider had scrawled *To Irwin from The Duke.* Wherever Irwin had gone in his more than thirty years of assignments all over the world, the picture, autographed by his childhood idol, had gone with him.

"I saw him hit twenty-five home runs at Ebbetts Field," he said. "It was the only year they won."

"And that's your wife and daughter?" Mary asked.

"Yes." Hansen beamed. "I hope you'll meet them some day soon."

Mary smiled.

"Well, I suppose we'd better get this party thing over with," Hansen said, putting on his jacket. Mary sensed his nervousness; he clearly did not relish the limelight.

In the news studio the floor director yelled "Clear!" The six o'clock news was over. Anchor Charles Davis, six foot four with a movie star's clean-cut good looks, removed the microphone from his trademark red silk necktie and laid it at a precise angle on the desk. He picked up his script printed on the yellow paper he insisted upon for superstitious reasons, and slowly rose from his chair.

"Another hour of TV history and journalism in the books." Davis's baritone boomed around the studio and he lingered on the first syllable of the word *journalism* so that it stretched into a howl. The technicians scurrying around the room dutifully smiled. When he first arrived from Pittsburgh over four years before, Davis's irreverence had picked up the crew at Channel 3, which had dropped to second place in the ratings. Now although they had tired of the ritual, the ripple of good humor represented their salute to the man who had brought the station back to the number-one position.

Davis ran his hand through his expensively cut black hair and walked up the flight of stairs that led from the studio to the second floor. At the top of the stairs he straightened his tie as he prepared to enter the newsroom where he had arranged a party to celebrate Hansen's first year as news director.

As he neared the newsroom, Davis saw Hansen and Mary, led by Margaret Lynch.

"You must be Mary Reed," Davis said, holding out his hand. "I'm Charles Davis, welcome to Channel 3." He looked at her appreciatively. "Now, if you'll excuse me, I have some business to do. Why don't you stay with Irwin until I introduce you both?" He paused at the door to the newsroom, and turned and winked at Mary and Irwin. "It's showtime!" he mouthed.

Margaret pushed Irwin through the door, and Mary followed him. After everyone had a glass in their hands, Davis waved for silence. "Ladies and gentlemen and those who fit somewhere in between, I give you Irwin Hansen, our eminent news director of one year, and with him Mary Reed, our newest reporter, whose fame and feistiness precede her." The assorted reporters, producers, writers, production staff, and technicians who were crowded into the balloon-decked newsroom, cheered and clapped.

"They said Irwin and I would never make it," he continued. "The original odd couple. Well, folks, year one has been a perfect one. Let's drink to another one just like it." Davis raised his glass of California champagne and waved it in Irwin's direction in a toast that everyone imitated.

"Oh, Irwin, before the festivities start, I want to offer you a token of our esteem." Davis pulled out his pocket a bottle of Thunderbird wine wrapped in a yellow ribbon and presented it to Hansen.

Irwin grinned. "Another year with me and *you* might need this, Charles," he said. Although it was clearly untrue that Irwin had any real control over his star employee, a few people laughed.

"Wait, wait," said Rick Worth. The young producer of the five o'clock news was surrounded by his usual coterie of admirers. "I would just like to read some telegrams I have here in honor of this occasion." People started to chuckle at Rick's mock serious tone of voice. "Here's one from Hong Kong. 'Dear Irwin,' it says, 'wish I was there, signed Bob Reynolds.' " The room broke up with laughter.

Bob Reynolds was Hansen's predecessor. When the position had opened up two and a half years earlier, Hansen, who had been executive producer at the station for five years, was the most obvious candidate for news director. Tom Baker, however, had shoehorned his own man into the job. Reynolds, a thirty-two-year-old Yale graduate had been the network's news manager. Hansen had almost quit but, on the advice of his wife, he stayed on. In the end it was Reynolds himself who did something that united two of the station's stars, Charles Davis and Bill Bryson, the sportscaster, behind Irwin. Not only did Reynolds hire a woman to report the sports but he also wanted to bust up the Davis-Bryson alliance on the six o'clock show by putting his woman on that show and moving Bryson to the less-prestigious five o'clock program. Together, Davis, Bryson, and Hansen had succeeded in getting Reynolds "promoted" to network bureau chief . . . in Hong Kong. With the powerful Davis backing him, Hansen finally became news director for the top-rated station in Los Angeles.

"And here's another one," said Worth, enjoying himself. " 'Dear Irwin, I love you, guy, signed Tom Baker.' "

Rick's back was to the newsroom entrance so he did not see Baker enter the room. "Hey, Rick. It's you I love, sweetheart, baby," the station manager drawled.

Startled, Rick turned around. Quickly responding to the situation, he gathered himself up and with a pirouette landed right in front of Baker, who was leaning on one of the many canes he used as a sartorial prop. Rick kissed the surprised station chief full on the lips. Everyone gasped.

Charles Davis could not tolerate being upstaged. "Order, order!" he cried. "As you know," he began seriously, "Irwin Hansen has covered more news events and won more

Emmys than all of us put together. His integrity, his journalism"—and here Davis extended the word as he had done in the studio—"have given our shows the quality that makes them number one. Speech, I beg you, sir. Speech."

Hansen cleared his throat. "I just want to say," he began in a low voice, and the crowd quieted and strained to hear him, "that I think there are two things I'm especially proud of doing this last year. One is to make sure that Charles Davis's golf cart arrives at the eighteenth hole in time for him to make it to the studio and keep the ratings sky-high." There was laughter. "And the other thing I'm particularly proud of," Irwin continued, "is the revitalization of the five o'clock news in the hands of our youngest news producer Rick Worth. To you, Charles and Rick, and all of you. It's been a great year." There were cheers and whistles. "And now enough about the past," Irwin went on. "I am delighted that Mary Reed has seen fit to join our team, and I know that she is going to help make next year our best ever." He raised his glass to more loud cheers.

"I thought she'd be taller than that," a writer commented to Rick Worth.

"Hey, I can handle it," Worth retorted. He strolled over to Mary. "Hi, I'm Rick Worth, producer of the five o'clock news. I've heard a lot about you."

"Well, I hope some of it was good," Mary said, looking the boyishly attractive Worth in the eye. "Because we'll be seeing a lot of each other from now on."

"Hey, Ricky," Charles Davis said, "stop monopolizing our new reporter. You know, guy, that kiss was a masterstroke. Some day when you least expect it, I'll use it against you."

"Who are you going to kiss? Irwin?" Rick joked.

Hansen crept out of the party. He went back to his office and called his wife to let her know that he was about to leave the station. Thirty minutes away in their Hancock Park home his wife and daughter would be waiting to celebrate his first year with his favorite meal: shrimp cocktail, chopped steak, well-done, and Barbara's mouthwatering coconut cream cake. The two women, the only people Irwin really cared about, and certainly the only people he felt cared about him, gave him many moments of quiet joy. The stucco and brick house with its lush green lawn, pots of plants, and gleaming swimming pool was very different from the Bensonhurst neighborhood in Brooklyn where he had grown up, but it was now home to Irwin Hansen. His parents, now dead, had never fully accepted Barbara, who was not Jewish, but they would have been very happy to know that their ornery and contrary son had found such happiness in family life.

Before leaving, he sought Mary out. "Do you need a ride home?" he asked.

"No, it's okay thanks. I brought my car. I think I should get going now, too." She looked at the owlish face of the news director. "Thanks for inviting me, Irwin. I enjoyed meeting everyone."

"Well, they must have looked like a bunch of crazies tonight, but they're good people." He grinned. "I'm really glad you're here, Mary." They walked down to the parking lot together.

Mary smiled as she pulled up to Mark's house because he had festooned the driveway with ribbons and balloons to welcome her on her first night. She turned the engine off, and sat for a moment in the dark. In the back of the car were a heap of boxes and glossy shopping bags, which Mary had picked up that afternoon. E. J. Edwards had insisted that his assistant take her shopping for new work clothes. The agent had criticized Mary's clothing—he had even shown her tapes and pointed out what was wrong. Edwards had persuaded her that she should dress more aggressively in sharply tailored suits that emphasized her shoulders. He also criticized the way Andrews had put her on air with distracting graphics in the background. Your face can fill a screen, the agent told her, I'm not going to let anyone else do that to you again. Edwards was not happy with her decision to live with Mark. Mary sensed that the agent's proprietary interest in her was offended by the other man in her life.

The door of the car opened. "Hey, look what I just found," Mark said, smiling at her. "You okay?" She nodded. "Welcome to L.A., honey."

"Who's there?" The voice was sharp and had an edge of querulousness. It belonged to a frail-looking woman in her mid-sixties who was hunched over a Formica-topped kitchen table. Strewn across the scratched surface were envelopes and papers. It was Sunday evening and a sermon boomed from the radio at a volume that indicated the woman was slightly deaf. Hearing nothing further, the woman went back to her task of stuffing envelopes with letters announcing a funding drive for the local Lutheran church.

"That you, Irma?" she asked, looking up as she heard the sound again. She massaged her hands, stiff with the arthritis that kept her in almost constant pain.

"Irma?" she called again as she walked into the living room. Someone was knocking at the front door. Nobody, not even the minister, knocked at the front door, most visitors knew to come in the back door, which was always open. She went back to the kitchen to turn the radio off. Now the knocking seemed impatient. Perhaps it was a stranger seeking directions. She smoothed her sweater at the neck and patted her hair in place.

"Who is it?" she asked, opening the door.

A man in a dark-blue suit stood on the stoop.

"Gerald?" the woman queried as if afraid to learn the answer.

"I've come to see you, Mom. Did you think you'd never hear from me again?" The man smiled.

"I've prayed every day of every year that I never lay eyes on you again," the woman said, recovering her tongue. "You've never been a son to me. I'm ashamed o' the day I bore you."

"Did you get my money, Mom? I never forgot you."

"I wouldn't touch anything you sent me if I had to beg on the streets for the want of it."

"What did you do with it?" the man asked curiously. "Gave it to the church, I suppose," he said, answering his own question.

"Flushed it down the sewer. It had the mark of Satan on't, like everything you touch."

"Mom, I've seen the error of my ways. I want to make amends."

"Hmmm." The woman rubbed her hands. She was getting cold in the doorway.

The man, seeing her weaken, pressed his point. "Let me come in, at least. If you don't want me to stay, I'll understand. Look, you're getting chilled standing there. And the arthritis has gotten worse. You need a man around, Mom."

"Well, I guess it won't hurt if you stopped in," she said grudgingly. "What's that, you've got a suitcase?" she said peering into the dusk.

"It's okay, I'll leave it there."

"No, bring it in, son."

Later that evening as he sat watching television while his mother cleaned up the dinner, Jerry Radamacker allowed himself to relax for the first time in two weeks.

After packing up his life in the desert compound, Radamacker had sent the men off in different directions. Some, including Finn Johnson, had gone to Bleech's old operation in Idaho and similar organizations in the mountains, others drifted into the big cities. Radamacker had left no forwarding address. After the Mary Reed interview he knew he had to lay low for a long time. He intended to hide in plain view in the little town of Timber Falls in the northeast corner of Washington State framed by the borders of Idaho and Canada. He knew the big sky there, the mountains that were brushed with blue, and the crisp, clear light. It was where his mother had grown up, the place she had moved back to after living in Chicago with her fifteen-year-old son. Radamacker had lived there, finishing high school, going to college, then teaching. It was in this peaceful corner of the country that he had developed many of his ideas and written the book he had published himself.

He rested his head thankfully against the back of the chair.

"You going to get a job, son?" his mother asked, emerging from the kitchen with a cup of tea.

ble they'll be ready this evening. If you like, I can take your number and we'll contact you."

"You know, I'm a reporter. I could ruin your business if I did a story on you." The pharmacist looked at her impassively. Mary chewed her nail. "I'm sorry," she said. "I've been under a lot of strain recently. Isn't there any way you can help me?" she pleaded.

"We'll try. Okay, miss?"

"Thank you." Mary laid the prescription down and left the drugstore. Her need for sleeping tablets had increased in recent weeks, and she depended on them to get the four or five hours of sleep she needed to function. As she walked down the street Mary admitted to herself with a trace of shame that she had lost control in the store. If only she could sleep better, she would be a nicer person, she thought.

"This your car, miss?"

"Yes, Officer. I was just about to leave." She smiled brilliantly at him.

"Say, aren't you Mary Reed?"

"That's me," she said, flashing a second smile at him.

"I watch you every night. You're a reporter for Channel Three, right?" He scratched his head. "What do you think is going to happen in that mayor's race?"

"You know, your guess is as good as mine. We're both going to vote, right?" Mary was alternately amused and irritated that her role in the news business gave people the idea that she could predict the future.

"Well, listen. I won't give you a ticket this time," the cop said, putting his book away, "just be careful where you park in the future."

"You don't know how much I appreciate this, Officer," Mary said gratefully. Her mood restored, she got into her white Mercedes SEL, a gift from E. J. Edwards a couple of months earlier. Although there were times when she felt she was missing something, there were some good things about her new life, she thought, gunning the powerful engine into gear and shooting into the street.

219

She put on KFWB, the all-news radio station, and opened the *Los Angeles Times* on the seat beside her as the car slid down the hill. At the bottom she picked up her car phone and dialed the station. "Hi—" she tried to remember the daytime assignment editor's name, then gave up. "It's Mary Reed. I'll be in in a few minutes, what's up? . . . Good, see you soon." She drove across the six-lane freeway and into the parking lot behind the faded green building where Channel 3's news and entertainment divisions worked. Mary, along with other stars and the executives, had a parking space marked by a whitewashed brick on which her name had been stenciled.

Mary strode past the guard toward the elevators, flashing her card. A frown line played between her eyes. Tonight was Monday, Emmy Award night in Los Angeles, and three of her pieces had been nominated for awards. She would have to tape her report for tonight's program, she decided, to give her enough time to get ready. Purposefully, she walked through the newsroom on the second floor to her desk in the long room full of reporters where she worked. Dumping her things on the messy surface, she immediately started back toward the newsroom and the assignment desk.

"Hi," said Tim Wallace, one of Channel 3's best reporters, looking up as she walked past.

"Oh, hi, Tim," she said.

"Listen, Mary, can I have the file tape on your airport safety story? The one you did in San Francisco. And do you have a contact with the controllers group you can give me?"

Most reporters do not share their sources, but Mary had often helped Tim out in return for his streetwise knowledge of Los Angeles, which she valued enormously. Wallace provided the depth of experience Mary felt she needed to cover stories in the new city in the same way David Roberti had in San Francisco.

Mary looked at him. "Sure. The tapes are down here." She indicated a file drawer filled with tapes. "It's marked 'Airport Safety.' You'll find it. I'll have to get you the contact later, I can't look for it right now."

"Thanks, Mary, I owe you," Wallace called after her.

She made her way back to the newsroom, where reporters and producers buzzed around the assignment desk. The assignment editor generally told the reporters what to do but Mary Reed had changed that, she told them what she wanted.

"I need two crews at the Board of Ed, no later than one-fifteen, Pete," she said, remembering his name.

"Okay," he said, glancing up at the big board where the crews and reporters were written. "Well, Kelly and Mack can do it for sure."

"Great, then I don't care who else you get. But, please, make sure they get there because I have to do the interview between sessions. There's no slack here, okay?"

"Will do."

"Oh, and I have to get it back here quickly, in time to pre-edit. Everything's going to be on tape tonight, because of the Emmys."

"Does Rick know?"

"Why don't you tell him?" She caught sight of Worth. "It's okay, I'll do it."

Mary walked toward the coffee machine where she had spotted her producer.

"Hi, Mary." He smiled at her. Worth knew that for the last six months Mary had been the highlight of his show. The hard-edged reports that E. J. Edwards had encouraged her to do had not only brought up the ratings but had attracted the demographically correct viewers, especially the coveted twenty-five to fifty-four-year-old women, the audience advertisers paid the most for. Last week, Rick had seen research showing that only four people at Channel 3 tested better than Mary Reed. All were on the top-rated six o'clock show: anchor Charles Davis, Bob Coleman, the nutty weatherman, sportscaster Bill Bryson, and conservative commentator Ralph W. Wilson.

"So, you all set for tonight?" he asked.

"Yes, that's what I wanted to talk to you about. I'm going

to pre-edit my piece, you know, the AIDS awareness one, so I have time to get dressed this evening."

The idea of Mary Reed getting dressed was almost too much for Rick, who thought that Mary was one of the most gorgeous woman he had not undressed since Gloria Milagros had kissed him behind the gym in high school. He had nicknamed Mary "Princess"—though he rarely used the name to her face—partly because of her imperious attitude and partly because she reminded him of Grace Kelly. "You better wear your running shoes," Rick said. "I expect you to get all four of those awards."

Mary smiled. Her producer had the most expressive eyes, she thought, not for the first time in her six months in Los Angeles. Though he was not classically handsome in the Charles Davis mold, many women found Rick's boyish appearance and gregarious personality irresistible. His corn-colored hair was straight and he wore it long enough that it fell over the collar of the striped dress shirts he liked to wear to work with faded blue jeans and sneakers. His face was lean, too thin to be perfect, and he was usually lightly tan. His smile was slightly lopsided, revealing perfect teeth, and he wore round horn-rimmed glasses because he hated contact lenses. Rick Worth had the ability to fasten his liquid brown eyes on a woman and talk to her with an intensity that made her feel as if she was the only one in the world. It was endearing, but also a sign of his insecurity, for Rick would use his charm on the cashier at the commissary and the stars at Channel 3 alike. Mary found herself looking for a moment too long into his eyes, and she pulled away. The man was married after all, she thought, walking toward the reporters' room.

Before she reached her destination, the assignment editor waved at her. "Hansen wants to see you."

"Now?"

"Yeah." She walked back past Tim Wallace, who gave her the thumbs up sign. "Yes, of course," he was saying into the phone. "Now, would you be willing to say this on-camera?"

Mary walked out of the room and instead of turning left

into the newsroom made a right. She made her way down the narrow hallway and through the glass doors that led to the carpeted inner sanctum of Channel 3's news management.

"Morning, Irwin," Mary said, walking through the open door of Irwin Hansen's office.

The news director was on the phone but he smiled and waved at Mary, indicating that she should sit down. He had a lot of respect for her work, and knew how much effort she put into it to make it good. In the last six months Hansen had tried to teach her as much as he could, as he had promised his old journalism school friend when he had pushed to take Andrews's protégée away from San Francisco. For her part, Mary had a great deal of affection for "old man Hansen" and had willingly absorbed what he had told her. Mary, who respected no one's judgment about her work but her own, had found that Irwin sometimes knew better.

In an incident that had actually changed Rick Worth's opinion of his new reporter, Mary and he were deadlocked over the length of one of her stories. "Inside the Shelter" was Mary's first investigative piece for Channel 3. It concerned a homeless boy, Johnny Faro, and the welfare system that cared for him. Mary had boiled the piece down to an intense twelve minutes and was furious when Rick had suggested that it was too long. After yelling, the producer and reporter refused to speak to each other again. Clint McCormick, executive producer for the news show, not knowing how to handle the situation, took it to Hansen. He, Mary, and Rick stood tensely in the editing room while Irwin screened the story without comment or perceptible reaction. At the end he rose out of his chair. "It's great," he said. "Run it as is, except for that fifty-five second conversation between the social worker and the lawyer. It's the kid's story. That slows it down." Hansen left the room. Carefully, Worth looked at Mary. "What do you think?" he asked. "He's right," Mary replied without hesitation, "I'll fix it." Worth had looked after her with grudging respect as she swept off with the tape. He had also liked the way his mentor Hansen had handled the situation. It was a lesson in problem solving he would remember.

"Sorry about that," Irwin said, as he replaced the receiver. "So, what are you working on today?"

"It's going to be a piece on the Board of Ed's decision to have AIDS awareness classes in grammar schools. I'm doing the interview between sessions at lunchtime."

"Good, good." Irwin leaned his elbows on the desk and clasped his hands together. "Listen, as you know by now, I don't go to these award ceremonies."

Mary nodded. She knew that the news director thought that a contest was not the way to judge news stories and so had not attended the Emmys for the previous nine years. "But even though I'm not making an exception in your case, I want you to know that I'm very proud of you, Mary. You have nominations in three different categories, I believe?"

"Four, actually," Mary said.

"I'm sorry, four. So, best interview, investigative report, writing, and the fourth?"

"Individual achievement," Mary supplied.

"I think this is a record, at least during my time here. Truly extraordinary." Irwin stood and held out his hand. "Listen, good luck tonight."

"Thanks, Irwin," Mary said, returning his handshake.

Mary left to go to the Board of Education ten miles away in downtown Los Angeles. At three forty-five she returned to the station and immediately went to the assignment desk where her producer on the piece was waiting.

"Okay," Mary said, handing her the tapes. "Take forty-five seconds on 'giving out condoms'—it's a minute-thirty into the interview." The producer nodded. "The guys against it, forty-five seconds, right from the top. Then, see if you can pull some file stuff of kids and also give me some of that parents' demo last week and put the sound bites on top."

"How long do you want it to run?"

"About three minutes. Oh, here." Mary gave the producer a piece of paper. "I wrote it all out for you here." She started to go.

"What about the narrative?"

"I'll come by editing in a half hour and lay down the track. Okay?"

"Sure." The producer walked off and Mary headed back to return calls and shape her narrative. First, though, she needed a Diet Coke. She grinned. After several years of doing all the work herself, Mary appreciated the expertise of the people who helped her at Channel 3. For every report she had a producer who did much of the drudgery, such as finding footage and supervising the editing, and a researcher, who worked on her stories, saving her yet more time. In addition, the camera crews knew what to do without her telling them, and she had a fully computerized library of stock footage and editors adept at fancy graphics at her fingertips. Now this was television, she thought, peeling back the aluminum tab on the can.

Jerry Radamacker pulled his parka tightly around him as he stepped out of his pickup truck. It was cold in December in Washington State. He walked toward an electronics store. A choir sang on the corner and Radamacker tossed them some loose change.

"I'd like the television and the VCR." He pointed out the items to the sales clerk. "Do you accept cash?"

The clerk nodded. "Wrap it with a ribbon or something," Radamacker said. He handed the clerk an envelope. "I think that covers it."

The clerk counted the bills. "I owe you a dollar ten," he said finally.

"Merry Christmas," Radamacker said, forcing a smile. "Can someone help me get the stuff into my truck?"

"Sure, I'll do it."

"Thanks. Oh, I just remembered, there's an important number on the envelope I gave you. Can I have it back?"

"Why, sure." Radamacker crushed the envelope in his

pocket and smiled. The envelope method was an excellent way to hand over cash without fingerprints.

They loaded the gifts into the truck, and Radamacker headed back to the little house on the edge of town where he had been hiding for six months. As he neared his mother's home, Radamacker saw two men get into a car and drive slowly down the street. His facial muscles twitched. He had a nose for cops. Mrs. Radamacker had been asking a lot of questions recently, mostly about how he had the money to buy a pickup truck and a lot of fancy video equipment. He had bought her the television in an effort to shut her up, but it seemed he was too late. Radamacker knew he had to get out. He turned the truck around, drove back through the small town, and down into Idaho. Sometime later, he stopped at a pay phone.

"Johnson?" he said. "Meet me in the usual place. I had to split. Bring a couple of sleeping bags. I'll explain later."

The Channel 3 table cheered loudly as Mary walked down from the stage at the Santa Monica Civic Center with her fourth Emmy. She threaded her way back to her table. She was sitting at a table, along with Rick Worth and his wife; Paul Gelson, producer of the six o'clock show and his wife; and reporter Tim Wallace and his girlfriend. At the last moment Mark had told her that he had to take a business trip that week. Mary had been hurt, but she bit back her disappointment, and invited Susan Schneider to come with her to the ceremony. Schneider was a producer of specials who had worked with her on a couple of pieces during the last six months; this invite would help keep Susan on her side.

"Hey, Mary, got anybody left to thank?" said Gelson as she returned.

"What are you going to do, Mary, melt them down?" Rick joked when she sat down at the table again, breathless from her walk. "This is becoming the Mary Reed show."

"And the winner is... Charles Davis," the announcer on stage said.

"Oh my God, fourth year running," Rick groaned. "It's the award for best anchor," he explained to his wife. "The man is going to be unbearable." He gave Charles a high five as he walked past their table. Davis was sitting at Channel 3's elite table, along with Tom Baker and his sales and publicity staff.

Later, as the evening broke up, Charles Davis came over to Mary. He towered over her. As Mary looked up, she noticed that the anchorman had kept on his makeup from the show. Even in a town where one became accustomed to physical perfection, Charles Davis, the living, breathing man, looked like an airbrushed *Interview* magazine cover.

"The first question is," Davis said in his deep tones, but leaning down toward her in a friendly way. "Why are you wasting yourself on the five o'clock show?"

"Why, Charles," said Mary, acting flirtatiously. "Most of my pieces run for at least four or five minutes and I know you can't stand to be off-camera for that length of time." She smiled knowingly up at him and batted her eyelashes with deliberate exaggeration.

Davis laughed and heads turned at his baritone chuckle. "You've got a point," he admitted. "But see here, Mary. Take a word of advice from an old hand. You're spreading yourself too thin with all these different awards. My one is worth more than your four put together. You know why?" Mary shook her head. "Because my award is for being a star." He grinned. "If you want to be anybody, take it from me, you let the writers write, producers produce, and the stars star."

"I always thought they twinkled," said Mary, looking up at him with a playful smile. "But thanks for the advice, Charles."

He bent down and put his mouth close to her ear. "And the second question is, do you have a ride home tonight?"

Mary wanted to raise her eyebrows: Charles Davis was coming on to her? This was something she definitely did not need. She indicated Susan, who was gathering her things together. "We have a car waiting for us outside, courtesy of my agent."

"That's E. J. Edwards, right?" asked Davis. He had stepped back from her and looked thoughtful.

"The same."

"I'll have to talk to him about all the attention he's giving you," Charles said. "He'll have no time left for me." Davis grinned, revealing two rows of perfect white teeth, and disappeared. Mary knew that the anchorman had been only half-joking, but she felt satisfied that he now knew that Mary Reed was on the map. She picked up her purse and led Susan out of the hall.

"Hey, E. J.," Charles Davis boomed into the speakerphone. "Did I wake you?" He had left the Santa Monica Civic Center, and now pointed his yellow Mercedes in the direction of his Brentwood home.

"Charles, don't you know by now, I never sleep?" Edwards was expecting the call, Davis always called him after the Emmys.

"I want the next Emmy I win to be a national one, E. J. Did you set up that meeting yet with the network fools?" Davis stretched out the vowels in the last word so that it rhymed with "jewels."

"We're getting there, Charlie. Probably next week."

"Good, because I'm getting tired of reporting the news." Although it would seem that Charles Davis, who was pulling in over a million dollars a year and was the undisputed king of Channel 3, had little to complain about, he was tired of the news treadmill he thought his life had become. He sensed that his quick wit, good looks, and sharp perceptions about people made him a natural talk-show host. Edwards was more cautious in his attitude, he did not want to lose money on one of his hottest clients.

"Don't knock the news, Charlie. Even if we get the talk-show deal, I want you to hang in there, cover your bets."

"But only for a while, right?"

The agent allowed himself a smile; who was Davis kidding? With a workday that started at four and ended at seven, the anchor had it made. "Don't sweat it, Charlie. There are other ways to lighten your load, trust me."

"So, you got the hots for Mary Reed?" Davis said, changing the subject. "Nice limo you gave her tonight."

"Forget it, Charlie. She's top-drawer material. There's no messing with her."

"Jesus, E. J. I just said it was a nice limo."

"I heard you. Charlie, do you want roses tomorrow for your award like the ones I'm going to send Mary?"

"No."

"Then, let's end this conversation, it's going nowhere." Edwards hung up.

Smiling, Davis walked through the garage into his two million-dollar bachelor's home. In the mail were a few bills and a letter from his daughter with pictures. Angela had moved back to Pittsburgh with her mother two years earlier. Grabbing a can of seltzer from the refrigerator, Davis headed for the den.

There, spread over a raised plywood base, which took up half the room, was an elaborate train set, complete with mountains and tunnels, bridges and farms, sidings and complicated intersections, a turntable, and stations. He pulled a switch on the transformer, and the many tiny bulbs placed in the miniature buildings, along the painted roads and in the Lilliputian depots, lit up.

The lamps around the room cast a dull glow upon the dark green walls lined with photographs, mostly of himself. Placing his fingers on the dials, Charles Davis became a child again, as the train set clicked and buzzed and hummed into life.

Mary walked through the front door of her house in the Hollywood Hills feeling happy but tired. She thought about calling her parents to let them know about the Emmys.

"Mary?" Her heart sank. Mark had got back a day earlier

than expected from his trip. She walked toward the door of the little room he used as an office. The television was on.

"Four Emmys, sweetheart. That's quite a coup."

"You watched it?"

"I got back early." He looked away. "Actually, I came back in time to go with you tonight." He paused. "I just couldn't face it, Mary." Mark held his head in his hands for a moment, then with a shrug he stood up and turned the television off. "I think I'd better go to bed now, before I say something I regret."

"Not so fast, tiger." Mary blocked the doorway. "What did you mean just now about not being able to face it? You can't say something like that and expect me to let it go." She flipped a switch, so that the room was flooded with bright light.

Mark blinked. "I said something stupid, okay?" he said. "And I'm sorry, I didn't mean it. But I'm tired—I've been on the road for four days—and I want to go to bed. Can we talk about this tomorrow?"

"Tomorrow never comes, remember?" Mary said angrily. "I think we should talk about this now. We haven't had a real conversation for a long time."

"Well that's not my fault."

"So, it's mine?"

"No, stop it, Mary. Let's go to bed. Please."

Mary's arms were crossed over her chest as she walked to the window. "It's the book, right? The police can't turn up a killer for Marvin Feld and the publisher cancels your book, so Mark Ashfield has been pissed off for a month. Listen, it happens, okay? This is real life. You just have to dust yourself down and find another project."

"Oh, spare me the advice, Mary. God! You should hear yourself. 'This is real life,'" he mimicked. "Listen, I am upset about the book, of course I am. I've spent six months working on the thing. Sure, I'm upset they canceled. But I'll get over it. No, what's far more worrying to me is what's happened to us over the last few months."

"It's because we're living in my house, isn't it?" Mary said. "You hate that."

"No, it's not the house I hate. It's what it represents."

"You mean E. J., right? You never did like him."

"Of course I mean E.J. The guy practically owns you, Mary."

"He's making me, Mark. Whatever happens, I'm going to be independent because of him."

"Oh, sure, Mary. Meanwhile the guy is taking your money and tying it up so you'll never leave him and, in addition, you're paying him for this house. Think about it, Mary. He lent you the money for the mortgage. What happens if you want to quit? You're on the street."

"I'm not quitting," Mary said coldly.

"Of course you're not, you can't!" Mark's eyes were blazing. "You never do anything without talking to this guy. He's not your agent, he's your oracle. God forbid you should cut your hair the way you like. No, E. J. has to be consulted. It's no fun anymore, Mary." Mark's voice was growing louder with every word.

"There's no need to yell," Mary said primly. Her bottom lip was trembling, but her back was stiff with anger.

"I don't know," Mark said more gently. Maybe I have a different perspective on all this. Because of my parents, I can afford to pursue a career I really enjoy, and take time off to do the things I like. It just seems to me, though, that you're getting in way too deep here." He paused. "You've changed, Mary. You're not the person I used to know. It's as if the more you achieve the more you have to achieve. Nothing satisfies you."

"Really?" said Mary. She was trying not to get pulled into the argument. Without being able to help herself, she pushed another button. "It's because I'm becoming better known, isn't it? Like the other week when you got upset because all those people came over to our table when we were having dinner."

Mark sighed deeply and, all at once, his fury subsided. "I

don't know, honey. I used to be so proud of what you do." He shook his head. "But something's happened. We used to do things, Mary. But now you're this television personality all the time, and we can't even go to dinner and leave her behind." He looked at her helplessly. "All I know is I didn't want to be with you tonight." His voice trailed off.

An uneasy silence fell between them. Mary felt tears welling in her eyes and, with an effort of will, she pushed them away. Her thoughts were so tangled she could not begin to unravel them. Suddenly, she felt too exhausted to even think.

Mark moved toward his desk and started tidying up his papers. "Listen, Mary," he said, turning around. "This isn't getting us anywhere. I think the best thing is that I move out. That will give us time to sort this whole mess out."

Mary looked at him helplessly. Part of her wanted to protest, but there was another voice in her head. "Remember, Mary, it's you, you, you," Edwards had said. "There can be no distractions. Show me you've got what it takes. You give me the next few years of your life and I'll give you everything you ever dreamed of."

"Good-bye, Mark," she said in a whisper. Without knowing how she did it, she walked slowly out of the room.

SEVENTEEN

EDDIE MARTINEZ HAD stared at the pamphlet he had found in Jim Wilkes's jacket pocket for several months before he turned it over and read what was written on the other side. Ever since he had established a link between the Presidio break in and the Goldor robbery, he had been stalled. Even his meeting with Mary Reed had not helped him much. She had offered him a description of the commander, he grinned when he thought about that—it was more than the feds had managed to get out of her. He had promised her that he would never reveal her name, but after that their meeting was cut short because she had to leave. The description could fit any number of people, he thought.

He had dismissed the pamphlet at first because it seemed

to be some religious rubbish, which he knew Wilkes would have laughed at sooner than read. However, as he read through it, he became curious. The first article was a doctrinal interpretation of the meaning of Armageddon, which was elaborate but standard in its tone. The second piece was far more militant, and contained racial and ethnic insults that made Martinez's blood boil. At the bottom was a post office box number, where the reader could send for more information. The address of the post office was Barstow, California. Martinez had walked out of his office and driven to Barstow.

That was several weeks ago. Now, as he sat in his car sucking on a grape juice, he saw a clergyman leave the post office. The articles had been written by someone who signed himself T. Taylor, Minister. Martinez hurried into the post office. Using his badge, he ascertained that the clergyman had picked up mail from the box number indicated in the pamphlet. Martinez ran out just in time to see the minister get into a beat-up car. He decided to follow him. They drove down the highway and into the desert. Two hours later the car disappeared down a track. Martinez followed a little way until he saw that beneath him in the valley a high wire mesh fence encircled several buildings, including a church which was built on top of a small hill. The minister unlocked the gates, and drove through. Martinez looked at his watch. It was six o'clock, he would be late for dinner again.

Tina Martinez covered the remains of dinner with aluminum foil, and washed up the dishes. Her son was upstairs doing his homework, her daughter had gone out for the evening with her fiancé. She sat down at the table and watched a game show she liked to play along with. Tina was a nurse at the local elementary school, and today she had had a grueling day of vaccinations. It felt good to sit down and take the weight off her feet.

When Martinez came in he found his wife slumped over the orange-and-white checkered tablecloth in the dining area of their kitchen. He moved quietly, warming up his dinner on the stove.

"Let me do that," Tina said, waking up and walking over to him.

"It's okay, you take it easy, mammy." He put a steaming plate of baked fish, rice, and black beans on the table, and sat down.

"I'll get you some iced tea," she said.

Martinez ate his dinner without talking. "Where have you been, Eduardo?" Tina asked. "I called the station. They said you left early in the afternoon."

"Had some business in Barstow," he said.

"What business?"

"Nothing important." He gave her a tired smile.

"It's that no-good Wilkes again, isn't it?"

He nodded. "So tell me about it," Tina said, sitting down heavily. "You never talk about your work no more."

"You wouldn't want to hear it," he said.

"Try, Eduardo, try. I need to know what's going on with you. You're my husband, not a visitor. We have to talk sometimes, right?"

"Okay." Martinez started to talk to his wife about the Wilkes murder. He was surprised how good it felt to talk, but though Tina was supportive he sensed her skepticism that anything would come of his investigation.

"Listen, my love, I know this is asking a lot of you," he said after he had finished. "But I was thinking in the car. I'd like to take a week off soon and watch that place in the desert. I know I'm onto something here."

Tina was incredulous. "Use your vacation time?" she said. "And there's so many things that need fixing around the house. Think what you could do with a week at home."

"I know, and I'm going to fix them all, Tina. I will," he said, seeing her disbelief. "I'll fix everything you want if you agree to this." He sighed. "I gotta find out what happened to Jim. I gotta do it, Tina." He looked at her pleadingly. There was a long silence.

"Okay, Eduardo, but one week is all," she said finally.

It was the day after the Emmy Awards and Irwin Hansen was in a good mood.

"Do you have the overnights yet?" he asked his secretary. The daily ratings were always Hansen's first item of business. Like report cards, they represented his success or failure as news director.

"Just came in," Margaret Lynch replied. "Oh, and Tom Baker's on the line."

Irwin's face fell. The last thing he wanted to deal with at nine in the morning was one of Baker's harebrained schemes.

"Irwin, greetings! I'm about fifteen minutes from the office." Hansen silently cursed the inventor of the cellular telephone. Baker had one in his car and another which he carried around with him. Hansen had often been surprised by a call when the station manager was watching his son play tennis or sitting in a restaurant with a client he found tedious.

"Clear the decks," Baker continued, "I've got a great idea."

"Really?" Irwin said. "Can't it wait till you get in?" The car phone cut out and Hansen put his own telephone down with relief. He had no curiosity about Baker's idea.

Hansen walked into the newsroom just as Mary strode in from the opposite direction looking, he thought, a little tired. As Mary reached the assignment desk the whole room burst into spontaneous applause for her Emmy sweep of the previous night.

"Way to go, Mare. Busted their nuts at Channel Seven." The writer of one of Mary's award-winning pieces congratulated her.

"Say, Mary?" Rick Worth said as she opened the door to her office. It was crammed with roses, mostly courtesy of Edwards.

"Yeah," she said, looking over her shoulder.

He walked toward her. "Why don't we do a piece on Edwards's flower budget? Probably feed an average family for a year, right?"

"Would you like me to put aside a few for you, Rick, so

you'll have them for the funeral when the weekly ratings come out tomorrow?" She took off her coat.

"Oooh, nasty, Mary, nasty." Rick pretended to cringe. He followed her into her office. "Did I see my friend Charles talking to you after the awards last night?"

"Whatever gave you that idea?"

"Just a feeling." Rick shrugged. "Listen, I know it's none of my business—"

"Right," Mary interrupted.

"But you know he's married, don't you?"

"Yes, Rick, I know."

"Just wanted to warn you, that's all." Worth stared absently at the wall. He was not quite sure why he had brought up the subject, and he felt uncharacteristically embarrassed.

"Well, gee, thanks, Rick, but rest assured I can take care of myself." She hung her coat on the back of the door. "Listen, I'm going to get a cup of coffee. Want one?"

"Sure." They walked out of her office together.

The newsroom suddenly fell silent as Tom Baker entered. It was not only the personal antipathy between Hansen and Baker that made the news division dislike Baker, although that certainly helped, it was also the classic divide between the station's revenue-producing arm and the lofty principles of news gathering.

"Hello, Margaret," Baker said sunnily as he sailed past her desk into Hansen's office and sat down on the Italian leather sofa.

"So, how are we going to save the station today, Tom?"

Hansen really made his skin crawl, Baker thought as he arranged the cuffs of his new suit the arms of which, he decided, were just a little too long. "Mary Reed," he said as if announcing her name at a ball.

"Mary Reed?" asked Hansen. "Is that the answer or the question?"

"She's been here six months now and she's done a first-rate job reporting. All those Emmys, Irwin, people love her. I think we should talk about making Mary co-anchor of the five o'clock this fall. She's been substituting for a while now and the research is first-rate. It's time to move old Amber on."

Amber Lyons had been co-anchor for the last five years, and had been at Channel 3 for fourteen years. She had started at age thirty-four reporting the weather, had moved on to become a features reporter, and eventually, she had been made co-anchor. Thanks mainly to the ingenuity of a plastic surgeon, Amber looked ten years younger than forty-eight, but she was no competition for Mary.

"Ratings are all right, but it's the demographics that have really changed over the years," said Hansen, thinking about the five o'clock show. "What do you propose doing with Amber?"

"Her contract has eight months to run. Put her on weekends until it expires and then, sayonara." Baker flourished his hand like a magician.

Hansen leaned forward. "That's what I like about you, Tom, you're all heart." Baker looked self-conscious. "You can't just dump Amber for a younger woman." Hansen paused. "Tell me, does the name Deborah Norville mean anything to you?" he asked sarcastically.

"Yeah, yeah, yeah." Hansen knew he had hit home. That was how Baker always responded when a plan of his was stymied. "So, okay, what would you do?"

Hansen was ready for the counterattack. "Listen, Tom. I agree with you about Mary. She'll do wonders for the five, which will help the six, which will help us all."

Baker was surprised, it was clear that Hansen had already thought about this topic. He raised his eyebrows.

Hansen thought fast. He happened to know that Amber Lyons was ready to quit the news and fulfill her aspirations for a syndicated talk show. The money and control that Oprah Winfrey enjoyed with her show had made a lot of people in the industry think about syndication. "As for Amber," he said after a moment, "let's develop a morning talk show for her. She'd be terrific and our daytime schedule has one less game show. If it works, we're geniuses; if not, she'll be gone in eight months."

"Sounds fine to me, but how do we get her to go for it?"

Hansen loved being in control. "I think I can persuade her to do this," he said, "but only if we offer her a percentage of the show. Her agent'll like that. If we guarantee to run the show here, they might just gamble."

"Good, good, I like it. Let's do it."

"One thing, Tom. You can't screw me on this. No backsliding when New York tells you how cheap game shows are. If we're going to do this, we've got to make sure that Amber feels good."

"Irwin, I hear you." Baker stood up and shook his leg so that the trouser fabric fell smoothly from his Gucci belt to his Gucci loafers. "So, let's arrange lunch with Edwards to set up the Reed deal first. You think he'll have any problems?"

The news director sat back. His pale eyes stared at Baker from behind his glasses. He looked wise and a little weary. "Are you kidding?" he said. "She'll be a co-anchor at twenty-six. He'll be very happy."

E. J. Edwards lunched at the Grill in Beverly Hills practically every day. He always sat in the front booth, so that he could watch everyone as they entered the restaurant. Many people nodded at the famous agent, and several stopped to chat for a couple of minutes. If no one was joining him, Edwards had no difficulty in picking out an amusing or profitable lunch companion. Regulars at the Grill included a lot of other agents since both CAA and the William Morris agency had offices nearby. There were also a growing number of entertainment lawyers, attorneys who were retained by stars in addition to their agents and business managers. Although Edwards was a lawyer, a qualification he believed was essential for his job, he hated the way it was currently fashionable to hire a lawyer on a deal, in addition to having a business manager and an agent. He recognized it as the paranoia of

Hollywood, but in the end, he thought, these slick Century City types ruined more deals than they ever made.

Edwards was absently picking at the bread and sipping an iced tea when he caught sight of Tom Baker and Irwin Hansen threading their way past the bar into the restaurant. Baker, sporting a pale yellow seersucker suit, white fedora, and cherrywood walking stick, led the stoop-shouldered Hansen to Edwards's table. To Edwards this odd twosome was a matched pair, combined they represented the voice of Channel 3. He got up and greeted each man with the affectionate hug that was his trademark.

Baker ordered a gin and tonic while Hansen, who privately viewed any drink with an *and* in it with mistrust, had his first Dewars on the rocks.

Baker put his elbow on the table and lowered his head in the agent's direction. "E. J.," he said in a deep, confiding voice that alerted the sharp-witted Edwards that something was brewing. "We've got an idea. A great idea." Baker's strategy was to sell the agent on his idea, leaving it to him to convince his client of its soundness. "We want to make an anchor out of Mary Reed."

Baker and Hansen independently scrutinized Edwards's face for a reaction; they were both disappointed. Like the good poker player he was, Edwards gave nothing away. "Oh," was all he said.

"Yes, we want her to anchor the five o'clock show instead of Amber. It'll help the five, but more importantly"—Baker leaned toward Edwards in a confiding manner—"it'll give Charles Davis a better lead-in for the six."

Edwards did not respond immediately. He took a sip of his iced tea. "Irwin," he said, putting down the glass. "You've been rather quiet. What do you think?"

Hansen swallowed his scotch. "I'm behind it. I think she's ready."

Edwards paused, savoring the power of having these men anxiously wait for his slightest reaction. "Let me ask you," he said neutrally. "What happens to Amber?" Edwards did not care about Amber Lyons. After all, he did not represent her, but he was well aware that her fate could have an impact on his client.

Baker, coached by his earlier conversation with Hansen, was ready. "Hey, we're not aiming to get into any ugly situations here. We'll offer her a morning talk show and the option to syndicate if it works." Baker was lordly and self-satisfied. He felt he had all the answers. Irwin kept his mouth shut and looked down at his second scotch.

"Gentlemen, let's order," said Edwards, summoning a waiter. Edwards did not actually order, which meant there would be no variation in his usual menu of a well-done chopped steak and salad with Russian dressing. Baker, ever trendy, ordered yellowtail tuna and Hansen chose something he knew he would regret but could not resist, a steak sandwich and onion rings.

After the waiter left with their orders, Edwards looked each man in the eye without speaking. "Well, guys," he finally said, "you are too much. Mary Reed is the hottest ticket in local television and you people want to use her on the five o'clock show. You must be joking."

Hansen quickly caught Baker's eye. This was not what they were expecting.

"Mary is no lounge act," the agent continued. "She doesn't do warm-ups, not even for Charles Davis." He looked coldly at each man, then smiled. "If you want to make Mary an anchor—an idea I endorse, by the way—team her up with Davis on the six o'clock."

Baker was taking a sip of mineral water and he spluttered into his drink. Edwards and Hansen pretended not to notice. Ever since he had become station manager two years earlier, Tom Baker had wanted a co-anchor for Davis. Hansen, too, felt they should attract the women that the demographics told him they were losing at that time. In addition, he was dreading the moment he knew would come, when Davis would tell Channel 3 that he was going to quit the news program to do his coveted talk show, leaving them without anybody for the six o'clock news. The stumbling block had always been the same: Davis's contract stipulated, without any ambiguity, that Davis was to be the sole anchor on the six o'clock news. This contract had been negotiated by his agent, Edwards, the same man who was sitting with them at lunch and was telling them that Reed should co-anchor with Davis. Baker dabbed at his chin with a napkin.

Hansen recovered more speedily than his boss. "I think that's a terrific idea. I'd do it tomorrow. But do you want to tell Charles or shall I have Tom do it?"

Edwards grinned. "I know you are both aware that for some time now I've been negotiating with the network for a late-night talk show for Charles Davis, who would be a natural for it. I met with them last week as a matter of fact and we're getting pretty close to a deal. Now, I want Charles to stay on the news while the talk show develops, but I don't think he should be carrying it alone. Reed and Davis—excuse me—Davis and Reed, are a great team. I think so and so does Charles. He has already told me that if the co-anchor is announced in tandem with the talk show, he is behind it one thousand percent." With that, Edwards cut into his steak.

"Mmm," said Baker, who had a mouth full of food. Hansen wished he could speak to Baker in private. He was not sure the man was on top of the situation.

Edwards sat back. "This is the way we do it. Tom," he said, turning to Baker, who looked at him expectantly, "you can call New York. Ask the network boys to give us the green light on the Charles Davis show." The agent looked at Baker straight in the eye.

"Yeah," said Baker. Hansen thought he looked mesmerized. "Well, I don't run the network, as you know," he said.

"Tom, Tom, Tom. You people in L.A. are responsible for about thirty percent of their profits. I'm sure I don't have to remind you of that. You call the tune, they'll dance, believe me. You're the guys making the profits now. Times have changed."

The idea that a man like Tom Baker could dictate network policy and programming disgusted Hansen. However, in this instance, both he and Baker were pawns in Edwards's game. The agent was using the co-anchor spot to pressure the network into giving Davis his show. Since Mary was the only co-anchor Davis would accept, Edwards had it all ways, promoting two of his clients in one beautifully coordinated move. In this instance, Hansen did not mind his role as a pawn: the prospect of Davis and Reed at six was magic to him.

"E. J.," Baker said, his voice tight with puffed-up vanity. "I'm going to do it." He looked at Hansen, who opened his eyes wide in an effort to communicate to Baker that he should slow down. "I'll call you later this afternoon at the earliest, tomorrow morning latest. I think we have a deal that makes sense."

Hansen thought that Baker had given in too easily, he should have put up more of a fight. Still, Baker was his boss so he sat still and nodded his agreement when Edwards looked over at him.

"Well, since we're this far along, I'd like you to know that I'd like to bring Mary's salary up to seven fifty for the first year, then we'll tie it to the numbers for years two and three. I'll thrash out the terms with your businesspeople."

"Be easy on me, E. J.," Baker said. "Don't play Jesse James."

"I won't." Edwards nodded. "Okay, guys, let's order some coffee," the agent said with a smile.

"There's one thing," Hansen said. He looked at Baker. "Tom and I have also discussed replacing Paul Gelson with Rick Worth—he's currently producing the five o'clock. A far better choice if there are to be two anchors. You know, it's a different ball game, more complicated. I think Rick would do a super job." Irwin wished he had been given a chance to get this in before Baker had so precipitously acquiesced, he might have had a chance of making it happen.

"Sorry, Irwin. I know your man Rick and I like him. He's got talent, but I know Charles wants to stay with Paul. They go back."

Hansen nodded. Sure Gelson and Davis went back. He was only Davis's third producer in four years at Channel 3, but he had lasted the longest, over two years. Davis was known to eat his producers for breakfast, terrifying them with his ad-libs and his nonchalant attitude toward work.

A waiter stood by the table and smiled. "Dessert, gentlemen?" he asked brightly.

Tony Caban walked into the little store, whistling the theme from *Deliverance*, which he had just seen in the movie house. He put down a one hundred dollar bill.

"Gimme a lotto ticket."

"You're the same 'un came in yesterday with a fifty note," the old man grumbled. "What do you think I am, a bank?" It was cold in the store, and the old man wore a wool vest under his windbreaker, and a handknit scarf around his neck.

"You want to sell me a lotto ticket, mister," Caban said nastily. He reached across the counter and seized the ends of the woollen scarf, dragging the old man's head toward the counter. "Or do you have a problem?"

"Take the ticket," the storekeeper said, struggling for breath. Caban let go. "I'm just going to have to go back and get some change for you," he continued, rubbing his neck with his fingers. "I don't keep that kind of money in the till these days. You never know who's going to walk in." As he spoke he edged sideways behind the counter, then he disappeared through a door at the back.

"Took your time," Caban said when he came back a few minutes later. He folded his change and the notes in his pocket. "Wish me luck, old man," he said, waving the lotto ticket. The door slammed.

The storekeeper leaned over the dusty boxes of toys in the window and pressed his nose to the glass. He was still watching when an unmarked car pulled up at the curb, and two police officers stepped out.

Two days later Caban sat in a cell at the Boise police station. He had not eaten since he had arrived, and his head felt clear and light. A warden appeared at the gate, and started unlocking the door. "There's some people want to talk to you," he said. He led the handcuffed man into a small room with a table and three chairs.

Sly Rigby and Frank Carson entered the room. The federal agents had just flown down from Spokane after an abortive mission in Timber Falls, Washington. After months of dead ends, the FBI had been very excited when they had got two breaks in a quick succession on the Zero case. The first was when they had busted the safehouse where the interview had taken place. The second had come from an unexpected quarter. A Mrs. Radamacker from Timber Falls, Washington, had contacted her sheriff's office with a suitcase of money. She said she had found the money in her son's bedroom. When the bills were traced to the Goldor robbery, Rigby had received a call. The FBI had surrounded the house only to discover that Radamacker had fled. They had hit yet another dead end.

Because of the things they knew about Zero and his like-minded friends, Carson had instructed Begay to stay out of the little room where they were going to talk to Tony Caban. They had a complicated mission, and they badly needed to get lucky. Smarting from Zero's close escape, the feds were looking for all the luck they could find.

Neither Carson nor Rigby sat down. "Three days ago," Rigby began, "you used a fifty dollar bill to purchase a fifty cent lotto ticket. This bill has been traced to a robbery that happened in May. The hundred dollar note you used two days ago has been established as a counterfeit. You're looking at a lot of time, Tony," he said.

Caban stared straight ahead. Radamacker had prepared him for a situation like this. He would be protected, they would release him on bail, and then he'd go into hiding with the Brotherhood. "I want a lawyer," he said. "I know my rights."

Carson sat on the metal table. "You're in a lot of trouble, Caban. You might think you can run, but we'll catch up with you. Before I leave you to call a lawyer, I want you to think about something. Promise me you'll think about it." Caban stared stonily ahead.

"There is another alternative," Carson continued, "and I think you might want to consider it. We can indict you and you can go to jail. You know we're going to come down on you hard, don't you Tony?" Carson thumped his fist on the metal table. "Or," he added softly, "there's the other option, the one where you tell us all you know about the Goldor robbery, and in return we will grant you immunity and protection."

"Protection?" Caban sneered. "You guys couldn't protect a can of tuna. Now let me talk to a lawyer. What you're doing is illegal."

"Okay, Tony. Talk to a lawyer. Tell him about the wife you married a couple of months ago. And the nice house and car you bought. Maybe you want to keep them, maybe this is your chance to protect them. Think about it," Carson advised as he stood to leave. "Think a lot. And we'll be back tomorrow for another nice friendly little chat."

Carson opened the door. He turned back. "Oh, and Tony," he said, "I hear this wife of yours is pregnant. Isn't that nice? You want your little boy growing up knowing his daddy is in jail? Be a shame, wouldn't it?"

Tony Caban held out for three days, then he accepted the deal. He implicated Radamacker in the Goldor robbery, and he told them about the Aryan Crusaders' camp in the Idaho mountains where he had seen Radamacker days earlier. Every now and then during his testimony, Caban's face would whiten with fear. "You're going to protect me, right?" he would ask. "Because you don't know what this man can do. You don't know anything."

EIGHTEEN

THE AIR SMELLED clean and cold, and the ground was lacey with frost as Sly Rigby and Ed Begay drove toward the Idaho National Guard Base in Boise.

"Wonder if we'll ever know what happened to Casey?" Begay mused. The FBI had just called off their search for the missing master sergeant.

"Probably not," Rigby responded. "I just hope we get Commander Zero before I retire." Rigby, nearing the end of his career with the bureau, thought longingly of his lakeside house in Northern California. He planned to retire up there, set up a fishing store. At that moment nothing seemed more pleasurable than talking about tackle and bait six days a week.

They pulled up at the base and flashed their identification. "So, let's nail this bastard," Rigby said as they drove through.

As directed, Rigby pulled his car onto the tarmac. When he got out the smell of kerosene burned in his nostrils.

"Over there." He pointed at a small building.

"What?" Begay asked. Rigby beckoned for him to follow. It was little use trying to yell over the earsplitting din of the fighter jet engines. The two agents made their way to the ready room.

"We're looking for Major Somers." Rigby said to the roomful of pilots.

"That'll be me," said a lean man in his forties, coming over to them. He was wearing an olive drab pressure suit. Somers held out his hand. "So you want us to take some pictures for you?"

Rigby felt out of place in his dark suit. "Yes," he said, trying to sound assertive. "Have a lead that someone we're looking for is hiding out in the mountains. Want to get the lay of the land before we go in." He found himself clipping his sentences, military-style, in front of the pilot.

Somers had flown Wild Weasel Thuds, or antiradar planes, in Vietnam. His task was to jam or destroy enemy radar ahead of a mission. After the war he became a commercial pilot and in his spare time he volunteered for the Idaho National Guard, so he could fly the machines he had come to love. His unit, composed of men of similar backgrounds and experience, had been flown out to the Persian Gulf during the brief war with Iraq. There they had taken laconic pride in beating the pants off of the twenty-five-year-old Air Force aces.

"Always glad to cooperate with the FBI," said Somers. Rigby could not tell if he was being sarcastic. He handed the pilot a map of the region. Tucked in a valley was the location of one of the Aryan Crusaders' camps where, Caban had informed them, Commander Zero was currently hiding. Rigby had marked the spot on the map.

"Best take two planes, looks like a normal pass that way.

Don't want to alert the target." He looked over his shoulder. "Captain Koller?" A second pilot joined the group. "Be back at thirteen hundred hours." He nodded at the two agents.

"Wait a minute. I thought, well, I thought maybe we could come along, get a look ourselves," said Rigby.

Somers stopped and appraised the two men with a hard stare. "Sure," he said finally. "Take you along for the ride, it'll be a nice, easy one." He gave a wide grin and winked at Koller. "Better get these gibs some speed slacks," he said, referring to the pressure suits they wore. Gib was an acronym for "guy in back."

Dressed in boots and suits and with helmets in their hands, Rigby and Begay stepped out of the building and onto the airstrip. Rigby picked out at least twenty-five Phantom jets lined up like droop-winged bats.

"Doesn't the noise bother you?" Begay *shouted*.

"What noise?" Somers *yelled*.

"The roar of jets is the sound of freedom," Koller added. The two men raised one hand and slapped their palms together in a well-rehearsed ritual.

Begay and Rigby exchanged glances. Both were having second thoughts about their little jaunt.

Rigby and Begay each slid into the cramped cabins of an R-F4 Phantom IIs. These were reconnaissance planes, popularly known as rhinos because the infrared cameras in their noses gave them a bulbous look. Sly could barely move and he seemed to be sitting on a rock. "You see this button," Somers said, leaning over and pointing to a black-and-yellow button on Rigby's right. "Now don't go pressing that baby unless you want to go flying up into the four hundred mile slipstream." He grinned. "Okay, let's do some yanking and banking," he said. If the agent wondered what that meant, he was soon to find out.

Rigby definitely regretted his request to accompany the pilots as the fighter plane took off and sped through the sky. As he strained to see something through the tiny windows on either side of him, the plane tilted at a 90 degree angle and dropped like a stone toward the earth. Five hundred feet above the ground, Somers rolled the jet on its back. "Thought I'd give you a better view," he said. At least, that's what Rigby thought the pilot said as his stomach hit his mouth and his head banged against the side of the cockpit. The Phantom was hurtling through the air at four hundred miles an hour upside down. Rigby could have done without a better view. The plane straightened, skimming over buildings, and the agent realized that they were nearing their target. As they reached the valley end beyond the buildings, Somers executed an aileron turn, rotating the plane 360 degrees in one second, as Rigby's head bounced from one side of the tiny cockpit to the other. Soon they were heading back to the base. As they landed, Rigby felt his stomach heave again, and the blood pounded behind his eyes and ears. He staggered onto the tarmac.

"Well, thanks for flying with the Idaho National Guard," said Somers with a wry grin. "Should have those pictures for you real soon."

Rigby and Begay walked shakily back to their car. The gravitational force had broken blood vessels in their eyes, giving them a ghoulish look.

"So, what did you think?" asked Begay, wondering if he looked as bad as his partner.

Rigby squared his shoulders. "The roar of jets is the sound of freedom," he said, imitating Killer's flat midwestern vowels. They both laughed.

"You see that?" Radamacker asked Finn Johnson.

"Sure, two fighter planes. We get a lot of those around here. It's the National Guard."

Radamacker's eyes narrowed. "You got to pay attention, Johnson. Those were two reconnaissance planes. Now why would they take planes from two different squadrons? And you notice they came over here straight and level, then they started fooling around. We got to get out of here."

"Yeah?"

"Yeah," Radamacker replied. He turned to Finn. "Someone has betrayed me, Johnson. There's only a few people who know about this place. We've got to be careful, real careful. The feds must've got to some of the AC-DC bunch," he said, referring to Bleech's Aryan Crusaders. "They must've told them about this camp. I'm beginning to feel like I know these guys who are tailing us, they move like a herd of fucking elephants. But they haven't touched the compound yet. Spoke to Taylor last week, says it's been real quiet down there. We're going back, Johnson, and we're going to continue our work. You got it?"

"Yeah," Finn said, "they're not going to stop us."

Mary was concerned. "I can't read this piece," she complained, waving her script at Rick Worth, who she had managed to track down in Davis's office fifteen minutes before the five o'clock show. She pulled him into the corridor. "It's horribly written and it's the lead story."

"Hey, don't sweat it," Rick said. "The important thing about anchoring is to develop a style of your own, then you can read anything and it will sound sort of the same, whoever wrote it."

Mary did not look reassured. "Sure, but, Rick, listen to this moronic first sentence: 'The president said today that the economic situation must be fixed before the tax situation can be addressed.' "

"Tell me how you would write it."

Mary started to get out her pen. "No, just say it," Rick said.

"Okay." Mary cleared her throat. "The president said today that nothing will be done about taxes until the economy recovers."

"Great, now go back to the original and read it as if you were reading what you just said."

She started. "Right," she said, reading it. "Okay, I've got it. If I stress *before* then I get the meaning across, and then I have to punch the big words—*taxes* and *economy*. Thanks, Rick."

"Watch Charles sometime, he's a real master at this."

Mary was remembering this conversation as she sat rather nervously in Channel 3's news studio on the ground floor.

"Bring the barn door down on the overhead light, will you? And, goddamn it, move camera three out of camera two's site!" yelled the director, Julian Phillips. He handled all technical aspects of the program. During the show he sat in the control room, but for the set up he ran between the studio and the control room, aiming for perfection and falling not very far short of it.

It was four on Sunday afternoon and in half an hour they were going to have a full rehearsal, meaning makeup, lights, and cameras, for the six o'clock news, which Mary and Davis were to co-anchor for the first time on Monday. Excitement at the station was running high, and full-page ads for the new Davis-Reed show had been taken out in newspapers for the following day.

When she had heard about the rehearsal, Mary had asked the perpetually anxious six o'clock producer, Paul Gelson, if she should get to the station at noon. Gelson was taken by surprise since he had grown used to Charles Davis's lackadaisical work habits; he hesitantly suggested that two would be fine. Mary had arrived, been made-up and had spent time getting comfortable with the new set and studying the script.

She looked up. The lights were growing hotter, and she could feel her makeup streaking. Her hair, damp with sweat, clung to her face, while her heart seemed to be racing. Suddenly, the new co-anchor felt sick to her stomach, she would rather be anywhere but where she was, sitting on an uncomfortable chair in Channel 3's news studio. She had never felt that anchoring was her main strength, she was much happier identifying herself as a reporter. There was something dumb about sitting here and parroting other people's words. Mary was also anxious about her co-anchor. Charles Davis might be brilliant, but unlike the placid Des Westin on the five o'clock show, Davis was famous for his mood swings, and for playing favorites. In Charles's mind, you were either for him or against him, it was very simple. Mary was not yet sure where she fit into his scheme. She had also heard about his notorious ad-libbing that kept the control room in a constant state of panic for large portions of the show. No wonder Gelson always looked so worried.

Mary looked at her watch. It was four-fifteen. Well, perhaps Davis would not show up, she thought. Mary jumped from her chair and left the studio in search of a drink of water and space to calm down. Maybe she should call E. J., he would cheer her up.

She walked out of the studio and past the control room, which was on the other side of the corridor. Paul Gelson emerged with a sheaf of paper in his hands. "Oh, Mary, just the person . . . your piece about the gangs, it's been moved. It's now going to come after the mayor's speech." There were beads of sweat on Gelson's forehead.

"But that means I'll be doing three pieces in a row," Mary objected.

Gelson looked up at her in wonder. She did not have her script with her, so she must have memorized it, he figured. "Yes, well, that's right as a matter of fact. Maybe we should think about changing it." He gave her a nervous smile.

Mary drank two cups of water and was making her way back to the studio when she saw Davis strolling down the corridor in the other direction. He was dressed in his usual impeccably pressed white shirt, blue blazer, red silk tie, matching red silk handkerchief along with a beat-up pair of white jeans that would not show on camera.

"Good afternoon, people. How good of all us to devote our Sunday afternoons to the great cause of journalism." Hearing Charles's voice, Gelson darted into the studio and ordered the makeup woman to tend to Davis on set, and handed him the script.

Davis, enjoying the attention his late entrance had

caused, barely looked at the producer. "Thanks, Paul. Hey, Barry," he said to the floor manager. "Did you see Robin Williams on the "Tonight Show" on Friday?"

"Not so thick," he advised the makeup woman. "Make me look like thirty, not like Michael Jackson." He beamed at Mary. Davis had not wanted to do the rehearsal but Edwards had persuaded him that if the papers picked up on the story, it would look like he did not want Mary as his co-anchor. Nothing could have been further from the truth, Davis was delighted to ease his workload. He got up as the makeup woman was dusting his face with powder, and pulled off the bib she had put around him. He went over to Mary and kissed her on the cheek. "Welcome," he said, "to my humble abode," and he whispered something in her ear. Mary, for all her usual quick wits, was still tense and his comment made her blush.

In the control room, the director counted down. "Eight, seven, six . . ." and the rehearsal started. As Mary read her lead-ins and stories, she grew more and more confident that this was something she could not only handle, but enjoy doing. She started to notice the rest of the world.

"So, Bill, what about those Rams?"

The floor director was frantically cuing Davis to get on with the lead-in to his report, but the anchor had ignored him. His ten-second lead-in had turned into an two-minute impromptu talk with his friend, sportscaster Bill Bryson.

"Well, Charles, they've had a lot of bad luck this season."

"Are they going to fire their coach?"

Bryson instinctively took an opposing position, one reason their on-air banter worked so well. *"Well, he's had a lot of injuries, Charles."*

"But, come on now. This guy's been around a long time. There's been some good times, they're not going to throw him out now when there's been a run of bad luck . . . ?"

In the control room, a collective sigh of relief was heaved when Davis finally read the lead-in. Gelson pushed the numbered button that connected him to microphones in the ears of both anchors. "After this piece," he said, "go to page twenty-four. This is your story, Mary."

Mary read the script, but Gelson had not made it clear to his director that he had skipped a story in order to compensate for the time Davis had taken to do his lead-in, so Phillips had not cued the tape.

"Here is Tim Wallace reporting to us from east L.A." Mary blinked as the monitor in front of her showed black.

Davis stood up. The studio door opened and Gelson rushed in. "Look, Charles," he said, seeing Davis had risen. "Let's go beyond five-thirty tonight. There are some things we've go to sort out."

"Not on your life, Paul," Davis said angrily.

The producer looked at Mary. She tried to lighten the atmosphere. "Well, I guess you're back to a single anchor," she said. "Me!" She forced a laugh.

Davis was grim. "Listen, it's five-twenty, this rehearsal is over." He unhooked his mike and put it on the desk. "Thanks, everybody, for coming in. See you all tomorrow. And, remember," he said, as he strolled toward the door. "Tomorrow it will be good, and it will be for real." The technicians started to clean up, knowing that Gelson had no authority over Davis.

Charles climbed into his yellow Mercedes and turned out of the parking lot. He picked up his cellular telephone and punched Edwards's number on his speed dial.

"Hey, listen, the rehearsal was a disaster. . . . What . . . no, no, no. Reed is a pistol, but Gelson's got to go. . . . Yes, I know, I wanted to hang on to him because he was easy, but that era has passed. . . . He can't handle a two-anchor show, didn't even have us talking to each other. . . ."

"Oh, Rick, it was awful." Mary was sitting in her office the next morning, drinking coffee with Rick Worth. "Gelson has no idea."

"Really?" said Worth. He had little respect for the man,

but it was interesting to hear from Mary how bad the six o'clock producer was.

"I mean he doesn't seem to be aware that times have changed. He only ordered five graphics." Mary rolled her eyes.

"What did he do the rest of the time?"

"Nada, we just read the piece cold, no nothing, just us. Oh, and even with the graphics he got, he messed up. I read a whole story about the mayor's speech with a picture of the president over my shoulder. Believe me, it was pitiful."

Mary stared out of the window. Before substituting as an anchor on the five o'clock news she had had little interest in what Rick liked to call the "gestalt" of a good news program, where the show had a rhythm which was greater than the sum of its parts. As a reporter, she had simply been interested in getting as much airtime as prominently as she could. Rick had taught her what a producer could contribute. He showed her, for instance, how to avoid predictability by mixing pieces of greater and lesser length. When she asked why he had headlines in the middle of the show, he replied that this "stacked" the show better, giving the second half a stronger, newsy feel. These long conversations about television had led her, over time, to respect his professional instincts unhesitatingly.

"What about the pacing, I would have thought just having the two of you together would bring up the heat a little?"

"Oh, God, that reminds me," Mary said, giggling, "that's what Charles said to me when he came in. He whispered that we should look like we're having an affair."

"Bad idea in reality," said Rick. "Good television. Did you get to talk to each other?"

Mary shook her head.

"What a waste of on-air talent," Rick said. "So the five o'clock still has a chance to catch up with you guys?"

"Oh, don't joke," said Mary. "I am so depressed. This show is going to be the biggest nonevent ever." She rested her forehead against the palms of her hands.

"Rick?" The door to Mary's office was pushed open and

Clint McCormick, the news division's orderly but ineffective executive producer, stood in the doorway. He beckoned Worth to come out. "Hansen wants you, me, and Gelson in his office now," he said in a low voice when they were both standing in the corridor. McCormick scurried away. Rick scratched his head.

"Hey, guys, so what's up?" Worth joined Gelson and the executive producer, who were standing around Margaret Lynch's desk. Hansen's office door was closed. Nobody answered. Rick winked at Margaret, who smiled at the young producer. After a few more minutes, Hansen buzzed Margaret and she waved them into the news director's office. Rick was surprised to see that Tom Baker was there. Something big was up.

The three men sat on chairs facing Hansen's desk while Baker paced around the room.

"Gentlemen," Hansen said. "I'll make this short and to the point. Starting tonight, we've decided to make Rick producer of the six o'clock show, Paul you'll do the five."

Rick could barely contain his excitement. He knew that the Davis-Reed team, handled right, was dynamite, and would put him at the top of the Los Angeles news world. His mind raced, this should also mean more money, perhaps fifty thousand, he figured rapidly. And, he would be working with his two pals, Charles and Mary.

"But, Irwin," Gelson was saying, "I rehearsed the dual anchor. I want to take a shot at it."

"Paul, this meeting is over," said Hansen, rising out of his chair. "My mind is made up. You can try the dual at five."

"What about the writers?" asked McCormick.

It was a good point. Hansen had not thought about the writers, but he came up with a solution. "They also switch. The whole team will switch, producer and writers together," he said decisively.

Gelson's face fell still further. He made his way out of the office, his shoulders bowed as he absorbed the full impact of his humiliation. Even his writers were going to be demoted.

Their fees would drop and they would lose the overtime they often got for cutting spots for the network's national morning show. He tried to pull himself together before he had to talk to his team.

Rick looked at his departing back; he knew that Gelson was a dead man. It might take weeks, maybe months, but Gelson was gone.

"Mr. Baker?" Margaret Lynch called out. "It's Michael Hartley." Baker, who had been talking to Hansen, jumped up. Hartley was his boss, the network vice-president in New York who was in charge of owned and operated stations, or O and Os as they were called. He took the call in the office next to Hansen.

"Rick," said Hansen, as Worth started to leave. "I am very happy this could work out. For some time now I've wanted it for you. You've done a great job at five and I know you're ready to handle the challenge." He beamed at Worth.

"Thanks, Irwin. It's going to be terrific, trust me."

"I do, Rick, that's what this is all about."

"Listen, I was wondering, should I talk to Charles and Mary about this?"

"Good idea. Set up a conference call, why don't you?" Hansen paused and looked at Rick. "By the way, Charles already knows about it," he said.

"Oh, right." Rick was not surprised to learn that Davis was calling the shots, he was still the station's kingmaker. It was useful, however, to know these things.

Baker came back into the office, rubbing his hands. "Davis, Reed, and Worth—the dream team," he said gleefully.

Rick and Irwin exchanged amused glances. "Hey, relax, Tom, I already got the job," Worth said.

"Then, what are you hanging around for?"

As they walked down the corridor, Baker put his hand on the younger man's shoulder. "We'll draw you up a new contract by the end of the week, Rick. This will mean a substantial raise, you know."

"With two kids it won't hurt," said Rick.

"No, of course not." Baker smiled. He stopped walking and leaned toward Worth. "Make the six o'clock a success, Rick, and I can see you as Channel Three's youngest news director ever." With a knowing wink, Baker headed off through the newsroom and back to his office in the other building.

Rick's head spun. The station chief was always full of hype, and Irwin Hansen was his leader and his mentor; but still, the idea of eventually replacing him was not altogether unattractive to the new producer of the six o'clock news.

Detective Eddie Martinez parked his car in the scrub so that it was only visible to a very searching eye, and climbed the hill above it. Just below the summit was a small indentation and here Martinez laid his backpack and sat down. He poured himself a cup of the sweet, milky coffee his wife brewed for him each morning and pulled a pair of binoculars from his pocket. Raising his head above the top of the hill, he trained the glasses on a complex of buildings on the valley floor. Satisfied that nothing unusual was going on, he took a gulp of the coffee.

This was Martinez's fifth day at the top of the hill and his time had nearly run out. Five days earlier the detective had seen the clergyman again. This time he had arrived at the post office in Barstow with a companion, who walked into a nearby hardware store. Martinez seized his chance.

"Is this one of your pamphlets?" he asked the clergyman as he walked out of the post office. He held the photocopy out.

"Why yes," said Thomas Taylor. "As a matter of fact it is. Why do you ask?"

"Do you know this man?" Martinez asked, showing the man a picture of Jim Wilkes.

The clergyman looked nervous. He licked his lips.

"This man bothering you, minister?" Finn Johnson returned from the hardware store. He held an ice-cream cone in his hand.

"Why, no, brother. He's just from the post office. Wanted to tell me about a letter which came in today." The clergyman had looked hard at Martinez, it was clear he was afraid of the man he had called brother.

Martinez had nodded and walked into the post office. From the window, he watched the two men drive off and after a few minutes he followed them. That was when he had decided to start his hillside vigil. For when he visited the compound a second time, he saw that things had changed. There were more men walking around, and several guards now stood at the gate.

It was late afternoon and Martinez was preparing to leave. He had one more day. The work of a detective requires a type of vigilance that is exhausting. More than once Martinez had been sorely tempted to call off his search into the cause of his late partner's death. As the sun sank lower, the detective took a last look through his binoculars. He was convinced that if he could get the clergyman alone, he could learn something from the man.

Radamacker walked into a motel on the outskirts of Boise, Idaho. He and Finn had left the mountain camp four days before it was raided by the feds. Radamacker had cleaned it up, and the disgruntled agents had found nothing but a few cases of vitamin tablets and some counterfeit money. They had run back to the desert compound and Radamacker had "reactivated" his most loyal supporters. However, when he had heard that Tony Caban wanted to speak with him, Radamacker had gone back to Idaho alone. He was worried about Caban. After the Presidio interview, he had given a few of his men, the ones he really trusted, a year's "salary" and a "bonus" for the work they had done. Caban had later asked permission to get married and Radamacker had acquiesced. Of course, he did not have much choice while he was in hiding, but he knew the minute he let go of his control over their daily lives, the men would grow slack. They would grow accustomed to an easier life, and would prefer riding around in the new cars his money had bought them to giving time to the Brotherhood. Caban had served him well. Without his electrical expertise, there would not have been a Goldor robbery. But Radamacker was well aware that a new wife can give a man other priorities, and he was anxious to gather Caban back into the fold. That was why they were meeting today. Radamacker wanted to convince him to come back with him to the California hideaway for the execution of his boldest plan. There would be time enough after that for the good life.

He approached the fake wood counter. "Key for Room Eight-oh-two please." The young receptionist smiled. "Here you are, sir. Oh," she added, "your guests are waiting for you already."

"Thank you." Radamacker turned around and started to walk out.

"That's the wrong way, sir. You gotta go through the back," she called out.

Outside in the street Radamacker saw a man coming toward him. He walked unhurriedly toward his car. As the agent came closer, Radamacker kept on walking as if he had not a care in the world. At the last moment, he pulled out his gun. At almost point-blank range, Ed Begay had no choice but to lay down on his back and put his feet in the air, a standard FBI maneuver in such a situation. The shot hit him in the foot. Without pausing, Radamacker headed for his car. As he opened the car door, the agent, still recumbent, fired a bullet which grazed his hand.

Radamacker started the car as other agents ran toward him from different directions. "Start, you fuckhead," Radamacker muttered. He floored the gas pedal and screamed away from the curb, nursing his wounded hand in the crook of his uninjured arm.

NINETEEN

"HELLO, CHARLES," IRWIN said pleasantly into his phone. It was Friday afternoon.

"What's the lineup for tonight, Irwin?"

"Oh, let me look. Well, there's a piece on the civil rights conference that's in town, and, you know, the usual. A story on valet parking rip-offs at the Forum . . ."

Davis chuckled. "Then you won't miss me if I take a day off today? It'll give Mary a chance to fly solo." Irwin put down the phone thoughtfully. Charles's talk show "Davis After Dark" was due to start airing the following week. He wondered if calls like the one he had just received were now going to become a regular feature. In his heart, Hansen hoped that "After Dark" would fail and a chastened Davis would return to the six o'clock news. He sighed. Not for the first time in recent months, he wondered if he should consider quitting while he was still on top.

"Do you think you can handle it?" Davis asked Mary, after getting the go-ahead from Hansen.

"Sure, Charles. You won't even be missed. By the way, how's the new show going?"

"Well, we've got a couple of things to iron out. But it's looking good," Charles said. "Looking good."

Mary hung up. Trust Charles to bug out on a slow news day, she thought as she went to warn Rick Worth.

It was close to six o'clock, and production assistants were scurrying around the newsroom, finishing their tasks. The day's lineup had been fixed at the daily three-thirty meeting and as the deadline approached, technicians prepared graphics, editors worked frantically on stories, and writers prepared the lead-ins. It never seemed to change, even on a light news day, the panic and confusion at the station was always the same as the show approached.

Charles Davis and Mary Reed had been co-anchoring the six o'clock news for five weeks. As everyone had predicted, the show was a success, garnering a 25 percent share of the local market each night.

"Help!" The assignment editor was frantic. The callboard had lit up after the station's conservative commentator, Ralph W. Wilson, had broadcast a piece advocating that women on welfare with more than two children be sterilized in order to save on costs.

"Okay, all yours, Rick." Paul Gelson handed over the control room to the six o'clock news producer. The two men had never discussed their change in fortunes, but Rick was uneasily aware that he was just as vulnerable as Gelson had been. He knew that in television you were only as good as last week's ratings.

Across the corridor in the news studio, Mary sat down, and hooked-up their microphones. Rick started the show. The tiny control room held two rows of people, who sat facing a wall of monitors. Rick sat in the back row, along with his production assistant, an associate producer, and a lighting director, who monitored the show on the screen in front of him. Rick's place was marked by a computer, hooking him up to the news wires, and two telephones. One was a regular telephone with outside lines, the other, a red telephone that connected directly to Irwin Hansen's office. Rick's production assistant knew her job was on the line if she allowed the red telephone to ring more than once, and she guarded it closely. Sitting in front of Rick was the associate director, whose task it was to call out time cues and also to prompt the supers, the identifying tags superimposed on the screen. Next to him director Julian Phillips coordinated the camera shots; he and Rick worked closely together and Rick depended on his good judgment. A technical director and production assistant completed the lineup.

A line rang on the regular telephone. "Rick, it's Pete," the production assistant said. "Seems there's a hostage crisis near the Forum."

Rick picked up the telephone and listened to the assignment editor. "Okay," he said. "When they get set up to shoot, we'll keep an eye on it."

A few minutes later during a taped report on the water shortage, pictures from the hostage scene started filtering on to one of the monitors in the control room. Police cars and hastily erected barricades kept people at bay. On screen, Tim Wallace talked to Rick through his microphone.

Rick pressed spoke into the microphone in front of him, which connected him to Wallace's earpiece. "What's going on, Tim?"

"Police think there are about twenty-five hostages in the apartment building behind me. You see the blue building? They were bursting a street gang for illegal weapons and three of the guys escaped, rounded up everyone in the building, and took over an apartment on the top floor. This is serious shit, Rick. The police are talking about storming the place."

"Okay, stay on top of it. Is anyone else there?"

"Nobody, and I think they've cordoned the place off now so no one can get through."

"How the hell did you hear about it?"

Wallace said grimly, "We were at the Forum to do our piece on valet parking and this happened. Rick, this could be an incredible exclusive. Believe me."

"Okay, listen, stay in touch." Rick turned the microphone off. Despite the reporter's excitement, he knew that many of these kinds of stories fizzled into nothing and he wanted to wait. The show continued as planned, while Worth kept glancing at the monitor to see if Wallace was getting better pictures.

When the camera crew managed to establish themselves with a clear shot of the front of the apartment building, Wallace spoke to Worth again. "Rick, you've got to go with this one. The police are going in."

"Okay, Wallace, hang in there."

Rick made his first move. "Julian," he said to the director. "Get the bulletin graphic ready and the 'live report' line with Reed and Wallace boxes. Marcia," he said to his production assistant, "get a map of Fourteenth Street, it's near the Forum." He pressed a button marked with the number one which connected him directly with Mary. The tape on the water shortage was still running. "Mary, we have a crisis in Inglewood. Wallace is there. Let's do it after this tape."

"Great, but don't all these situations look the same, Rick?" Mary's voice echoed in the control room.

"I think we're going to get some action on this one. Police are talking about storming the building. And we're the only people there. Wallace is no fool."

"Thirty seconds!" yelled the associate director from the front desk. This meant that the taped story on the economy had thirty seconds more to run. In the studio the floor director signaled the time to Mary.

"Okay," said Mary, her voice betraying her excitement, "we can drop the hospitals piece."

"Right. And, who knows, we could get lucky," Rick said.

A few seconds later Mary leaned into the screen dramatically, racking up the tension. Her voice was low. *"There is a hostage crisis in Inglewood. Channel Three's Tim Wallace is the first reporter on the scene. Tim? What is going on?"*

In his office, Irwin Hansen tensed. He hated the sleazy crime coverage that the local news in many big cities had developed. In his view, a bulletin story should be weighty, not tabloid in style. In the adjoining building, Tom Baker was also watching intently. He, however, liked the approach. The research had shown him that Channel 3 was the leader in breaking news stories and this attracted desirable, younger viewers to the show.

"Mary, I have with me one of the eight people who managed to flee the building before the siege began . . ."

"Give Wallace a one-minute cue," Worth told the associate director. This meant Wallace would know when to throw the story back to the studio. Rick had kicked his chair away, and was standing like a quarterback in shotgun formation, giving his orders.

On the screen the man Wallace was interviewing wept. *"My son was killed by these people nine months ago. I hope the cops kill every one of them."*

In his office, Hansen relaxed. This was a good story. He called the assignment desk and told them to send out two more crews to the scene.

The minute was up. *"Now, back to Mary Reed in the studio."*

Mary looked unsmiling into the camera. *"Thank you, Tim."* In front of her a small monitor fed her the pictures from Wallace's camera crew. Out of the corner of her eye she saw the reporter move out of view and the camera zoomed in on a flurry of police activity at the side of the building. She made a split-second decision. *"I'm supposed to go to a commercial break right now, but I see that police are moving in on the building where the seventeen hostages are being held in Inglewood, so let's go back to our reporter on the scene, Tim Wallace. Tim, what's happening?"*

"*Mary, as you can probably hear, two police helicopters, no, wait a minute, there's a couple more on the way, four police helicopters are flying in.*" Shots could be heard. "*Shooting has broken out. Come on, guys!*" Wallace shouted to his camera crew. "*Follow me!*" They moved closer to the side of the building where police were scaling a fire escape.

In the control room, Rick looked at the two other stations. Neither of them were showing anything about the Inglewood shoot-out. Strangely, moments of tension calmed Rick's normally flippant temperament, and he was icily cool. "Julian, put the 'exclusive' super on." He called the newsroom. "I want a police spokesman," he told one of the writers. Then he spoke to Hansen, "Listen, we're coming up to the hour. I'm assuming there's no problem in staying with this story. It's getting really hot."

"You're doing great. I'll get back to you." Hansen called Baker. He had to get the station chief's agreement to cut into the station's local programming, in this case two game shows. "Tom, this story's really going. You have a problem with running over?"

"Go for it," Baker said. Hansen called Rick and told the producer that he could stay with the story. He walked out of his office and stood by the assignment desk in the newsroom. At the assignment desk he could monitor the feeds from Wallace's crews, the studio, and other reporters. He could also listen to the police radio. When the news was big, Hansen wanted to know exactly what was happening. However good his producer, two heads were better than one, he figured.

Mary was still on the air. "*We cannot speak to our reporter Tim Wallace who is on the spot at this shoot-out in Inglewood because his microphone was hit. He is unhurt and we hope to be in contact with him soon.*"

"We're still trying, Mary," Rick said into his microphone. "Keep winging it."

"*I want to repeat that our reporter is not hurt. Until we hook-up with him again, I think you can say that the pictures are telling us the story. Just to recap, three armed gang members in a top floor apartment in this building started firing when police attempted to enter the building. Wait a minute, it looks like...*"

Worth pressed the button on his desk. "Mary, we've got Tim back."

"We've reestablished contact with Tim Wallace. Tim?"

"Mary, I've been told that six hostages were killed, the other eleven have been rescued. I can now count six police helicopters and they are hovering above the building. Repeated calls for surrender have been met with more gunfire."

The camera panned out to show the helicopters moving in and, as if on cue, they began firing at the top floor of the building. Suddenly a massive explosion erupted from one of the windows, sucking a hovering helicopter into its flaming mass. Smoke poured from the top of the building as the staggering helicopter crashed in fiery fragments onto the roof. Everything was captured on screen by Wallace's crew.

It was seven-thirty when Hansen called Baker a second time. "Listen, we might have to extend this thing beyond eight."

Baker hated the idea, knowing that his network bosses would be very unhappy if he preempted prime-time shows from the second-largest market in the country. "Let me think about it," he said. Baker called Worth. "What do you think, Worth? Is this story going to run over eight?"

"Nah. It's practically over now and it's only seven thirty-five. We'll probably be filling for the last fifteen minutes before eight anyway."

"Okay. Hey, Rick, this is just between us, understand?"

"Sure." It wasn't hard for Rick to figure out what was going on.

"Okay, Hansen," Baker called back, knowing it would not happen, "if we have to, we'll pre-empt at eight."

"Mary, the siege is over. The remains of the three gang members are burned beyond recognition along with the six hostages they killed. Nineteen people went through a terrible ordeal but are alive to tell the story. Two police officers were killed, Mary."

"Thank you, Tim. This was a daring police operation, but

was it a success? I have Shana Cusack from the L.A.P.D. here in the studio, and later we will go live for an interview with Oswald Simpson, the mayor of Los Angeles. . . ."

Hansen told Rick to run the explosion tape over and over again as Cusack spoke. The other two stations had called asking for pictures, and Hansen took pleasure in allowing them only thirty seconds of footage, which they had to run with a large super reading "Courtesy of Channel 3" across the bottom.

As Worth had estimated, the show wound up at eight. When the associate director yelled "Clear!" in the control room, Rick stepped down to the front of the control room and worked his way along the rows, shaking the hand of everyone in the room.

Then he sprinted across to the studio. Mary, planted a warm kiss on his cheek. "Good work, boss," she said.

Rick silently cursed himself for blushing. "Well, guys," he said, regaining his composure, "you were the greatest." And he swept his hands around the studio to include everyone. "What a show, boy! You know what I always say, it's better to be lucky than good but when you're both, like we were tonight, no one can touch you." He beamed, still riding on the high that the show had produced.

Rick and Mary walked up to the newsroom together where they were greeted with cheers and congratulations. Tom Baker entered the newsroom with a flourish of his cane.

"Now," Worth said, "for those of you who have to put on the eleven o'clock news, I am sorry. One, because we're a tough act to follow and two, because Tom is going to buy everyone drinks across the street!"

"That's right, Rick," said Baker, cornered.

In the bar across the street, spirits already high become noisy and exclamatory as the evening wore on. Tom Baker left after an hour for dinner at one of the glamorous spots he liked to be seen at. Ironically, the real hero of the evening,

Tim Wallace, was absent. He was still at the scene, working on a report for the eleven o'clock news.

"Mary?" She turned around to find Charles Davis at her elbow.

"Hi, Charles."

"Judging by your work today, it looks like I'm going to have to take more Fridays off." The mild tension that his presence had created snapped, and everyone laughed.

"Seriously, Mary. You did great. I couldn't have done better myself."

Mary was flattered. "Thank you, Charles. It was nice of you to come by."

At the end of the evening, Mary walked to her car for the short drive home. She was pleased with herself. She knew she had handled the challenge well, grasping the situation quickly, ad-libbing fluently, and her decision not to go to a commercial break had proven inspired.

The air was cool and Mary breathed it in hungrily. She had put her keys in the car door when, suddenly, a hand fell heavily on her shoulder. Mary jumped and turned around.

"My God, I didn't mean to scare you," said Rick Worth, taken aback by her reaction. "I was just getting into my car and I saw you. Thought I'd say good night."

"I'm sorry, Rick. I'm tired, that's all."

"Well, I just wanted to tell you again that you did a great job tonight."

"Thanks."

"Go get some sleep, you deserve it."

As she let herself in her front door, Mary sighed. The trouble was she had not had a good night's sleep in several weeks now. She wondered if Mark had seen the show. They had not been in touch since he left, except that he had given her his new home number, telling her to call if she needed to. She wanted to tell him about how she'd handled the hostage crisis, to share it with him. Without taking off her coat, she dialed his number. She heard his answering machine, and hung up without leaving a message. Wearily, Mary prepared herself for another night of tossing and turning.

As the lights went out upstairs Jerry Radamacker smiled. He started his car, and slipped along the street past Mary's house, and turned toward the freeway.

TWENTY

RADAMACKER PACED ANGRILY up and down his underground office in the desert. "You see that?" he yelled at Finn. "You see those jumped-up street kids who should be chewing watermelon seeds?" Radamacker jabbed his finger at the television, where a prominent national politician was being interviewed, along with the mayor of Los Angeles. Both were African-American. "These men never should have been born. You know that?"

Johnson nodded. Radamacker turned his attention back to the architectural blueprint he had been studying. The plans were spread out over his desk. He had returned to the compound after the incident at the motel. Thomas Taylor had not exactly welcomed the fugitives when they first arrived, but Radamacker took him aside. Now, the minister scuttled around, keeping away from them like a cockroach avoiding the light, Jerry joked.

In a series of rituals, they had sworn allegiance to one another and to the cause they all believed in. As a final ceremony Radamacker had given them names he had taken from graves in Idaho. In that state birth certificates are not stamped when a person dies, and Radamacker was able to obtain legal copies of the documents and with them social security numbers and driver's licenses. Newly christened, they would execute his most ambitious mission.

On the television screen, the interview had been followed by pictures of the hostage crisis from the day before, and the riots among street gangs that it had sparked. The gangs were protesting what they saw as the use of excessive force by the L.A.P.D. People were worried. It was a volatile situation, and they had all seen before where such tensions could lead. Radamacker clasped his hands together; he was well pleased. Since he had been back at the compound, he had sold weapons indiscriminately to the street gangs. For once he did not care about color or race. His intent was to arm the people of Los Angeles so that, when the time came, there would be anarchy in the streets. That was when he, Jerry Radamacker, would step in.

"For more than six months I have beaten the FBI at their own game, Johnson"—Radamacker turned to him—"and it has become clear to me that I have been saved for a reason. The Great One"—he nodded at the picture on the wall—"has shown me the way." His face twitched. "Johnson, are the men prepared for the hanging?"

"Yessir."

"Then let us begin."

The men had assembled outside the entrance to the church in front of a crude scaffold. It was dark, and great torches of flame had been lit and attached to the outer walls of the church. The men all wore hoods and were chanting in a low murmur that swelled as Radamacker and Johnson, also wearing hoods, emerged from the church. "Kill, kill, kill, kill," the men chanted. Roped to the scaffold, his hands tied behind his back, his head in the noose, stood Tony Caban, the only man without a hood. On his face was an expression of mingled fear and supplication.

Radamacker stood on the steps of the church and waved for silence. "When Christ was sold for thirty pieces of silver," he began, "he was not angry at the traitor Iscariot." Jerry shook his head. "No, he looked with sorrow at his betrayer, knowing well that his sin would torment the man, would make his life a living hell so that he would end his wretched existence by hanging himself." Radamacker paused. "Tony Caban has told us that he will never live in peace again. But we are going to help him." He turned to the condemned man. "We are not going to kill you tonight," he said softly.

"Oh, please, don't!" Caban screamed, sensing hope.

"No, we're not going to kill you. Instead, you, like Judas, will hang yourself."

There was silence as the men grasped Radamacker's diabolical reasoning. "Press that button"—Radamacker pointed to a button within the man's reach—"and you will end it all."

Radamacker fell silent. The men started a low, ragged chant led by Johnson. "Judas, Judas, Judas," they intoned.

Twice Caban reached out his hand, and twice with an expression of anguish, he pulled it back. Radamacker nodded at Johnson, who walked over. "Like this," Finn sneered, taking Caban's index finger and stabbing the button. The makeshift trapdoor opened and Caban's terrified visage was frozen in death.

Radamacker turned to face the men gathered together in the desert night. "The Day of the Rope has dawned," he said.

"Come on, tell me. Was it a surprise?" E. J. Edwards asked eagerly.

"Never in a million years . . ." Mary was speechless.

274

"Well, you know Channel Three's too cheap to buy you a cup of coffee."

"It's incredible," Mary said. She turned again to look at the billboard on Sunset Boulevard that Edwards had bought her. Despite the excellent numbers for the hostage crisis, the ratings on the six o'clock news had begun to dip recently, and Edwards had decided Mary needed cheering up. They were sitting in his car on Sunset Boulevard.

"You see how big it is? Bigger than most of the others?" Edwards could not restrain himself. He was enjoying the moment as much as if it had been for him.

"Yes, E. J. If it's from you, I know it's going to be larger than life." Mary laughed. They were sitting in his car. She turned back to face him. "Do you remember sending me three hundred roses? I'll never forget the look on the guard's face. Nobody had any idea what to do with them."

"Hey, it got your attention, didn't it?"

"Oh, it was wonderful," Mary said, "and you are wonderful, E. J. I owe you a lot. I don't think I could have survived this town without you."

"Never undersell yourself, kid. You did it, and I know what it took." He smiled at her. "Do you ever see that fellow Mark, by the way?"

Mary shook her head.

"Well, there's plenty of people I know—"

"For God's sake, E. J., don't even think about it. I can get a date if I need one."

"Just a thought. Now, where you want to have lunch?"

"The Grill, of course. Where else?"

"For you, Mary, I'll try anything, but"—he turned to his driver—"the Grill it is."

As they sped up Mary grasped her agent's hand. "Thanks, E. J., thanks for an outrageous surprise." She kissed him on the cheek. "Now, all we've got to do is fix the ratings."

"I'm glad you liked it." He ducked her last remark. "Listen, Mary, I've been meaning to tell you. They've been using that same promo of you with that old blue suit for too long.

I'm getting tired with it. Don't you have any other clothes?"

"We're meant to be shooting another one soon. I'll talk to Irwin about it. You really noticed it, uh?"

Edwards nodded. "I like the way your investigative pieces on the entertainment industry are turning out. That was some story on the Teamsters last night."

"Smart idea to do hard news on a soft industry. And it was yours, I believe, E. J., in case you've forgotten. It keeps both Irwin and Tom happy!"

"Listen, Rather cut his teeth on the civil rights movement, Brokaw had the riots in Berkeley and Jennings was in Beirut. You can't afford to be perceived as a news bimbo." Mary nodded, she had heard this line a dozen times before. "Tell me, Mary. How did you get that producer to talk about paying out favors?"

"He was terrified the union would find him out and he'd wind up like Jimmy Hoffa. That's why I couldn't show his face."

"How did you get him?"

"Commander Zero. I said if the FBI hadn't made me back down about those tapes, I wouldn't back down on him. And I guaranteed I'd alter his voice and shoot in silhouette so no one would know."

"So, who was it, Mary? I won't tell."

"Sure, E. J."

"I guess that's a no, huh? Did you ever hear from that Zero guy again?"

Mary shook her head regretfully. "No, it's a shame. I tried really hard for a while to track him down, but no luck. The FBI haven't found him yet either, at least that was the last I heard. I haven't heard anything since a couple of months ago when they busted his safehouse in San Francisco, and linked him to that robbery. You remember I did a piece around then, just before I became anchor? I should probably do another follow-up piece on him, see where the investigation's at now."

"Sure, it can't hurt." Edwards pulled a thick invitation

card out of his breast pocket. "Before I forget, Mary. I'd like to take you to the opening of that new restaurant Premiere." He handed her the card. "It's next week."

Mary looked at the card. "I usually hate these type of events," she said.

"Hey, listen, this is your new news beat. Investigative reporter to the stars."

"Right, see how fast they dump me when my reports air."

"Don't underestimate your importance to them, Mary. They need you much more than you need them—you can always report on something else. Anyway, there's another reason I think you should go. An old friend of mine is going to be in town. I think it's time you met him."

"As usual, E. J., there's no business without some pleasure," Mary said ironically. "So, who is this mystery guest?"

"You'll find out soon enough."

"Listen, E. J., about these ratings. I'm really worried. Charles has got to decide whether he's a talk-show host or an anchorman; we're getting killed."

"Stick with me," he said. "I'll see you through this, I promise."

"How can you, E. J.? You can't represent both of us. Let's be honest."

Edwards gave Mary one of his penetrating looks. "Believe me, Mary, I'm looking out for you," he said.

The car glided to a halt and the agent and the anchorwoman walked into the restaurant arm in arm. Across the street a dark blue sedan pulled up. The driver unfolded a newspaper and prepared to wait.

"Hi, Joe," said Irwin Hansen to the ninety-year-old man who worked the shoeshine stand. It was ten o'clock and he and Rick Worth were walking past the news and entertainment studios on the ground floor. They were heading for a meeting at Tom Baker's sixth-floor penthouse office complex in the adjacent building. Both men were deep in thought. They knew the meeting was about the six o'clock show, whose ratings had fallen steadily over the past couple of weeks.

"How's 'After Dark' doing?" Rick asked, though he knew the answer. His relationship with his old pal had cooled recently; partly because Davis was busy, and partly because he was avoiding Rick, who he knew was upset that he had not been offered a job on the new show.

"Well, it did well the first couple of weeks, now it's doing okay, nothing spectacular. A new show needs time early on, time to settle in."

They crossed the parking lot to the other building, and walked by the ground-floor commissary to the elevator bank, then rode up to the place Rick liked to call "carpet canyon." Here, the leather furniture, perfectly placed coffee tables topped with sheaves of shiny industry magazines, and cut flowers in porcelain vases, was a marked contrast with the functional, engine-room decor of the newsroom. Hansen and Worth walked past the rows of neatly framed pictures of network and station stars lining the corridor to Baker's office.

"Mr. Hansen, Mr. Worth, Mr. Baker will be with you soon," said Baker's secretary.

"Come in," Tom Baker said a moment later. He was unusually subdued and businesslike. Hansen and Worth sat down.

"Gentlemen," Baker began. "I think you both know why I called this meeting." He looked down at a small notepad in front of him where rows of figures were neatly inked. "The six o'clock show is fading. Channel Seven is nipping at our heels, and E. J. Edwards is playing us for suckers. Think about it, the only person who stands to win from this situation is Charles Davis."

"We're the ones that let it happen, Tom. Remember that," Hansen said.

Baker waved his hand. "We had to break Charles's contract, and this was the only way we could get him to accept a co-anchor. I did what was best for the station, and, I think, the research on Reed proves that I made an excellent decision."

"Oh, you did more than that," Arledge said thoughtfully. He nodded at a figure, who was beckoning him over.

"I have to go, I'm afraid, Mary. But I'm in town for a couple of days. How about breakfast tomorrow or dinner on Friday?"

"Dinner Friday night would be great." Mary preferred a time when she did not have to worry about getting back to work.

Arledge moved away. Now Mary knew why Edwards had been so anxious for her to come to the party. For Roone Arledge, or any of the network news chiefs, personal contact was a prerequisite for any major deal. Their investment was in people and they had to know you before they would sign you. Another door was opening for her.

Across the room, Mary caught sight of Mark Ashfield. Curiously, she negotiated a path across the chattering, excited crowd. "Hi, Mark. This is a surprise."

"Mary!" he said, clearly pleased to see her. "How are you?"

"Fine," she said, noting that he looked cheerful and relaxed. "You?"

"Great." He paused. "I saw your piece last night. I'm glad they still let you report."

"It's the best part," Mary said. "So, what've you been up to?" The conversation was a little strained but she felt the strong pull of her attraction to this man, which she realized with surprise had not subsided in the weeks since he left. She thought about inviting him to have dinner with her.

"You'll never believe this, but they've optioned my manuscript on Feld for a movie," Mark said, grinning.

"Hey, that's marvelous," Mary said with genuine delight. "Listen, how about dinner sometime? We could catch up. I'd love to hear about the movie."

"Sure," said Mark slowly, "that'd be nice."

"What about tomorrow?" Mary pressed. "Well, I mean, we can always make it next week, or the week after if you're busy," she added hastily.

Mark smiled. "No, I can make it tomorrow," he said.

"Mark?" A woman came up and seized his arm familiarly. "There's someone I want you to meet." She ignored Mary.

"Sure," Mark said. "But first, Alexis, this is Mary Reed. Mary, Alexis Court."

If looks could kill, thought Mary as Alexis gave her the once-over. She held out her hand. Alexis had a head of wavy auburn hair that hung down to her waist and a delicately beautiful oval face. Only her stony glare betrayed her total lack of desire to meet Mark's former girlfriend.

"I always thought you were taller," Alexis said.

"Yes, well, it was nice meeting you," Mary said. She smiled at Mark. "Good to see you," she said to Mark. She walked off to find Edwards. Suddenly she wanted to leave.

Martinez hung up the pay phone in Bob's Cafe, and got into his car. Earlier that morning, Martinez had seen a line of trucks pull out of the compound. Through the powerful lens of his binoculars he had recognized the face of the man who had come to Barstow with the clergyman. In the passenger seat beside him sat a man of slender build and brown hair wearing wire-framed glasses. He fit the description of Commander Zero Mary Reed had given him. As the convoy pulled on to the road, Martinez hurriedly gathered up his gear and scrambled down the hill. Crouching behind his car, he waited for them to pass. He had followed the trucks to the outskirts of Los Angeles where he lost them. Disappointed, he returned to the desert. Like a dog worrying at a bone, Martinez was drawn back to the compound.

He drove fast down the now-familiar route until he got to the dirt track that wound around the hill. Hiding his car behind the scrub, he climbed to his place near the top of the hill and trained his binoculars on the compound. It seemed deserted. So, they had not come back. Martinez stayed there watching for over an hour until he felt certain that the place was empty.

Leaving his car in the scrub, the detective walked along the dirt track for a long, hot mile until he arrived at the chained gates of the compound. He could tell the gates were not wired. Throwing his jacket over his shoulder, Martinez crawled painfully up the high wire mesh fencing and half way down the other side. He dropped heavily down to the ground. Looking warily around him, he walked to the end of the paved road. Ahead was a path leading up to the church. He headed toward the church since he had seen a lot of people coming and going from it during his hillside vigil. Martinez made his way up the steps.

As he neared the top of the small hill, he heard the creak of wood in the wind. Martinez reached the top, and saw the hideous rictus of a hanged man. As a homicide detective, Martinez prided himself on having seen it all, but the shock of finding the body on top of a morning of bad coffee and a frustrating car chase undid him. His stomach heaved and churned, and a clammy sweat beaded and broke from the pores of his skin.

Recovering, he fancied he heard a low moan issuing from the interior of the church. Walking to the entrance, the detective kicked open the wooden door with his foot, and pressed himself against the wall, his gun poised in his hand. Nothing happened. He peered into the church and, seeing no one, went inside. Keeping his back to the wall, and looking warily around him, he edged his way toward the door at the back. The moans were growing louder.

"Oh, help me, please."

In a room at the back of the church Martinez recognized the black robes of the minister he had seen in town, the same one who had written the poisonous article in Jim Wilkes's pamphlet, he realized with disgust. Taylor lay doubled up on the floor. An uneven stain of darker black had spread across his skirts. He was badly wounded in the stomach.

"Help me," the minister said again.

"I will," Martinez said. "But first you're going to answer some questions."

"You're the man who asked me about that cop, aren't you?" Taylor's eyes were dim. "They killed him. He helped them rob that depot and they killed him. Now they've killed me," the cleric was wailing. "But, listen, there's worse to come. I overheard them planning something new. They didn't know I was listening. I fooled them." Taylor grimaced in pain. "They're going to assassinate someone big, not like that talk-show host or any of the others. I heard them talking. Before they left, I went down to the office. It was dark, but I found these plans. I copied them, see, in case they came in useful. Now it doesn't matter."

"Okay, enough. Now, shut up," Martinez ordered. Struggling to remember his training, the detective started to tend to Taylor's wound.

TWENTY-ONE

"TOM BAKER'S ON the line," Margaret Lynch said.

Hansen sighed, remembering their conversation the previous day.

"Irwin," Baker had said. "I've just been going over the latest budget figures you gave me. I'm afraid I still need a million dollars from you."

"Come on, this is absurd. The news department generated six million more in total billing this year; it makes no sense for you to penny-pinch."

"Listen, if it were up to me I'd give you a million dollars next year. But it's not up to me, Irwin. The network's really hurting. They're getting killed in prime time and the daytime numbers are practically nonexistent."

"So, we should pay for their mistakes. Is that what you're saying? Why don't you tell them to get better shows." When Baker did not respond, Hansen realized he had gone too far. "Listen, Tom," he said more reasonably, "you cut my budget and my ratings go down. This is something we can't afford to play with right now."

Baker knew that Hansen was right. He tried a different tack. "Times are hard. We've all got to tighten our belts a little while we ride over this rough patch. We're all in this together, and I think we should pull together on this one."

"Well maybe we should both fly up to New York, Tom, and discuss how this pulling together actually works."

Hansen had hit a raw nerve. Baker hated the fact that Hansen still had a lot of contacts in New York from his old days as head of the London bureau, and he did not hesitate to use them when he wanted to put pressure on the station chief. "I'm giving you till four tomorrow to come to your senses." Baker slammed the telephone down.

Hansen picked up the phone and dialed Baker's extension. "Hi, Tom," he said when Baker answered.

"Irwin, I hope we can settle these budget numbers now. Can you get me that million dollars?"

"Tom, I know we're both tired of fighting about this. So I've been thinking. What I can do is combine some parts of our operation. I'll cut back on some crew hours and editing time. That way I can give you five hundred thousand." His spies in New York had told him that was the real figure Baker needed.

"Hmm," Baker responded. "Okay, Irwin, you win."

"Tell me, what did I win?"

"You won the argument." Baker paused. "But I'll take the money." Both men laughed uneasily at the attempted humor. "Listen, I'm going to come over to your office right now. This way we can go over the numbers and I'll be able to fax them up to New York tomorrow."

"Fine," Hansen said.

Mary was in her office when the phone rang.

"Mary?" The voice was subtle and oily, suggesting an intimacy that was disturbing because she could not place the voice.

"Yes," she said cautiously.

"You've done well for yourself since we last met. Are you enjoying your success, Mary?"

"Who is this?"

"Mary," the voice reproached her. "I helped you, put you where you are, you might say. And you helped me, too. I won't forget that. You are a brave woman." The voice paused. "The two of us helping each other, isn't that the way it's supposed to be?"

"Oh, God!" Mary said, suddenly recognizing the voice. "Commander Zero?"

"That's right, Mary. Your old friend."

"Where are you?" said Mary, her reporter's instincts coming to life.

"Hey, not so fast, Mary. I'm alive and out of jail, isn't that enough?" He paused for effect. "And, it's all thanks to you, Mary, isn't it? We're in this thing together. You saw me, Mary, didn't you?" he asked. "If you did and you didn't report me, you don't have to say anything more. You're for me. You proved yourself."

Mary thought rapidly. She realized she could be in real danger. If the Commander knew for sure she had seen him, she was a potential threat, and Mary shuddered to think of what he would do to her. If she denied it, she lost any chance she had of finding the elusive Zero. "I don't know what you're talking about," she said quickly. She felt icy drops of perspiration on her temples. "I'd like to talk to you, Commander," she said, collecting herself. "Perhaps you can tell me what you've been doing. I could get you on television again," she wheedled. "Same deal as before. Nobody would know who you are."

"That's an interesting idea, Mary," he said. "Be careful, it might happen sooner than you think." He hung up.

Mary pulled at the drawers of her file cabinets. Somewhere she had a number of a detective she had spoken to once. Mary kept organized files on all her research, including individual rolodexes for major stories. As she searched through her papers, she tried to remember his name. Yes, it was there. She pulled the card out excitedly and dialed the number.

"Is Detective Martinez there?" she asked the Bakersfield police department.

"He'll be back later," an officer replied. Mary left a message. She dialed Edwards's number. He was soothing, and offered her a bodyguard. "I don't think it's gone that far," she said.

"You ready?" Radamacker barked at his men.

"Yessir," they said in unison, and they held up their guns in a salute. Twenty men were crowded into the motel room. Jerry had laid a map out on one of the beds.

"The first step of our operation was completed with total success under the leadership of Johnson. His squadron infiltrated the target area last night. This morning they opened the side door that we will enter exactly one hundred and twenty-two minutes from now. Is that clear?

"Does everyone have a hood?" he asked. The men nodded. "I want to see them." The men obediently pulled the hoods from their pockets.

"Now, we're going to go out there, and we're going to fight for our country, our women, our children, and the truths we hold dear. Remember, that, brothers. If you want something changed, you got to do something about it. Right?"

"Right," the men echoed in unison.

"Before we go, brothers, I would like for us to pray together." Radamacker gathered his men around him, and with moist eyes he gave voice to their prayers.

Martinez drove back to the police department in Bakersfield. He had checked Taylor into the hospital, informing the surprised hospital staff that the minister was wanted for questioning by the police, and that he would return with an armed guard.

After the detective had dressed the ugly wound, Taylor had lapsed in and out of consciousness, his muttered ramblings making no sense to Martinez. He had collected his car and loaded the minister into the back. The whole operation had taken several hours, and he had barely had time to think. Now, as he digested the information that Jim Wilkes had robbed the depot in San Francisco, he felt a stab of conscience—he should have stayed in touch more. What a mess. He looked down at his bloodstained clothing, and for the first time realized what a sight he looked. No wonder the hospital staff had looked at him so queerly.

Back in his office, he put his messages to one side. He took out the card that Frank Carson had given him seven months earlier when he had met with the FBI in Los Angeles. Reluctantly he dialed the number. He knew this case was too big for him, and he did not want to get bogged down in the bureaucracy of the sheriff's office who would want to handle the minister's arrest.

Frank Carson was very interested in Martinez's story. Furious about Radamacker's escape from the motel in Boise, and the disappearance of their informant Tony Caban, the feds were taking a lot of heat. Carson alerted the FBI office in Los Angeles and instructed Rigby and Begay to fly with him to Bakersfield. Begay still limped slightly from the wound Radamacker had inflicted on his foot.

The detective hung up the phone with satisfaction. He noticed a call from Mary Reed among his messages and called her office. It was five forty-five, he was informed, and Mary was preparing for the six o'clock show. He left a message. Leaning back in his chair, Martinez pulled out the papers Taylor had given him and, once again, tried to make sense of them. He could have drawn the plans himself he had looked at them so hard. Where was this building? What did it contain?

Mary took her seat on the studio set. On her right a technician helped the mayor hook-up his microphone, and a makeup woman dusted his face with powder. Mayor Simpson had had a tough time as mayor in a city riven with racial and economic discord, but he had won the grudging respect of the citizenry for his folksy, hands-on management of the various crises that had plagued his administration. His flair for self-promotion, which had alienated some people initially, had over time endeared him to his constituents through simple familiarity. He had become another feature of the sprawling urban landscape that was reassuring just because it endured.

Charles Davis ambled on to the set at the last minute. "Good evening Mayor, good evening everybody."

"Okay," said Worth in the control room. "Let's rock and roll."

"Good evening and welcome to Channel Three news at six. Tonight we have a guest, Mayor Simpson, who is going to answer questions from you. The number to call is . . ."

Mary looked around the studio. She wondered how dinner with Mark would go that evening. It had been so good to see him again.

"So, Mary, are you doing anything special tonight?" Davis asked his co-anchor before they went to the first commercial break.

"Actually, Charles, I am."

"Wait a minute, that's not what you're supposed to say," Davis said. *"You're supposed to say, yes, I'll be watching your exclusive with the president tonight on 'After Dark.'"*

"Oh, is that so?" Mary said, laughing. *"But tell me, Charles, how is the president going to do your show when he's meant to be flying to the Middle East tonight?"*

"Well, Mary, that's why you and everybody else will have to watch 'After Dark' to find out. And we'll be back right after these messages."

"Hey thanks, Mary, for that little plug," Davis said as the commercials started.

"You didn't give me much choice, did you?" she replied.

"I guess not. I just want to get it rolling."

"Relax, Charles, it'll happen."

"A little free advertising at the local news's expense, Charles?" Rick Worth had strolled onto the set to chat with his stars.

"Hey, I need everything I can get, Ricky."

"Mayor Simpson"—Rick extended his hand—"I'm the producer over in the control room across the corridor. We're glad to have you on the show tonight." He turned to Mary. "Mary, are you ready with the interview?" She nodded. "So, first we'll do the headlines, then we'll start with the interview. You have four minutes, a break for commercials, then we'll wind up the interview. After that we'll open up the switchboard. Okay?" They agreed. Rick was in his element. He loved his job and he communicated his enthusiasm to everyone around him.

"Fifteen," the floor director called.

"Okay, guys, back to the grindstone," Rick said. "Can't leave Julian alone in the control room too long, he's afraid of the dark." Worth ran across the hallway. It flashed across his mind that the corridor was unusually deserted for that time of the evening, but he soon became caught up in the show again.

"*The trial of Dr. Drubin, the plastic surgeon who—*"

The control room door suddenly burst open and seven armed men in the white overalls of the A & E Cleaning Service and masks leveled their semiautomatic machine guns at the shocked occupants. Finn Johnson marched up the narrow aisle.

"What's going on?" said Rick. He found it hard to absorb what was happening.

"You the chief?" Worth nodded yes.

"Tell them to keep the program on," Johnson said. He looked at the monitors. "Which one is the one people see?"

Rick pointed. "That stays on, okay? We have men watching. We will know if you take the show off and we will kill every fucking idiot in this room. Understand?"

"Do as the man says," Rick ordered. The telephone in front of him rang.

"Who's that?" Johnson asked.

"I don't know," said Rick.

"Well, leave it the fuck alone," Johnson said.

The telephone continued to ring. With a swift motion, Rick reached for the phone, but Johnson lunged at him, hitting him on the head with the butt of his weapon. "I said leave it the fuck alone!" Johnson grabbed the ringing telephone and ripped it out of its socket. Rick put his hand to his temple and saw blood on his fingers. He felt dizzy.

Johnson called two of his men in two different motel rooms to check that Channel 3 was still broadcasting. He looked back at the monitors, seemingly satisfied. "Okay," he said. "We want you to show this tape on television." He handed Rick a videocassette tape. "And then we want Mary Reed to interview our leader. We have surrounded the building, and our men are about to capture the studio. If you don't obey instructions"—Johnson surveyed the control room—"everyone of you will be shot." He fired his gun in the air. "Bang, just like that," he said to the terrified faces in front of him.

The walkie-talkie buzzed again. "Okay," Johnson said. "Situation's stabilized, Commander. They have the tape and will follow orders."

"Good work," Radamacker said into the walkie-talkie.

Irwin Hansen was concerned. He was watching the six o'clock news with Tom Baker, who had remained in his office after they had hashed out the budget figures. During Davis's reading of the headlines something seemed wrong. The graphics were out of order and slow to change, giving the show an off-key effect.

As he reached for the red phone on his desk, his eyes

were riveted to the screen. Charles Davis was gone and in his place an American flag waved to the accompaniment of band music. In a clever technical effect, the flag dissolved into shots of riot scenes in Los Angeles, men beating other men to the ground, panicked people looting stores. These were followed by pictures of the poorer sections of Los Angeles, the homeless, the destitute, the drug-users. Pictures of smog and pollution, a policeman's funeral. In the background a choir sang and a man's voice exhorted white people to spontaneously rise up and claim their heritage.

"Is this part of the mayor's interview?" Baker asked.

"I don't know." Hansen shook his head. "But I don't think so." Angrily he picked up the red phone.

"Another fucking telephone!" Johnson yelled in Rick's ear as the red phone rang.

"This one's important," Rick said, trying to sound calm. His voice sounded to him as if it came from far away. His head hurt. "These people can take the show off the air."

Johnson snatched up the phone. "Listen, mister," he growled, "I don't know who you are, but this show is staying on, or everyone of your people down here are dead. You fucking get that, mister?"

In the studio, there was panic and confusion. Contact with the control room had been lost, and on the monitors a tape was running that no one knew anything about.

"I don't know what's going on," the mayor said, red-faced with fury, as the voice on the tape spewed racial obscenities, "but if this is your idea of a journalism, I'm leaving." He got up and started walking toward the door.

Before he reached it, the door banged open and eight armed men, also wearing white overalls and masks, stormed the studio. The mayor was seized by two men, while the other six men took up strategic positions around the room. Mary could feel a gun pointed at her neck.

"We've been taken over by janitors!" Davis exclaimed.

The man who had entered last walked up to the desk.

"What do you want?" Davis asked.

"Shut up, faggot."

"But it's my show."

"It's my show now." Radamacker walked over to Mary. "You said you wanted to see me again, Mary," he said.

"Commander Zero," Mary gasped.

"I have a message for your viewers, Mary." He turned around. "Tie him up to that chair," he ordered, gesturing at the mayor.

"What are you going to do?" Mary asked, the color draining from her face.

"You'll see, Mary, you'll see. Remember, I know you're for me." He walked away.

Hansen called the station's security desk. There was no answer. Radamacker's men had already taken care of that. The night before they had entered the building disguised as the cleaning crew, and chloroformed the night guards, replacing them with their own men. When the day shift arrived, they were locked up in the basement along with the others.

He called the L.A.P.D. "Don't move," the chief told him. "They've probably surrounded the place. We'll be there right away."

Hansen looked at the monitor, and was so shocked that he dropped the phone. The tape had ended and onscreen was a wide shot of the Channel 3 news studio. In the middle, the mayor of Los Angeles sat roped to a chair, while guns were trained at the heads of Mary Reed, Charles Davis, Ralph Wilson, and Bill Bryson. The terrorists had taken off their white cleaners' coveralls, revealing the military camouflage uniforms they were wearing underneath. For a moment Irwin found it hard to believe that it was actually happening, that it was not a movie.

Hansen's private line rang. It was E. J. Edwards. "What in heaven's name is going on there, Hansen?"

"I've called the police."

"You better call the fucking Marines. I've got three million dollars of talent in that studio." The line went dead. Hansen picked up his other phone.

"The outside lines have been cut," he said to Baker.

"Oh, my God," Baker moaned.

"Come on, man. We've got a lot of very scared people out there to talk to."

Martinez drove toward the small airport outside Bakersfield into which Carson and his agents were flying in on an FBI helicopter. He turned up the radio, which was playing country music. Martinez liked to think to country music. *"I lie back on my pillow / And try to fight the tears."* He tapped his foot.

The music stopped and an announcer started speaking. *"We interrupt our program with this news bulletin. The Channel Three news program has been taken over by armed terrorists headed by a man calling himself Commander Zero. They are threatening to assassinate Mayor Simpson, who was a guest on the show tonight. We will bring you more . . ."*

Martinez rammed his foot on the gas pedal. So that was it. As the helicopter hovered over the tarmac, Eddie Martinez rushed toward it in his bloody clothing, waving furiously. "We're going to Burbank!" he yelled at Frank Carson. "Hurry! I'll explain it to you when we're in the air." A few minutes later the helicopter took off and flew south.

Rick could feel the nose of Johnson's semiautomatic in his back. He watched the monitors.

"Shoot him!" Radamacker ordered.

A cameraman had backed toward the studio door, using his camera as a shield. Pushing the heavy camera into the room, he made a dash for the door. A single shot rang out, and the cameraman slumped against the wall.

"This has got to stop!" Rick said.

"Oh, no. It's only just beginning," Johnson hissed. "Now, do your job, you dumbfuck idiot." He pushed his gun under Worth's chin.

"*Order!*" Radamacker called in the studio. He surveyed the terrified captives. "*That's what happens if any of you try to escape.*" He looked at Mary. "*I want you to interview me, Mary. You know, like we did before. You said you wanted to do that again, Mary.*"

Mary was unable to speak. She had been profoundly shocked by the shooting and now she was shivering, unable to move.

"*He wants me to interview him,*" she said in a high, unnatural voice.

"I know, Mary," Worth said, pressing the button that connected him to her. "Go ahead, do what he says," Rick soothed the near-hysterical Mary. "We're counting on you, Mary."

"*Mary, do what he says,*" Davis said in his most commanding voice. It was enough to bring Mary back to her senses.

"Okay," she said, her voice barely audible.

"You've got sixty seconds to get into place, then we'll open out to a two shot." Rick's familiar dialogue from the control room calmed her.

"Where do you want me to go, Commander?" she asked.

"Over here." Radamacker indicated a sofa and chair where interviews were sometimes conducted.

"Right, get a tight shot of the leader, and another one of Mary," Rick ordered. Julian Phillips found a good shot of Radamacker. "I want you to lead with a wide shot," Rick said. Julian obeyed. The camera panned to a wide shot of the studio. "Now, show the mayor, and intercut with some shots of the others," said Worth. The jagged camera shots started to play more rhythmically as Julian Phillips, following Rick's instructions as if in a dream, started to make television out of the confusion. "Now back to the commander. That's good."

"What the fuck are you doing?" said Johnson.

"We're professionals," Rick said. "We're going to make this look like real television, not amateur hour." For the first time Johnson had no reply.

"Okay, go ahead, Mary," Rick said to Mary as he settled on a shot of Mary and the Commander.

Mary looked at the Commander. If she could get the same rapport with him that she had in San Francisco, then things might work out. If she could just stall for time, someone might be able to rescue them. She tried to speak gently. *"Commander,"* she said. *"I am just going to read our standard disclaimer and then we'll hear from you."* She looked into the camera. The tight lines around her mouth and her voice, which was still close to hysteria, revealed her state of mind. *"The tape you have just seen in no way represents the views of Channel Three. We have been forced—"*

"Oh, but there you're wrong, Ms. Reed. It represents the views of many people out there." Radamacker was courteous. *"I've done some research on this. You people out there are the people who will make our revolution work. Come on, now, aren't you sick to your gut of some illegal alien stealing your job? Aren't you tired of politicians who are controlled by big money and international conspiracies? Aren't you ready to stop the banks that are robbing you of your homes, the drug pushers that are poisoning your children? Your neighborhoods are dangerous, there aren't enough cops for the job. We have to rise up, we have to fight might with might."* Radamacker had stood up, and now he crashed his fist against the back of the chair.

In the studio everyone jumped.

TWENTY-TWO

OUTSIDE THE CHANNEL 3 building, the L.A.P.D. had been joined by a FBI swat team radioed in by Carson. Men with loudspeakers coordinated the rescue effort, and helicopters hovered in the sky like spiny insects. Three hours had passed since the six o'clock news had been taken over, and the mass of bodies and equipment waited for a way to storm the studio without killing everyone inside. Eddie Martinez conferred with a group of agents. With Carson's blessing, he had devised a plan he thought could work.

In contrast to the noise outside, it was eerily quiet in the soundproofed studio.

"Commander," Mary said. "How is this going to help your *cause?"* By now Radamacker had lost control. *"It will*

show that niggers and Mexicans should be rounded up and killed. You there"—he pointed at the mayor—*"you will be the first.*

"And you"—he pointed at Bill Bryson—*"will be the next."* He looked at his men. *"The day of the rope has begun,"* he announced.

Sweat poured down from Martinez's forehead as he inched on his hands and knees along the air-conditioning ducts of the building. Behind him, Rigby and Begay echoed his grunts. The plans had indicated this narrow crawlspace, and, Martinez suspected, it was the route Zero and his men planned to use for their escape after the bloody assassination. In a coordinated three-pronged attack they were going to try to get into the studio this way at the same time as two swat teams stormed the control room and the door to the studio.

He reached an intersection, and flashing a light briefly on his plans, he turned left. If the plans were accurate, the first small door on his right would lead him into the studio ceiling. He radioed Carson.

The trussed-up mayor had been forced to stand. A noose had been thrown around his neck.

"Now, what have you to say to the people of Los Angeles?" Radamacker jeered. Two gunmen trained their weapon at the terrified man's head.

"No," said Mary, getting up. Her head was suddenly clear. She placed herself in front of the mayor. *"Stop it. You will have to shoot me first. This can't go on."*

"Hold your fire!" Radamacker screamed. *"Don't kill her."* Mary stepped toward him. *"Commander, can't we work something out? We will do whatever you want us to."*

"Will you, Mary?" Radamacker was momentarily distracted.

At that moment the police broke down the door of the studio and the room was filled with confusion.

"Shoot!" Radamacker ordered his men. *"Shoot!"* He grabbed Mary's arm and started running toward a ladder at

the back of the room. "We're going to get out of here!" he said to her.

Reaching the ladder, Radamacker started climbing, pulling Mary behind him. In a moment he had snatched off his hood, and when she looked up Mary saw the frenzied twitching of his facial muscles, the pitted scars on his skin.

Martinez crawled out on to a beam threaded by cable on which some of the studio lights were hung. In the confusion below him, Martinez could make out nothing clearly, and the shots temporarily deafened him. Swaying a little as he crept out on to the beam, he seized a cable to stop himself from falling. Suddenly, he looked back, and saw Radamacker and Mary Reed a few feet up the ladder. They had not seen him. Carefully, he laid his body along the beam, winding the cable around his wrist to steady himself.

"Freeze!" he said. "I've got you covered."

Radamacker's head darted up. Without loosening his vicelike grip on Mary's arm, he pulled a gun from his chest and aimed it at Martinez just as Martinez shot and missed. Radamacker's bullet also missed, hitting a light which shattered and crashed to the floor beneath.

The motion threw Martinez off-balance, and he grasped for the beam as he fell, held only by the cable wrapped around his wrist. Dangling thirty feet above the studio floor, Martinez was not aware of danger. He had one thought. Grunting with the exertion, the detective tried to haul himself back on to the relative safety of the beam. A second bullet narrowly missed his leg, he felt the wind of its trajectory. "Up . . . over . . . higher . . . breathe . . . steady," he muttered. He could feel the blood pumping in his wrist and he hid in a strange silent world where the sights and sounds around him were obliterated by his angle purpose. He was lying on the beam, his forearm broad.

"Freeze motherfucker," he said, the gasping tinny voice given face by a hatred he did not know he could feel. He fired at Radamacker, the killer of his friend, the would-be killer of his people and he fired again and again and again.

A bullet ripped through Radamacker's heart.

It was the second bullet that went through Radamacker's heart. With a look of infinite surprise, the terrorist fell back, knocking Mary off the ladder. They dropped to the floor and lay there side by side.

As she fell, Mary felt a sensation of instant heat travel through her body. Looking down, she saw a bloodstain blossoming on her blouse. As if living in slow motion, she connected the two perceptions, the heat and the bloodstain. "I'm shot," she declared, both surprise and a curious detachment sounding in her voice. And then a terrifying idea hit her: I am not ready to die, she thought, this can't be. Without hearing herself, she made a keening, wailing noise, which unnerved those who heard it, and sank to the floor. Around her, the sound of gunshots mixed with screaming.

In the control room Rick was rooted to the spot. With icy horror he watched the scene unfold in the studio through the unmanned cameras—Channel 3 was still on the air. Ralph Wilson lay wounded beside the cameraman; the floor director was moaning. He had no idea where Mary was. As the agents swarmed into the tiny room, Worth saw Johnson face him and aim his gun at Rick's head. Suddenly, Johnson turned the gun around, put the barrel of it into his mouth, and fired. Viscera from the back of his head splattered on the monitors and his body staggered backward under the impact of the shot, collapsing finally in the narrow passageway. Losing heart, the remaining men threw down their arms and submitted peaceably to arrest.

The red telephone rang and Rick automatically picked it up. The inside line had not been cut. "Worth, are you there? Pull the plug, man, go to black! This is a horror show!" Hansen cried.

Rick heard the sound of a scuffle. Hansen had dropped the receiver. Then he heard Baker's voice. "Don't do it Worth. We can't go off the air now. I'm in charge. Do as I say, you hear me?"

"People are dying," Rick heard Hansen say. "You want a TV show and people are dying. I won't allow it."

"Hansen, you're fired. You haven't got the guts."

"Wrong, asshole," he heard Hansen say. "I quit."

"Worth, Worth, are you still there?" It was Baker.

"Yes."

"Listen to me. Get Davis on now. We've got to wrap this up, let the audience know what the hell is going on."

Moving like a zombie, Rick stepped over the body of Finn Johnson. He ordered Julian to train a camera on Davis and pushed down the button that connected him with the anchor.

"Charles, you're on . . . wrap this up somehow."

As the police moved around the studio, Davis spoke intimately into the camera, talking directly to his viewers as he tried to make sense of the events.

"As you saw, a group of right-wing terrorists took over the show while we were on the air this evening. Their plan was to assassinate Mayor Simpson, a guest on the show. In that they have failed. The mayor is said to be unhurt, repeat unhurt by the event. The terrorists forced Channel Three to play their tape and then co-anchor Mary Reed was ordered to conduct an interview with their leader. We were all held at gunpoint and had no choice." Charles's voice grew stronger as he spoke, it was his show again now. *"We did everything these people wanted us to but just as they were threatening to assassinate the mayor, the police moved in. A cameraman, the floor director, Ralph Wilson, and Mary Reed have all been injured and are being taken to the hospital now."* He looked sorrowfully into the camera. *"We will have bulletins throughout this evening and more at eleven when we will have a special expanded edition of the late news."*

Davis was frowning. *"Most of the time, we at Channel Three report the news. Tonight the news came to us in a terrifying drama of hate, gunfire, and death. Now that this is all over, we all have to sort it out. For now, I'm Charles Davis. Good night."*

"Fade to black," Rick ordered. He heard the sirens wailing in the distance.

TWENTY-THREE

RICK WORTH DROVE carefully to work the next morning. His doctor had dressed his head wound, and given him some medication for the shock that made him feel as though his brain were wrapped in gauze. His wife had tried to persuade him to stay at home, but he insisted that going to work would be good for him. Jane's concern was too much, he did not want to talk about what happened the night before.

At Channel 3, the atmosphere was subdued. People talked in whispers, they walked rather than ran around the newsroom, and gathered in little clusters, some of them sobbing. Somehow, like Rick, they all needed to be at work, to be with the people who had shared the same experience. Policeman were positioned at all the entrances to the building.

Baker called Rick on the telephone. "Have you seen the ratings?"

"A fifty-six share," Worth said. "It's incredible."

"Listen, Rick. I've cleared this with the network. We're going to do a special tonight, across the board." This meant a nationally broadcast show. "A one-hour show on what happened last night. I want you to produce. Davis has agreed to anchor."

"Oh," said Rick. This would be the first time that he had produced a national show.

"So, get started on it right away." Baker paused. "Oh, and Rick, we have to talk about this news director spot. I assume you're interested?"

"Yes, sure I'm interested," said Rick in a trance.

"We'll talk about it tomorrow."

Rick hung up. Maybe tomorrow he would be able to think straight. In the meantime, he had a show to put together.

In her hospital room, Mary stirred out of the general anaesthetic to a foggy consciousness. There was something she should remember, but the effort of thinking exhausted her. She closed her eyes. When she woke up again, she noticed that a nurse was sitting by her bed.

"Oh, my," the nurse said when she saw Mary's eyes open. "Hello, there."

"What happened?" Mary asked.

"They operated on you early this morning to extract the bullet from your chest. It was the same one that hit the other guy, so by the time it reached you it couldn't do much damage. Missed all the major spots," she said. "You lost a lot of blood," she said, "it's made you very weak. We were very worried for a while."

"So was I," said Mary. "I thought that was it." She shuddered. "Oh, God," she said, shutting her eyes. "So, it's all real? Is that awful man dead now?"

"Yes," the nurse soothed her. "There's nothing to worry about anymore."

"What about the others?"

The nurse shook her head. "Why don't you try to get some more rest, miss. Everything's going to be all right."

"No, I want to know what happened." Before she could protest further, Mary dozed off again.

When she woke up several hours later, Mark was sitting by her bed, stroking her hand and looking anxiously down at her.

"What are you doing here?" she asked Mark with surprise.

"Well, we had a dinner date, right?" Mark said lightly.

"Then it really is true. It wasn't a bad dream. What about the others, Mark? The nurse wouldn't tell me."

Mark frowned. His inclination was not to tell her yet, but he figured it was better he told her than she found out more abruptly. "It's not good news. The cameraman and Wilson both died."

"Oh, no."

"And the floor director, Chris, he's in critical condition here in the hospital."

"Oh, dear," said Mary.

"You were very lucky, Mary. Someone up there must love you."

"Mark?"

"Yes."

"I've been thinking."

"So've I."

"I'm sorry for some of the things I said to you. I was unfair."

"So am I. For the things I said to you, I mean," Mark said.

"I missed you," Mary said.

"Did you really, honey? I missed you, too. You were the best thing that happened to me and I screwed it up. A thousand times I went to pick up the phone and stopped myself because I figured you had about ten million guys on your arm by this point."

"It's funny. I've dated a few people, but they all know me as an anchorwoman, and I figured it was hard for them to break through. But then I thought of something you said, about my being on all the time, and I realized that perhaps I didn't give them any help." She looked at him. "You know I haven't made any friends here. I mean there's lots of people I know, people I work with, people I meet and interview, but no one who really knows me. Even E. J. . . . ." she trailed off. "You're the only one."

"Would you like to try again?"

"What about that woman you were with?"

"What woman? Oh, you mean Alexis? She's my agent. She wasn't very nice to you, was she?"

"Oh, I thought . . ."

"You thought . . . ?"

They both laughed.

"Listen, Mark," Mary said. "Let's go away. For a long, long time, I mean. I need to take a break."

"Sounds like a wonderful idea. Leave it to me."

"Mmm, okay," Mary said dreamily. "Uh-oh," she said, "I think I'm falling asleep again." Her head fell back against the pillow.

A couple of hours later the door of her hospital room opened, and Irwin Hansen poked his head around it.

"She's up!" He smiled.

"Irwin, why aren't you at work?" Mary was sitting up. She was far more alert. The doctor had just visited her and told her she was recovering remarkably well. Mark had left her to call his office.

"I quit," said Hansen. He sat down by her bed.

"No," said Mary. "I don't believe it."

"Yeah, that idiot Baker. After you were shot, I wanted to go to black. But not Baker. He wanted more. It was the last straw." Hansen shrugged, but Mary could see that he was still struggling with the idea."

308

"What are you going to do?"

"Teach, I guess," said the former news director. "Can't let the Tom Bakers of this world go completely unopposed."

The telephone rang. It was Rick Worth. "Yes, the doctor said I'm doing great. He said another week and I'll be out. Isn't that incredible?" Rick told her about the death of the commentator and the cameraman. "Yes, I heard. It's awful, I can't believe—" Rick cut her off. She listened. "A special? Tonight?" she repeated. "You want to interview me?" Mary looked at Irwin. "I've just had surgery, Rick. The answer's no. . . . No, no means I'm not going to do it. . . . No, don't even try. Bye."

"Can you believe it?" she asked Hansen.

"Don't blame Rick, it's Tom Baker's doing," he said. "I'm glad you said no, though," he added. "This is no time for a television interview."

"You know, if you'd asked me a few months ago, I would have said that I would do anything for a story." Mary looked at Hansen. "But I've learned something. There is a line between what I do and what I am. Not doing the interview was part of that. I think I'm going to live differently from now on."

Hansen smiled at her. "It's a good lesson, and one that many people don't learn."

"But I feel responsible," Mary continued. "By interviewing Commander Zero, I gave him the attention he craved and paved the way for all this. I helped kill those people last night, Irwin," she said soberly, her eyes filling with tears.

"Don't be so hard on yourself," Hansen said, "There are other lines, too, ones that divides personal responsibility from generalized guilt. Don't indulge in the second, it's not healthy. You got caught up in a machine that generated terror and fear, but you did not invent the machine. And, in a small way, you helped stop it. You behaved with great courage in that studio, Mary. The distraction you created gave the police a chance to come in. Nobody who saw you will forget that." He patted her hand.

Irwin got up. "I should go now. They told me to stay only ten minutes. Good luck, Mary." He bent down and kissed her on the cheek. Mary looked affectionately at his departing back.

"Hi," Mark came back into the room. "You look much better," he said. "You'll never guess, I was just talking to the detective that figured the whole thing out. His name's Martinez."

"He's the one that I called," Mary said.

"He's outside and wants to talk to you when you're up to it. He feels bad because it was his shot that hit you, after it hit the commander. He says he didn't think he had a choice."

"I think I'll let him off the hook," Mary said. "I wouldn't even be here if it wasn't for him."

"He told me something else, too," Mark said. "You know our idea that the commander was behind the Feld murder? It was right, he has a witness!"

"Really?" said Mary. "Another mystery solved. Now," she said mischievously, "you can finish your book!"

The telephone rang. "Hello, E. J.," Mary said. "Fine, I'm going to be fine, and yes I got your flowers." She smiled at the roomful of roses. "Yes, you heard right, I'm not interviewing for the special. . . . I'm not sure. . . . No, I'm not, I'm going to take some time off. . . . You know something? I don't care about a fifty-six share." She laughed, and Mark looked at her in delight. It was a long time since he had heard Mary laugh with such infectious joy. "I'm serious, I don't care. I'm alive, E. J., that's all I can think about right now. I'm going away. . . . I don't know for how long, we haven't decided. . . . Yes, with Mark." Mary looked at Mark and smiled. "Well, how about we call you when we get back. . . . Sure, bye." As Mary hung up, she could hear Edwards expostulating on the other end of the telephone. She smiled serenely at Mark.

"Do you think they have any decent food in this dump?" she said. "I'm starving."

Eddie Martinez stood in Radamacker's underground office in the desert. In the months since the takeover of Channel 3, the FBI had combed through the compound, taking it apart and hauling off the vast supply of weapons, the jars of botulin and anthrax bacteria stored in freezers, the printing press, the counterfeiting machinery and wads of money left over from the Goldor depot and other robberies. The rotting body of informant Tony Caban had been cut down and buried.

Behind Martinez, the once gleaming bank of monitors had rusted, and sand was scattered over the floor of the office—the desert was claiming its own. On the wall, Radamacker's picture of the one he called The Great One had been taken down to reveal a safe that contained the number of a Swiss bank account and several cyanide pills.

The detective had been decorated for his actions in the studio, but, more important to him, he felt he had avenged the death of his former partner Jim Wilkes. He picked up a remote control device the feds had left and played with it as he looked around the office. Finally, with a last glance around, he closed the door behind him for the last time. Martinez walked through the church and down the zigzag path to his car. As he opened the door, Martinez heard a low rumble. The ground beneath him seemed to groan and shake and he feared an earthquake. He slammed the door and started the car, speeding out of the compound as the noise grew louder. Only when he had climbed up on the dirt road that curved around the hill, did he stop and look back. Great jagged cracks were snaking across the compound pavement. The sound reached an explosive crescendo and, right before the detective's startled gaze, the hill under the church exploded in a great round fiery ball that leapt high into the sky. When Martinez next looked, the hill and church had disappeared and in their place was a huge crater. Small pieces of debris fell from the sky and were swallowed by the gaping hole in the ground.

The remote control, Martinez figured, had been left by the feds and was what had set off Jerry Radamacker's final act of violence in this world. Trust him to have the last word. He shuddered suddenly, realizing how close he had come to being buried alive. Something bounced on the hood of his car, and he picked it up. The black plastic had twisted in the heat, but Martinez could make out the shape of a videocassette. On the side, in neat handwriting, was written *Interview with Mary Reed.* Martinez tossed the tape aside and started his car. It was time to go home.